FUN 學
英語故事閱讀訓練 1

Michael A. Putlack & e-Creative Contents_著

陳怡靜／彭尊聖_譯

Super
Reading
Story
Training
Book

培養閱讀原文書實力的
課本（Main Book） ➕ 文章即讀、即解、即背的
訓練書（Training Book） ➕ 生動、道地的
故事朗誦MP3 + MP3

FUN 學
英語故事閱讀訓練 1

Michael A. Putlack & e-Creative Contents_著

陳怡靜／彭尊聖_譯

Super
Reading
Story
Training
Book

MAIN
BOOK

以名著閱讀法，
打造閱讀原文書的實力

　　一旦掌握英語閱讀的技能，就能藉由閱讀拓展國際視野，因此閱讀訓練非常重要，是一定要打好基礎的入門功夫，《Fun學英語故事閱讀訓練》要把閱讀訓練法中最有效的「名著閱讀法」傳授給你，幫助讀者培養閱讀原文書的實力，體驗不用頻查字典就能品味原文小說的感動。

1 本套書精選**15篇世界經典文學名著及改編童話故事**，如丹麥安徒生童話之中的《小美人魚》、英國大文豪狄更斯的《聖誕頌歌》、俄國寫實作家托爾斯泰的《人靠什麼活著》等大作，帶你品味文學芬芳，提升人文素養；搭配彩繪插圖，賞心悅目，增添學習樂趣。

2 本書共有六個學習階段（6 steps），依文章難易度分為兩冊：

　　Book 1 包含Step 1~Step 3，適合初學者
　　Book 2 包含Step 4~Step 6，適合進階學習者

3 每一冊各分兩大部分，精心設計各種實用學習幫手，讓你更有效率、更輕鬆地學會閱讀原文書：

　　課本 Main Book：全英語呈現，藉由學習幫手不需字典也能讀懂
　　訓練書 Training Book：英文語句、文法結構大解密

4 讀完一段課文後，隨即有Stop & Think測驗掌握主旨及細節的能力，以及有 Check Up練習各種常見的閱讀測驗題型，如字彙選填、是非題及配合題等 5種題型變化，不僅驗收閱讀理解成效，也為日後參加英語檢定作準備。

強力推薦給這些人！

- 想把英語根基扎得又深又牢的人。
- 想順暢閱讀《時代》雜誌推薦小說原著的人。
- 想在多益、托福等各種英文考試中得高分的人。
- 想上全英語教學或雙語教學課程的人。
- 正準備出國留學的人。

培養不用字典就能讀原文小說的實力，
現在，就讓它變成你的競爭力吧。

How to Use This Book

本書的使用步驟

《Fun學英語故事閱讀訓練》共兩冊，每冊各分兩大部分，第一部分為全英文的課本，第二部分為拆解英文語句的訓練書，訓練書是為提升「即讀即解」的能力和「理解英語句子結構」的能力而編寫的。

Main Book 課本　　六個學習階段（6 steps），共15篇故事。

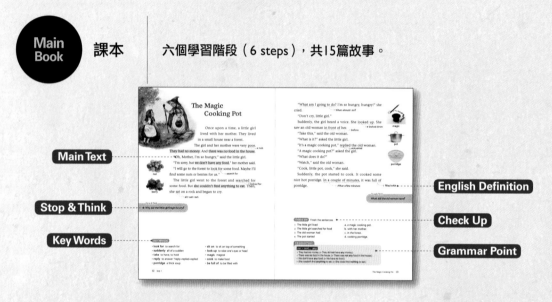

- Main Text
- Stop & Think
- Key Words
- English Definition
- Check Up
- Grammar Point

1 讀課文（Main Text）

首先，只看全英文的課文，不懂的單字或用語，可以透過精心設計的學習幫手了解字義，因此不需字典也能讀懂課文：

- 彩圖字彙解說，圖像學習超easy。
- 英英單字注釋（Key Words），快速擴充字彙量。
- 課文中附註英文釋義（English Definition），搭配上下文，熟練字彙運用。
- 文法解析（Grammar Point）學習常見句型。

2 試做練習題（Stop & Think / Check Up）

讀完課文後，立即透過5種測驗題型，檢核字彙能力及文章理解程度。

Stop & Think ➡ 引導式問題，訓練你抓出文章主旨（main idea）及細節（details），以及培養獨立思考的能力。

Check Up ➡ 英語檢定常見題型，是非題、字彙選填、選擇題及配合題，為參加考試作準備。

Training Book 訓練書

訓練書提供了即讀即解的課文，以意義為單位來斷句，以斜線（∕）標示句子的結構，還設計了**用法特寫**（Close Up）和**文法解析**（Grammar Point），加強英文句型及文法能力。書末附有課本的正確答案和翻譯。

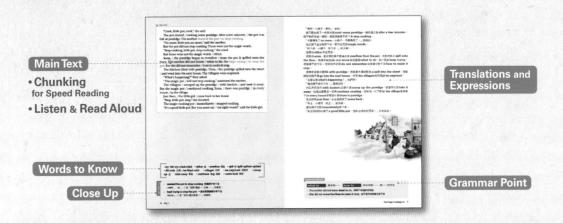

Main Text
• **Chunking** for Speed Reading
• **Listen & Read Aloud**

Words to Know
Close Up

Translations and Expressions

Grammar Point

3 查看訓練書
首先將單字學習（Words to Know）裡重要關鍵英單的中文釋義瀏覽一遍，接著讀斷句課文（Chunking），藉由清楚劃分句子的結構，可達到「即讀即解」的成效。再對照中文翻譯與重要片語中英對照（Translations and Expressions），以意義為單位來理解英文課文，同時亦作為中英翻譯練習參考，還可透過學習幫手Close Up，和Grammar Point學習片語、句型及文法。

4 挑戰看斷句課文自行翻譯
現在不看翻譯，參考活用斷句標示（∕），試著自己翻譯英文課文。若有不明之處，就再確認中文釋義和英文用法，反覆查看，直到完全理解為止。

5 聽MP3朗讀並複誦
背英文時，一面看一面讀出聲音，記得更牢。本書隨書附贈MP3，課文皆由英語母語人士以正確、清晰的發音朗讀。聽課文時，要注意斜線（∕）斷句的地方，並注意聽母語人士的發音、語調及連音等。最好自己在課文上把語調和連音標示出來，然後大聲地跟著MP3朗誦，盡量跟上英語母語人士的速度。

6 不聽MP3，自己朗讀課文
接著，不聽MP3，自己唸課文，並盡量唸得母語人士一樣。若有發音或語調不順的地方，就再聽一次MP3，反覆練習。

7 重新閱讀英文課文
現在再回來看課本，再讀一次英文課文，並試著解題，如果讀得很順，練習題也都答對，訓練就成功了。

★ 正確答案請見訓練書書末的〈Answers & Translations〉。

The Introduction of Training Book

訓練書特色説明

透過「斷句」掌握「即讀即解」的竅門

　　為了能更快、更正確地閱讀英文，就需要能夠掌握英文的句子結構。而要培養英文句子結構的敏銳度，最好的方法就是以各「意義單元組」來理解句子，也就是將英文句子的「意義單元組」（具一個完整意義的片語或詞組），用斷句（chunk）的方式分開，然後再來理解句子。只要能理解各個「意義單元組」，那麼再長的句子，都能被拆解與理解。

　　聽力也是一樣，要區分「意義單元組」，這樣能幫助很快聽懂英文。例如下面這個句子可以拆解成兩個部分：

I am angry / at you.
我生氣　　　對你

　　我們會發現，這個句子由兩個「意義單元組」所組成。不管句子多長多複雜，都是由最簡單的基本句型（主詞＋動詞）發展而成，然後再在這個主要句子上，依照需求，添加上許多片語，以表現各式各樣的句意。

　　在面對英文時，腦子裡能立刻自動快速分離基本句型和片語，就能迅速讀懂或聽懂英文。在讀誦英文時，從一個人的斷句，大致就能看出個人的英文能力。現在再來看稍微長一點的句子。經過斷句以後，整個句子變得更清楚易懂，閱讀理解就沒問題了：

Beauty was not only pretty / but also kind and smart.
美麗不僅漂亮　　　　　　　還很善良、聰明

一個句子有幾個斷句？

一個句子有幾個斷句？有幾個「意義單元組」？這是依句子的情況和個人的英語能力，而有不同的。一般來說，以下這些地方通常就是斷句的地方：

★ 在「主詞＋動詞」之後
★ 在 and、but、or 等連接詞之前
★ 在 that、who 等關係詞之前
★ 在副詞、不定詞 to 等的前後

另外，主詞很長時，時常為了要區分出主詞，在主詞後也會斷句。例如：

A man / who wants to learn / can learn anything.
人　　　　願意學習　　　　　就能學會任何事

對初學者來說，一個句子裡可能會有很多斷句的斜線，而當閱讀能力越來越強之後，你需要斷句的地方就會越來越少，到後來甚至能一眼就看懂句子，不需要用斷句的方式來幫助理解。

本訓練書因為考慮到初學者，所以盡可能細分可斷句處，只要是能分為一個「意義單元組」的地方，訓練書上就標示出斷句。等你的英文實力逐漸提升，到了覺得斷句變成是一種累贅，能夠不用再做任何標記就能讀懂課文時，就是你的英文能力更進一階的時候了。透過斷句的練習，熟悉英語的排列順序和結構，你會驚訝地發現到，自己的閱讀能力突飛猛進！

Table of Contents

BOOK 2

Super Reading Story Training Book

Step

1

The Magic Cooking Pot

♪ 01

Once upon a time, a little girl lived with her mother. They lived in a small house near a forest.

The girl and her mother were very poor. `≠ rich`
They had no money. And there was no food in the house.

"Oh, Mother, I'm so hungry," said the little girl.

"I'm sorry, but we don't have any food," her mother said.

"I will go to the forest to look for some food. Maybe I'll find some nuts or berries for us." `→ search for`

nut

The little girl went to the forest and searched for `→ looked for` some food. But she couldn't find anything to eat. Then, she sat on a rock and began to cry.

berry

`→ sit–sat–sat`

Stop & Think

Why did the little girl begin to cry?

KEY WORDS

- **look for** to search for
- **suddenly** all of a sudden
- **take** to have; to hold
- **reply** to answer *reply–replied–replied
- **porridge** a thick soup

- **sit on** to sit on top of something
- **look up** to raise one's eyes or head
- **magic** magical
- **cook** to make food
- **be full of** to be filled with

"What am I going to do? I'm so hungry, hungry!" she cried.

> *What should I do?*

"Don't cry, little girl."

Suddenly, the girl heard a voice. She looked up. She saw an old woman in front of her.

> *≠ looked down*
> *before*

magic

"Take this," said the old woman.

"What is it?" asked the little girl.

"It's a magic cooking pot," replied the old woman.

> *answered*

pot

"A magic cooking pot?" asked the girl.

"What does it do?"

"Watch," said the old woman.

"Cook, little pot, cook," she said.

porridge

Suddenly, the pot started to cook. It cooked some nice hot porridge. In a couple of minutes, it was full of porridge.

> *After a few minutes*
> *filled with*

Stop & Think

What did the old woman have?

CHECK UP Finish the sentences.

1 The little girl lived
2 The little girl searched for food
3 The old woman had
4 The pot started

a. a magic cooking pot.
b. with her mother.
c. in the forest.
d. cooking porridge.

GRAMMAR POINT

no = not ... any

- They had **no** money. (= They did **not** have **any** money.)
- There was **no** food in the house. (= There was **not any** food in the house.)
- We don't have **any** food. (= We have **no** food.)
- She couldn't find **anything** to eat. (= She could find **nothing** to eat.)

amazing

delicious

magic words

"Wow!" said the girl.

"That's amazing. Let's eat the porridge."
⟶ *very surprising*

"Wait," said the old woman.

"First, the pot must stop."

Then, she said to the pot, "Stop, little pot, stop."

The pot immediately stopped cooking.
⟶ *instantly*

"You must always say those words, or the pot will
⟶ *or else, otherwise*

keep cooking porridge. Now, you can eat."

"It's delicious!" said the little girl.

"You can have this pot," said the old woman.
⟶ *take*

"Oh, I am so happy. Thank you so much."

"Just don't forget the magic words," said the old
⟶ *remember*

woman.

The little girl took the pot and ran back to her home.
⟶ *take–took–taken*   ⟶ *run–ran–run*

"Mother," shouted the little girl.

"Look at what I have. It's a magic cooking pot."

Stop & Think
What should the little girl do
to stop the pot from cooking?

KEY WORDS

- **amazing** very surprising
- **keep -ing** to continue doing something
- **magic words** words that can do magic
- **run back** to return
- **go out** to leave *go–went–gone

- **immediately** instantly; at once
- **forget** to not remember
- **take** to hold; to carry *take–took–taken
- **shout** to yell loudly
- **be out** to be away

The girl's mother looked at the pot.

"Magic? Are you sure?"

"Of course. Watch this," answered the little girl.

"Cook, little pot, cook."

Immediately, the pot cooked some nice hot porridge. In a couple of minutes, it was full of porridge.

"Wait a minute, Mother," said the little girl.
→ *Wait a second, Hold on*
"We have to say the magic words to stop the pot. Stop, little pot, stop," she said.

The pot immediately stopped cooking.

The little girl and her mother ate porridge every day. They were not hungry anymore.

One day, the little girl went out to play with her friends. She was out for a long time.
→ *go–went–gone*
Her mother became very hungry. So she decided to eat without her daughter.

play

daughter

Stop & Think
Why did the mother decide to eat without her daughter?

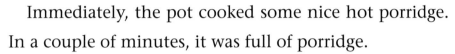

CHECK UP Put the right words.

| full | immediately | porridge | ran back |

1 The little girl took the pot and _____ to her home.
2 Soon, the pot was _____ of porridge.
3 The pot _____ stopped cooking.
4 The little girl and her mother ate _____ every day.

GRAMMAR POINT

stop -ing / keep -ing / decide to

- The pot immediately **stopped** cooking.
- The pot will **keep** cooking porridge.
- She **decided to** eat without her daughter.

overflow

spill

surprised

"Cook, little pot, cook," she said.

The pot started cooking some porridge. After a few minutes, the pot was full of porridge. The mother wanted the pot to stop cooking.

"No more, little pot, no more," said the mother.

But the pot did not stop cooking. Those were not the magic words.

"Stop cooking, little pot, stop cooking," she cried.
→ shouted

But those were not the magic words either.

Soon, the porridge began to overflow from the pot. It
→ run over
spilled onto the floor. The mother did not know what
→ overflowed
to do. She kept trying to stop the pot. But she did not
→ continued *keep–kept–kept
remember how to make it stop.

forgot ←

The kitchen filled with porridge. Then, the porridge spilled into the street and went into the next house. The villagers were surprised.

"What's happening?" they asked.

What's going on? ←

"The magic pot will not stop cooking," answered the mother.

Stop & Think

Why did the pot keep making porridge?

KEY WORDS

- **cry** to shout *cry–cried–cried
- **spill** to flow over; to fall *spill–spilled–spilled
- **villagers** the people who live in a village
- **scoop up** to draw up
- **continue -ing** to keep doing something

- **overflow** to run over; to flow over
- **fill with** to be full of; to be filled with
- **be surprised** to be shocked
- **take away** to remove
- **come back** to return

The villagers scooped up the porridge with buckets
and took it away. But the magic pot continued cooking.
Soon, there was porridge in every house in the village.

> removed it — *(scooped up)*
> kept — *(continued)*

Just then, the little girl came back to her home.

> returned — *(came back)*

"Stop, little pot, stop," she shouted.

The magic cooking pot immediately stopped cooking.

"It's a good little pot. But you must say the right words!"
said the little girl.

> ≠ wrong — *(right)*

scoop up

bucket

CHECK UP Choose the right words.

1 The mother did not remember _____ make it stop. (how to | what to)

2 The porridge _____ onto the floor. (filled | spilled)

3 Every house in the village had _____ in it. (porridge | pot)

GRAMMAR POINT

what to . . . / how to . . .

- The mother did not know **what to** do.
- She did not remember **how to** make it stop.

The Magic Cooking Pot   **7**

The Shoemaker and the Elves

shoemaker

a pair of shoes

gold coin

There was once an old shoemaker. He owned an old shoe shop. He worked on the first floor, and he and his [→ had] wife lived on the second floor. The shoemaker and his wife were very poor. Few people visited his shop, so he [→ not many] did not make much money. [→ earn much money]

One day, the shoemaker told his wife.

"One last pair of shoes. That's all I can make. We [→ final] don't have any money. What are we going to do?"

"It is late. So we should go to bed. Make the shoes [→ go to sleep] in the morning," answered the shoemaker's wife. The shoemaker and his wife went upstairs and went to bed. [→ ≠ downstairs]

The next morning, the shoemaker and his wife went downstairs. There was something on the table. It was a pair of shoes.

Stop & Think

Were there many customers in the shop?

KEY WORDS

- **shoemaker** a person who makes shoes
- **make money** to earn money
- **pair** two same things that are used together
- **go upstairs** ≠ go downstairs
- **magic** super powers
- **own** to have *own–owned–owned
- **wife** ≠ husband
- **go to bed** to go to sleep
- **a pair of** a couple of
- **gold coin** a coin that is made of gold

"Look at these," the shoemaker said. "What beautiful shoes! It's magic."

walked into ←

Just then, a lady came into the store. The lady looked at the shoes and said, "What beautiful shoes! I'll take them."

I'll buy them. ←

She gave the shoemaker three gold coins for the shoes.

"Three gold coins! Now I can make two more pairs of shoes," the shoemaker said. So he went out and bought some more leather. He came back and cut the leather.

→ buy–bought–bought

leather

cut–cut–cut ←

"It is late. Make them in the morning," said his wife. The shoemaker and his wife went upstairs and went to bed.

Stop & Think

Who made the beautiful shoes?

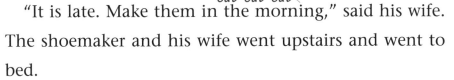

CHECK UP   True or false?

1 The shoemaker was very poor. _____
2 The shoemaker finished his last pair of shoes. _____
3 The lady gave the shoemaker three gold coins for the shoes. _____
4 The next morning, the shoemaker made two more pairs of shoes. _____

GRAMMAR POINT

What . . . ! / How . . . ! (exclamation)

• **What** beautiful **shoes!**
• **How beautiful** they are!

The next morning, the shoemaker and his wife came down. They saw two beautiful pairs of shoes on the table.

came downstairs ←

"Look at these," he said. "More magic."

The shoemaker put the shoes in the window. A man

→ *placed, displayed*

saw them. He walked into the shop. "How beautiful

see–saw–seen ←

→ *came into*

they are! I must buy them. Here are six gold coins."

What beautiful ←
shoes they are!

"Now I can buy enough leather to make four pairs of shoes," the shoemaker said. So he went out and bought some more leather. He came back and cut the leather.

"It is late," said his wife. "So we should go to bed." The shoemaker and his wife went upstairs and went to bed.

KEY WORDS

• **come down** to go down
• **a while later** after a while; later on
• **pay** to give money *pay–paid–paid
• **wonder** to be curious about

• **put** to place; to display
• **customer** someone who buys goods; a shopper
• **twelve** 12; a dozen
• **hide** to keep from being seen *hide–hid–hidden

The next morning, the shoemaker and his wife came down. They saw four beautiful pairs of shoes on the table.

customer

"Look at these," he said. "They're beautiful. Even more magic."

→ After a while   → came into

A while later, two customers entered the store. They looked at the shoes and said, "Those shoes are beautiful. We'll take them." They paid the shoemaker twelve gold coins for the shoes.

⋯→ pay-paid-paid

twelve

The shoemaker and his wife were very happy. But they wondered, "Who is making these shoes? We must know."

⋯→ were curious

wonder

That night, the shoemaker cut the leather for the shoes. But he and his wife did not go upstairs. Instead, they hid downstairs. They waited and waited.

⋯→ hide-hid-hidden

hide

Stop & Think

Why did the shoemaker and his wife hide downstairs?

CHECK UP Put the right words.

twelve	hid	came down	pairs of

1 The next morning, the shoemaker and his wife _____.
2 They saw two beautiful _____ shoes on the table.
3 The two customers paid _____ gold coins for the four pairs of shoes.
4 The shoemaker and his wife _____ downstairs.

GRAMMAR POINT

enough . . . to . . .

• Now I can buy **enough leather to** make four pairs of shoes.

elf

sew

At midnight, two elves came into the shoemaker's shop. They jumped onto the table.

→ *sg. elf*

"Look at this leather," one said.

"Let's make some beautiful shoes with it," said the other.

The elves worked hard all night long. They made several beautiful pairs of shoes. When the sun rose, they left.

→ a few

rise–rose–risen ←

→ leave–left–left

"Those elves are very kind," said the shoemaker.

"You're right," answered his wife. "We should do something for them."

"What can we do?" asked the shoemaker.

"I know," said his wife. "Their clothes looked poor. Let's make some clothes for them."

So the shoemaker and his wife made some tiny clothes for the elves. They sewed

→ very small

sew–sewed–sewed ←

Stop & Think

Who made the beautiful shoes?

KEY WORDS

- **midnight** twelve at night
- **jump onto** to leap onto
- **rise** move upward *rise–rose–risen
- **look poor** to appear to have no money
- **sew** to make clothes *sew–sewed–sewed
- **stay** to be in one place (≠ leave)

- **elf** fairy *pl. elves
- **several** a few; more than two but not many
- **leave** ≠ arrive; stay
- **tiny** very small
- **put on** to put clothes on (≠ take off)
- **sg.** singular
- **pl.** plural

tiny pants, shirts, hats, and boots for the elves. Then, they put the new clothes on the table.

pants

That night, the shoemaker and his wife hid again. At midnight, the elves came into the shoemaker's shop. When they jumped onto the table, they saw the clothes.

shirt

"What are these?" one said. "Are these clothes for us?"

"Yes," said the other. "They are for us."

The elves put their new clothes on. Then, they
↪ ≠ take off
danced with each other.
↪ no longer

hat

"We cannot stay here any longer," said the first elf.

"You're right. They know about us. Now it's time for us to go," said the second elf.

"Goodbye, shoemaker," they said.

The elves left and never came back. But now the

boots

shoemaker could make good shoes. He worked hard, too. So he and his wife became very rich. And they
↪ become–became–become
lived happily ever after.
↪ forever

Stop & Think

Why did the elves leave?

CHECK UP Choose the right words.

1 Two _____ made the shoes at night. (elves | customers)
2 The shoemaker and his wife made tiny _____. (clothes | shoes)
3 The _____ left and never came back. (elves | customers)
4 The shoemaker and his wife became _____. (rich | poor)

GRAMMAR POINT

it's time for . . . to . . .

• Now **it's time for** us **to** go.

Jack and the Beanstalk

♪ 03

cottage

cow

bean

Long ago, there lived a mother and her son. The son's name was Jack. They lived in a small cottage. They were very poor. Their only valuable possession was an old cow.

> property

One day, the mother said to Jack.

"We've got no money, Jack. Go and sell the cow."

> We have no money

So Jack took the cow and walked toward the town. On his way to the town, he met a strange old man. He

> While going to   > odd

asked Jack, "Where are you going with that cow?"

"I'm going to town to sell the cow so that we can buy some food," said Jack.

"Ah . . . but the town is so very far away . . . I will gladly buy the cow from you," the old man said.

happily

Look at

"Take a look at these." The old man showed Jack some beautiful beans.

"These are magic beans. I will give you five magic beans for your cow," he offered.

> proposed

Stop & Think

What did the strange old man offer Jack?

KEY WORDS

- **valuable** worth a lot of money
- **on one's way to** on the way to; while going to
- **be far away** to be a long distance from
- **be impressed by** to be amazed by
- **amazing** very surprising; incredible

- **possession** something a person owns
- **so that** in order that
- **offer** to suggest; to propose
- **throw out** to throw away
- **climb up** to go up (≠ climb down)

Jack was impressed by the magic beans. So he sold
→ was amazed by   sell–sold–sold ←
the cow to the old man for five beans. Jack was very
proud of himself.
→ arrived
But when he got home, his mother was angry.

"What? Beans!" she cried. "You sold our cow for five
beans? You fool! Only a fool would exchange a cow for
                    → idiot
five beans. No supper for you. Go to bed right now,"
                    → dinner
she told him. Then, Jack's mother threw the beans out
                        throw–threw–thrown ←
the window.

The next morning, Jack looked out the
window and saw an amazing sight. There was an
    → huge, very big
enormous beanstalk growing next to the window.
It rose so high that he could not see where it ended.
→ rise–rose–risen
"The old man was right," said Jack. "They were
magic beans." Jack started climbing up the beanstalk.
He climbed for hours and hours. Finally, he got to
the top of the beanstalk.   At last ←   reached ←

beanstalk

CHECK UP   Answer the questions.

1 What did Jack sell the strange old man?
   a. magic beans   **b.** some food   **c.** a cow

2 What did Jack's mother do with the beans?
   a. She ate them.   **b.** She threw them out the window.   **c.** She planted them.

GRAMMAR POINT

so that . . . / so . . . that . . .

- I'm going to town to sell the cow **so that** we can buy some food.
- It rose **so** high **that** he could not see where it ended.

Jack and the Beanstalk   **15**

There, high in the clouds, was a huge castle.

→ while

"I wonder who lives there," thought Jack as he walked toward the castle. When Jack got to the castle, he tripped over an enormous foot. It belonged to the

→ fell over

biggest woman he had ever seen.

"You, boy," said the woman. "What are you doing here? My husband is a giant. He loves to eat little boys like you."

→ likes to

castle

"Please don't let him eat me," answered Jack. "I just came here because I smelled breakfast, and I am so hungry."

→ kind, nice ≠ mean

The giant's wife was kindhearted, so she gave Jack some food. All of a sudden, the ground began to shake.

→ Suddenly

"Hide, boy," said the woman. "My husband is coming."

giant

"Fee, fi, fo, fum, I can smell a little boy," said the giant when he walked into the kitchen. "Are you

→ came into

cooking a boy for me for breakfast?"

"No, dear," she answered. "You probably smell the boy you ate last week."

→ eat–ate–eaten

smell

Stop & Think

Who lived in the castle?

KEY WORDS

- **castle** a palace
- **enormous** huge; very large
- **kindhearted** nice; kind (≠ mean)
- **ground** land; earth
- **take out** to put out; to pull
- **run out** to use all of something

- **trip over** to fall over
- **giant** a very tall person
- **all of a sudden** suddenly
- **shake** to move back and forth
- **fall asleep** to get to sleep (≠ wake up)
- **go away** to leave

The giant sat down and ate his breakfast. Then, he took out a huge bag. It was filled with gold. After a while, he fell asleep at the table. Then, Jack came out quietly. He took the bag of gold and ran out of the castle. He climbed down the beanstalk and showed his mother the gold. She was very pleased with him.

→ put out
≠ woke up
→ grabbed, stole
→ run-ran-run
≠ climbed up
→ very happy

Jack and his mother lived happily. But they soon ran out of gold. Jack decided to climb the beanstalk again. He got to the top of the beanstalk and walked to the castle.

→ used up

bag

fall asleep

hide

find

"Oh, it's you again?" said the giant's wife. "Go away! You're a bad boy. Didn't you take my husband's gold?"

Get out! / Leave! ←

"That wasn't me. That was another boy," answered Jack.

The giant's wife believed Jack. She gave him some food. Then, the ground began to shake. "He's coming," said the woman. "Hide, or he will find you."

Stop & Think

Why did Jack climb the beanstalk again?

CHECK UP   Finish the sentences.

1 The giant's wife
2 The giant's huge bag
3 Jack stole

a. the giant's gold.
b. was kindhearted.
c. was filled with gold.

GRAMMAR POINT

Hide, or . . . (imperative + or . . .)

• **Hide, or** he will find you. (= **If you don't hide,** he will find you.)

hen

lay an egg

thief

harp

"Fee, fi, fo, fum, you have a boy for me today, don't you?" said the giant.

"Sorry, dear. I don't. But here are some bacon and eggs for you," she said.

After breakfast, the giant said, "Wife, bring me my hen. I want some golden eggs." So she brought the hen to the
bring-brought-brought
table. "Lay," said the giant. The hen laid a golden egg.
lay-laid-laid

After a while, the giant fell asleep at the table. Then, Jack came out of his hiding place. He grabbed the
took
hen and ran out of the castle. He climbed down the beanstalk and showed his mother the hen. They became very rich.
became bored

But Jack got bored one day, so he climbed up the beanstalk again. He went to the castle, but he hid from the giant's wife this time.
yelled loudly

"Fee, fi, fo, fum, I can smell a little boy," roared the giant.

"Can you? Maybe it's that thief again," said the giant's wife. "Let's find that boy."

They looked in the kitchen, but they could not find Jack. Soon, they gave up and ate breakfast. Then, the
stopped
giant got his harp. "Play," he said. The harp began to
grabbed, took
play some beautiful music.

KEY WORDS

- **lay an egg** to produce an egg
- **get bored** to become bored (≠ get excited)
- **give up** to stop doing; to abandon
- **steal** to take without permission
- **cut down** to chop down

- **grab** to take *grab–grabbed–grabbed
- **thief** a person who steals things
- **master** an owner
- **chase** to run after
- **fall down** to fall to the ground

After a while, the giant fell asleep at the table. Then, Jack came out of his hiding place. He grabbed the harp and ran out of the castle. But the harp called out, "Master, save me! The boy is stealing me!"

~~shouted~~

~~called out ---> help me~~

axe

The giant woke up and chased Jack. Jack ran to the beanstalk and began climbing down it. The giant started climbing down, too.

~~≠ fell asleep <---~~   ~~---> ran after~~

~~---> going down~~

"Mother, get the axe. Quick! The big giant is coming," shouted Jack. When he reached the bottom, he grabbed the axe. He cut down the beanstalk.

~~---> got to~~

The beanstalk fell, and the giant fell down with it. His head hit the ground. Thump! He was dead. Jack never went back to the giant's castle.

~~fall–fell–fallen <---~~

~~---> fell to the ground~~

Stop & Think

Why did Jack cut down the beanstalk?

CHECK UP   Put the right words.

| laid | stole | harp | cut down |

1 The hen _____ golden eggs.
2 The _____ played beautiful music.
3 Jack _____ the harp and ran out of the castle.
4 Jack _____ the beanstalk with an axe.

GRAMMAR POINT

. . . , don't you? (tag question)

- You have a boy for me today, **don't you?**

Jack and the Beanstalk   **19**

The Ugly Duckling

♪ 04

duck

crack

duckling

One summer in a country farmyard, Mother Duck was sitting on her new eggs. She sat on them for a long time. Finally, the eggs began to crack. Six little ducklings popped out and started to cry out, "Quack, quack!"
→ came out
Mother Duck was very pleased. "My little ducklings!" she said.
→ happy

She looked inside her nest. One egg had not opened.

"That's strange," she thought. "This egg is bigger than the other ones."
→ odd

→ remember
Mother Duck couldn't recall laying that seventh egg. How did it get there? "Did I count the eggs wrongly?" Mother Duck wondered.
incorrectly ≠ rightly
→ stopped by
An old duck came by to see the ducklings.

"Hello, Mother Duck. I see your eggs have hatched. How are the ducklings?" the old duck asked.

Stop & Think

How did the seventh egg look?

KEY WORDS

- **farmyard** the area around a farm
- **duckling** a baby duck
- **recall** to remember
- **hatch** to come out of an egg

- **crack** to break open
- **pop out** to come out
- **wonder** to think about
- **look like** to resemble; to look the same as

"Almost all of them have hatched. There is only one egg left," Mother Duck answered.

"That egg looks strange. It looks like a turkey egg. Leave it alone," said the old duck.
---→ Do not take care of it.

"No, I can't do that. It's my egg, so I must wait for it," said Mother Duck. She got back into her nest and sat on the big egg. After a while, the egg finally hatched.
---→ went back

nest

hatch

They looked at the last baby duckling with great surprise. He looked nothing like the other ducks. In fact, he did not look like much of a duck at all. He was big, gray, ugly, and strange looking.
---→ with shock
---→ did not look like
---→ Actually
---→ ≠ beautiful, handsome

turkey

"Well, he certainly is an unusual-looking duckling," said the old duck.
---→ surely
---→ strange-looking

"Hmm," said Mother Duck, "he was in the egg for so long, so he must be so big. I am sure he will become a proper-looking duck."
---→ normal-looking

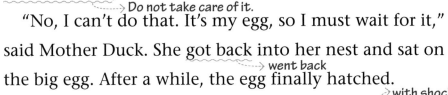

Stop & Think

How did the ugly duckling look?

CHECK UP True or false?

1 Mother Duck did not remember the seventh egg. _____
2 The last baby duckling looked strange. _____
3 The ugly duckling looked like the old duck. _____

GRAMMAR POINT

look + adjective / look like + noun

- That egg **looks** strange.
- It **looks like** a turkey egg.
- He **looked** nothing **like** the other ducks.
- He did not **look like** much of a duck at all.

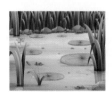

pond

peck at

laugh at

goose

Mother Duck took her children to the pond. They all jumped into the pond one by one. The ugly duckling swam very well. *swim-swam-swum* Actually, he swam even better than the others. *In fact* Mother Duck was pleased.

All of the animals gathered around *came around* Mother Duck and her ducklings. "What a beautiful family!" they all said. Then, they noticed *saw, found* the ugly duckling. "What is wrong with that big duckling? He's very ugly," they said. One of the ducks even pecked at *What happened to* the ugly duckling. This made the ugly duckling very sad.

Mother Duck and her ducklings went swimming in the pond every day. And, every day, the ducks and other animals laughed at *made fun of* the ugly duckling. Even the farm girl disliked *≠ liked* the ugly duckling. "Go away," she said. "You are an ugly duckling."

The ugly duckling felt very sad. "Nobody loves me. They all tease me! *make fun of* Why am I different from my brothers?"

Stop & Think

Why was the ugly duckling sad?

KEY WORDS

- **gather around** to come around
- **laugh at** to make fun of
- **tease** to make fun of
- **run away** to flee
- **noise** a sound
- **scared** afraid

- **notice** to be aware of; to pay attention to
- **dislike** to hate; to not like
- **be different from** to not be the same
- **loud** noisy (≠ quiet)
- **rifle** a long gun
- **hunter** a person who hunts animals

One night, he ran away from the farm. He traveled a

→ fled

long, long way until he finally found a huge field. He

soon fell asleep. When he woke up, he was by a lake. He

→ wake–woke–woken

looked up in the sky and saw two geese.

→ sg. goose

rifle

hunter

"You look very strange," they said. "But we like

you. Do you want to fly with us?" they asked the ugly

duckling.

The ugly duckling agreed, but he suddenly heard a

loud noise. "Bang! Bang!"

→ very big sound

The two geese fell to the ground.

→ fall–fell–fallen

They were dead. In the distance, the

From a distance ←

ugly duckling saw some men with

hunting rifles. He got very scared.

→ was very afraid

He ran away from the hunters. He ran

and ran until he was very far away.

Stop & Think

Who killed the two geese?

CHECK UP Choose the right words.

1 The ugly duckling was a _____ swimmer. (good | bad)
2 The farm girl _____ the ugly duckling. (liked | disliked)
3 The ugly duckling _____ the farm. (ran to | ran away from)
4 Hunters with _____ killed the two geese. (rifles | knives)

GRAMMAR POINT

-er + than . . . (comparative)

• He swam even **better than** the others.

hut

at sunrise

swan

Finally, he found an old hut in the forest. He entered the hut. There were a woman, a cat, and a hen. The woman was very old. "What are you? A duck?" she asked. "How wonderful! You can stay here and lay eggs for me."

The next day, the cat asked the ugly duckling, "Where are your eggs?"

"I don't have any eggs," he answered.

"Then you are useless. You must leave," the hen said.

> worthless ≠ valuable

The ugly duckling left the hut. The weather was getting colder.

> ≠ getting hotter

One day at sunrise, he saw something beautiful and strange overhead.

> over his head

It was a flight of beautiful

> a group of

birds—three swans! They had long necks and soft white wings. They were migrating south.

> moving south

Stop & Think

What did the ugly duckling see in the sky?

KEY WORDS

- **hut** a small house
- **useless** worthless
- **flight** a group of flying birds
- **freeze** to become ice
- **pick up** to lift
- **survive** to live; to not die

- **lay eggs** to produce eggs
- **overhead** over one's head; up in the air
- **migrate** to move somewhere else to live
- **lie** to be on the ground
- **be able to** can; to have an ability to
- **set free** to let go; to release

"Oh, what beautiful birds!" he thought. He called to them. "Who are you? Take me with you." But they did not hear him.

Winter came, and the water in the lake froze. The

freeze–froze–frozen

poor ugly duckling could not even swim in the water.

unlucky, unhappy

He was cold and had no food to eat.

A farmer walked by the lake. He saw the ugly duckling lying on the ice. "You poor bird," he said. "I

lie–lay–lain

will take you home and help you." He picked up the

lifted

ugly duckling and took him home. The man had a wife, a son, and a daughter. They took good care of the

looked after

ugly duckling. Slowly, he started to get better. Thanks to them, the ugly duckling was able to survive the cold winter.

could   stay alive

However, by springtime, he had grown so big. The

grow–grew–grown

farmer decided to set the ugly duckling free by the pond.

let go, release

lie

pick up

set free

Stop & Think

How did the ugly duckling survive the winter?

CHECK UP   Answer the questions.

1 Why couldn't the ugly duckling swim in the lake?
   a. There was no water.   **b.** He was a bad swimmer.   **c.** The water froze.

2 When did the farmer set the ugly duckling free?
   a. in the winter   **b.** in the spring   **c.** in the summer

GRAMMAR POINT

can / be able to

• The poor ugly duckling **could** not even swim in the water.
• Thanks to them, the ugly duckling **was able to** survive the cold winter.

flap

garden

shy

reflection

The ugly duckling was alone again. He was swimming [→ by himself] alone in the pond. Then, suddenly, he started to flap his wings and flew into the sky. "I can fly. I can fly!" [move quickly ←] shouted the ugly duckling. "This is amazing." [← fly–flew–flown]

The ugly duckling flew all around the land. Then, he looked down and saw a garden. It was a garden with a pond. "That's a beautiful garden," he thought. "I will go there."

He landed in the pond in the garden. He looked over [→ went down onto] [→ looked around] and saw three swans. They were the three swans he had seen in winter. "Oh, they are so beautiful," he thought. "I have to speak to them."

But the ugly duckling did not know what to say. He suddenly felt shy. He looked down into the water. Then, [→ ≠ looked up] he saw his reflection in the water. He looked just like [→ image] the swans. He was not an ugly duckling. He was a swan. "I'm a swan!" he cried.

Stop & Think

What was the ugly duckling?

KEY WORDS

- **alone** by oneself
- **fly into** to fly up into
- **shy** ≠ brave
- **throw** to toss *throw–threw–thrown
- **flap one's wings** to move one's wings quickly
- **land** to go down to the ground from flying
- **reflection** an image reflected by a mirror or water
- **pleased** happy; glad

"Mother, look," some children shouted. "There's a new swan. Isn't he beautiful? He's the most beautiful of all the swans."

throw

→ throw–threw–thrown

The children threw some bread into the pond for him to eat. He was so pleased. All his life, people had

→ happy, glad

thought he was ugly. Now, they told him how beautiful he was. It was the happiest moment of his life.

→ ≠ the saddest

CHECK UP   Put the right words.

the most	flew	reflection	ugly

1 The ugly duckling _____ into the sky.
2 The ugly duckling saw his _____ in the water.
3 He was not an _____ duckling anymore.
4 The ugly duckling was _____ beautiful of all the swans.

GRAMMAR POINT

the + -est (superlative)

• It was **the happiest** moment of his life.
• He's **the most beautiful** of all the swans.

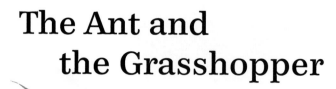

The Ant and the Grasshopper

 05

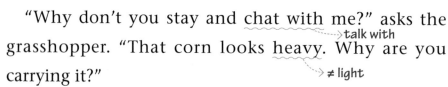

One summer day, a grasshopper hops into a field. He sings happily
`---> jumps into`
because it is a beautiful summer day. He sees an ant pass by. The ant
`---> go by`
is working hard. It is carrying some corn to its home.

grasshopper

"Why don't you stay and chat with me?" asks the
`--->talk with`
grasshopper. "That corn looks heavy. Why are you
`---> ≠ light`
carrying it?"

ant

"I'm saving food for the winter," answers the ant. "I
`---> keeping`
recommend that you do the same thing. Then, you will
`---> advise, suggest`
have plenty of food for the winter."
`---> a lot of, lots of`

"Winter?" says the grasshopper. "Why worry about that? We have lots of food right now. And winter is a long time away."
`---> far in the future`

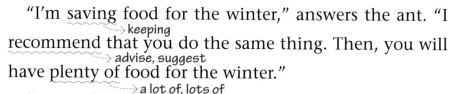

Stop & Think

Why does the ant work hard every day?

KEY WORDS

- **hop** to jump
- **recommend** to advise
- **gather** to collect
- **disappear** to vanish
- **look over** to look around

- **pass by** to go by
- **a long time away** far in the future
- **completely** entirely; totally
- **discover** to see; to realize
- **prepare for** to be ready for; to get ready for

The ant leaves the grasshopper. The ant works hard every day, so it gathers lots of food. After a while, the
<u>collects</u>
ant completely fills its house with food.
<u>entirely, totally</u>

Meanwhile, the grasshopper stays in the field. But he
<u>In the meantime</u>
does not work at all. Instead, he plays and sings every day.

carry

Soon, summer turns to fall, and fall turns to winter.
<u>changes to</u>
When the weather gets colder, the food starts to disappear. The grasshopper discovers that he has no
<u>vanish ≠ appear</u>   <u>realizes</u>
food to eat. He looks over at the ant's house. The ant has plenty of food and a nice, warm house. The grasshopper realizes how foolish he was.
<u>silly</u>

plenty of

weather

That winter, there is lots of snow. Later, when spring arrives, the ant comes out of its house. The ant had
<u>comes</u>
enough food during winter. Now, it is ready to start gathering food for the next winter. When the ant looks around the field, there is no sign of the grasshopper.

- *Moral: Work hard today to prepare for tomorrow.*
  be ready for

Stop & Think

What does the grasshopper do every day?

CHECK UP   Choose the right words.

1 The ant _____ a lot of food for the winter. (gathers | eats)
2 In winter, the _____ has no food to eat. (grasshopper | ant)
3 The grasshopper realizes how _____ he was. (fun | foolish)
4 Is the grasshopper in the field in the next spring? (Yes | No)

GRAMMAR POINT

see + O(object) **+ V**(verb)

- He **sees** an ant **pass** by.

The Hare and the Tortoise

hare

tortoise

race

One day, a hare was bragging about how fast he could
run. "I am the fastest animal in the entire forest," he
said. All the animals were tired of hearing the hare brag.
They had heard his bragging many times before.

> boasting
> sick of

The hare started to make fun of the tortoise. "You
are so slow," laughed the hare. "A snail could run faster
than you."

> laugh at

The tortoise smiled at the hare and replied, "Yes, I am
slow. But I bet I can reach the end of this field before
you. Let's run a race."

> I'm sure

"Oh, really? It's a bet," said the hare. "All right,
everyone. Let's find out who the faster animal is."

> betting

The tortoise and the hare went to the starting line.
All the animals in the forest gathered to watch. "Ready.
Go," shouted the fox.

> learn, discover
> ≠ finish line

Stop & Think

Why did the tortoise and the hare race?

KEY WORDS

- **brag** to boast
- **be tired of** to be sick of
- **find out** to learn; to discover
- **leave . . . behind** to get ahead of
- **far behind** far away from ≠ far ahead of
- **cross** to go across; to pass

- **entire** all; total
- **bet** to be sure; to challenge; betting
- **race off** to run quickly
- **look back** to look behind oneself
- **get rest** to rest; to relax
- **steady** constant; regular

The hare raced off and left the tortoise behind. The
↗ ran quickly   ⤍ got ahead of
tortoise simply kept moving as fast as he could.

When the hare was halfway across the field, he
looked back. The tortoise was far behind him. "Ha,"
↝ looked behind   ↝ far away from
thought the hare. "It will take the tortoise all day to
finish. I'm going to get some rest here." The hare rested,
↝ take some rest
but he soon fell asleep in the warm sunshine.

get rest

cross

The tortoise, in the meantime, walked and walked.
↝ meanwhile
He never stopped until he got to the finish line.

A few hours later, the hare woke up. "Oh, no!" the
hare thought. He looked ahead toward the finish line.
The tortoise was about to cross it. The hare ran as fast
↝ was going to
as he could, but it was too late. The tortoise crossed the
finish line first. The tortoise had won.
win–won–won ←
• *Moral: Slow and steady wins the race.*
constant ←

CHECK UP Finish the sentences.

1 The hare bragged
2 The tortoise bet
3 The tortoise
4 The hare woke up

a. kept walking to the finish line.
b. about how fast he could run.
c. too late.
d. he could beat the hare.

GRAMMAR POINT

as . . . as one can / could

- The tortoise simply kept moving **as fast as he could**. (= as fast as possible)
- The hare ran **as fast as he could**. (= as fast as possible)

The Sick Lion

♪ 07

hunt

forest

cave

Once, there was a very old lion. As he got older, he became weak and slow. He could no longer hunt animals. So he was not able to eat any food.
> grew older
> ≠ strong
> could not

The lion was sure he would soon die. He was very sad. As he slowly walked home, the lion told a bird about his sad situation. Soon, all of the animals in the forest heard about the lion.

The other animals felt sorry for the lion. "That's terrible," they said. "We should visit the lion and see how he is doing." So, one by one, they went to visit the lion in his cave.
> felt bad for
> awful, very bad
> one after another

The lion was old and weak, but he was also very wise. As each animal came into his cave, they were easy to catch and eat. Soon, the old lion became fat.
> clever, smart
When ←

Still, he kept pretending to be sick. And the animals kept going into the lion's cave. After a while, many of the animals of the forest had disappeared.
> acting
> vanished

Stop & Think

What did the lion do?

KEY WORDS

- **situation** a condition
- **wise** very clever; smart
- **disappear** to vanish
- **die** to become dead
- **footprint** an impression of one's foot
- **terrible** awful; very bad
- **pretend** to act
- **call out** to yell; to shout
- **closely** carefully
- **misfortune** bad luck

One day, early in the morning, the fox went to the lion's cave. The fox was very wise, too. He slowly walked close to the cave. Standing outside the cave, the fox called out, "Hello. How are you feeling now?"

footprint

The lion answered, "I am not doing very well. Why
↪ *yelled, shouted*
don't you come in? I can't see you very well. Come closer and tell me some kind words.
I am old and will die soon."

While the lion was talking, the fox was looking closely at the ground. The fox suddenly
↪ *carefully*
realized what the lion was doing.

Finally, the fox looked up and answered, "No, thank you. I can see many footprints entering your cave. But I cannot see any footprints
↪ *footsteps*
leaving your cave."
↪ *going out of*

• *Moral: A wise person learns from the misfortunes of others.*

bad luck ↩

Stop & Think
Why did the fox refuse to enter the cave?

CHECK UP   Put the right words.

| hunt | footprints | sorry | pretended |

1 The lion could not _____ animals anymore.
2 The animals felt _____ for the lion.
3 The lion _____ to be sick.
4 The fox looked at the _____ outside the cave.

GRAMMAR POINT

as (conjunction)

• **As** he got older, he became weak and slow.
• **As** he slowly walked home, the lion told a bird about his sad situation.
• **As** each animal came into his cave, they were easy to catch and eat.

The Boy Who Cried Wolf

shepherd

a flock of sheep

pipe

There once was a shepherd boy. He watched a flock of sheep at the bottom of a mountain. The shepherd boy was bored watching the sheep all day by himself. So he sometimes talked to his dog or played his pipe.

→ a group of
≠ at the top of
≠ was excited
alone

One day, he became very bored. So he thought of a plan to have some fun. He decided to play a trick on the villagers. He ran down toward the village and cried out, "Wolf! Wolf!"

→ idea
→ fool, trick

The villagers heard the shepherd boy. The kind villagers ran up the mountain to help him. But when they arrived, they found no wolf.

≠ ran down

"Where is the wolf?"

→ there was no wolf

The boy laughed at the sight of their angry faces.

"Ha, ha, ha! I fooled all of you," he said.

→ tricked

"Don't cry 'wolf,' shepherd boy," said the villagers, "when there's no wolf!" They went back down the mountain.

→ shout

Stop & Think
Why did the shepherd boy yell, "Wolf!" the first time?

KEY WORDS

- **shepherd boy** a boy who watches sheep
- **bored** ≠ excited
- **play a trick on** to trick; to fool
- **fool** to trick
- **louder** ≠ quieter
- **scatter** to spread out

- **flock** a group of animals
- **by oneself** alone
- **run up** to go up quickly
- **frightened** scared
- **trick** to fool
- **liar** a person who tells lies

A few days later, the shepherd boy was bored again. So the boy cried out again, "Wolf! Wolf!" When the villagers arrived, the shepherd boy was laughing at them again. → as

One day while the boy was watching the sheep, a wolf really did come. It started attacking his sheep. The frightened boy ran toward the village and shouted even → scared louder than before.

frightened

"Wolf! Wolf! A wolf is killing my sheep!"

But the villagers thought he was fooling them again. So they didn't come. "He will not trick us fool ← again," they said. Because none of them went to help the boy, the wolf killed many of the sheep. And the flock scattered.
spread out ←

- *Moral: No one believes liars* → trusts *even when they tell the truth.*
≠ lie

Stop & Think
Why did the villagers not go to help the shepherd boy?

CHECK UP True or false?

1 The shepherd boy tricked the villagers by crying out, "Wolf!" _____
2 A wolf attacked the shepherd boy's sheep. _____
3 The shepherd boy killed the wolf. _____

GRAMMAR POINT

to + V (purpose)

- He thought of a plan **to have** some fun.
- The kind villagers ran up the mountain **to help** him.
- None of them went **to help** the boy.

Super
Reading
Story
Training
Book

Step

2

The Little Mermaid

— Hans Christian Andersen

The Little Mermaid

mermaid

tail

Deep beneath the sea, the Sea King lived. He lived
----> under
with his six daughters, very beautiful mermaids,
in a palace. His wife died many years ago. Their
----> looked after
grandmother took care of the mermaid princesses.
----> ≠ princes

Each princess was beautiful, but the youngest was the
loveliest of all. Her skin was like a rose. Her eyes were
----> lovely–lovelier–loveliest
deep sea-blue. Her long hair flew smoothly in the sea.
And she had the most beautiful singing voice in the
world. When she sang, the fish flocked from all over the
----> gathered around
sea to listen to her. She seemed like other girls on land.
But, like all mermaids, she had no legs. She had a tail
like a fish.

KEY WORDS

- **take care of** to look after; to care for
- **loveliest** most beautiful
- **seem like** to resemble; to be similar to
- **for oneself** by oneself
- **stand by** to stand next to

- **princess** ≠ prince
- **flock** to gather around
- **keep . . . company** to be with another
- **hardly** barely
- **look up** to look toward the sky

The Little Mermaid had a wonderful life. She played and sang with her sisters all day long. She also liked to spend her time in her wonderful sea garden. The seahorses kept her company, and sometimes a dolphin would come and play.
→ played with her

seahorse

But the Little Mermaid was happiest when her grandmother told her stories. Her grandmother told her all about the world above the sea. She told her about beautiful ships, villages, and the people above.

dolphin

The Little Mermaid never went out of the sea.

"Oh, how I'd love to go up there and see the sky at last!"
→ I really want to
"You're still too young," said her grandmother.

ship

"When you are fifteen, you can swim to the top of the ocean and see the wonderful things for yourself," said her grandmother.
→ by yourself

→ could not wait
The Little Mermaid could hardly wait. Every night, she stood by the window and looked up through the water. She often dreamed of the land above the water.
→ stand-stood-stood

CHECK UP Choose the right words.

1 The Little Mermaid had a _____ singing voice. (terrible | beautiful)
2 All mermaids have a _____ instead of legs. (tail | head)
3 The Little Mermaid dreamed of the _____ above the water. (land | sea)

GRAMMAR POINT

the loveliest of all (superlative + a group or place)
- The youngest was **the loveliest of all**.
- She had **the most beautiful** singing voice **in the world**.

comb

wave

lightning

break apart

At last, the Little Mermaid turned fifteen.
became fifteen years old

"There, now you can go to the surface," said her father.

The Little Mermaid was so excited. She combed her
thrilled ≠ bored
long golden hair. She polished the scales on her tail. She
shined
kissed her grandmother goodbye.

Quickly *swim–swam–swum*
In a second, the Little Mermaid swam up toward the
surface of the sea. She swam so fast that even the fish
could not keep up with her.
follow, run after

Suddenly, she popped out of the water. How
came out of
wonderful! For the first time, she saw the great sky. It
was full of red and orange clouds. The sun was setting.
going down
"It's so lovely!" she exclaimed happily.
shouted

In front of her was a big ship. She swam close to the
ship and looked inside. There was a big party. There
were many handsome gentlemen, but the finest of all
fine–finer–finest
was a prince. He was laughing and shaking hands with
everyone. She had never seen anyone like him before.
She could not take her eyes off him.
stop looking at him

All of a sudden, the weather changed. The sky became
Suddenly
dark, and heavy rain started to fall. The waves became
very rough. Lightning flashed, and thunder boomed
≠ smooth *made a loud sound*

Stop & Think

Who did the Little Mermaid see inside the ship?

KEY WORDS

- **polish** to shine; to clean
- **keep up with** to follow
- **flash** to make a bright light
- **roll up and down** to move up and down

- **in a second** quickly; swiftly
- **pop out of** to come out of
- **thunder** the loud sound caused by lightning
- **break apart** to come apart; to go to pieces

throughout the sky. The ship rolled up and down on the

→ moved up and down

waves. Then, the ship broke apart and started to sink.

The Little Mermaid saw the prince fall into the sea.

go beneath the water ←

"People cannot breathe underwater," she thought. "I

breathe

must save him." The Little Mermaid went diving down

to look for him. He was sinking deep into the ocean.

She seized his shoulder and took him to the surface.

→ grabbed

storm

When she got to land, she pushed the prince's body

→ reached

onto the shore. The prince was still not awake. The

≠ asleep

Little Mermaid looked into his handsome face all night

long.

By the morning, the storm was finished, and the

warm sun appeared. In the sunlight, the prince looked

→ ≠ disappeared

more handsome. His eyes were still

closed. "Wake up. Please don't die,"

she whispered.

spoke softly ←

CHECK UP   True or false?

1 The Little Mermaid thought the prince was handsome.   _____

2 The prince could breathe underwater.   _____

3 The Little Mermaid saved the prince's life.   _____

GRAMMAR POINT

so . . . that . . .

• She swam **so** fast **that** even the fish could not keep up with her.

beach

rock

sorrow

look out

Now, she could see dry land ahead. She took the prince onto a pretty beach with calm water. She laid the prince on the warm sand. At that moment, she saw some girls walking along the sand. Quickly, she swam away and hid behind some rocks. She watched the prince. "I must stay here until someone comes to save him," she thought.

≠ wet

quiet ←

put down

hide–hid–hidden

rescue

After a while, a pretty girl came along the beach. She saw the prince and ran to him. At that moment, the prince opened his eyes and smiled at the girl. The girl called for help. Soon, some people came and took the prince away.

→ yelled for

carried away

The Little Mermaid felt so sad because she could not see him anymore. She swam back home full of sorrow.

full of sadness ←

"What did you see?" her sisters asked. But she told them nothing. She was too sad to speak. She was quiet all day long.

→ passed

Days and weeks went by. The Little Mermaid could only think about the prince. She missed him so much. At night, she often swam to the beach. She looked for the prince, but she did not see him.

→ wanted to see

Stop & Think

Who found the prince on the beach?

KEY WORDS

- **calm** peaceful
- **take away** to carry away; to remove
- **go by** to pass
- **foam** bubbles

- **lay** to put down *lay–laid–laid
- **sorrow** sadness
- **wish** a desire; a dream
- **soul** a spirit

One day, she finally told her sisters her

> at last

story. One of the sisters took her to his palace. He lived in a great palace by the sea. She could see the prince looking out his window. She was so happy. Every night, she swam near the palace and watched the prince.

The Little Mermaid loved the world above the sea more and more. Now she had only one wish—to become a human.

> desire, dream

"Grandmother," she asked one day. "Can humans live forever?"

> without end

"No, they can't," said her grandmother. "Humans die. They live shorter lives than we do. Mermaids live for three hundred years, and then we become foam on the

*sg. life

> bubbles

sea. But humans have souls. Their souls live forever."

> spirits

foam

Stop & Think

What did the Little Mermaid wish?

CHECK UP Put the right words.

| mermaids | souls | prince | rocks |

1 The Little Mermaid hid behind some _____.
2 The Little Mermaid only thought about the _____.
3 _____ live for three hundred years.
4 Humans have _____, but mermaids do not.

GRAMMAR POINT

see + O(object) + V(verb) / V-ing

• The Little Mermaid **saw** the prince **fall** into the sea.
• She **saw** some girls **walking** along the sand.
• She could **see** the prince **looking** out his window.

marry

witch

scary

bone

"I want to be like a person. Can I get a human soul?" asked the Little Mermaid. _→human_ _→ have_

"Don't say that," said her grandmother.

"Is there any way that I can get a soul?" she asked over and over again. _→repeatedly_

At last, her grandmother replied. _→ Finally_

"There is only one way. If a man loves you with all his heart and marries you, then his soul can enter your _→ truly_ body. Then, you would have a soul and would live forever," she continued. "But that will never happen _→ occur_ because we have tails. Humans think tails are ugly. They prefer legs. No man will want to marry a mermaid."

The Little Mermaid looked at her tail and thought.

"I want to have two legs. I must win the prince's love _→ ≠ lose_ and marry him. I love him. I will do anything for him. Maybe the sea witch can help me."

She swam off to see the sea witch. The sea witch lived _→ swam away_ in a horrible, scary place. Her house was made from _awful ←_ _→ frightening_ the bones of dead sailors. And there were sea snakes

Stop & Think

How can a mermaid get a soul?

KEY WORDS

- **over and over again** repeatedly
- **prefer** to like one thing more than another
- **scary** frightening
- **grant one's wish** to make one's wish come true
- **hurt** to feel pain; to cause pain

- **marry** to get married to; to wed
- **horrible** awful
- **afraid** scared; frightened (≠ brave)
- **split in** to divide into
- **bear pain** to stand being hurt

everywhere. The Little Mermaid felt very afraid. She almost left. Then, she thought, "The prince! And my soul! I must not be afraid."

scared ←
nearly went away →

sailor

The Little Mermaid swam up to the sea witch. When the witch saw the Little Mermaid, she said, "I know what you want. I can give you a pair of human legs. Then, you will be able to walk on land. Come in."

→ can

magic drink

The Little Mermaid followed the witch into the bone house.

"You are a stupid girl. You will be sorry. But I will grant your wish," the witch said.

→ foolish
→ regret
→ make your wish come true

"I will make a magic drink for you. Tomorrow morning, before sunrise, you must swim to land and drink it. Then your tail will split in two, and you will have two legs. But it will be very painful. It will hurt every time you walk. Can you bear the pain?"

≠ sunset ←
divide into ←
→ cause pain
→ stand, deal with

Stop & Think

How can the Little Mermaid become a human?

CHECK UP   Finish the sentences.

1 Humans think
2 The sea witch's house
3 The Little Mermaid
4 The Little Mermaid's tail

a. wanted a pair of human legs.
b. was made from bones.
c. will split in two.
d. tails are ugly.

GRAMMAR POINT

will be able to / must be able to

- You **will be able to** walk on land. (*NOT* will can)
- I **must be able to** talk to the prince. (*NOT* must can)

painful

tears

"Yes," replied the Little Mermaid. "It doesn't matter!" whispered the Little Mermaid with tears in her eyes. "As long as I can go back to him!"
⤳ If

"But remember one more thing," the sea witch added. "Once you become a human, you can never become a mermaid again. You will never return to your
⤳ go back
father's palace. And if the prince marries another girl, you will turn into foam on the sea."
⤳ change into

"I will do it," the Little Mermaid said.

"Ah, but there is one more thing," said the sea witch. "You must pay me. I want your voice. You have the prettiest voice in the world."
⤳ pretty–prettier–prettiest

"My voice? Then how can I speak?" the Little Mermaid asked. "How will I make the prince fall in love with me? I must be able to talk to him."

love me

pay

"You are beautiful," said the sea witch. "You can dance. You can smile at him. Your deep blue eyes will speak for you. You do not need to talk."

"All right," the Little Mermaid agreed to the price.

→ Immediately

Instantly, her voice was gone.   → disappeared

knife

The sea witch made the magic drink for her. The Little Mermaid took the drink and swam to land. She reached the beach and then drank the magic drink.

→ drink–drank–drunk

Suddenly, she felt a horrible pain. It was like a knife in her body. She passed out in the sand.

→ fainted

pass out

The next morning, the Little Mermaid woke up. She looked at her body. Her tail was gone. She had the prettiest legs on Earth. Then, she saw a shadow. She looked up. The prince was standing over her and looking down at her.

shadow

Stop & Think
What did the sea witch take from the Little Mermaid?

CHECK UP   Answer the questions.

1 What will happen to the Little Mermaid if the prince marries someone else?
   a. She will lose her voice.   **b.** She will turn into foam.   **c.** She will get a soul.

2 What happened right after the Little Mermaid drank the magic drink?
   a. She became a human.   **b.** She found the prince.   **c.** She passed out.

GRAMMAR POINT

as long as / once

• **As long as** I can go back to him!
• **Once** you become a human, you can never become a mermaid again.

castle

jewelry

"Who are you? Where did you come from?" asked the prince.

But the Little Mermaid could not speak. She just looked deeply into his eyes with her sad blue eyes. At that moment, the prince had very strong feelings for her.

→ take care of

"I'll take you to the castle and look after you," he said. The prince took the Little Mermaid inside his castle. Every step felt like sharp knives. But she was with the prince, so she was happy.   → ≠ dull

In the days afterward ←

In the days that followed, the Little Mermaid started a new life. The prince gave the Little Mermaid her own room. He gave her beautiful clothes and jewelry to wear, too. She was the most beautiful girl in the kingdom. But the Little Mermaid could not say anything to the prince. All she could do was smile at him.

→ had many parties

The prince held many parties. One night, some girls sang for the prince. They sang well, but the Little

sing-sang-sung ←

Mermaid was sad. "I used to sing much better than

Stop & Think

Where did the prince take the Little Mermaid?

that," she thought. "I wish the prince could hear my singing voice."

Then, the girls started to dance. Now, the Little Mermaid could dance for the prince. She danced and danced. She suffered terrible pain throughout her body,

--> felt, experienced

--> horrible

but she danced so beautifully. Everyone was amazed by

was surprised by <--

the Little Mermaid's dancing. The prince could not stop watching her.

take his eyes off <--

have a picnic

go riding

After the party, the Little Mermaid and prince did everything together. They had picnics on the beach. They went riding together. They walked beside the calm ocean. The Little Mermaid's feet ached, but she did not care. She was happy to be with the prince.

--> went to ride a horse

--> hurt

--> did not mind

Sometimes at night, she went to the ocean. She put her feet into the cool water. It always felt so good. At those times, she thought of her family. She missed them so much. "I hope they are well. I hope they understand me," she thought.

Stop & Think

What did the Little Mermaid do at the prince's party?

CHECK UP Choose the right words.

1 _____ sang for the prince at the party. (Some girls | The Little Mermaid)
2 The Little Mermaid and the prince did _____ together. (everything | nothing)
3 The Little Mermaid _____ her family. (forgot about | missed)

GRAMMAR POINT

I wish . . . (subjunctive)

• **I wish** the prince **could hear** my singing voice.

drown

get married

sail

marry ←---

> As days went by

Day by day, the prince loved the Little Mermaid more and more. But he loved her like a sister. He did not think of marrying her.

One day, the prince told the Little Mermaid, "You are the sweetest girl I know. You remind me of a girl.
> make me think of

This girl saved my life when my ship sank. I almost
> rescued

drowned. I only saw her once, but I cannot forget her. She is the only girl I can ever love."

"I wish I could tell him it was me!" the Little
> I wish I were able to, I want to

Mermaid thought. "I saved you. But you don't know me." She felt so sad.
> commanded

One day, the king ordered the prince to visit the next kingdom. The king wanted the prince to marry the princess of the kingdom.

"I must go there because my father ordered me," said the prince, "but no one can make me marry this princess. You remind me more of my lost love. If I must
> not found, missing

get married, I will marry you." He kissed the Little Mermaid. "Will you come with me? I want you to sail with me," he asked.

Stop & Think

How did the prince feel about the Little Mermaid?

KEY WORDS

• **sweetest** the nicest; the kindest
• **save one's life** to rescue someone
• **come true** to become real; to happen
• **remind** to make one remember something
• **drown** to die in the water
• **be broken** to be shattered

The prince, the Little Mermaid, and many others got on a ship and sailed across the sea. At last, they arrived at a beautiful town. Many people came to the ship and welcomed the prince. And there was the princess. She had deep blue eyes, just like the Little Mermaid.

broken

"It is you," cried the prince. "My true love! You are the girl who saved my life. Let us get married tonight."

The prince turned to the Little Mermaid. He said, "My wish has come true.

faced

become real

I am so happy. I have found my true love. And I know you will be happy for me because you love me."

The Little Mermaid's heart was broken. She would never marry the

break–broke–broken

prince now. His wedding meant one thing.

She must die.   *mean–meant–meant*

CHECK UP   True or false?

1 The prince did not think of marrying the Little Mermaid. _____
2 The king ordered the prince to marry the Little Mermaid. _____
3 The prince met the girl he had been looking for. _____
4 The princess of the next kingdom saved the prince's life. _____

GRAMMAR POINT

who / whom (relative pronoun)

- You are *the girl* **who** saved my life.
- You are *the sweetest girl* **(whom)** I know.
- She is *the only girl* **(whom)** I can ever love.

angel

bride

stay awake

That night, the prince and the princess got married on his ship. The wedding was beautiful. There was joyful music everywhere. But the Little Mermaid did
----> happy
not hear the music.

"This is my last night on Earth," she said to herself. "Tomorrow, I will die and become foam on the sea."

At the wedding, the Little Mermaid danced for the last time. She moved like an angel. She danced more
----> ≠ for the first time
beautifully than ever. But her feet and heart were in pain. After that night, she would not see the prince
----> hurt
again.

At midnight, the music stopped, and the prince led his bride away. All was silent, yet the Little Mermaid
----> took away   ----> quiet
stayed awake. She went out to look at the water by
----> ≠ fell asleep
herself.
----> alone

Just then, the Little Mermaid's sisters swam up to the ship. They looked different. Their beautiful hair was gone.
----> missing

Stop & Think

What did the Little Mermaid do at the wedding?

KEY WORDS

- **joyful** happy
- **lead away** to take away
- **silent** quiet (≠ loud)
- **rise** to come up
- **sneak** to move silently
- **be in pain** to hurt
- **bride** a wife (≠ groom)
- **stay awake** to remain alert (≠ fall asleep)
- **splash** to splatter; to spray
- **peacefully** quietly

"Little sister!" they cried. "We gave our hair to the

↗ In response, As payment for it

sea witch. In return, she gave us a knife. Before the

sun rises, you must kill the prince. When his blood

splashes on you, your tail will return. You will become

⤳ splatters   ⤳ come back

a mermaid again. Hurry up and do it. You must kill him

before the sun rises, or it will be too late."

⤳ otherwise, or else

The Little Mermaid took the knife from her sisters.

⤳ walked into very quietly

It was very sharp. She sneaked into the prince's room.

≠ dull ⤶

The prince and the princess were sleeping peacefully.

⤳ quietly

The Little Mermaid took the knife out.

She looked at the knife. Then, she

looked at the prince. No, she

could not do it. She loved him.

She threw the knife into the sea.

⤳ throw–threw–thrown

Then, she jumped into the sea.

The sun was rising.

splash

CHECK UP Finish the sentences.

1 The prince and the princess   **a.** got married on the ship.
2 The Little Mermaid's sisters   **b.** couldn't kill the prince.
3 The Little Mermaid had to kill   **c.** gave their hair to the sea witch.
4 The Little Mermaid   **d.** the prince before the sun rose.

GRAMMAR POINT

give A to B (= give B A)

- We **gave** our hair **to** the sea witch. (= We **gave** the sea witch our hair.)
- She **gave** us a knife. (= She **gave** a knife **to** us.)

The Little Mermaid felt cold water. "I am dying," she thought.

change into ⤶

But the Little Mermaid did not <u>turn into</u> foam. Suddenly, she felt her body <u>rising into the air.</u> She

⤷ going up

saw other lovely <u>floating</u> children. They were singing around her.

⤷ flying

"Where am I? Who are you?" asked the Little Mermaid. She could speak again! She had a new voice. It was even more beautiful than before.

"You're with us in the sky. We are the fairies of the air," they <u>responded.</u> "You are now a fairy of the

⤷ replied

air. There are many ways to win a soul. We can <u>get souls</u> by doing good <u>deeds,</u>" they continued.

⤷ get a soul

⤷ acts

"Mermaids only get souls if humans love them. But the fairies of the air can live for three hundred years. If we do good deeds for three hundred years, we can <u>earn souls.</u>

win souls, get souls ⤶

Stop & Think

What did the Little Mermaid become?

KEY WORDS

- **turn into** to change into; to become
- **lovely** beautiful
- **deed** an act
- **fly down** ≠ fly up

- **rise** to go up (≠ fall)
- **floating** flying
- **earn a soul** to win a soul; to get a soul
- **heaven** the place where souls go

You tried so hard to earn a soul. You loved the prince so much that you gave your life for him. We will help you get a soul. Your soul will live forever."

"I can earn a soul? This is wonderful."

fairy

The Little Mermaid looked down at the ship. She saw the prince and the bride. The prince was looking sadly

≠ happily

into the ocean. He seemed to have guessed what had happened to her.

≠ flew up *fly–flew–flown

fly down

She flew down to them. Of course, they could not see the Little Mermaid. She moved her body around them. They felt the cool air move around them. The Little Mermaid kissed the prince and his bride. Then, she smiled and flew up into the sky.

fly up

"In three hundred years, I will have a soul," she said. "And I will see my prince in heaven."

Stop & Think

Why did the prince look sad?

CHECK UP Put the right words.

guessed   fairy   soul   kissed

1 The Little Mermaid became a _____ of the air.
2 The Little Mermaid can get a _____.
3 The prince _____ what had happened to the Little Mermaid.
4 The Little Mermaid _____ the prince and princess.

GRAMMAR POINT

feel + O (object) + V (verb) / V-ing

- They **felt** the cool air **move** around them.
- Suddenly, she **felt** her body **rising** into the air.

Super
Reading
Story
Training
Book

3

Beauty and the Beast
— Madame de Beaumont

•

The Stars
— Alphonse Daudet

Beauty and the Beast

♪ 12

Once, there was a rich merchant who had many
ships. He bought and sold things from around the
world. He lived in a big house by the sea. He had three
daughters. The daughters were all very beautiful, but
the youngest was the most beautiful of all. In fact, she
was so beautiful that everyone called her "Beauty."

Beauty was not only pretty but also kind and smart.
She loved reading. Her two sisters were not very nice
though. They were selfish and greedy. They liked to go
to parties and to wear nice dresses. They were always
mean to Beauty. They laughed at her when she read
books. They only thought about marrying rich men.

wealthy ≠ poor

≠ eldest

As a matter of fact

self-interested ←

≠ generous

unkind ←

made fun of

merchant

greedy

Stop & Think

What kind of a person was Beauty?

KEY WORDS

- **youngest** ≠ oldest; eldest
- **selfish** caring only for oneself
- **marry** to get married to; to wed
- **earn money** to make money

- **not only A but also B** B as well as A; both A and B
- **greedy** wanting more of everything
- **sink** to go beneath the water
- **be supposed to** to be expected to

One day, there was a terrible storm at sea. All the merchant's ships sank, so he lost everything. The man had to sell his big house and move into a small house in the countryside.

sink–sank–sunk ←⋯

⋯→ lose–lost–lost

storm

"I'm sorry, my children. All my ships sank," said the man. "We have no money, so we have to work to earn money."

make money ←⋯

"But, Father," said the eldest daughter, "we have never worked in our lives. We don't know how to work."

⋯→ ≠ youngest

⋯→ *sg. life

sink

"We can't work. No rich man will want to marry us!" the middle daughter cried.

The family moved to the small country house.

"This house is so tiny," said the eldest daughter.

⋯→ very small

"How are we supposed to live here?" the middle daughter cried.

⋯→ How can we live here?

countryside

Stop & Think

What happened to the merchant's ships?

CHECK UP Put the right words.

> tiny   countryside   selfish   enjoyed

1 Beauty's sisters were _____ and greedy.
2 Beauty was beautiful and _____ reading.
3 The merchant sold his house and moved to the _____.
4 Their new house was very _____.

GRAMMAR POINT

not only . . . but also . . .

• Beauty was **not only** pretty **but also** kind and smart.

sit around

port

jump for joy

The two sisters did not stop complaining. But Beauty did not complain at all. Instead, she tried to be happy and to make everyone else happy.

→ grumbling

"I will clean the house, Father," she said. "This house is small, but we can be happy here."

Beauty worked hard every day. She woke up early in the morning and cleaned the house. She cooked breakfast, lunch, and dinner for her family. But her sisters never did any work. They sat around and complained all the time.

→ got up

→ sat and did nothing

One day, Beauty's father received a letter. He read the letter and instantly cheered up.

→ got

→ immediately, at once

"Children, I just heard some good news," he said. "One of my ships did not sink. It is bringing back lots of gold and silver for us. We are rich again. I must go to the port now."

→ hear–heard–heard

→ coming back with

Beauty's sisters jumped for joy. "We are rich! We are rich!" they cried.

→ were very happy

"Oh, Father, you must buy us some new dresses," said the two older sisters.

Stop & Think

How did Beauty's sisters like their new house?

KEY WORDS

- **complain** to express dissatisfaction
- **cheer up** to become happy
- **jump for joy** to be very happy
- **steal** to rob; to take without permission
- **afford to** to have enough money to

- **sit around** to sit and do nothing
- **bring back** to come back with
- **pirate** a thief on the ocean
- **fix** to repair; to mend

"Yes, my dears, I will," said their father.

"And you, Beauty, what would you like me to get you?" asked her father.

give, buy ←

rose

Beauty did not want anything. She was happy just because she could see her father happy. "Please bring me a rose, Father," said Beauty. "There are no roses in our garden."

→ went quickly

pirate

Beauty's father hurried to the port. When he arrived there, he heard some bad news.

→ ≠ good news

"The gold and silver are gone," his friend told him.

→ go-went-gone

"Pirates stole it. There is your ship. It has many holes

→ steal-stole-stolen

in it, so you must fix the holes before the ship can sail again."

→ repair

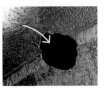
hole

→ fell down

Beauty's father fell to the ground.

→ don't have enough money to

"Without any gold or silver, I cannot afford to fix my ship," said Beauty's father sadly. "I will leave the ship there for now and return to the countryside."

→ go back

Stop & Think
What happened to Beauty's father's ship?

CHECK UP   Finish the sentences.

1 Beauty worked hard and
2 One of Beauty's father's ships
3 Some pirates stole
4 Beauty's father could not

a. cleaned every day.
b. afford to fix the ship.
c. did not sink.
d. the gold and silver.

GRAMMAR POINT

would like . . . to . . .

• What **would** you **like** me **to** get you?

pocket

coin

howl

Then he remembered his daughters. He looked in his pockets and found only a few coins. "I don't have enough money to buy any dresses." Sadly, he started to walk back home.

recalled (→ remembered)

Suddenly, the weather became terribly cold. It began to snow, and the wind blew heavily. Soon, he was lost in a forest.

very, really (→ terribly)
blow–blew–blown (← blew)
strongly (→ heavily)
got lost (→ lost)

"This is very strange," he said to himself. "I have never seen this forest before. I must be lost."

He heard wolves howling loudly. He began to feel very afraid. "I must find some shelter. There is no way I will get home tonight," he said.

someone who steals (→ shelter)

He looked around and saw a light at some distance. "What is that? Is there a house there?"

in the distance (→ at some distance)

KEY WORDS

- **terribly** very; really
- **howl** to make a sound like a dog or wolf
- **look around** to look at everything in an area
- **burn** to be on fire
- **be full of** ≠ be empty

- **heavily** strongly; powerfully
- **shelter** a place that protects a person
- **wonder** to be curious about
- **fireplace** an indoor place to have a fire
- **starving** very hungry

Beauty's father followed the light. After a few minutes, he found a castle.

"I wonder who lives here," he said. He went to the door of the castle.
~~~> am curious about

"Hello?" he called. But there was no answer. The door was open, so he walked inside. He saw no one. It was cold, and he was tired. He entered a large hall. It was a dining room. A huge fire was burning in the fireplace.
~~~> walked into
~~~> on fire
And the dining table was full of food. There was a single plate on the table with a knife and fork beside it.
~~~> one

"This must be someone's dinner," he thought. He waited for the person to arrive, but no one came. Finally, after he had waited for a couple of hours, he sat down at the table and ate the food. Because he was starving, he ate all of the food. Then, he found a
~~~> two, a few
~~~> very hungry
bedroom and fell asleep immediately.
~~~> instantly, at once

dining room

fireplace

plate

bedroom

Stop & Think
What did Beauty's father see in the dining room?

CHECK UP   Choose the right words.

1 The weather suddenly became very _____. (cold | hot)
2 Beauty's father saw a _____ in the forest. (light | wolf)
3 There was _____ in the castle. (someone | no one)
4 Beauty's father sat down at the table and _____ the food. (ate | cooked)

GRAMMAR POINT

have/has + p.p. (present perfect: experience)

• I **have** never **seen** this forest before.

Beauty and the Beast   **63**

snowstorm

promise

rose bush

pick

In the morning, Beauty's father woke up. He looked around the room. He saw some breakfast on the table. But he did not see anybody. He sat down at the table and enjoyed breakfast. While he ate, he looked outside.
---> ate, had
He saw a beautiful garden full of flowers.

"That's strange," he thought. "Last night, there was a huge snowstorm, but the sun is shining now, and the
---> very big
flowers are blooming."

Just then, he remembered the promise that he had made to Beauty. "A rose!" he said aloud. "I promised Beauty I would bring her a rose."   made a promise

He went out to the garden and found a rose bush. It was full of beautiful red roses. He picked one. But as soon as he picked the rose, he heard a loud roar. And he
---> the moment   ---> a loud sound
saw a frightful, angry beast coming toward him.
scary <---
"You dirty thief!" cried the Beast.
---> someone who steals
"I saved your life and gave you food and a bed. But, in return, you are stealing my flowers. Now you're
as payment for it <---
going to pay for it. I'm going to kill you."
---> be punished for

Stop & Think

Why did Beauty's father go to the garden?

KEY WORDS

- **snowstorm** heavy snow
- **frightful** scary
- **forgive** to pardon

- **bloom** to open, as in a flower
- **pay for** to be punished for; to suffer
- **angrily** with anger

Beauty's father fell to the ground and cried out, "Forgive me. I only wanted a single rose for my daughter. I promised to bring a rose to my youngest daughter, Beauty. Please do not kill me."

~~Forgive~~ ⟶ *Pardon*

angrily

The Beast looked down at him angrily and said, "All right. You may go home. But you have to send me your daughter. She must come here and live in this castle with me. If not, then you must return here and die. Go back to your bedroom. There is a box of gold there. Take it and go."

~~angrily~~ ⟶ *with anger*

~~If not~~ ⟶ *Otherwise*

box of gold

Stop & Think
What did the Beast want Beauty's father to do in return for sending him home?

CHECK UP True or false?

1 The garden had many yellow roses. _____
2 The Beast wanted to eat Beauty's father. _____
3 The Beast gave Beauty's father a box of gold. _____

GRAMMAR POINT

the usage of "promise"

- I **promised** Beauty **(that)** I would bring her a rose.
- I **promised to** bring a rose to my youngest daughter, Beauty.

say goodbye

ugly

as fast as possible

Beauty's father hurried away from the castle as fast as he could. When he got home, he told his children what had happened.

"I must return to the castle," he said. "I just wanted to say goodbye to all of you."

upset with

Beauty's sisters suddenly became angry at her.

"Beauty, what have you done?" they shouted. "It's your fault. You wanted the rose, and now Father must die. You stupid girl!"

responsibility

foolish

scared

"Father, I'll go to the Beast. I'm not afraid. I will go and live with the Beast," Beauty said quietly.

"No, Beauty, no."

calmly

"There is no choice," she said. "The Beast will kill you and our family if I do not go."

Beauty's father was very sad. He went to his bedroom. Beauty followed him there.

"What is the Beast like, Father? Is he very ugly?" she asked.

bad-looking

"Yes, the Beast is ugly, but he can also be kind. Look. He gave me this box of gold. But do not tell your

Stop & Think

What did Beauty ask her father about the Beast?

KEY WORDS

- **suddenly** instantly; at once
- **stupid** foolish; not smart
- **walk up to** to approach
- **weird** strange

- **angry at** upset with; mad at
- **arrive at** to get to
- **yell** to shout; to speak loudly
- **favorite food** the food that one likes the most

sisters about it. They will only want to spend it on new dresses."

"Father, please give the money to them," Beauty told her father. "While you <u>were away</u>, two men came here.

marry
------> were out, were not here
My sisters are going to marry them, so they will have to buy many things. They need that money."

The next morning, Beauty said goodbye to her family and left for the castle. She was very sad, but she did not cry. Late in the evening, she finally <u>arrived at</u> the Beast's

yell
------> ≠ left for
castle. The door was open, so she <u>walked up to</u> it. She saw nobody. "Hello?" she <u>yelled</u>, but no one answered.
went near, approached <------

favorite

"What a <u>weird</u> place!" thought Beauty. But she was
------> strange
very <u>brave</u>. She walked around the castle and found the
------> not afraid
dining room. There was a table with lots of food on it. All her <u>favorite</u> foods were on the table. There were two
------> most liked
plates, two glasses, two forks, and two knives. Beauty <u>sat down</u> and ate the food.
------> ≠ stood up

Stop & Think
Who met Beauty at the castle?

CHECK UP   Answer the questions.

1 What did Beauty's father show her?
   a. a box of gold   **b.** a picture of the Beast   **c.** a red rose

2 What was on the dining table?
   a. nothing   **b.** Beauty's favorite foods   **c.** some cakes and pies

GRAMMAR POINT

had + p.p. (past perfect: earlier past)

• When he <u>got</u> home, he <u>told</u> his children what **had happened**.

sign

pick up

note

After supper, Beauty started to look around the castle.
→ dinner

It was a beautiful castle with many fine rooms. When
→ very good, expensive

Beauty got to one room, she looked at the door. There

was a sign on the door. It read "Beauty's Room."

"Is this my room? Well, if he gives me a special room,

maybe he will not kill me," she thought.

Beauty opened the door and went inside. It was the

most beautiful room she had ever seen. It was full of

flowers, books, and beautiful clothes. She picked up one
→ lifted

book and opened it. Inside, there was a note. It read:

> Welcome, Beauty.
> Do not be afraid. → ≠ in danger
> You will be safe and happy here.
> I will do anything you want.
> You may have all of this.

"He must be very kind," Beauty thought. Beauty was

very tired. She went to bed and fell asleep instantly.

Beauty spent the next day alone. In the evening,
→ by herself

Beauty put on the most beautiful dress and went to the
→ ≠ took off

Stop & Think

What did Beauty find in the book?

KEY WORDS

- **look around** to explore
- **pick up** to lift
- **alone** by oneself
- **growl** a low sound an animal makes

- **kill** to make a living thing die
- **safe** secure
- **put on** to wear clothes or accessories
- **seem to** to appear; to look like

dining room. All of her favorite foods were on the table.

Beauty sat down. Suddenly, she heard a gentle growl,
soft

and the Beast came in. He was wearing fine clothes, but
he had as much hair as a lion.
a lot of hair like

present

Beauty said, "Thank you for my present, sir."
gift

"Call me Beast," said the Beast.

"Tell me, Beauty. Am I very ugly? Are you afraid of me?"
scared of

"Yes, Beast, you are ugly," said Beauty slowly. "But you
seem to be very gentle. I'm not afraid
look   _nice, kind_

of you because you're nice to me."

"Thank you for saying that,"
said the Beast.

That evening, Beauty and the
Beast sat down and ate dinner
together. They talked about
many topics. By the end of
the dinner, Beauty thought
that the Beast was not so
frightening.
scary

CHECK UP Put the right words.

| lion | frightening | ugly | sign |

1 The _____ on the door read "Beauty's Room."
2 The Beast had hair like a _____.
3 Beauty told the Beast that he was _____.
4 Beauty thought the Beast was not so _____.

GRAMMAR POINT

as much/many . . . as . . .

• He had **as much** hair **as** a lion.

mirror

heart

propose

The next day, Beauty went downstairs. There, she saw the Beast waiting for her.

≠ went upstairs

"There is a mirror in your bedroom," the Beast said. "It is a magic mirror. When you want to see your father, look into that mirror."

"That is very generous of you. Thank you," replied Beauty.

kind

"Beauty, I know that I am ugly," said the Beast. "I must be stupid as well because I cannot think of anything smart to say to you."

≠ smart   *also*

Beauty felt bad. "I know many people who look beautiful but have ugly hearts," she said. "I like you better than those people, Beast."

felt sorry

"Then will you marry me?" asked the Beast.

"Marry you? Oh, no. I'm sorry, but I cannot do that," she said.

Beauty lived in the castle with the Beast, and they were very happy. Every night at nine o'clock, Beauty and the Beast had dinner together and chatted. At the end of every dinner, the Beast always proposed, "Will you marry me?" And Beauty always answered, "I like you, but I cannot marry you."

chat–chatted–chatted

asked to get married

Stop & Think

What did the Beast ask Beauty to do?

KEY WORDS

- **generous** kind; sweet
- **feel bad** to feel sorry; to feel sad
- **propose** to ask someone to get married
- **be sick in bed** to be ill in bed

- **stupid** foolish; dumb
- **chat** to talk
- **sick** ill
- **all by oneself** all alone

For three months, Beauty lived at the castle. She was happy there. She read books and walked through the garden every day. But, one day, she looked into the magic mirror. She saw her father. He was sick in bed and was all by himself.

all alone

"I must go and see my father. I must talk to the Beast at dinner," Beauty thought.

At nine o'clock, Beauty and the Beast had dinner together. The Beast said, "If you will not marry me, then will you be my friend? I want you to stay with me forever."

always

"Of course I will," Beauty answered. "You are kind to me. I will stay here with you, but there is a problem. I looked into the magic mirror and saw my father. He is sick in bed and all by himself. Will you please let me go to visit him?"

be sick in bed

Stop & Think

Why did Beauty want to go home?

CHECK UP Finish the sentences.

1 The Beast gave Beauty
2 Beauty and the Beast
3 Beauty saw her father

a. had dinner together every night.
b. sick in bed.
c. a magic mirror.

GRAMMAR POINT

want + O(object) + to + V(verb) / let + O + V

- I **want** you **to stay** with me forever. (*NOT* want you stay)
- Will you please **let** me **go** to visit him? (*NOT* let me to go)

"If you leave, you will not come back," the Beast said.

> go away
> won't

"I promise to come back," said Beauty. "But let me go there for one week."

The Beast thought for a moment and then said, "Okay. You may go."

> for a while
> wear ≠ take off

He gave Beauty a ring and said, "Take this. Put on this ring and go to bed. Tomorrow, you will wake up in your father's home. After seven days, take the ring off and put the ring by your bed. You'll wake up in this castle."

> ≠ put on
> place

"Goodbye, Beauty. Don't forget your promise. Come back in seven days."

Beauty thanked the Beast. She put the ring on and went to sleep. In the morning, when she woke up, she was in her father's home. She got up and ran to her father.

> woke up

"Father, I'm home," she said.

"Oh, Beauty," he cried, "you have returned. I thought the Beast ate you. I'm so ill, and I am all alone. Your sisters are married, and they never visit me."

> sick

ring

put on

take off

Stop & Think

Why did the Beast give Beauty a ring?

KEY WORDS

- **put on** ≠ take off
- **take care of** to look after
- **respond** to answer
- **handsome** good-looking

- **promise** a vow
- **feel better** to get better
- **be good to** to be nice to
- **unkind** mean (≠ kind)

"Father, I am only here for one week, but I will take good care of you. You will feel better soon," Beauty responded.
→ look after
→ get better
→ answered, replied

husband

Beauty's father looked at her. "You look beautiful," he said. "Your dress looks very nice. Is the Beast good to you?"
Is the Beast nice to you? ←

handsome

"Yes, he is very kind to me. I like him very much. Perhaps I almost love him," Beauty said.
→ Maybe
→ nearly

Her older sisters heard that Beauty was back. They came to visit her with their husbands. Both sisters were unhappy. **One had a very handsome husband,** but he was unkind. **The other had a very smart husband,** but he talked too much. When they saw Beauty in her beautiful dress, they both became angry.
→ ≠ kind
→ got angry

"Why is she always happy?" said one.

"I can't stand this. Let's keep Beauty here longer than a week. Then, the Beast will become angry with her. Maybe the Beast will eat her then." The other sister agreed.
→ can't bear
→ ≠ disagreed

Stop & Think
How did Beauty feel about the Beast?

CHECK UP   Choose the right words.

1 Beauty _____ the ring and went to bed. (put on | took off)
2 In the morning, Beauty was in _____. (the Beast's castle | her father's house)
3 Beauty's sisters were very _____. (happy | unhappy)

GRAMMAR POINT

one / the other

• **One** had a very handsome husband. **The other** had a very smart husband.

have a dream

lie

grass

So they said to Beauty, "Oh, Beauty, we are so happy to see you. Please stay here for a few more days."

Beauty disliked seeing them sad. So a week passed, ⤳ ≠ liked
but Beauty did not go back to the castle.   went by

Then, one night, Beauty had a dream. In her dream, ⤳ dreamed
she saw the Beast. The Beast was lying on the grass. He was very sick and sad. He seemed to be dying. Beauty
looked like he was dying ↞
heard the Beast saying, "Oh, Beauty! Beauty, why haven't you come back yet? I am dying."

Beauty woke up and jumped out of bed. It was the middle of the night.   ⤳ midnight   ⤳ took off

"I'm coming back, Beast!" she said. She removed the ring quickly and put it beside her bed. Then, she went back to sleep.   ⤳ next to

Beauty woke up in the castle. She jumped up and went looking for the Beast. She tried every room in the
⤳ searching for
castle, but she could not find the Beast anywhere.

Stop & Think

Where did Beauty see the Beast?

Then, she remembered her dream. She ran into the garden and saw the Beast.

"Wake up, Beast. Wake up," she cried. "I'm back. I'm so sorry."

die

→ raised

The beast slowly lifted his head. "I waited for you, Beauty. But you didn't come. Now it is too late. I'm going to die soon."

→ ≠ early

"No, Beast, you cannot die. I need you," said Beauty.

"I love you, Beast. Please don't die. I want to marry you." Beauty kissed his ugly face.

Stop & Think

What did Beauty tell the Beast?

CHECK UP True or false?

1 The Beast was dying in Beauty's dream. _____
2 Beauty woke up from the dream and removed the ring. _____
3 Beauty found the Beast in the dining room. _____

GRAMMAR POINT

dislike -ing / go -ing

• Beauty **disliked** see**ing** them sad. (*NOT* disliked to see)
• She jumped up and **went** look**ing** for the Beast. (*NOT* went to look for)

prince

fairy

magic wand

At that moment, something magical happened. The sky was filled with bright light. In a moment, Beauty found herself inside the castle. The room was filled with flowers. But the Beast was not there. Next to Beauty was a very handsome young man. He was dressed like a prince.

> magic
> shining
> was wearing clothes

"What's going on here? Where is Beast?" Beauty asked.

> What is happening here?

"I am here, Beauty," said the prince. "I am the Beast. Well, I was the Beast."

"A long time ago," said the prince, "I was selfish and unkind. A fairy touched me with her magic wand and put a spell on me. She turned me into a beast. She cursed me to be a beast forever until someone loved me. You broke the spell, Beauty. I became a man again because you love me."

cast a spell <
> changed . . . into
> stopped magic from happening

Then, the fairy suddenly appeared and said, "Yes, Beauty, you understand that kindness is more important

> came into sight

Stop & Think

What did the fairy do to the prince?

KEY WORDS

- **magical** related to magic
- **be filled with** to be full of
- **fairy** an elf
- **curse** to use bad magic on someone
- **appear** to come into sight
- **invite** to ask someone to go somewhere; to ask for
- **happen** to take place; to occur
- **prince** ≠ princess
- **put a spell on** to cast a spell on
- **break a spell** to stop magic from happening
- **grant** to give

than looks. Your sisters don't understand that. So now they are unhappy ⤳ *appearance* with their husbands. But you will be happy with your prince. You are the most beautiful couple in the world. I will marry you and give you happiness for the rest of your lives. And I will grant you many beautiful children, too." ⤳ *until you die*   ⤳ *give*

wedding

Beauty and the prince married soon. They had a wonderful wedding. Beauty invited her father to live in the castle with her. Beauty and the prince lived happily ever after.

CHECK UP Answer the questions.

1 How did Beauty break the spell?
  a. She kissed the Beast.   **b.** She married the Beast.   **c.** She loved the Beast.

2 What did the fairy promise Beauty and the prince?
  a. many children   **b.** long lives   **c.** lots of money

GRAMMAR POINT

-thing + adjective

• At that moment, **something magical** happened. (*NOT* magical something)

The Stars

♪ 15

Once I was

I used to be a shepherd in the Luberon region of France. It was a very isolated place, so I was often all alone in the pasture. Sometimes, I did not see many people for weeks. During those weeks, I only had my dog and the flocks of sheep to accompany me.

remote

be with

Sometimes

From time to time, I saw a loner who lived on Mount Lure. He would come down to hear some news of the outside world. Also, I sometimes saw coal miners. They worked in the coal mines near my field, so I spoke with them as they went back and forth to the coal mines.

were coming and going

Once every two weeks, I got a visitor from the farm. This person was usually the farm boy or an old woman who worked at the farm. They were sent to bring me

shepherd

pasture

coal miner

Stop & Think

Who did the shepherd sometimes see?

KEY WORDS

- **isolated** remote; separated from other things
- **accompany** to go with; to be with
- **supplies** food and other essential goods
- **delivery** the bringing of goods to someone's place
- **flock** a group of animals
- **loner** a person who spends much time alone
- **master** a boss; an employer
- **run out of** to become used up

→ food and other essential goods

supplies on a mule. I was always happy to see them. They would tell me all of the news from the lowlands.

However, the news that interested me the most was an area of low ← about my master's daughter. Her name was Stephanette, and she was the most beautiful girl in the surrounding around the area ← area. Without seeming to take too much interest, → Pretending not to have much interest I would ask how Stephanette was doing. I asked if there were any young men who wanted to marry her.

mule

delivery

Of course, I was just a lowly shepherd who worked → unimportant, humble for her father. I had to remind myself that there was no → make myself remember way that Stephanette would be interested in me. After → Anyway all, there were many wealthy and handsome young → rich men in the area.

One Sunday, I was waiting for the delivery boy to arrive. It had been two weeks since my last delivery, so I was running out of supplies. By ten o'clock, no one had arrived yet. → almost used up

> *Stop & Think*
>
> **What news interested the shepherd the most?**

CHECK UP True or false?

1 The shepherd spent most of his time alone. _____
2 A person delivered supplies to the shepherd every week. _____
3 The shepherd often spoke with Stephanette. _____
4 One Sunday, the delivery boy arrived at ten o'clock. _____

GRAMMAR POINT

would

- He **would** come down to hear some news of the outside world.
- They **would** tell me all of the news from the lowlands.
- I **would** ask how Stephanette was doing.

noon

dark clouds

ray

farmhand

"That's odd," I thought. "There must be a problem at my master's house."

> strange

I continued to wait, but no one came by noon. "They must have forgotten to send my supplies," I said to myself.

Around noon, I noticed that a big storm was coming. In the distance, some dark clouds were gathering. Soon, heavy rain began to pour down. "Now I understand," I said to myself. "The bad weather has delayed the delivery person. The roads must be muddy by now. I should not expect him to arrive yet."

> realized

> fall heavily

> made the delivery person late

> full of mud

A few hours later, the storm was over. The sun shone high in the sky, and its warm rays spread bright light all over the fields.

> shine–shone–shone

All of a sudden, I heard the familiar sound of the mule's bells. I eagerly looked to see if it was the farmhand or the old woman. However, it was neither the farmhand nor the old woman. It was the beautiful Stephanette! Oh, what a wonderful surprise that was!

> well-known

> excitedly

> whether

She got off the mule, and then she said to me, "I got lost on my way up the hill."

> was lost

"Are you all right, mistress?" I asked.
She smiled and nodded at me.

> ≠ master

KEY WORDS

- **odd** strange
- **delay** to make someone to be late
- **spread** to stretch out
- **eagerly** excitedly; enthusiastically
- **get off** ≠ get on

- **notice** to realize; to become aware of
- **muddy** full of mud; dirty
- **all of a sudden** suddenly
- **farmhand** a person who works on a farm
- **get lost** to lose one's way

"The farmhand is sick," said Stephanette, "and the old woman is visiting her children to spend the holiday with them. So my father sent me instead."

> vacation

I could not take my eyes off her. She looked so beautiful in that fresh afternoon air. In fact, I had never seen her so close before. And I had never spoken to her. I had only ever seen her from a distance.

> stop looking at her

> from far away

When I returned to the lowlands in the winter, her father would invite me to dinner at his farm. At those times, she would walk silently across the room and not say a word to any of the servants. She had

household workers

always looked very proud during those times. And now she was standing in front of me.

Stop & Think

Why did Stephanette come to the field?

CHECK UP Choose the right words.

1 The heavy _____ delayed the delivery person. (snow | rain)
2 The person on the mule was _____. (the old woman | Stephanette)
3 Stephanette _____ on her way to the field. (got lost | took a nap)
4 Had the shepherd ever spoken to Stephanette before? (Yes | No)

GRAMMAR POINT

neither . . . nor . . .

• It was **neither** the farmhand **nor** the old woman.

barn

straw

cape

stick

After she took my supplies off the mule, Stephanette looked around the area. She seemed curious about the pasture and the small barn.
> interested in

"So this is where you live, shepherd?" she asked. She noticed my bed in the barn. It was a simple bed made of straw and sheepskin. There were a cape and a stick hanging on the wall above my bed.

"You must be lonely and bored because you are always alone," she continued. "What do you do all day long?"

I wanted to answer, "I only think about you, Stephanette," but I did not. As a matter of fact, I could not say a single word to her. How embarrassed I was.
> In fact
> a word
> ashamed

Stephanette must have noticed my embarrassment. She started to tease me.
> make fun of

"Do the fairies come to see you sometimes?" She was laughing with a twinkle in her eyes. I thought she was like a fairy, but I did not say those words. Instead, I said nothing.
> pleasantly, happily

Stop & Think

What did the shepherd say to Stephanette?

KEY WORDS

- **hang** to suspend
- **embarrassed** ashamed or nervous
- **tease** to make fun of
- **footstep** the sound or mark of walking
- **chore** a small duty or job
- **shiver** to shake
- **cross** to go across

- **lonely** lonesome
- **embarrassment** the state of being embarrassed
- **disappear** to vanish; to go away
- **remain** to stay
- **soaking wet** very wet
- **flood** to overflow
- **tremble** to shake

"Well, I must leave now," she said. Stephanette got

≠ got off

back on the mule and said goodbye to me. Then, the
mule led her back toward the farm. I watched her as

---> lead–led–led

she disappeared down the hill. The sound of the mule's

----> went away

footsteps continued for a while. The sound of those
footsteps remained with me for a long time.

----> stayed

Later in the evening, I brought the flock of sheep
back in from the fields. As I was completing my chores,

finishing <------

I heard a voice calling my name. It was Stephanette. She
had returned. But she was not smiling anymore. Now,
she was soaking wet and shivering from the cold.

very wet <-----   -----> shaking

"At the bottom of the mountain, there is a river as
you know. The rain from the storm caused the river to
flood. The water has risen very high. I tried to cross the

overflow <----   -----> rise–rose–risen

river, but I almost drowned in the water. I was so scared

drown–drowned–drowned <-----   ----->was very afraid

and didn't know what to do. So I just returned here,"
she said in a trembling voice.

----> shaking

footstep

soaking wet

flood

Stop & Think

Why did Stephanette return to the shepherd?

CHECK UP   Finish the sentences.

1 The shepherd's bed was
2 The shepherd was
3 Stephanette left to go
4 The water in the river

a. embarrassed in front of Stephanette.
b. had risen too high.
c. made of straw and sheepskin.
d. back to the farm.

GRAMMAR POINT

"-ing" form (present participle)

• There were a cape and a stick **hanging** on the wall above my bed.
• She was **laughing** with a twinkle in her eyes.
• As I was **completing** my chores, I heard a voice **calling** my name.

→ ≠ wrong

I was not sure what to do. It was not right for her to spend the night on the mountain. I also could not leave the flock of sheep to take her home. But then I thought, "The nights in July are short. It's only one night."

make a fire

→ just

I immediately made a fire so that she could dry
→ at once
her feet and clothes. Then, I gave her some milk and cheese, but Stephanette was not interested in eating. She burst into tears. And I almost felt like crying, too. It
→ started crying

burst into tears

was completely dark outside. I took her to the barn, and
→ totally, entirely
made a bed ←⸱⸱ I prepared a bed for her. I laid out a new sheepskin on
→ set out *lay–laid–laid
the fresh straw so that she could rest. I said goodnight
→ new   → relax
and went outside.

I sat down in front of the door. I tried not to think of the young lady who was resting in my house. But all that I could think of was her. I was proud because I had
helped ← assisted her. Tonight, it was my responsibility to keep
duty ←
her safe. In happiness, I looked up in the sky. The stars
→ Happily, Gladly
shone more beautifully than ever that night.

Stop & Think

How did the shepherd feel about
taking care of Stephanette?

KEY WORDS

- **burst into tears** to start crying
- **completely** totally; entirely
- **lay out** to set out
- **keep . . . safe** to protect someone or something
- **frighten** to scare; to make someone afraid

- **almost** nearly
- **prepare** to get ready
- **be proud** to have a feeling of pride
- **normal** usual; regular
- **shooting star** a meteor

A while later, the barn door opened, and Stephanette came out.

"I cannot sleep," she said. "Do you mind if I sit next to the fire?"
→ Is it okay if

frog

shooting star

She sat down by the fire. I gave her a goatskin to wrap around herself. We sat by the fire in silence. That
→ quietly
night, every creature seemed to come alive. The frogs in
→ living thing
the pond croaked louder than normal. The insects sang
→ usual
loudly as well. The fire made a brilliant bright light as it
→ very bright
burned through the night. Even the night air seemed to be fresher than normal.
→ fresh–fresher–freshest
Some noises in the night frightened her. She moved
→ sounds
closer to me. Just then, a shooting star passed in the sky above us. It was the most beautiful shooting star I had ever seen.

Stop & Think
What did Stephanette suddenly do?

CHECK UP   Answer the questions.

1 Where did the shepherd make a bed for Stephanette?
   a. by the fire   **b.** in the barn   **c.** in the pasture

2 How did the noises make Stephanette feel?
   a. warm   **b.** frightened   **c.** angry

GRAMMAR POINT

it . . . to + V (preparatory "it")

- Tonight, **it** was my responsibility **to keep** her safe.
- **It** was not right **for her to spend** the night on the mountain.

plain

Milky Way

point out

"What is that?" asked Stephanette.

"A soul that has entered Heaven," I responded.

Stephanette looked at me and said, "You are not like the other young men I know."

I answered, "I am probably like most other men, but my life in the field is very different from theirs. Here, I live close to the stars. I know what happens up there better than people from the plains."

similar to

perhaps, maybe

Stephanette looked up into the sky and said, "Look! There is another shooting star." She pointed to a shooting star streaking across the sky.

moving quickly

"It's so beautiful. I have never seen so many beautiful stars in my life. Do you know the names of the stars?"

KEY WORDS

- **soul** a person's spirit
- **stretch** to extend
- **constellation** a group of stars
- **streak of light** a long band of light
- **point out** to show
- **form** to make; to create

"Of course, mistress, I do," I answered. "Look up there. Do you see the streak of light that travels across the sky? That is the Milky Way. The Milky Way stretches all across France and goes into Spain. Soldiers often use the Milky Way to find their way home."

> long band of light

> extends

constellation

I continued to point out some of the stars to her. I explained constellations to her.

"Many stars combine to form constellations. They are like pictures in the sky. Can you see that group of stars? That is the Big Dipper. The three stars in front are the Three Animals. And there is Orion the Hunter up there."

> make

come together, unite

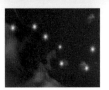

Big Dipper

"Did you know that we shepherds are able to use the sky like a clock? I can tell the time by looking at the stars. For instance, right now, it is almost midnight." I kept talking.

> can

> know what time it is

> continued

Stop & Think

What did the shepherd show Stephanette in the sky?

CHECK UP   Put the right words.

| tell | shooting star | Milky Way |

1 Stephanette pointed to a _____ in the sky.
2 The _____ stretches across all of France.
3 Shepherds can _____ time by looking at stars.

GRAMMAR POINT

to + V (purpose)

- Soldiers often use the Milky Way **to find** their way home.
- Many stars combine **to form** constellations.

Evening Star

Saturn

"All of the stars are beautiful. But the most beautiful star of all is the Evening Star. It comes out first every night. It is the shepherd's friend. She lights our way at dawn when we take our flocks out to the fields —→ lead outside and also in the evening when we return. We call her Maguelonne. Maguelonne chases Saturn in the sky and marries him every seven years." —→ follows

"What? The stars can marry?" she exclaimed.

"Oh, sure. The stars can get married," I told her.

KEY WORDS

- **dawn** daybreak
- **enchanting** charming; attractive
- **march** a movement
- **brilliant** very bright and strong

- **exclaim** to yell; to shout
- **fade** to become weaker; to disappear gradually
- **imagine** to think; to consider
- **lose one's way** to get lost

I was just about to explain how the stars get married.
→ was going to
Then, I felt as Stephanette laid her head on my shoulder
→ lay–laid–laid
and fell asleep. In the cool breeze, the ribbons in her
→ a light wind
hair danced, and I felt the touch of her curls against my

curls

neck. It was the most enchanting feeling.
→ charming, attractive
We stayed like that until the stars began to fade and
disappear gradually ←
the first rays of dawn appeared. I wanted that night to
last forever.
→ movement
All above us, the stars continued their march across
thought, considered ←
the night sky. I imagined that one of the stars, the finest
→ fine–finer–finest
and the most brilliant, had lost her way and was resting
her head on my shoulder.

Stop & Think

How did Stephanette fall asleep?

CHECK UP   Choose the right words.

1 The _____ is the most beautiful star of all. (Evening Star | Saturn)
2 Stephanette _____ in front of the fire. (woke up | fell asleep)
3 Stephanette _____ her head on the shepherd's shoulder. (laid | stayed)

GRAMMAR POINT

the + -est (superlative)

• It was **the most enchanting** feeling.
• One of the stars, **the finest** and **the most brilliant**, had lost her way.

Super
Reading
Story
Training
Book

TRAINing
BOOK

Table of
Contents

BOOK 1

BOOK 2

Super
Reading
Story
Training
Book

Step

1

The Magic Cooking Pot

·

The Shoemaker and the Elves

·

Jack and the Beanstalk

·

The Ugly Duckling

·

Aesop's Fables

The Magic Cooking Pot

Once upon a time, / a little girl / lived with her mother. They lived / in a small house / near a forest.

The girl and her mother / were very poor. They had no money. And there was no food / in the house.

"Oh, Mother, / I'm so hungry," said the little girl.

"I'm sorry, / but we don't have any food," her mother said.

"I will go to the forest / to look for some food. Maybe / I'll find / some nuts or berries / for us."

The little girl / went to the forest / and searched for some food. But she couldn't find / anything to eat. Then, / she sat on a rock / and began to cry.

"What am I going to do? I'm so hungry, hungry!" she cried.

"Don't cry, / little girl."

Suddenly, / the girl heard a voice. She looked up. She saw an old woman / in front of her.

"Take this," said the old woman.

"What is it?" asked the little girl.

"It's a magic cooking pot," replied the old woman.

"A magic cooking pot?" asked the girl.

"What does it do?"

"Watch," said the old woman.

"Cook, little pot, cook," she said.

Suddenly, / the pot started to cook. It cooked / some nice hot porridge. In a couple of minutes, / it was full of porridge.

- **once upon a time** 從前從前　• **live with** 跟⋯⋯住在一起　• **poor** 窮的
- **look for** 尋找　• **nut** 核果 *複數 **nuts**　• **berry** 莓果 *複數 **berries**
- **search for** 尋找　• **sit on** 坐在⋯⋯上 *sit-sat-sat　• **be going to** 將要
- **suddenly** 突然間　• **look up** 仰視　• **in front of** 在⋯⋯前面　• **take** 收下；拿去
- **magic** 魔法的　• **pot** 鍋子　• **cook** 煮　• **porridge** 麥片粥　• **be full of** 充滿

CLOSE UP

1　**to look for some food** 去找點食物 /
I'll find some nuts or berries 我會找到一些核果或莓果
look for是對需要的東西或遺失的東西刻意地去「尋找」的意思；find是在某個地方無意間「找到」、「發現」的意思。

2　**in a couple of minutes** 過了幾分鐘
〈in＋時間〉是「在⋯⋯之後」的意思，表時間的經過。

3　**was full of porridge** 滿滿一鍋的麥片粥
〈be full of . . .〉是「充滿了⋯⋯」的意思，也可以改寫成be filled with。

魔法鍋子

從前從前 **once upon a time**，有一個小女孩 **a little girl** 跟媽媽住在一起 **live with her mother**。她們住在森林附近 **near a forest** 的一間小屋子裡 **in a small house**。

小女孩和媽媽很窮 **be very poor**，她們沒有錢 **have no money**，屋子裡 **in the house** 也沒有食物 **no food**。

「喔！媽媽，我好餓 **be so hungry**。」小女孩說。

「對不起，我們沒有半點食物 **don't have any food**。」媽媽說。

「我去森林 **go to the forest** 裡找點食物 **look for some food**，也許 **maybe** 我可以找到一些核果或莓果 **some nuts or berries**。」

小女孩走進森林找食物 **search for some food**，但是她找不到 **can't find** 任何可以吃的東西 **anything to eat**，後來，她坐在一塊大石頭上 **sit on a rock**，哭了起來 **begin to cry**。

「我該怎麼辦？我好餓，好餓。」她大哭。

「小女孩 **little girl**，別哭 **don't cry**。」

突然間 **suddenly**，女孩聽到了一個聲音 **hear a voice**，她抬頭看 **look up**，看到她前面 **in front of her** 有個老婆婆 **an old woman**。

「收下這個 **take this**。」老婆婆說。

「這是什麼？」小女孩問。

「這是一個有魔法的鍋子 **a magic cooking pot**。」老婆婆回答。

「有魔法的鍋子？」小女孩問。

「它會做什麼？」

「妳看 **watch**。」老婆婆說。

「煮吧 **cook**，小鍋子 **little pot**，煮吧。」她說。

突然間，鍋子開始煮東西 **start to cook** 了。它煮了一些又香又熱的麥片粥 **some nice hot porridge**，過了幾分鐘 **in a couple of minutes**，就煮了滿滿一鍋的麥片粥 **be full of porridge** 了。

"Wow!" said the girl. "That's amazing. Let's eat the porridge."

"Wait," said the old woman. "First, / the pot must stop."

Then, / she said to the pot, / "Stop, little pot, stop."

The pot / immediately / stopped cooking.

"You must always say / those words, / or the pot will keep cooking porridge. Now, / you can eat."

"It's delicious!" said the little girl.

"You can have this pot," said the old woman.

"Oh, I am so happy. Thank you so much."

"Just don't forget / the magic words," said the old woman.

The little girl took the pot / and ran back to her home.

"Mother," shouted the little girl.

"Look at / what I have. It's a magic cooking pot."

The girl's mother / looked at the pot.

"Magic? Are you sure?"

"Of course. Watch this," answered the little girl.

"Cook, little pot, cook."

Immediately, / the pot cooked / some nice hot porridge. In a couple of minutes, / it was full of porridge.

"Wait a minute, / Mother," said the little girl.

"We have to say / the magic words / to stop the pot. Stop, little pot, stop," she said.

The pot / immediately / stopped cooking.

The little girl and her mother / ate porridge / every day. They were not hungry / anymore.

One day, / the little girl went out / to play with her friends. She was out / for a long time. Her mother / became very hungry. So she decided to eat / without her daughter.

- **amazing** 神奇的　　• **immediately** 立刻　　• **keep V-ing** 繼續做某事　*keep-kept-kept
- **delicious** 好吃的　　• **forget** 忘記　　• **magic words** 咒語　　• **take** 帶　*take-took-taken
- **run back** 跑回　　• **shout** 大喊　　• **look at** 看著某物　　• **anymore** 不再
- **go out** 出去　*go-went-gone　　• **be out** 不在　　• **decide to** 決定　　• **without** 沒有
- **daughter** 女兒　≠ son

CLOSE UP

1　**the pot must stop** 鍋子必須停止 / **you must always say those words** 妳每次都要說這些咒語 / **we have to say the magic words** 我們必須說咒語

　　must 和 have to 是「必須要去做……」的意思，表必要或義務。

2　**you can eat** 妳可以吃 / **you can have this pot** 妳可以擁有這個鍋子

　　這裡的 can 是表許可的意思。

3　**what I have** 我得到的

　　名詞子句〈what＋主詞＋動詞〉是「主詞所……的什麼」的意思。

　　例 what I do（我所做的事）/ what I need（我所需要的東西）。

「哇 **wow**！」小女孩説，「真神奇 **be amazing**，我們來吃麥片粥吧 **let's eat the porridge**。」

「等一下 **wait**，」老婆婆説，「首先 **first**，鍋子必須停止 **must stop**。」

然後，她對鍋子説：「停止 **stop**，小鍋子，停止。」

鍋子立刻 **immediately** 停下來不煮了 **stop cooking**。

「妳每次 **always** 都要説這幾個字 **say those words**，不然 **or** 鍋子會一直煮麥片粥 **keep cooking porridge**。現在 **now**，妳可以吃 **can eat** 了。」

「真好吃 **be delicious**！」小女孩説。

「妳可以擁有這個鍋子 **have this pot**。」老婆婆説。

「喔！我真是太高興了 **be so happy**，真是謝謝妳 **thank you so much**。」

「別忘了 **don't forget** 咒語 **the magic words**。」老婆婆説。

小女孩帶著鍋子 **take the pot**，跑回她的家 **run back to her home**。

「媽媽。」小女孩大喊 **shout**。

「妳看我得到什麼 **what I have**，這是個魔法鍋子。」

女孩的媽媽看著鍋子 **look at the pot**。

「魔法 **magic**？妳確定嗎 **are you sure**？」

「當然 **of course**，注意看這兒喔 **watch this**。」小女孩回答。

「煮吧，小鍋子，煮吧。」

鍋子立刻煮了一些又香又熱的麥片粥。過了幾分鐘，它已經煮好滿滿一鍋粥 **be full of porridge**。

「等一下 **wait a minute**，媽媽。」小女孩説。

「我們必須念咒語 **say the magic words** 讓鍋子停下來 **stop the pot**。停止，小鍋子，停止。」她説。

鍋子立刻停下來，不再繼續煮了。

小女孩和媽媽每天 **every day** 都吃麥片粥 **eat porridge**，她們再也不用挨餓了 **be not hungry**。

有一天 **one day**，小女孩出門 **go out** 和朋友玩 **play with her friends**。她去了 **be out** 很久 **for a long time**。媽媽餓了 **become hungry**，於是她決定不等女兒，自己先吃飯 **decide to eat without her daughter**。

GRAMMAR POINT

stop V–ing：停止做…… **keep V–ing**：繼續做…… **decide to V**：決定做……

⇨ 有些動詞要以動名詞 (V–ing) 作受詞，有些要以不定詞 (to V) 作受詞，像這樣的動詞特徵，要分辨清楚並熟記。

- The pot immediately **stopped** cook**ing**. 鍋子立刻停下來不煮了。
- The pot will **keep** cooking porridge. 鍋子會一直煮麥片粥。
- She **decided to** eat without her daughter. 她決定不等女兒，自己先吃飯。

"Cook, little pot, cook," she said.

The pot started / cooking some porridge. After a few minutes, / the pot was full of porridge. The mother **wanted the pot** / **to stop cooking.**

"No more, little pot, no more," said the mother.

But the pot did not stop cooking. Those were not the magic words.

"Stop cooking, little pot, stop cooking," she cried.

But those were not the magic words / either.

Soon, / the porridge began to overflow / from the pot. It spilled onto the floor. The mother did not know / what to do. She **kept trying** / **to stop the pot**. But she did not remember / how to make it stop.

The kitchen filled with porridge. Then, / the porridge spilled into the street / and went into the next house. The villagers were surprised.

"What's happening?" they asked.

"The magic pot / will not stop cooking," answered the mother.

The villagers / scooped up the porridge / with buckets / and took it away. But the magic pot / continued cooking. Soon, / there was porridge / in every house / in the village.

Just then, / the little girl / came back to her home.

"Stop, little pot, stop," she shouted.

The magic cooking pot / immediately / stopped cooking.

"It's a good little pot. But you must say / the right words!" said the little girl.

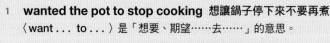

- **cry** 大喊 *cry-cried-cried • **either** 也（用於否定句中）• **overflow** 溢出
- **spill** 流出 *spill-spilled-spilled • **fill with** 充滿 = **be filled with**
- **villager** 村民 • **be surprised** 很驚訝 • **scoop up** 舀 • **take away** 帶走
- **continue V-ing** 繼續做某事 • **come back** 回來

1 **wanted the pot to stop cooking** 想讓鍋子停下來不要再煮
〈want . . . to . . .〉是「想要、期望……去……」的意思。

2 **kept trying to stop the pot** 一直試著想讓鍋子停下來
〈try to . . .〉是「努力、盡力去做……」的意思。

「煮吧，小鍋子，煮吧。」她説。

鍋子開始煮了一些麥片粥 **cook some porridge**，幾分鐘之後 **after a few minutes**，鍋子煮好滿滿一鍋粥。媽媽想讓鍋子停下來 **stop cooking**。

「不要再煮了 **no more**，小鍋子，不要再煮了。」媽媽説。

但是鍋子並沒有停下來，那不是咒語 **magic words**。

「停下來，小鍋子，停下來。」她大叫。

但那也 **either** 不是咒語。

很快地 **soon**，麥片粥開始從鍋子裡溢出來 **overflow from the pot**，流到地板上 **spill onto the floor**。媽媽不知道 **do not know** 該怎麼辦 **what to do**。她一直試著 **keep trying**，想讓鍋子停下來，但是她不記得 **do not remember** 怎麼讓它停下來 **how to make it stop**。

廚房裡都是麥片粥 **fill with porridge**，接著麥片粥流到街上 **spill into the street**，流進隔壁的房子裡 **go into the next house**。村民 **the villagers** 都很驚訝 **be surprised**。

「怎麼回事 **what's happening**？」他們問。

「魔法鍋子停不下來。」媽媽回答。

村民們用桶子 **with buckets** 舀麥片粥 **scoop up the porridge**，把粥帶回家 **take it away**，但魔法鍋還是一直煮 **continue cooking**。不久，村子裡 **in the village** 每棟房子 **in every house** 都有麥片粥 **there is porridge**。

就在那時 **just then**，小女孩回到家了 **come back to her home**。

「停止，小鍋子，停止。」她大喊。

魔法鍋子立刻 **immediately** 停下來不煮了。

「這是很好的小鍋子 **a good little pot**，但妳必須説對咒語！」小女孩説。

The Shoemaker and the Elves

There was once / an old shoemaker. He owned / an old shoe shop. He worked / on the first floor, / and he and his wife / lived / on the second floor. The shoemaker and his wife / were very poor. **Few people / visited his shop, /** so he did not make / much money.

One day, / the shoemaker / told his wife.

"One last pair of shoes. That's / **all I can make.** We don't have any money. What are we going to do?"

"It is late. So we should go to bed. Make the shoes / in the morning," answered the shoemaker's wife. The shoemaker and his wife / went upstairs / and went to bed.

The next morning, / the shoemaker and his wife / went downstairs. There was something / on the table. It was / **a pair of shoes.**

"Look at these," the shoemaker said. "What beautiful shoes! It's magic."

Just then, / a lady / came into the store. The lady / looked at the shoes / and said, "What beautiful shoes! I'll take them." She gave the shoemaker / three gold coins / for the shoes.

"Three gold coins! Now I can make / **two more pairs of shoes**," the shoemaker said. So he went out / and bought / some more leather. He came back / and cut the leather.

"It is late. Make them / in the morning," said his wife. The shoemaker and his wife / went upstairs / and went to bed.

- **shoemaker** 鞋匠　• **own** 擁有　• **work** 工作　• **first floor** 一樓　• **second floor** 二樓
- **make money** 賺錢　• **wife** 妻子　• **last** 最後的　• **pair** 一雙　• **go to bed** 上床睡覺
- **go upstairs** 上樓　• **magic** 魔法　• **gold coin** 金幣　• **leather** 皮革
- **cut the leather** 裁切皮革

1. **few people visited his shop** 很少人光顧他的鞋店
   few 指數量「不多的」、「幾乎沒有的」，有否定的含意。

2. **all I can make** 我只能做
   〈all＋主詞＋動詞〉是「（主詞）所⋯⋯的全部」及「（主詞）就只能做⋯⋯」的意思。
   例 all I have（我所擁有的全部）/ all I want（我想要的全部）

3. **a pair of shoes** 一雙鞋　/ **two more pairs of shoes** 再兩雙鞋
   a pair 是由兩個組成「一雙、一對」的意思，two pairs 就是「兩雙」。
   例 a pair of socks（一雙襪子）/ a pair of pants（一條褲子）/ a pair of earrings（一副耳環）

鞋匠和小精靈

　　從前 **once** 有一個老鞋匠 **an old shoemaker**，他擁有 **own** 一間老鞋店 **an old shoe shop**，他在一樓 **on the first floor** 工作 **work**，和他的太太住 **live** 二樓 **on the second floor**。鞋匠夫婦很窮 **be very poor**，很少人 **few people** 光顧他的鞋店 **visit his shop**，所以他錢賺得不多 **do not make much money**。

　　有一天 **one day**，鞋匠告訴他太太。

　　「最後一雙鞋 **one last pair of shoes**，我只能做這麼一雙了 **all I can make**，我們沒有錢 **don't have any money**，該怎麼辦？」

　　「很晚了，我們該上床睡覺 **go to bed** 了，明天早上再做鞋吧！」鞋匠太太回答。鞋匠和太太上樓 **go upstairs** 去睡覺 **go to bed**。

　　隔天早上 **the next morning**，鞋匠和太太下樓 **go downstairs**，桌上 **on the table** 有個東西 **there is something**，是一雙鞋 **a pair of shoes**。

　　「看看這雙鞋 **look at these**，」鞋匠說，「好漂亮的鞋子 **what beautiful shoes**，這是魔法 **magic**。」

　　就在那時 **just then**，一位女士 **a lady** 走進店裡 **come into the store**，她看到這雙鞋 **look at the shoes**，就說「好美的鞋子！我要買這雙 **I'll take them**。」她付了三枚金幣 **three gold coins** 給鞋匠。

　　「三枚金幣！現在我可以再做兩雙鞋 **can make two more pairs of shoes** 了。」鞋匠說。於是 **so** 他出門 **go out** 買更多的皮革 **buy some more leather**，回來 **come back** 後，就開始裁切皮革 **cut the leather**。

　　「很晚了，明早再做吧！」鞋匠太太說。鞋匠和太太就上樓睡覺了。

What . . . ! / How . . . !（感嘆句）

- **What** beautiful shoes! 多漂亮的鞋子！（What＋形容詞＋複數名詞！）
- **How beautiful** they are! 這些鞋子多麼美麗！（How＋形容詞＋主詞＋動詞！）
- -
- **What a** wonderful **surprise**! 多美妙的驚喜！（What a/an＋形容詞＋單數名詞！）
- **How fast** it flies! 它飛得多快！（How＋副詞＋主詞＋動詞！）

The next morning, / the shoemaker and his wife / came down. They saw / two beautiful pairs of shoes / on the table.

"Look at these," he said. "More magic."

The shoemaker / put the shoes / in the window. A man saw them. He walked into the shop. "How beautiful / they are! I must buy them. Here are / six gold coins."

"Now I can buy / enough leather / to make four pairs of shoes," the shoemaker said. So he went out / and bought / some more leather. He came back / and cut the leather.

"It is late," said his wife. "So we should go to bed." The shoemaker and his wife / went upstairs / and went to bed.

The next morning, / the shoemaker and his wife / came down. They saw / four beautiful pairs of shoes / on the table.

"Look at these," he said. "They're beautiful. Even more magic."

A while later, / two customers / entered the store. They looked at the shoes / and said, "Those shoes are beautiful. We'll take them." They paid the shoemaker / twelve gold coins / for the shoes.

The shoemaker and his wife / were very happy. But they wondered, "Who is making these shoes? We must know."

That night, / the shoemaker / cut the leather / for the shoes. But he and his wife / did not go upstairs. Instead, / they hid downstairs. They waited and waited.

• come down 下來　• put 放置　• walk into 走進　• enough 足夠的　• go out 出門
• even more 更加　• a while later 過了一會兒　• customer 顧客　• enter 走進
• pay for 買……付錢　*pay-paid-paid　• wonder 好奇　• instead 反而
• hide 躲藏　*hide-hid-hidden　• wait 等

CLOSE UP

1　**Here are six gold coins.** 這裡是六枚金幣。
〈here is/are . . . 〉把什麼東西交給對方的時候，意思就是「你要的……在這裡」或「給你……」。

2　**They paid the shoemaker twelve gold coins for the shoes.**
他們付了12枚金幣給鞋匠買鞋。
〈pay＋人＋錢〉是「支付給某人多少錢」的意思，要表示「為……付錢」時，要用介系詞for。

隔天早上，鞋匠和太太下來 **come down** 以後，他們看到 **see** 桌上有兩雙漂亮的鞋子 **two beautiful pairs of shoes**。

「看看這些鞋子，」他說，「更神奇 **more magic** 了。」

鞋匠把鞋子放進櫥窗裡 **put the shoes in the window**，一個男士 **a man** 看到它們 **see them**，走進鞋店 **walk into the shop**。「這些鞋子多麼美麗 **how beautiful they are** 啊！我一定要買 **must buy**。這裡是六枚金幣 **six gold coins**。」

「現在我可以買 **can buy** 足夠的皮革 **enough leather**，做四雙鞋子 **four pairs of shoes** 了。」鞋匠說。於是他出門買更多皮革，回來以後，又開始裁切皮革。

「很晚了，」鞋匠太太說，「我們應該上床睡覺了。」鞋匠太太說。鞋匠和太太就上樓睡覺了。

隔天早上，鞋匠和太太下樓，他們看到桌上有四雙漂亮的鞋子 **four beautiful pairs of shoes**。

「看看這些鞋子，」他說，「真漂亮，更加神奇 **even more magic** 了。」

過了一會兒 **a while later**，兩位顧客 **two customers** 走進店裡 **enter the store**。他們看到鞋子，就說：「這些鞋子真漂亮，我們要買下來。」他們付了 12 枚金幣 **pay twelve gold coins** 給鞋匠。

鞋匠和太太非常高興 **be very happy**，但他們很納悶 **wonder**，「是誰做了這些鞋子 **make these shoes**？我們一定要查出來 **must know**。」

那天晚上 **that night**，鞋匠裁好鞋子的皮革，但是他和太太沒上樓，而是 **instead** 躲在樓下 **hide downstairs**，他們等了又等 **wait and wait**。

enough . . . to . . . ：有足夠的……可以去……
⇨ 要注意 enough 的位置，它要放在名詞之前、形容詞之後。

• Now I can buy **enough** leather **to** make four pairs of shoes.
現在我可以買足夠的皮革，做四雙鞋子。

• She had **enough** money **to** pay for the clothes. 她有足夠的錢支付買衣服的花費。

• You are old **enough to** help your mother with housework.
你年紀夠大，可以幫媽媽做家事。

At midnight, / two elves / came into the shoemaker's shop. They jumped onto the table.

"Look at this leather," one said.

"Let's make / some beautiful shoes / with it," said the other.

The elves / worked hard / all night long. They made / several beautiful pairs of shoes. When the sun rose, / they left.

"Those elves / are very kind," said the shoemaker.

"You're right," answered his wife. "We should do something / for them."

"What can we do?" asked the shoemaker.

"I know," said his wife. "Their clothes / looked poor. Let's make some clothes / for them."

So the shoemaker and his wife / made some tiny clothes / for the elves. They sewed / tiny pants, shirts, hats, and boots / for the elves. Then, / they put the new clothes / on the table.

That night, / the shoemaker and his wife / hid again. At midnight, / the elves / came into the shoemaker's shop. When they jumped onto the table, / they saw the clothes.

"What are these?" one said. "Are these clothes / for us?"

"Yes," said the other. "They are for us."

The elves / put their new clothes on. Then, / they danced / with each other.

"We cannot stay here / any longer," said the first elf.

"You're right. They know about us. Now it's time / for us to go," said the second elf.

"Goodbye, / shoemaker," they said.

The elves left / and never came back. But now the shoemaker / could make good shoes. He worked hard, / too. So he and his wife / became very rich. And they lived happily / ever after.

- **midnight** 午夜　• **elf** 小精靈 *複數 **elves**　• **jump onto . . .** 跳到什麼上面
- **all night long** 整夜　• **several** 很多的　• **rise** 日出 *rise-rose-risen
- **leave** 離開　• **clothes** 衣服　• **look poor** 看起來很舊　• **tiny** 微小的　• **sew** 縫
- **put on** 穿上（衣服）　• **stay** 留下　• **any longer** 不再　• **happily** 快樂地
- **ever after** 從此以後

1 **Their clothes looked poor.** 他們的衣服看起來很舊。
〈look＋形容詞〉是「看起來……的」的意思。

2 **The elves put their new clothes on.** 精靈穿上他們的新衣服。
〈put . . . on〉是將衣服、鞋子、帽子、眼鏡、手套等「穿上、戴上」的意思。
補充：put on是指「穿上」的動作，而wear是「穿著」的狀態。

半夜時 **at midnight**，兩個小精靈 **two elves** 來到鞋匠的店裡 **come into the shoemaker's shop**，他們跳到桌子上 **jump onto the table**。

　　「看看這件皮革 **look at this leather**，」一個小精靈說。

　　「讓我們用它 **with it** 做出一些漂亮的鞋子吧 **let's make some beautiful shoes**！」另一個精靈說。

　　小精靈整夜 **all night long** 辛苦地工作 **work hard**，做出好幾雙美麗的鞋子 **several beautiful pairs of shoes**，太陽升起 **the sun rises** 時，他們就離開 **leave** 了。

　　「這些精靈真是好心 **be kind**。」鞋匠說。

　　「你說的對，」鞋匠太太回答，「我們應該為他們做點事 **do something for them**。」

　　「我們可以做些什麼呢？」鞋匠問。

　　「我知道，」鞋匠太太說，「他們的衣服 **their clothes** 看起來很舊 **look poor**，我們來幫他們做些衣服 **make some clothes** 吧。」

　　於是鞋匠和太太替精靈做了一些小小的衣服 **some tiny clothes**，他們縫 **sew** 了小褲子、小上衣、小帽子和小靴子 **tiny pants, shirts, hats, and boots**。然後 **then**，他們把新衣服 **the new clothes** 放在桌上。

　　當晚，鞋匠和太太又躲起來了 **hide again**，到了半夜，小精靈來到鞋匠的店裡。當他們跳上桌子時，看到桌上的新衣服 **see the clothes**。

　　「這是什麼？」一個精靈說。「這些衣服是給我們 **for us** 的嗎？」

　　「是的 **yes**，」另一個精靈說，「這是給我們的。」

　　精靈穿上他們的新衣服 **put their new clothes on**，然後一起跳舞 **dance with each other**。

　　「我們不能再待在這裡了 **cannot stay here any longer**。」第一個精靈說。

　　「沒錯，他們已經知道我們的存在 **know about us** 了，現在我們該走的時候到了 **it's time for us to go** 了。」第二個精靈說。

　　「再見 **goodbye**，鞋匠。」他們說。

　　精靈離開 **leave** 以後，再也沒回來過 **never come back**，但現在 **but now** 鞋匠可以做出好鞋子 **make good shoes**。他工作很認真，所以他和太太變得很有錢 **become very rich**。從此以後 **ever after**，他們過著幸福快樂的日子 **live happily**。

GRAMMAR POINT

it's time for ... to ...：……的時候到了

- Now **it's time for** us **to** go. 現在我們該走的時候到了。
- **It's time for** you **to** do something for your family. 為你的家人做點事的時候到了。

Jack and the Beanstalk

Long ago, / there lived / a mother and her son. The son's name / was Jack. They lived / in a small cottage. They were very poor. Their only valuable possession / was an old cow.

One day, / the mother said to Jack.

"We've got no money, / Jack. Go and sell the cow."

So Jack took the cow / and walked toward the town. **On his way to the town,** / he met / a strange old man. He asked Jack, "Where are you going / with that cow?"

"I'm going to town / to sell the cow / so that we can buy some food," said Jack.

"Ah . . . / but the town is / so very far away . . . I will gladly / buy the cow / from you," the old man said.

"Take a look at these." The old man showed Jack / some beautiful beans. "These are magic beans. I will give you / five magic beans / for your cow," he offered.

Jack was impressed / by the magic beans. So he sold the cow / to the old man / for five beans. **Jack was very proud of himself.**

But when he got home, / his mother was angry.

"What? Beans!" she cried. "You sold our cow / for five beans? You fool! Only a fool / **would exchange a cow** / **for five beans.** No supper / for you. Go to bed / right now," she told him. Then, / Jack's mother / threw the beans / out the window.

The next morning, / Jack looked out the window / and saw an amazing sight. There was / an enormous beanstalk / growing next to the window. **It rose so high** / **that he could not see** / **where it ended.**

"The old man was right," said Jack. "They were magic beans." Jack started / climbing up the beanstalk. He climbed / for hours and hours. Finally, / he got to the top of the beanstalk.

- **cottage** 農舍　　• **valuable** 有價值的　　• **possession** 財產　　• **strange** 奇怪的
- **far away** 很遠　　• **gladly** 樂意地　　• **take a look at . . .** 看看某物　　• **offer** 提議
- **be impressed by . . .** 被某物吸引　　• **be proud of . . .** 感到驕傲　　• **fool** 笨蛋
- **exchange** 交換　　• **throw** 丟 *throw-threw-thrown　　• **amazing** 不可思議的
- **sight** 景象　　• **enormous** 巨大的　　• **beanstalk** 豌豆莖
- **climb up** 往上爬 ≠ **climb down**　　• **get to . . .** 到達某處

1　**on his way to the town** 在往城裡的路上
〈on one's way to . . .〉是「在往……的路上」的意思。

2　**Jack was very proud of himself.** 傑克沾沾自喜。
〈be proud of . . .〉是「對……感到驕傲」的意思。

3　**would exchange a cow for five beans** 用五顆豆子換一頭牛
〈exchange . . . for . . .〉是「用……來換……」的意思。

傑克與魔豆

　　很久以前 long ago，那裡住著一個媽媽和她的兒子 a mother and her son，兒子的名字 the son's name 叫傑克 Jack。他們住在一個很小的農舍裡 live in a small cottage，非常地窮困 be very poor，他們唯一有價值的財產 valuable possession 是一頭老牛 an old cow。

　　有一天 one day，媽媽告訴傑克。

　　「我們沒有錢了 have got no money，傑克，去把牛賣掉 sell the cow 吧！」

　　於是傑克牽著牛，往城裡走 walk toward the town，在往城裡的路上 on his way to the town，他遇見 meet 了一個奇怪的老人 a strange old man，老人問傑克：「你牽著牛 with that cow 要去哪裡？」

　　「我要進城 go to town 賣牛，這樣我們才能買些食物 buy some food。」傑克說。

　　「啊……但城裡離這裡遠得很 so very far away……我很樂意 gladly 向你 from you 買下這頭牛 buy the cow。」老人說。

　　「看看這些 take a look at these，」老人給傑克看一些漂亮的豆子 some beautiful beans，「這些是魔豆 magic beans，我用五顆魔豆 five magic beans 跟你換牛 for your cow。」他提議 offer。

　　傑克被魔豆 by the magic beans 吸引 be impressed，所以他以五顆豆子的代價把牛賣給老人，傑克沾沾自喜 be proud of himself。

　　但當他到家 get home 以後，他媽媽很生氣 be angry。

　　「什麼 what？豆子 beans！」她大叫，「你用五顆豆子把我們的牛賣掉了？你這個笨蛋 you fool！只有笨蛋 only a fool 才會用五顆豆子換一頭牛 exchange a cow for five beans。你不准吃晚餐 no supper，馬上 right now 去睡覺 go to bed。」媽媽跟傑克說。接著，傑克的媽媽把豆子丟到窗戶外面 throw the beans out the window。

　　隔天早上 the next morning，傑克往窗外看 look out the window，看到一個不可思議的景象 an amazing sight。有一條巨大的豌豆莖 an enormous beanstalk 長在窗戶旁邊 next to the window，長得很高 rise so high，傑克甚至看不到 cannot see 它的盡頭 where it ends。

　　「那老人是對的，」傑克說。「這些真的是魔豆。」傑克開始沿著豌豆莖往上爬 climb up the beanstalk，爬了好幾個小時 for hours and hours，最後 finally，爬到豌豆莖的頂端 get to the top of the beanstalk。

There, / high in the clouds, / was a huge castle.

"I wonder / who lives there," thought Jack / as he walked / toward the castle. When Jack got to the castle, / he tripped over an enormous foot. **It belonged to / the biggest woman / he had ever seen.**

"You, boy," said the woman. "What are you doing here? My husband / is a giant. He loves to eat / little boys like you."

"Please / **don't let him eat me**," answered Jack. "I just came here / because I smelled breakfast, / and I am so hungry."

The giant's wife / was kindhearted, / so she gave Jack / some food. All of a sudden, / the ground / began to shake. "Hide, boy," said the woman. "My husband is coming."

"Fee, fi, fo, fum, / I can smell a little boy," said the giant / when he walked into the kitchen. "Are you cooking a boy / for me / for breakfast?"

"No, dear," she answered. "You probably smell the boy / you ate last week."

The giant sat down / and ate his breakfast. Then, / he took out a huge bag. It was filled with gold. After a while, / he fell asleep / at the table. Then, / Jack came out / quietly. He took the bag of gold / and **ran out of the castle.** He climbed down the beanstalk / and showed his mother the gold. She was very pleased with him.

Jack and his mother / lived happily. But they soon / **ran out of gold.** Jack decided / to climb the beanstalk again. He got to the top of the beanstalk / and walked to the castle.

"Oh, it's you again?" said the giant's wife. "Go away! You're a bad boy. Didn't you take / my husband's gold?"

"That wasn't me. That was another boy," answered Jack.

The giant's wife / believed Jack. She gave him / some food. Then, / the ground / began to shake. "He's coming," said the woman. "Hide, / or he will find you."

- **huge** 非常大的　• **castle** 城堡　• **trip over** 絆倒　• **belong to** 屬於　• **husband** 丈夫
- **giant** 巨人　• **kindhearted** 善良的 ≠ **mean**　• **all of a sudden** 突然間　• **shake** 震動
- **probably** 大概　• **sit down** 坐下來　• **take out** 拿出　• **be filled with** 裝滿
- **fall asleep** 睡著 ≠ **wake up**　• **take** 拿 *take-took-taken
- **run out of** 跑出、逃出；用完　• **be pleased with . . .** 很滿意　• **go away** 走開
- **find** 發現 ≠ **hide**

1　**It belonged to the biggest woman he had ever seen.** 它屬於他所見過最巨大的女人。
〈最高級＋主詞＋have/had ever seen〉是「看過最……的」的意思。

2　**don't let him eat me** 請妳不要讓他吃掉我
〈let＋受詞＋原形動詞〉是「讓／允許……去做……」的意思。

3　**ran out of the castle** 跑出城堡
〈run＋out of＋地方〉是「從……逃／跑出去」的意思。

4　**ran out of gold** 把金子花光了
〈run out＋of＋東西〉是「用完……」的意思。

高高的雲層裡 **high in the clouds** 有一座大城堡 **a huge castle**。
「我想知道 **wonder** 是誰住在那裡 **who lives there**。」傑克走向
城堡 **walk toward the castle** 的時候心裡這麼想。當傑克走到
城堡 **get to the castle** 的時候，他被一隻巨大的腳絆倒 **trip
over an enormous foot**，那是一個他所見過最巨大的女人
the biggest woman 的腳。

　　「你，男孩 **you, boy**，」女人説。「你在這裡做什麼？我丈夫 **my husband** 是巨人
giant，他喜歡吃 **love to eat** 像你這樣的小男孩 **little boys like you**。」

　　「請妳不要讓他吃掉我 **don't let him eat me**，」傑克回答。「我是因為聞到早餐的味道
smell breakfast，才來這裡 **come here**，我很餓 **be so hungry**。」

　　巨人的妻子 **the giant's wife** 很善良 **be kindhearted**，所以她給傑克一些食物
give Jack some food。突然間 **all of a sudden**，地 **the ground** 開始震動 **begin to
shake**。「男孩，快躲起來 **hide**，」女人説，「我丈夫來了 **be coming**。」

　　「啊哈哈，我聞到小男孩的味道 **smell a little boy** 了，」當巨人走進廚房 **walk into the
kitchen** 的時候，他説，「妳在煮小男孩 **cook a boy** 給我當早餐 **for breakfast** 嗎？」

　　「不，親愛的 **no, dear**，」她回答，「你大概是聞到上星期你吃掉的小男孩的味道。」

　　巨人坐下來 **sit down** 吃早餐 **eat his breakfast**，然後，他拿出一個大袋子 **take out a
huge bag**，裡面裝滿了金子 **be filled with gold**。過了一會兒 **after a while**，他趴在餐
桌上 **at the table** 睡著了 **fall asleep**。然後，傑克悄悄地出來 **come out quietly**，拿了
那袋金子 **take the bag of gold**，跑出城堡 **run out of the castle**，爬下豌豆莖 **climb
down the beanstalk**，把金子拿給媽媽看 **show his mother the gold**，媽媽很滿意 **be
pleased with him**。

　　傑克和媽媽過著幸福快樂的日子 **live happily**，但不久他們就把金子花光了 **run out of
god**。傑克決定再爬一次 **decide to climb again** 豌豆莖，他爬到了豌豆莖頂端，走向城
堡。

　　「噢！又是你 **you again**？」巨人的妻子説，「走開 **go away**！你這個壞男孩 **a bad
boy**。你不是把我丈夫的金子拿走 **take my husband's gold** 了嗎？」

　　「那不是我 **not me**，那是另一個男孩 **another boy**。」傑克回答。

　　巨人的妻子相信傑克的話 **believe Jack**，她給他一點食物。然後，地開始震動，「他來
了，」女人説，「快躲起來 **hide**，不然 **or** 他會發現你 **find you**。」

"Fee, fi, fo, fum, / you have a boy / for me / today, / don't you?" said the giant.

"Sorry, dear. I don't. But here are / some bacon and eggs / for you," she said.

After breakfast, / the giant said, "Wife, / bring me my hen. I want / some golden eggs." So she brought the hen / to the table. "Lay," said the giant. The hen / laid a golden egg.

After a while, / the giant fell asleep / at the table. Then, / Jack came out of his hiding place. He grabbed the hen / and ran out of the castle. He climbed down the beanstalk / and showed his mother the hen. They became very rich.

But Jack got bored / one day, / so he climbed up the beanstalk / again. He went to the castle, / but he hid from the giant's wife / this time.

"Fee, fi, fo, fum, / I can smell a little boy," roared the giant.

"Can you? Maybe / it's that thief / again," said the giant's wife. "Let's find that boy."

They looked in the kitchen, / but they could not find Jack. Soon, / they gave up / and ate breakfast. Then, / the giant got his harp. "Play," he said. The harp / began to play / some beautiful music.

After a while, / the giant fell asleep / at the table. Then, / Jack came out of his hiding place. He grabbed the harp / and ran out of the castle. But the harp called out, "Master, save me! The boy is stealing me!"

The giant woke up / and chased Jack. Jack ran to the beanstalk / and began climbing down it. The giant / started climbing down, / too.

"Mother, / get the axe. Quick! The big giant is coming," shouted Jack. When he reached the bottom, / he grabbed the axe. He cut down the beanstalk.

The beanstalk fell, / and the giant fell down / with it. His head / hit the ground. Thump! He was dead. Jack never went back / to the giant's castle.

- **bring** 拿 *bring-brought-brought • **hiding place** 藏身之所 • **grab** 抓
- **get bored** 無聊的 ≠ excited • **roar** 大吼 • **thief** 小偷 • **give up** 放棄
- **call out** 大聲喊叫 • **master** 主人 • **steal** 偷 • **wake up** 醒來 ≠ fall asleep
- **chase** 追 • **cut down** 砍斷 • **fall down** 摔下來 • **be dead** 死掉

CLOSE UP

1 **Jack got bored** 傑克覺得很無聊
〈get＋形容詞〉是「感覺／使得……」的意思，表示狀態。

2 **get the axe** 拿斧頭
get 也當作「拿取……」的意思。

「啊哈哈，妳今天為我準備了一個小男孩 **have a boy for me**，對不對？」巨人說。

「對不起，親愛的 **sorry, dear**，我沒有。不過，這裡有一些培根和蛋 **some bacon and eggs**。」她說。

早餐後 **after breakfast**，巨人說：「老婆，把我的母雞拿來 **bring me my hen**，我想要些金蛋 **want some golden eggs**。」於是她把母雞帶到桌上。「下蛋 **lay**。」巨人說。母雞下了一顆金蛋 **lay a golden egg**。

過了一會，巨人在餐桌上睡著了，然後傑克從藏身的地方 **his hiding place** 悄悄地走出來，他抓了母雞 **grab the hen**，跑出城堡。他爬下豌豆莖，把母雞給媽媽看 **show his mother the hen**。他們變得非常有錢 **become very rich**。

但有一天傑克覺得很無聊 **get bored**，所以他又爬上豌豆莖，去了城堡 **go to the castle**，但這次 **this time** 他避開巨人的妻子 **hide from the giant's wife**。

「啊哈哈，我聞到小男孩的味道。」巨人大吼 **roar**。

「你聞到了嗎？或許又是那個小偷 **that thief again**，」巨人的妻子說，「我們把他找出來 **let's find that boy**。」

他們找了廚房 **look in the kitchen**，但是找不到傑克 **cannot find Jack**。很快地，他們放棄 **give up** 了，開始吃早餐。然後，巨人拿了他的豎琴 **get his harp** 說：「彈奏 **play**。」然後，豎琴開始演奏美麗的音樂 **play some beautiful music**。

過了一會，巨人在桌上睡著了，傑克從藏身的地方走出來 **come out of his hiding place**，他抓了豎琴 **grab the harp**，跑出城堡，但是豎琴大聲喊 **call out**，「主人 **master**，救我 **save me**！男孩要把我偷走 **steal me**！」

巨人醒來 **wake up** 追傑克 **chase Jack**，傑克跑到豌豆莖 **run to the beanstalk**，開始往下爬 **climb down it**，巨人也開始往下爬。

「媽，拿斧頭 **get the axe**。快！大巨人來了。」傑克大喊。當他到地面上時，他拿了斧頭，把豌豆莖砍斷 **cut down the beanstalk**。

豌豆莖倒下來 **fall**，巨人跟著摔下來 **fall down**，頭撞到地面 **hit the ground**。砰 **thump**！他死了 **be dead**。傑克再也沒 **never** 回巨人的城堡 **go back to the giant's castle**。

GRAMMAR POINT

附加問句的用法　⇨　前面的句子是肯定句，附加問句就要用否定句；前面的句子是否定句，附加問句就要用肯定句。

- You **have** a boy for me today, **don't you?** 妳今天為我準備了一個男孩，對不對？

- You **are** cooking a boy for me, **aren't you?** 妳正在煮男孩給我吃，對不對？
- You **don't** have much money, **do you?** 你沒有很多錢，對嗎？
- You **are not** the thief, **are you?** 你不是小偷，對嗎？

The Ugly Duckling

One summer / in a country farmyard, / Mother Duck / was sitting on her new eggs. She sat on them / for a long time. Finally, / the eggs / began to crack. Six little ducklings / popped out / and started to cry out, / "Quack, quack!" Mother Duck was very pleased. "My little ducklings!" she said.

She looked inside her nest. One egg / had not opened.

"That's strange," she thought. "This egg is bigger / than the other ones."

Mother Duck / couldn't recall / laying that seventh egg. How did it get there? "Did I count the eggs / wrongly?" Mother Duck wondered.

An old duck / came by / to see the ducklings.

"Hello, / Mother Duck. I see / your eggs / have hatched. How are the ducklings?" the old duck asked.

"Almost all of them / have hatched. There is / only one egg left," Mother Duck answered.

"That egg / looks strange. It looks like / a turkey egg. Leave it alone," said the old duck.

"No, / I can't do that. It's my egg, / so I must wait for it," said Mother Duck. She got back into her nest / and sat on the big egg. After a while, / the egg finally hatched.

They looked at the last baby duckling / with great surprise. He looked nothing like / the other ducks. In fact, / he did not look like / much of a duck / at all. He was big, gray, ugly, and strange looking.

"Well, / he certainly is / an unusual-looking duckling," said the old duck.

"Hmm," said Mother Duck, "he was in the egg / for so long, / so he must be / so big. I am sure / he will become / a proper-looking duck."

- farmyard 農家庭院　　• crack 裂開　　• duckling 鴨寶寶　　• pop out 探出頭
- nest 鳥窩　　• recall 記得　　• wrongly 錯誤地　　• wonder 納悶；想知道　　• hatch 孵化
- look like 看起來像　　• with great surprise 很驚訝地　　• in fact 事實上　　• ugly 醜的
- unusual-looking 長相奇特　　• proper-looking 長相正常

CLOSE UP

1. **couldn't recall laying that seventh egg** 鴨媽媽記不得她下了那第七顆蛋
   recall 是「回想起……」的意思。can't recall 則是「想不起來」的意思。

2. **there is only one egg left** 只剩下一顆蛋
   〈there is/are . . . left〉是「留下／剩下……」的意思。

3. **I must wait for it** 我必須等它 / **he must be so big** 他才會長這麼大
   must 是「（有義務、有需要）必須去……」以及「（推測）一定是……沒錯」的意思，要依句意來決定是哪個意思。

醜小鴨

　　有一年夏天 one summer，在一個鄉下的農家庭院 in a country farmyard，鴨媽媽 Mother Duck 坐在她剛生的蛋上 sit on her new eggs，坐了很久 for a long time，終於 finally 蛋裂開 begin to crack 了，六隻鴨寶寶 six little ducklings 探出頭來，開始大叫，「呱、呱 quack, quack！」鴨媽媽非常高興 be very pleased。「我的小鴨寶寶 my little ducklings！」她說。

　　她往鳥窩一看 look inside her nest，有一顆蛋還沒孵化。

　　「真奇怪 be strange，」她想，「這顆蛋比其他的還要大 be bigger。」

　　鴨媽媽記不得 cannot recall 她下了那第七顆蛋 lay that seventh egg，這顆蛋是怎麼 how 來的 get there 呢？「我算錯 count the eggs wrongly 了嗎？」鴨媽媽很納悶 wonder。

　　一隻老鴨子 an old duck 來 come by 看看這群鴨寶寶 see the ducklings。

　　「哈囉 hello，鴨媽媽 Mother Duck，我看妳的蛋 your eggs 孵化 hatch 了，鴨寶寶們們好不好？」老鴨子問。

　　「幾乎全部 almost all of them 都孵化了，只剩下一顆蛋 only one egg left 還沒。」鴨媽媽回答。

　　「那顆蛋看起來很奇怪 look strange，看起來很像火雞的蛋 look like a turkey egg，別管它 leave it alone。」老鴨回答。

　　「不 no，我不能這麼做 can't do that，那是我的蛋 my egg，我必須等它 wait for it 孵出來。」鴨媽媽回答。她回到她的窩裡 get back into her nest，坐在那顆巨蛋上 sit on the big egg，過了一會兒 after a while，蛋終於孵化 finally hatch 了。

　　他們很驚訝地 with great surprise 看著最後一個孵出來的鴨寶寶 the last baby duckling，他看起來完全不像其他的鴨子 look nothing like the other ducks。事實上 in fact，他看起來根本不像鴨子 do not look like much of a duck，他又大 big、又灰 gray、又醜 ugly，而且長得很奇怪 strange looking。

　　「好吧 well，他絕對 certainly 是一隻長相奇特 unusual-looking 的鴨寶寶」，老鴨子說。

　　「嗯 hmm，」鴨媽媽說，「他待在蛋裡 in the egg 這麼久 for so long，才會長這麼大 be so big，我相信他將來會變成長相正常的 proper-looking 鴨子。」

GRAMMAR POINT

look + 形容詞：看起來……的　　**look like + 名詞**：看起來像……

- That egg **looks** strange. 那顆蛋看起來很奇怪。
- It **looks like** a turkey egg. 它看起來很像火雞蛋。
- He **looked** nothing **like** the other ducks. 他看起來完全不像其他的鴨子。
- He did not **look like** much of a duck at all. 他看起來根本不像鴨子。

[pp. 22−23]

Mother Duck / took her children / to the pond. They all / jumped into the pond / one by one. The ugly duckling / swam very well. Actually, / he swam even better / than the others. Mother Duck was pleased.

All of the animals / gathered around / Mother Duck and her ducklings. "What a beautiful family!" they all said. Then, / they noticed / the ugly duckling. "What is wrong / with that big duckling? He's very ugly," they said. One of the ducks / even pecked at the ugly duckling. This made the ugly duckling / very sad.

Mother Duck and her ducklings / went swimming / in the pond / every day. And, / every day, / the ducks and other animals / laughed at the ugly duckling. Even the farm girl / disliked the ugly duckling. "Go away," she said. "You are an ugly duckling."

The ugly duckling / felt very sad. "Nobody loves me. They all tease me! Why am I different / from my brothers?"

One night, / he ran away / from the farm. He traveled / a long, long way / until he finally found / a huge field. He soon fell asleep. When he woke up, / he was by a lake. He looked up in the sky / and saw two geese.

"You look very strange," they said. "But we like you. Do you want / to fly with us?" they asked the ugly duckling.

The ugly duckling agreed, / but he suddenly heard / a loud noise. "Bang! Bang!"

The two geese / fell to the ground. They were dead. In the distance, / the ugly duckling / saw some men / with hunting rifles. He got very scared. He ran away / from the hunters. He ran and ran / until he was very far away.

- **pond** 池塘　• **swim** 游泳 *swim-swam-swum　• **better than . . .** 比……還要好
- **gather around . . .** 聚在……附近　• **notice** 注意　• **peck at** 啄……
- **laugh at** 嘲笑……　• **dislike** 不喜歡　• **tease** 嘲笑　• **run away from** 逃離……
- **wake up** 醒來　• **goose** 鵝 *複數 geese　• **fly** 飛　• **agree** 同意　• **loud** 大聲的
- **noise** 聲響　• **in the distance** 遠處　• **rifle** 來福槍　• **get scared** 害怕的
- **hunter** 獵人　• **far away** 很遠的

CLOSE UP

1　**This made the ugly duckling very sad.** 這讓醜小鴨非常傷心。
〈make＋受詞＋形容詞〉是「使……感覺…」的意思。

2　**went swimming in the pond** 到池塘游泳
〈go＋V－ing〉是「去做……」的意思。例 go fishing（去釣魚）/ go climbing（去登山）

3　**Why am I different from my brothers?** 為什麼我長得跟哥哥不一樣？
〈be different from . . .〉是「和……不同」的意思。

4　**ran away from the farm** 逃離農場 / **ran away from the hunters** 逃離那些獵人
〈run away from . . .〉是「從……逃脫／逃跑出去」的意思。

鴨媽媽帶孩子們到池塘**take her children to the pond**，他們一個接一個**one by one**跳進池塘裡**jump into the pond**，醜小鴨**the ugly duckling**游得非常好**swim very well**，事實上**actually**，他比其他鴨子游得還要好**even better**，鴨媽媽很高興。

所有動物**all of the animals**聚集**gather**在鴨媽媽和鴨寶寶附近，「真是漂亮的一家人**what a beautiful family**！」他們全都這麼說。然後，他們注意到醜小鴨**notice the ugly duckling**，「那隻大的鴨寶寶是怎麼回事**what is wrong**？他好醜**be very ugly**。」他們說。其中一隻鴨子**one of the ducks**還啄了醜小鴨一下**peck at the ugly duckling**，讓醜小鴨非常傷心**make the ugly duckling very sad**。

鴨媽媽和鴨寶寶每天**every day**都到池塘**in the pond**游泳**go swimming**，每天鴨子和其他動物都嘲笑醜小鴨**laugh at the ugly duckling**，連農場裡的女孩**the farm girl**都不喜歡醜小鴨**dislike the ugly duckling**。「走開**go away**，」她說，「你是隻醜小鴨。」

醜小鴨很難過**feel very sad**，「沒有人**nobody**愛我**love me**，他們都嘲笑我**tease me**！為什麼**why**我長得跟哥哥們不一樣**be different**？」

有天晚上**one night**，他逃離農場**run away from the farm**，走了很遠很遠的路**travel a long, long way**，最後他發現一大片田野**find a huge field**，他很快就睡著**fall asleep**了，醒來**wake up**的時候，到了湖邊**by lake**，他抬頭看天空**look up in the sky**，看到了兩隻鵝**see two geese**。

「你長得好奇怪，」他們說，「但是我們喜歡你**like you**，你想要跟我們一起飛**fly with us**嗎？」他們問醜小鴨。

醜小鴨同意**agree**了，但他突然**suddenly**聽到一聲巨響**a loud noise**。「砰**bang**！砰！」

兩隻鵝摔到地上**fall to the ground**，死了**be dead**。在遠處**in the distance**，醜小鴨看到一些拿著獵槍的人**some men with hunting rifles**，他非常害怕**get scared**，趕快逃離那些獵人**run away from the hunters**，一直跑，一直跑**run and run**，直到離獵人很遠很遠**very far away**。

Finally, / he found an old hut / in the forest. He entered the hut. There were / a woman, a cat, and a hen. The woman was very old. "What are you? A duck?" she asked. "How wonderful! You can stay here / and lay eggs for me."

The next day, / the cat asked the ugly duckling, "Where are your eggs?"

"I don't have any eggs," he answered.

"Then you are useless. You must leave," the hen said.

The ugly duckling / left the hut. The weather / was getting colder.

One day / at sunrise, / he saw / something beautiful and strange / overhead. It was / a flight of beautiful birds / –three swans! They had long necks / and soft white wings. They were migrating south.

"Oh, what beautiful birds!" he thought. He called to them. "Who are you? Take me with you." But they did not hear him.

Winter came, / and the water in the lake / froze. The poor ugly duckling / could not even swim / in the water. He was cold / and had no food to eat.

A farmer / walked by the lake. He saw the ugly duckling / lying on the ice. "You poor bird," he said. "I will take you home / and help you." He picked up the ugly duckling / and took him home. The man had / a wife, a son, and a daughter. They took good care of / the ugly duckling. Slowly, / he started to get better. Thanks to them, / the ugly duckling / was able to survive / the cold winter.

However, / by springtime, / he had grown so big. The farmer decided / to set the ugly duckling free / by the pond.

- hut 小屋 - lay an egg 下蛋 - useless 毫無用處 - get colder 變冷
- overhead 上頭 - flight 一群 - migrate 遷徙 - freeze 結冰 *freeze-froze-frozen
- lie 躺 *動名詞：lying - poor 可憐的 - pick up 撿起來
- take good care of . . . 細心地照顧 - be able to 能夠 - survive 熬過
- set free 釋放

CLOSE UP

1 **The weather was getting colder.** 天氣變冷。/ **he started to get better** 他好起來了
〈get＋比較級〉是「漸漸變得更……」的意思。

2 **They took good care of the ugly duckling.** 他們細心地照顧醜小鴨。
〈take care of . . .〉是「照顧……」的意思，要強調「細心地照顧／照顧得很好」的話，就加上 good 變成 take good care of 就可以了。

3 **decided to set the ugly duckling free** 他決定放醜小鴨走
〈decide to . . .〉是「決定要……」的意思，〈set……free〉是「放……自由」的意思。

最後，他在森林裡 in the forest 找到一間小屋 find an old hut，他走進小屋 enter the hut，屋裡有一個女人 a woman、一隻貓 a cat 和一隻母雞 a hen，那女人非常老。「你是什麼東西？一隻鴨嗎？」她問。「太棒了 how wonderful！你可以留在這裡 stay here，為我下蛋 lay eggs。」

隔天 the next day，貓問醜小鴨：「你的蛋 your eggs 在哪裡 where？」

「我沒有蛋 don't have any eggs。」他回答。

「那你毫無用處 be useless，你得離開 must leave 這裡。」母雞說。

醜小鴨離開小屋 leave the hut。天氣 the weather 變冷 get colder 了。

有一天 one day 太陽升起 at sunrise 的時候，他看到頭頂上 overhead 有個東西又漂亮又奇怪 something beautiful and strange，是一群 a flight 美麗的鳥在飛——三隻天鵝 three swans！他們有長長的脖子 long necks 和軟軟的、白色的翅膀 soft white wings，正在往南遷徙 migrate south。

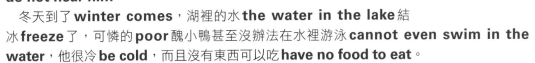

「噢！多美麗的鳥啊 what beautiful birds！」他想。他對著他們大叫 call to them：「你們是誰 who are you？帶我一起走 take me with you。」但是他們沒有聽見他的聲音 do not hear him。

冬天到了 winter comes，湖裡的水 the water in the lake 結冰 freeze 了，可憐的 poor 醜小鴨甚至沒辦法在水裡游泳 cannot even swim in the water，他很冷 be cold，而且沒有東西可以吃 have no food to eat。

有一個農夫 a farmer 經過湖邊 walk by the lake，看到醜小鴨躺在冰上面 lie on the ice。「可憐的小傢伙 you poor bird，」他說。「我會帶你回家 take you home，幫助你 help you。」他把醜小鴨撿起來 pick up，帶他回家，那男人有一個妻子、一個兒子和一個女兒。他們細心地照顧醜小鴨 take good care of the ugly duckling。慢慢地 slowly，他好起來 get better 了，多虧他們的照顧 thanks to them，醜小鴨才能熬過了寒冬 survive the cold winter。

春天到了 by springtime，他長很大 grow so big 了，農夫帶他來到池塘邊 by the pond，他決定讓醜小鴨自由 set the ugly duckling free。

GRAMMAR POINT

can：能…… ⇨ 表能力，過去式是 could。

be able to：能做…… ⇨ 和 can 意思一樣，過去式是 was/were able to。

- The poor ugly duckling **could** not even swim in the water.
  可憐的醜小鴨甚至沒辦法在水裡游泳

- Thanks to them, the ugly duckling **was able to** survive the cold winter.
  多虧有他們的照顧，醜小鴨才能熬過寒冬。

[pp. 26–27]

The ugly duckling / was alone again. He was swimming alone / in the pond. Then, suddenly, / he started to flap his wings / and flew into the sky. "I can fly. I can fly!" shouted the ugly duckling. "This is amazing."

The ugly duckling / flew all around the land. Then, / he looked down / and saw a garden. It was a garden / with a pond. "That's a beautiful garden," he thought. "I will go there."

He landed in the pond / in the garden. He looked over / and saw three swans. They were the three swans / he had seen in winter. "Oh, they are so beautiful," he thought. "I have to / speak to them."

But the ugly duckling / did not know / what to say. He suddenly felt shy. He looked down / into the water. Then, / he saw his reflection / in the water. He looked / just like the swans. He was not / an ugly duckling. He was a swan. "I'm a swan!" he cried.

"Mother, look," some children shouted. "There's a new swan. Isn't he beautiful? He's the most beautiful / of all the swans."

The children / threw some bread / into the pond / for him to eat. He was so pleased. All his life, / people had thought / he was ugly. Now, / they told him / how beautiful he was. It was / the happiest moment / of his life.

- **alone** 孤單的 • **flap one's wings** 拍翅膀 • **fly into . . .** 飛到 • **garden** 花園
- **land** 降落 • **look over** 放眼望去 • **shy** 很害羞 • **look down into . . .** 低頭往……看
- **reflection** 倒影 • **the most beautiful** 最美麗的 • **throw** 丟 *throw-threw-thrown
- **pleased** 開心的 • **the happiest moment** 最快樂的時刻

CLOSE UP

1. **the ugly duckling was alone** 醜小鴨孤孤單單的 / **he was swimming alone** 他一個人在池塘裡游泳
   alone是「單獨一個人」的意思，可當形容詞也可當副詞，不過不能放在名詞前。
   例 the alone ugly duckling (✕)

2. **They were the three swans he had seen in winter.** 他們是他曾經在冬天看到的那三隻天鵝。
   基準的時間是過去（were），因為看到天鵝的時間比基準時間早，所以要用更早的時式和時態——過去完成式（had seen）。

3. **for him to eat** 給他吃
   to不定詞意思上的主詞，用〈for＋受格〉來表現，且放在to不定詞前。

4. **all his life** 他人生中
   all one's life是「一輩子」、「從出生到死亡」的意思。例 all my life（我這一生）

醜小鴨又孤孤單單的 **be alone** 了，他一個人 **alone** 在池塘裡游泳 **swim**，突然他拍拍翅膀 **flap his wings**，飛到天上 **fly into the sky**。「我可以飛了，我可以飛了！」醜小鴨大叫。「太不可思議了 **be amazing**！」

醜小鴨在田野間四處飛 **fly all around the land**，然後，他往下看 **look down**，看到一座花園 **see a garden**，這座花園有一個池塘 **with a pond**。「這真是一座美麗的花園 **a beautiful garden**。」他想，「我要去那裡 **go there**」。

他在花園的池塘裡降落 **land in the pond**，放眼望去 **look over**，他看到三隻天鵝 **see three swans**，是他曾經在冬天看到 **see in winter** 的那三隻天鵝。「喔！他們真美麗，」他想，「我一定要跟他們說話 **speak to them**。」

但是醜小鴨不知道 **do not know** 要跟他們說什麼 **what to say**，突然覺得很害羞 **feel shy**。他低頭往水裡一看 **look down into the water**，他看到自己水中的倒影 **his reflection in the water**，他看起來就像那些天鵝一樣 **look just like the swans**，他不是一隻醜小鴨，他是天鵝。「我是天鵝！」他大叫。

「媽媽，你看，」一些小孩大叫，「那裡有一隻新的天鵝 **a new swan**，他是不是很美麗？他是所有天鵝中 **of all the swans** 最美麗的一隻 **be the most beautiful**。」

孩子們把一些麵包 **some bread** 丟 **throw** 到池塘裡給他吃，他很開心 **be pleased**。在他一生中 **all his life**，大家都認為他很醜 **be ugly**，現在 **now** 他們卻說他多麼美麗 **how beautiful he was**，這是他人生中 **of his life** 最快樂的時刻 **the happiest moment**。

GRAMMAR POINT

the ＋ 最高級：最……的、最……地

⇨ 最高級，在形容詞或副詞後加 –est；三個音節以上的字，要在前面加 most。

- It was **the happiest** moment of his life. 這是他人生中最快樂的時刻。
- He's **the most beautiful** of all the swans. 他是所有天鵝中最美麗的一隻。

The Ant and the Grasshopper

One summer day, / a grasshopper / hops into a field. He sings happily / because it is / a beautiful summer day. He sees an ant / pass by. The ant is working hard. It is carrying some corn / to its home.

"Why don't you stay and chat / with me?" asks the grasshopper. "That corn looks heavy. Why are you carrying it?"

"I'm saving food / for the winter," answers the ant. "I recommend / that you do the same thing. Then, / you will have / plenty of food / for the winter."

"Winter?" says the grasshopper. "Why worry about that? We have lots of food / right now. And winter is / a long time away."

The ant leaves the grasshopper. The ant works hard / every day, / so it gathers / lots of food. After a while, / the ant completely / fills its house / with food.

Meanwhile, / the grasshopper / stays in the field. But he does not work / at all. Instead, / he plays and sings / every day.

Soon, / summer turns to fall, / and fall turns to winter. When the weather gets colder, / the food starts to disappear. The grasshopper discovers / that he has no food / to eat. He looks over / at the ant's house. The ant has plenty of food / and a nice, warm house. The grasshopper realizes / how foolish he was.

That winter, / there is / lots of snow. Later, / when spring arrives, / the ant comes out of its house. The ant had enough food / during winter. Now, / it is ready / to start gathering food / for the next winter. When the ant looks around the field, / there is / no sign of the grasshopper.

• Moral: Work hard today / to prepare for tomorrow.

- hop 跳　• pass by 經過　• carry 扛　• stay 留　• save 積存　• recommend 建議
- plenty of 足夠的　• a long time away 很遙遠（時間）　• gather 收集
- completely 完全地　• meanwhile 同時　• get colder 變冷　• disappear 消失
- discover 發現　• look over 看到　• realize 明白　• foolish 愚蠢的
- be ready to . . . 準備　• sign 蹤跡　• prepare for . . . 為……做準備

CLOSE UP

1 **Why don't you stay and chat with me?** 你何不留下來和我聊天呢？
〈Why don't you . . . ?〉是「你為什麼不去做……呢？」的意思，表建議或勸誘。

2 **plenty of food** 足夠的食物 / **lots of food** 很多食物 / **lots of snow** 很多雪
〈plenty of . . . 〉和〈lots of . . . 〉兩個都是「很多……」的意思。

3 **fills its house with food** 家裡堆滿了食物
〈fill . . . with . . . 〉是「用……填滿……」的意思。

4 **it is ready to start gathering food** 開始要為下一個冬天收集食物
〈be ready to . . . 〉是「準備好要去做……」、「隨時都可以去做……」的意思。

螞蟻和蚱蜢

夏天的某一天 one summer day，一隻蚱蜢 a grasshopper 跳進田裡 hop into a field。因為那一天是一個美麗的夏日 a beautiful summer day，蚱蜢很高興地唱著歌 sing happily，他看到一隻螞蟻 an ant 經過 pass by。那隻螞蟻很辛勤地工作 work hard，扛著穀粒回家 carry some corn to its home。

「你何不留下來 stay 和我 with me 聊天 chat 呢？」蚱蜢問，「那顆穀粒 that corn 看起來很重 look heavy，你為什麼要扛著它呢？」

「我在為冬天 for the winter 積存食物 save food。」螞蟻回答。「我建議你也這麼做 do the same thing，這樣，你才有足夠的食物 have plenty of food 可以過冬。」

「冬天？」蚱蜢說，「幹嘛 why 擔心那個 worry about that？我們現在 right now 有很多食物 have lots of food 啊，冬天還很遙遠 a long time away。」

螞蟻離開蚱蜢 leave the grasshopper 以後，每天 every day 辛勤地工作，所以他收集了很多食物 gather lots of food，過一陣子 after a while，螞蟻家裡堆滿了食物 fill its house with food。

同時 meanwhile，蚱蜢留在田野裡 stay in the field，但他完全不工作，而是每天玩耍和唱歌 play and sing。

不久 soon，夏天變成秋天 turn to fall，秋天變成冬天 turn to winter。當天氣 the weather 變冷 get colder，食物 the food 也開始消失 disappear 了。蚱蜢這才發現 discover 他沒有食物可以吃 have no food to eat，他看到螞蟻的家 look over at the ant's house，螞蟻有很多食物，他的家又好又溫暖 a nice, warm house。蚱蜢這才明白 realize 他之前有多愚蠢 how foolish。

那個冬天 that winter 下了很多雪 lots of snow。之後 later，當春天來臨 spring arrives，螞蟻走出他的家 come out of its house。冬天的時候 during winter 他有足夠的食物 have enough food 可以吃。現在他準備好要為下一個冬天 for the next winter 收集食物 gather food 了。螞蟻在田野間四處查看 look around the field，卻再也看不見蚱蜢的蹤跡 no sign of the grasshopper 了。

- 寓意：今日辛勤的工作是為明日作準備 *prepare for tomorrow*。

The Hare and the Tortoise

One day, / a hare was bragging about / how fast he could run. "I am / the fastest animal / in the entire forest," he said. All the animals / **were tired of hearing / the hare brag**. They had heard his bragging / many times before.

The hare started / to make fun of the tortoise. "You are so slow," laughed the hare. "A snail could run faster / than you."

The tortoise smiled at the hare / and replied, "Yes, I am slow. But I bet / I can reach / the end of this field / before you. Let's run a race."

"Oh, really? It's a bet," said the hare. "All right, / everyone. Let's find out / who the faster animal is."

The tortoise and the hare / went to the starting line. All the animals / in the forest / gathered to watch. "Ready. Go," shouted the fox.

The hare raced off / and left the tortoise behind. The tortoise / simply kept moving / as fast as he could.

When the hare was halfway / across the field, / he looked back. The tortoise was / far behind him. "Ha," thought the hare. "**It will take the tortoise all day / to finish.** I'm going to / get some rest here." The hare rested, / but he soon fell asleep / in the warm sunshine.

The tortoise, / in the meantime, / walked and walked. He never stopped / until he got to the finish line.

A few hours later, / the hare woke up. "Oh, no!" the hare thought. He looked ahead / toward the finish line. The tortoise / **was about to cross it**. The hare ran / as fast as he could, / but it was too late. The tortoise / crossed the finish line / first. The tortoise had won.

• *Moral: Slow and steady / wins the race.*

- **brag** 吹噓　　• **entire** 整個的　　• **forest** 森林　　• **tired of** 厭倦於　　• **make fun of** 嘲笑
- **bet** 打賭　　• **run a race** 賽跑　　• **find out** 查明　　• **race off** 跑開
- **leave . . . behind . . .** 把……留在後面　　• **halfway** 半路　　• **across** 跨越
- **look back** 回頭看　　• **far behind . . .** 遠遠在……的後面　　• **get some rest** 休息一下
- **fall asleep** 睡著　　• **in the meantime** 同時　　• **wake up** 醒來　　• **finish line** 終點線
- **be about to** 將要　　• **cross** 跨越　　• **steady** 沉著

1　**were tired of hearing the hare brag** 聽膩了兔子說的大話
　　〈be tired of . . .〉是「對……感到厭倦」、「對……感到疲累」的意思。

2　**It will take the tortoise all day to finish.** 烏龜要花一整天才能跑完。
　　〈it takes (＋A)＋時間＋to . . .〉是「(A) 花了多少時間去做……」的意思。

3　**was about to cross it** 快要越過它
　　〈be about to . . .〉是「正要去……」的意思。

龜兔賽跑

有一天 one day，兔子 a hare 吹噓 brag about 自己能跑 can run 多快 how fast。「我是整座森林裡 in the entire forest 跑得最快的動物 the fastest animal。」他説。所有的動物 all the animals 都聽膩 be tired of hearing 了兔子説的大話，他們聽 hear 他吹噓 his bragging 很多次 many times。

兔子開始嘲笑烏龜 make fun of the tortoise。「你太慢 be so slow 了，一隻蝸牛 a snail 都跑得比你快 run faster than you。」

烏龜對兔子微笑 smile at the hare，回答説：「是，我很慢，但我打賭我可以比你先 before you 到田野的盡頭 reach the end of this field，我們來比賽 run a race。」

「喔，真的嗎 oh, really？我跟你打賭 a bet，」兔子説，「好吧，各位 all right, everyone，我們來看 find out 誰跑得比較快 the faster animal。」

兔子和烏龜到起跑線 starting line，森林裡所有動物都來看 gather to watch。「預備 ready，跑 go！」狐狸大喊。

兔子開始跑 race off，把烏龜拋在後面 leave the tortoise behind，烏龜只能 simply 繼續盡他所能地快跑 keep moving as fast as he could。

當兔子跑過田野的一半 halfway across the field，他回頭看 look back，烏龜遠遠落後 far behind him，「哈 ha」，兔子想，「烏龜要花一整天 take all day 才能跑完 to finish，我要在這裡休息一下 get some rest。」兔子停下來休息 rest，但在溫暖的陽光下 in the warm sunshine，他很快地睡著 fall asleep 了。

這時候 in the meantime，烏龜走啊走 walk and walk，到終點線 the finish line 之前，他不曾停下來 never stop 休息。

幾個小時以後 a few hours later，兔子醒來 wake up 了，「喔，不 oh, no！」兔子想。他朝終點線看 look ahead toward the finish line，烏龜快越過終點線 be about to cross it 了，兔子盡他所能地快跑，但太遲了 be too late。烏龜先通過了終點線 cross the finish line，烏龜贏 win 了。

• 寓意：緩慢、沉著 *slow and steady* 贏得比賽 *win the race*。

as . . . as one can/could：盡……所能地 ⇨ 也可以換成 as . . . as possible

• The tortoise simply kept moving **as** fast **as he could**.
  烏龜只能繼續盡他所能地快跑。(= **as** fast **as possible**)

• The hare ran **as** fast **as he could**. 兔子盡他所能地快跑。(= **as** fast **as possible**)

- -

• Try **as** hard **as you can**. 盡你可能地努力。(= **as** hard **as possible**)

The Sick Lion

Once, / there was / a very old lion. As he got older, / he became weak and slow. He **could no longer** / **hunt animals**. So he was not able to / eat any food.

The lion was sure / he would soon die. He was very sad. As he slowly walked home, / the lion told a bird / about his sad situation. Soon, / all of the animals / in the forest / heard about the lion.

The other animals / **felt sorry for the lion**. "That's terrible," they said. "We should visit the lion / and see / how he is doing." So, / one by one, / they went to visit the lion / in his cave.

The lion was old and weak, / but he was also very wise. As each animal came into his cave, / they were easy / to catch and eat. Soon, / the old lion / became fat.

Still, / he kept pretending / to be sick. And the animals / kept going / into the lion's cave. After a while, / many of the animals / of the forest / had disappeared.

One day, / early in the morning, / the fox went to the lion's cave. The fox was very wise, / too. He slowly walked / close to the cave. Standing outside the cave, / the fox called out, "Hello. How are you feeling now?"

The lion answered, "I am not doing / very well. Why don't you come in? I can't see you / very well. Come closer / and tell me / some kind words. I am old / and will die soon."

While the lion was talking, / the fox was looking closely / at the ground. The fox suddenly realized / what the lion was doing.

Finally, / the fox looked up / and answered, "No, thank you. I can see many footprints / **entering your cave**. But I cannot see any footprints / **leaving your cave**."

• *Moral: A wise person learns / from the misfortunes of others.*

• **weak** 虛弱的 ≠ **strong**   • **hunt** 追捕   • **die** 死   • **situation** 處境
• **feel sorry for . . .** 為……感到難過   • **terrible** 糟糕的   • **one by one** 一個接一個
• **cave** 洞穴   • **wise** 聰明的   • **pretend** 假裝   • **disappear** 消失   • **stand** 站
• **call out** 大叫   • **closer** 更靠近的   • **closely** 仔細地   • **realize** 明白   • **footprint** 腳印
• **misfortune** 不幸

CLOSE UP

1 **could no longer hunt animals** 沒辦法再追捕動物
no longer 是「不再……」、「現在不再是……」的意思。

2 **felt sorry for the lion** 為獅子感到難過
〈feel sorry for . . .〉是「對……感到抱歉」、「對……感到憐憫」的意思。

3 **footprints entering your cave** 走進你洞穴的腳印 /
footprints leaving your cave 走出你洞穴的腳印
分別用 entering . . . 和 leaving . . . 來修飾 footprints，形成意思對比的形態。

生病的獅子

　　從前 **once**，有一隻很老的獅子 **a very old lion**，隨著年紀變老 **get older**，他變得又虛弱又緩慢 **become weak and slow**，沒辦法再 **no longer** 追捕動物，所以他沒有食物可以吃。

　　獅子確信 **be sure** 自己快死 **will soon die** 了，他很傷心 **be sad**，當他慢慢走回家 **walk home** 的時候，獅子告訴小鳥他可憐的處境 **his sad situation**，不久，森林裡所有動物 **all of the animals in the forest** 都聽到獅子的消息 **hear about the lion**。

　　其他的動物都為獅子感到難過 **feel sorry for the lion**，「真是太糟糕了 **that's terrible**，」他們說，「我們應該去拜訪獅子 **visit the lion**，看看他過得怎麼樣 **how he is doing**。」於是，他們一個接一個 **one by one**，到獅子的洞穴裡 **in his cave** 探望他 **go to visit the lion**。

　　獅子又老又虛弱 **be old and weak**，但他也很聰明 **be wise**。當動物 **each animal** 走進他的洞穴 **come into his cave**，他就可以把他們抓來吃 **catch and eat**，不久 **soon**，老獅子變胖 **become fat** 了。

　　儘管如此 **Still**，他繼續假裝 **keep pretending** 生病 **be sick**，動物不斷地走進 **keep going into** 獅子的洞穴。過了一段時間後 **after a while**，森林裡許多動物消失 **disappear** 了。

　　有一天 **one day**，大清早的時候 **early in the morning**，狐狸 **the fox** 到獅子的洞穴去 **go to the lion's cave**，狐狸也非常聰明，他慢慢走近洞穴 **walk close to the cave**，站在洞穴外 **stand outside the cave**，大叫 **call out**：「哈囉 **hello**，你現在覺得怎麼樣 **how are you feeling now**？」

　　獅子回答：「我不舒服 **I am not doing very well**，你怎麼不進來 **why don't you come in**？我看不清楚 **can't see you very well**，你靠近點 **come closer**，跟我說一些好話 **some kind words** 吧，我很老，不久就要死了。」

　　獅子在說話的時候，狐狸仔細地看地上 **look closely at the ground**，狐狸突然明白 **realize** 獅子在做什麼 **what the lion was doing** 了。

　　最後，狐狸抬頭，回答說：「不，謝謝，我看到很多走進你洞穴的腳印 **footprints entering your cave**，但我沒看到走出你洞穴的腳印 **footprints leaving your cave**。」

- 寓意：一個有智慧的人 *a wise person* 能從別人的不幸 *from the misfortunes of others* 當中學到教訓。

GRAMMAR POINT

as (連接詞)：一……就……／當……的時候／因為…… ⇨ 依句意挑選適合的用法。

- **As** he got older, he became weak and slow. 隨著年紀變老，他變得又虛弱又緩慢。
- **As** he slowly walked home, the lion told a bird about his sad situation. 當他慢慢走回家的時候，獅子告訴小鳥他可憐的處境。
- **As** each animal came into his cave, they were easy to catch and eat. 當動物走進他的洞穴，他就可以把他們抓來吃。
- -
- **As** it's raining, we should stay at home. 因為下雨，我們應該待在家裡。

The Boy Who Cried Wolf

There once was / a shepherd boy. He watched / a flock of sheep / at the bottom of a mountain. The shepherd boy / was bored / watching the sheep / all day / by himself. So he sometimes / talked to his dog / or played his pipe.

One day, / he became very bored. So he thought of a plan / to have some fun. He **decided** / **to play a trick on the villagers.** He ran down / toward the village / and cried out, "Wolf! Wolf!"

The villagers / heard the shepherd boy. The kind villagers / ran up the mountain / to help him. But when they arrived, / they found no wolf.

"Where is the wolf?"

The boy laughed / **at the sight of** / **their angry faces.**

"Ha, ha, ha! I fooled all of you," he said.

"Don't cry 'wolf,' / shepherd boy," said the villagers, "when there's no wolf!" They went back / down the mountain.

A few days later, / the shepherd boy / was bored again. So the boy / cried out again, "Wolf! Wolf!" When the villagers arrived, / the shepherd boy / was laughing at them / again.

One day / while the boy was watching the sheep, / **a wolf really did come.** It started / attacking his sheep. The frightened boy / ran toward the village / and shouted even louder / than before.

"Wolf! Wolf! A wolf / is killing my sheep!"

But the villagers thought / he was fooling them / again. So they didn't come. "He will not trick us / again," they said. Because none of them / went to help the boy, / the wolf killed / many of the sheep. And the flock scattered.

• *Moral: No one / believes liars / even when they tell the truth.*

- **shepherd** 牧羊人　　• **flock of sheep** 羊群　　• **at the bottom of . . .** 在……底下
- **bored** 無聊的　　• **by oneself** 自己一人　　• **pipe** 笛子　　• **play a trick on . . .** 捉弄……
- **villager** 村民　　• **run down** 跑下來 ≠ **run up**　　• **fool** 愚弄　　• **cry** 大叫
- **laugh at . . .** 嘲笑某人　　• **while . . .** 當……的時候　　• **attack** 攻擊　　• **frightened** 嚇壞的
- **louder** 更大聲　　• **kill** 殺害　　• **trick** 耍　　• **scatter** 散布　　• **liar** 說謊者　　• **truth** 實話

CLOSE UP

1 **The Boy Who Cried Wolf** 大喊狼來了的男孩
Who Cried Wolf 是修飾 The Boy 的關係子句。

2 **decided to play a trick on the villagers** 他決定要戲弄村民
〈play a trick on . . .〉是「欺騙……」、「對……耍小技倆」的意思，動詞 fool 和 trick 意思相同。

3 **at the sight of their angry faces** 看到他們生氣的臉
〈at the sight of . . .〉是「看到……」的意思。sight（看、看到的景象）是動詞 see（看）的名詞。

4 **a wolf really did come** 一隻狼真的來了
這裡的 did come 是強調 came 的形態，助動詞 do 可以加在肯定句的主要動詞前，用來加強語氣。
例 I do love you.（我真的很愛你。）/ She does look happy.（她真的看起來很快樂。）

放羊的孩子

　　從前 **once** 有一個牧童 **a shepherd boy**，他在山腳下 **at the bottom of a mountain** 看守 **watch** 羊群 **a flock of sheep**。牧童覺得整天 **all day** 獨自 **by himself** 看守羊群 **watch the sheep** 很無聊 **be bored**，所以他有時候 **sometimes** 會跟他的狗說話 **talk to his dog**，或是吹笛子 **play his pipe**。

　　有一天 **one day**，他覺得很無聊 **become bored**。他想到 **think of** 一個找樂子的辦法 **a plan to have some fun**，他決定要戲弄村民 **play a trick on the villagers**，他跑下山 **run down** 往村莊去，大喊 **cry out**：「狼 **wolf** 來了！狼來了！」

　　聽見牧童的聲音 **hear the shepherd boy**，好心的村民跑上山 **run up the mountain** 幫助他 **help him**，但是他們到 **arrive** 山上的時候，卻找不到狼 **find no wolf**。

　　「狼在哪裡？」

　　男孩看到他們生氣的臉 **at the sight of their angry faces**，便大笑 **laugh**。

　　「哈，哈，哈 **ha, ha, ha**！我騙你們的 **fool all of you**。」他說。

　　「牧童，沒有狼的時候 **when there's no wolf**，不要喊『狼來了』**don't cry wolf**」村民說完，就下山了。

　　幾天後 **a few days later**，牧童又覺得很無聊 **be bored again**，於是他又大叫 **cry out again**，「狼來了！狼來了！」村民到了以後，牧童又嘲笑他們 **laugh at them**。

　　有天，牧童在看守羊群時，一隻狼 **a wolf** 真的 **really** 來 **come** 了，牠開始攻擊羊隻 **attack his sheep**，牧童嚇壞了 **the frightened boy**，往村裡跑去 **run toward the village**，叫得比以前更大聲 **shout even louder than before**。

　　「狼來了！狼來了！有隻狼在殺我的羊 **kill my sheep**！」

　　但是村民認為牧童又在捉弄他們 **fool them again**，所以都不肯去，「不能再讓他耍我們 **trick us again** 了。」他們說。因為沒有人 **none of them** 去幫男孩 **go to help the boy**，狼殺了很多羊 **kill many of the sheep**，羊群也走散 **scatter** 了。

- 寓意：沒有人會相信騙子 **liars**，即使他們說的是實話 **tell the truth**。

GRAMMAR POINT

to 不定詞（目的）：為了要去做……，要去做……

- He thought of a plan **to have** some fun. 他想到一個找樂子的辦法。
- The kind villagers ran up the mountain **to help** him. 好心的村民跑上山來幫助他。
- None of them went **to help** the boy. 沒有人去幫男孩。

Super
Reading
Story
Training
Book

Step

2

The Little Mermaid

— Hans Christian Andersen

The Little Mermaid

Deep beneath the sea, / the Sea King lived. He lived with his six daughters, / very beautiful mermaids, / in a palace. His wife died / many years ago. Their grandmother / took care of the mermaid princesses.

Each princess was beautiful, / but the youngest was the loveliest / of all. **Her skin was like a rose.** Her eyes were deep sea–blue. Her long hair flew smoothly / in the sea. And she had / the most beautiful singing voice / in the world. When she sang, / the fish flocked / from all over the sea / to listen to her. **She seemed like / other girls on land.** But, **like all mermaids,** / she had no legs. She had a tail / **like a fish.**

The Little Mermaid / had a wonderful life. She played and sang / with her sisters / all day long. She also liked / to spend her time / in her wonderful sea garden. The seahorses kept her company, / and sometimes / a dolphin would come and play.

But the Little Mermaid was happiest / when her grandmother told her stories. Her grandmother told her / all about the world above the sea. She told her / about beautiful ships, villages, and the people above.

The Little Mermaid / never went out of the sea.

"Oh, how I'd love to go up there / and see the sky at last!"

"You're still too young," said her grandmother.

"When you are fifteen, / you can swim to the top of the ocean / and see the wonderful things / for yourself," said her grandmother.

The Little Mermaid / **could hardly wait**. Every night, / she stood by the window / and looked up through the water. She often dreamed of the land / above the water.

- **beneath . . .** 在……之下　　• **mermaid** 人魚　　• **palace** 皇宮
- **take care of . . .** 照顧　　• **princess** 公主　　• **loveliest** 最漂亮的　　• **flock** 聚集
- **tail** 尾鰭　• **wonderful** 美妙的　• **spend time** 花時間　• **seahorse** 海馬
- **keep . . . company . . .** 與……相伴　　• **dolphin** 海豚　　• **ship** 船
- **I'd love to . . .** 我真想　• **for oneself** 親自　• **stand by . . .** 站在……旁　• **look up** 往上看
- **dream of . . .** 幻想

1　**Her skin was like a rose.** 她的皮膚像玫瑰一樣。
　She seemed like other girls on land. 她看起來就像陸地上的女孩。
　這裡的 like 是介系詞，〈be like……〉是「和某物很像」的意思；〈seem like……〉是「看起來和……很像／很類似」的意思。

2　**like all mermaids** 和所有人魚一樣 / **like a fish** 像魚一樣
　這裡的 like 是介系詞「就像……」、「和……一模一樣」、「宛如……」的意思。

3　**could hardly wait** 等不及
　hardly 是「幾乎不」的意思，和 can 一起使用的話，是「幾乎不能……」、「做……非常吃力」的意思。

小美人魚

深海裡 deep beneath the sea 的皇宮 a palace 住著 live 一位國王 the Sea King 和他的六個女兒 his six daughters，他們都是美麗的人魚 beautiful mermaids。國王的妻子 his wife 許多年前 many years ago 去世 die 了，所以由公主的奶奶 their grandmother 照顧 take care of 人魚公主 the mermaid princesses。

每個公主 each princess 都很漂亮 be beautiful，但其中年紀最小的 the youngest 公主最漂亮 be the loveliest。她的皮膚 her skin 像玫瑰一樣 be like a rose；她的眼睛 her eyes 像深海一樣藍 deep sea-blue；她的長髮 her long hair 隨著海水飄蕩 fly smoothly in the sea；她的歌聲 singing voice 是世上 in the world 最動聽 the most beautiful 的聲音。當她唱歌，魚 the fish 會從四面八方 from all over the sea 圍 flock 過來聽她 listen to her 唱歌。她看起來就像陸地上的女孩 seem like other girls on land，只是她和所有人魚一樣 like all mermaids，沒有腳 have no legs，像魚一樣 like a fish 只有尾鰭 have a tail。

小美人魚 the Little Mermaid 過得很快樂 have a wonderful life，整天 all day long 和姊姊們 with her sisters 玩耍和唱歌 play and sing。她也喜歡待在她美麗的海中花園 sea garden 裡，海馬 the seahorses 會來和她作伴 keep her company，有時海豚 a dolphin 也會來玩 come and play。

小美人魚最快樂的時光是奶奶跟她說故事 tell her stories 的時候。奶奶會告訴她陸地上發生的事 the world above the sea，告訴她美麗的船隻 ships、村莊 villages 和陸地上的人類 the people above。

小美人魚從沒離開過大海 never go out of the sea。

「喔！我真想上去那裡 go up there，看看天空 see the sky！」

「妳還太年輕 be too young 了。」奶奶說。

「等妳15歲 be fifteen，妳可以游到海面上 swim to the top of the ocean，親自 for yourself 看看這些美好的事物 see the wonderful things。」奶奶說。

小美人魚等不及了 can hardly wait，每天晚上 every night，她站在窗戶旁 stand by the window，從水裡往上看 look up through the water，她常常幻想陸地上的事 dream of the land。

GRAMMAR POINT

最高級＋範圍 ⇨ 最高級之後出現 of all、in the world 這些表大範圍的片語。

- The youngest was **the loveliest of all**. 年紀最小的最漂亮。
- She had **the most beautiful** singing voice **in the world**. 她的歌聲是世上最動聽的聲音。
- He is **the richest** man **in the country**. 他是國內最有錢的人。

At last, / the Little Mermaid / turned fifteen.

"There, / now you can go to the surface," said her father.

The Little Mermaid / was so excited. She combed / her long golden hair. She polished / the scales on her tail. She kissed her grandmother goodbye.

In a second, / the Little Mermaid swam up / toward the surface of the sea. She swam so fast / that even the fish / could not keep up with her.

Suddenly, / she popped out of the water. How wonderful! For the first time, / she saw the great sky. It was full of / red and orange clouds. The sun was setting. "It's so lovely!" she exclaimed happily.

In front of her / was a big ship. She swam close to the ship / and looked inside. There was / a big party. There were / many handsome gentlemen, / but the finest of all / was a prince. He was laughing / and shaking hands with everyone. She had never seen / anyone like him / before. She could not take her eyes off him.

All of a sudden, / the weather changed. The sky became dark, / and heavy rain started to fall. The waves became very rough. Lightning flashed, / and thunder boomed / throughout the sky. The ship rolled up and down / on the waves. Then, / the ship broke apart / and started to sink.

The Little Mermaid / saw the prince / fall into the sea. "People cannot breathe / underwater," she thought. "I must save him." The Little Mermaid / went diving down / to look for him. He was sinking / deep into the ocean. She seized his shoulder / and took him to the surface.

When she got to land, / she pushed the prince's body / onto the shore. The prince was still not awake. The Little Mermaid / looked into his handsome face / all night long.

By the morning, / the storm was finished, / and the warm sun appeared. In the sunlight, / the prince looked more handsome. His eyes were still closed. "Wake up. Please don't die," she whispered.

- **turn** 達到（年齡） • **comb** 梳理 • **polish** 擦亮 • **in a second** 很快地
- **keep up with** 追上 • **pop out of** 探出 • **set** 太陽西沉 • **finest** 最帥的
- **shake hands with** 跟⋯⋯握手 • **rough** 洶湧的 • **lightning** 閃電 • **flash** 發出
- **thunder** 雷聲 • **boom** 隆隆作響 • **roll up and down** 忽高忽低搖晃
- **break apart** 解體 • **sink** 下沉 • **breathe** 呼吸 • **dive down** 往下潛
- **seize** 抓住 • **get to land** 到陸地 • **shore** 海岸 • **be awake** 醒 • **all night long** 整夜
- **storm** 暴風雨 • **appear** 出現 • **whisper** 輕聲低語

CLOSE UP

1 **There was a big party.** 有一個盛大的舞會。
   There were many handsome gentlemen. 有很多英俊的紳士。
   〈there is/are . . .〉是「在某個地方有⋯⋯」的意思，後接的名詞若是單數則用 is，若是複數則用 are，過去式則用 was 或 were。

2 **She could not take her eyes off him.** 她的視線離不開他。
   〈take one's eyes off . . .〉是「將視線離開⋯⋯」的意思，常和 cannot 一起出現，表感嘆某個東西相當有魅力，無法轉移視線。

終於 **at last**，小美人魚滿15歲 **turn fifteen** 了。

「現在妳可以到水面上去 **go to the surface** 了。」她爸爸說。

小美人魚很興奮 **be excited**，她梳理 **comb** 她長長的金髮 **her long golden hair**，擦亮 **polish** 尾鰭的鱗片 **the scales on her tail**，跟奶奶親吻道別。

很快地，小美人魚游向海面 **swim up toward the surface of the sea**，她游得很快 **swim so fast**，連魚都追不上她 **cannot keep up with her**。

突然間 **suddenly**，她探出水面 **pop out of the water**。多美啊 **how wonderful**！她第一次 **for the first time**，看到廣大的天空 **the great sky** 布滿了紅色、橘色的雲 **red and orange clouds**，太陽漸漸西沉。「真美 **it's so lovely**。」她快樂地驚呼 **exclaim happily**。

在她前面 **in front of her** 有一艘大船 **a big ship**。她游到船附近 **close to the ship**，往船裡看 **look inside**。船上正在舉行一個盛大的舞會 **a big party**，有很多英俊的紳士 **handsome gentlemen**，但當中最帥的 **the finest** 是一個王子 **a prince**，他正笑著和每個人握手。她從未見過 **never see** 像他這種人 **anyone like him**，王子是如此地英俊，她看得目不轉睛 **take her eyes off him**。

突然間 **all of a sudden**，天氣 **the weather** 驟變 **change**，天空 **the sky** 變黑 **become dark**，開始下起 **fall** 起大雨 **heavy rain**。波濤 **the waves** 洶湧 **become rough**，閃電 **lightning** 閃過 **flash**，雷聲 **thunder** 隆隆作響 **boom**。船隨著浪忽高忽低搖晃 **roll up and down**，最後，船解體 **break apart**，開始往下沉 **sink**。

小美人魚看到王子掉入海裡 **fall into the sea**，「人類在水裡 **underwater** 無法呼吸 **cannot breathe**，」她想，「我一定要救他 **save him**。」小美人魚往下潛 **go diving down**，找尋王子 **look for him**，他沉到大海深處 **deep into the ocean**，她抓著他的肩膀 **seize his shoulder**，把他帶到水面上 **take him to the surface**。

她到陸地 **get to land** 以後，把王子的身體 **the prince's body** 推到岸上 **push onto the shore**，王子還沒醒來 **be not awake**。小美人魚整夜 **all night long** 看著他英俊的臉龐 **look into his handsome face**。

到了早晨 **by the morning**，暴風雨 **the storm** 止息 **be finished**，溫暖的太陽 **the warm sun** 出現 **appear** 了。在陽光下 **in the sunlight**，王子看起來更英俊 **look more handsome**，但他的眼睛 **his eyes** 仍然閉著 **be closed**。「醒一醒 **wake up**，請不要死去 **don't die**。」她輕聲低語。

The Little Mermaid　**41**

Now, / she could see / dry land ahead. She took the prince / onto a pretty beach / with calm water. She laid the prince / on the warm sand. At that moment, / she saw some girls / walking along the sand. Quickly, / she swam away / and hid behind some rocks. She watched the prince. "I must stay here / until someone comes / to save him," she thought.

After a while, / a pretty girl / came along the beach. She saw the prince / and ran to him. At that moment, / the prince opened his eyes / and smiled at the girl. The girl called for help. Soon, / some people came / and took the prince away.

The Little Mermaid / felt so sad / because she could not see him / anymore. She swam back home / full of sorrow.

"What did you see?" her sisters asked. But she told them nothing. She was too sad / to speak. She was quiet / all day long.

Days and weeks / went by. The Little Mermaid / could only think about the prince. She missed him / so much. At night, / she often swam to the beach. She looked for the prince, / but she did not see him.

One day, / she finally told her sisters / her story. One of the sisters / took her to his palace. He lived in a great palace / by the sea. She could see the prince / looking out his window. She was so happy. Every night, / she swam near the palace / and watched the prince.

The Little Mermaid / loved the world above the sea / more and more. Now / she had only one wish / –to become a human.

"Grandmother," she asked one day. "Can humans live forever?"

"No, they can't," said her grandmother. "Humans die. They live shorter lives / than we do. Mermaids live for three hundred years, / and then we become / foam on the sea. But humans have souls. Their souls live forever."

• dry land 陸地　•ahead 在前面　•calm 平靜的　•lay 放　•swim away 游開
• hide 躲　•smile at . . . 對……微笑　•call for . . . 求救……　•take away 帶走
• full of sorrow 滿帶悲傷　•quiet 安靜 ≠ loud　•all day long 整日
• go by （日子）過去　•miss 想念　•finally 終於　•look out 往外看　•wish 願望
• human 人類　•forever 永遠　•life 壽命 *複數 lives　•foam 泡沫　•soul 靈魂

CLOSE UP

1 **took the prince onto a pretty beach** 把王子帶到美麗的沙灘上 /
took the prince away 把王子帶走 / **took her to his palace** 帶她去王子的皇宮
這裡的take是「帶領／帶（某人）」的意思。

2 **She was too sad to speak.** 她傷心地說不出話。
〈too . . . to . . . 〉是「太……以致不能……」的意思。
例 **You are too young to go up there.** （妳年紀太小，不能上去那裡。）

現在，她看到前面有陸地 **see dry land ahead**，她把王子帶到美麗的沙灘上 **onto a pretty beach**，那裡的浪很平靜 **calm water**，她把王子放在溫暖的沙子上 **lay the prince on the warm sand**。那時候 **at that moment**，她看到幾個女孩 **some girls** 沿著沙灘散步 **walk along the sand**。她很快地游開 **swim away**，躲在岩石後面 **hide behind some rocks**，看著王子 **watch the prince**。「我必須留在這裡 **stay here** 直到有人來救王子 **come to save him**。」她想。

過了一會兒 **after a while**，有個漂亮的女孩 **a pretty girl** 來到沙灘上 **come along the beach**，看到王子 **see the prince**，就跑到他身邊 **run to him**。那一刻王子睜開他的眼睛 **open his eyes**，對著女孩微笑 **smile at the girl**。女孩大聲呼救 **call for help**，不久，有幾個人 **some people** 來了，他們把王子帶走 **take the prince away**。

小美人魚覺得很傷心 **feel sad**，因為她再也看不到王子 **cannot see him anymore** 了。她滿懷悲傷 **full of sorrow** 地游回家 **swim back home**。

「妳看到什麼了？」她的姊姊問她，但她什麼也不說 **tell othing**。她傷心得說不出話 **too sad to speak**，整日 **all day long** 都安安靜靜的 **be quiet**。

日子一天天過去。小美人魚腦海中只有王子 **only think about the prince**，她非常想念他 **miss him so much**。她常常趁晚上 **at night** 游到沙灘 **swim to the beach**，找尋王子的蹤影 **look for the prince**，但是並沒有見到他 **do not see him**。

有一天 **one day**，她終於 **finally** 跟姊姊說了她的故事 **tell her sisters her story**。其中一個姊姊 **one of the sisters** 帶她去王子的皇宮 **take her to his palace**。王子住在海邊的一座大皇宮裡 **live in a great palace by the sea**。她看到王子正看著窗外 **look out his window**，她很開心，於是每晚 **every night**，她都游到皇宮附近 **swim near the palace**，去看王子。

小美人魚越來越 **more and more** 喜歡陸地上的世界 **the world above the sea**，現在她只有一個願望 **have only one wish**——變成人類 **become a human**。

有一天她問奶奶：「奶奶，人類 **humans** 可以永遠活著 **live forever** 嗎？」

「不，他們不能，」奶奶說，「人類會死 **die**，他們的壽命比我們短 **live shorter lives**，人魚可以活 300 年 **live for three hundred years**，人魚死了以後，會化成海上的泡沫 **foam on the sea**，但人類有靈魂 **have souls**，他們的靈魂永恆不朽。」

---

see ＋受詞＋原形動詞／現在分詞 ⇨ 感官動詞的受詞之後，要接原形動詞或現在分詞。

- The Little Mermaid **saw** the prince **fall** into the sea. 小美人魚看到王子掉入海裡。
- She **saw** some girls **walking** along the sand. 她看到一些女孩沿著沙灘散步。
- She could **see** the prince **looking** out his window. 她看到王子正看著窗外。

"I want to be like a person. Can I get a human soul?" asked the Little Mermaid.

"Don't say that," said her grandmother.

"Is there any way / that I can get a soul?" she asked / over and over again.

At last, / her grandmother replied.

"There is / only one way. If a man loves you / with all his heart / and marries you, / then his soul can enter your body. Then, / **you would have a soul / and would live forever,**" she continued. "But that will never happen / because we have tails. Humans think / tails are ugly. They prefer legs. No man will want / to marry a mermaid."

The Little Mermaid / looked at her tail / and thought.

"I want to have two legs. I must win the prince's love / and marry him. I love him. I will do anything / for him. Maybe the sea witch / can help me."

She swam off / to see the sea witch. The sea witch / lived in a horrible, scary place. Her house **was made / from the bones of dead sailors.** And there were sea snakes / everywhere. The Little Mermaid / felt very afraid. She almost left. Then, she thought, "The prince! And my soul! I must not be afraid."

The Little Mermaid / swam up to the sea witch. When the witch saw the Little Mermaid, / she said, "I know / **what you want.** I can give you / a pair of human legs. Then, / you will be able to / walk on land. Come in."

The Little Mermaid / followed the witch / into the bone house.

"You are a stupid girl. You will be sorry. But I will grant your wish," the witch said.

"I will make a magic drink / for you. Tomorrow morning, / before sunrise, / you must swim to land / and drink it. Then your tail will split in two, / and you will have two legs. But it will be very painful. It will hurt / every time you walk. Can you bear the pain?"

- **over and over again** 不停地 • **with all one's heart** 全心全意 • **marry** 結婚
- **continue** 繼續 • **ugly** 醜的 • **prefer** 喜歡 • **sea witch** 海巫 • **swim off** 游走
- **horrible** 可怕的 • **scary** 恐怖的 • **be made from . . .** 用什麼做的 • **sailor** 水手
- **sea snake** 海蛇 • **swim up to . . .** 游向 • **a pair of** 一雙 • **be able to . . .** 可以
- **stupid** 笨的 • **grant one's wish . . .** 實現某人的願望 • **magic drink** 魔法藥水
- **sunrise** 日出 • **split in . . .** 裂成兩半 • **painful** 痛苦的 • **hurt** 痛的
- **every time** 每次 • **bear pain** 承受痛苦

CLOSE UP

1 **you would have a soul and would live forever** 妳就能擁有靈魂，永恆不朽
這裡的 would（將）表未來不太可能會實現的事。

2 **was made from the bones of dead sailors** 用死去水手的骨頭建造的
〈be made from . . .〉是「由……做成的」的意思。例 Cheese is made from milk.（起司是用牛奶做的。）

3 **what you want** 妳想要什麼
〈what＋主詞＋動詞〉是「主詞所做（或其他動詞）的東西」的意思。例 what you have（你所有的）

「我想像人類一樣 **be like a person**，我能擁有人類的靈魂 **get a human soul** 嗎？」小美人魚問。

「別說這種話 **don't say that**。」奶奶說。

「有沒有什麼辦法可以讓我擁有靈魂 **get a soul**？」她不停地 **over and over again** 問。

最後，她的奶奶回答了。

「只有一個辦法 **only one way**，如果有個男人 **a man** 全心全意 **with all his heart** 地愛妳 **love you**，跟妳結婚 **marry you**，那麼他的靈魂 **his soul** 就可以進到妳的身體裡 **enter your body**，然後 **then** 妳就能擁有靈魂 **have a soul**，長生不死 **live forever**。」她繼續說，「但是這恐怕不會發生 **never happen**，因為我們有尾鰭，人類認為尾鰭很醜 **be ugly**，他們比較喜歡腳 **prefer legs**，沒有人想要娶人魚 **marry a mermaid** 的。」

小美人魚看著她的尾鰭 **look at her tail**，想「我想要一雙腿 **two legs**，我一定要贏得王子的愛 **win the prince's love**，嫁給他 **marry him**，我愛他 **love him**，願意為他做任何事 **do anything for him**，也許 **maybe** 海巫 **the sea witch** 可以幫我 **help me**。」

她游開 **swim off**，去見海巫 **see the sea witch**，海巫住在一個令人毛骨悚然的地方 **a horrible, scary place**，她的家是用死去水手的骨頭 **the bones of dead sailors** 建造而成的，到處 **everywhere** 都是海蛇 **sea snakes**。小美人魚很害怕 **feel afraid**，差一點就要離開 **almost leave**，然後，她想，「為了王子 **the prince**！為了我的靈魂 **my soul**！我一定不能害怕 **must not be afraid**。」

小美人魚游向海巫 **swim up to the sea witch**。當海巫看到小美人魚，她說：「我知道妳想要什麼 **what you want**，我可以給妳一雙人類的腳 **a pair of human legs**，讓妳可以在陸地上行走 **walk on land**，進來吧 **come in**。」

小美人魚跟著海巫 **follow the witch** 進入人骨建造的房子 **into the bone house**。

「妳這個笨女孩 **a stupid girl**，妳會後悔的 **will be sorry**，但我會實現妳的願望 **grant your wish**。」海巫說。

「我會為妳調製一瓶魔法藥水 **a magic drink**，明天早上 **tomorrow morning**，日出之前 **before sunrise**，妳必須游到陸地 **swim to land**，喝下魔藥 **drink it**，妳的尾鰭會一分為二 **split in two**，然後妳就會有一雙腿，但這會很痛苦 **be painful**，妳每次走路的時候 **every time you walk**，腿都會很痛 **hurt**，妳受得了這種痛苦 **bear the pain** 嗎？」

"Yes," replied the Little Mermaid. "It doesn't matter!" whispered the Little Mermaid / with tears in her eyes. "As long as I can go back to him!"

"But remember / one more thing," the sea witch added. "Once you become a human, / you can never become a mermaid again. You will never return / to your father's palace. And if the prince marries another girl, / you will turn into foam on the sea."

"I will do it," the Little Mermaid said.

"Ah, / but there is / one more thing," said the sea witch. "You must pay me. I want your voice. You have the prettiest voice / in the world."

"My voice? Then how can I speak?" the Little Mermaid asked. "How will I make the prince / fall in love with me? I must be able to / talk to him."

"You are beautiful," said the sea witch. "You can dance. You can smile at him. Your deep blue eyes / will speak for you. You do not need to talk."

"All right," the Little Mermaid / agreed to the price. Instantly, / her voice was gone.

The sea witch / made the magic drink / for her. The Little Mermaid / took the drink / and swam to land. She reached the beach / and then / drank the magic drink. Suddenly, / she felt a horrible pain. It was like / a knife in her body. She passed out / in the sand.

The next morning, / the Little Mermaid / woke up. She looked at her body. Her tail was gone. She had the prettiest legs / on Earth. Then, / she saw a shadow. She looked up. The prince was standing over her / and looking down at her.

- with tears in one's eyes 眼中含淚　• as long as 只要　• remember 記得
- once 一旦　• return 返回　• turn into 變成　• pay 付代價
- fall in love with . . . 愛上……　• instantly 立刻　• knife 刀　• pass out 昏倒
- shadow 影子　• look up 抬頭看　• look down at . . . 低頭看某物

CLOSE UP

1　**will turn into foam on the sea** 變成海上的泡沫
　〈turn into . . .〉是外貌或性質「變成了……」、「轉換成……」的意思。

2　**make the prince fall in love with me** 讓王子愛上我
　〈make＋受詞＋原形動詞〉是「使……去做……」的意思。〈fall in love with……〉是「和……談戀愛」、「愛上……」的意思。

3　**her voice was gone** 她的聲音不見了 / **Her tail was gone.** 她的尾鰭不見了。
　〈be gone〉表什麼東西消失了，或沒有留下什麼就離開了的狀態。

「可以，」小美人魚回答，「沒關係 it doesn't matter！」小美人魚眼眶含淚 with tears in her eyes，她低聲回答：「只要我能回到他身邊 go back to him。」

「還要記得 remember 一件事 one more thing」海巫補充道，「一旦 once 妳變成人類 become a human，就再也不能變回人魚 never become a mermaid again，也不能回到 never return 妳父親的皇宮 to your father's palace。如果王子娶了別的女孩 marry another girl，妳就會變成海上的泡沫 turn into foam on the sea。」

「我願意這麼做。」小美人魚說。

「啊，還有一件事，」海巫說，「妳必須給我報酬 pay me，我要妳的聲音 want your voice，妳擁有世上最動聽的聲音 the prettiest voice。」

「我的聲音 my voice？那我怎麼 how 說話 speak？」小美人魚問，「我要怎麼讓王子愛上我 fall in love with me？我必須和他說話 talk to him。」

「妳很美麗 be beautiful，」海巫說，「妳可以跳舞 dance，可以對他微笑 smile at him，妳那雙深藍色的眼睛 your deep blue eyes 會為妳說話 speak for you，妳不需要說話 do not need to talk。」

「好吧 all right。」小美人魚同意付出這個代價 agree to the price，剎那間 instantly，她的聲音 her voice 消失 be gone 了。

海巫為她調製了魔法藥水 make the magic drink，小美人魚拿到藥水 take the drink 後，就游到陸地，她到沙灘上 reach the beach，喝下藥水 drink the magic drink，突然間，感到一陣劇痛 feel a horrible pain，身體裡好像有把刀 a knife in her body，在沙灘上 in the sand 昏了過去 pass out。

隔天一早 the next morning，小美人魚醒來 wake up 了。她看看自己的身體 look at her body，她的尾鰭 her tail 不見 be gone 了。她有天底下 on Earth 最美的一雙腿 the prettiest legs。她看到一個陰影 see a shadow，抬頭一看 look up。王子就站在她的上方 stand over her，低頭看著她 look down at her。

"Who are you? Where did you come from?" asked the prince.

But the Little Mermaid / could not speak. She just looked deeply / into his eyes / with her sad blue eyes. At that moment, / the prince had very strong feelings / for her.

"I'll take you to the castle / and look after you," he said. The prince took the Little Mermaid / inside his castle. **Every step / felt like sharp knives.** But she was with the prince, / so she was happy.

In the days that followed, / the Little Mermaid / started a new life. The prince gave the Little Mermaid / her own room. He gave her / beautiful clothes and jewelry to wear, / too. She was the most beautiful girl / in the kingdom. But the Little Mermaid / could not say anything / to the prince. **All she could do / was smile at him.**

The prince held many parties. One night, / some girls / sang for the prince. They sang well, / but the Little Mermaid was sad. "**I used to sing / much better than that,**" she thought. "**I wish / the prince could hear / my singing voice.**"

Then, / the girls started to dance. Now, / the Little Mermaid could dance / for the prince. She danced and danced. She suffered terrible pain / throughout her body, / but she danced so beautifully. Everyone was amazed / by the Little Mermaid's dancing. The prince could not stop watching her.

After the party, / the Little Mermaid and prince / did everything together. They had picnics / on the beach. They went riding together. They walked / beside the calm ocean. The Little Mermaid's feet ached, / but she did not care. She was happy / to be with the prince.

Sometimes at night, / she went to the ocean. She put her feet / into the cool water. **It always felt so good.** At those times, / she thought of her family. She missed them / so much. "I hope / they are well. I hope / they understand me," she thought.

- **deeply** 深深地　　• **feeling** 情感　　• **look after** 照顧　　• **sharp** 銳利的
- **in the days that follow** 接下來的日子　　• **jewelry** 珠寶　　• **kingdom** 王國
- **hold a party** 舉辦宴會　　• **suffer** 承受痛苦　　• **be amazed by** 為某事而驚訝
- **have a picnic** 野餐　　• **go riding** 騎馬　　• **ache** 痛　　• **do not care** 不在乎
- **put A into B** 把A放在B裡　　• **at those times** 那時候　　• **hope** 希望

CLOSE UP

1　**Every step felt like sharp knives.** 每走一步都像銳利的刀子。/
　It always felt so good. 這讓她覺得很舒服。
　feel的主詞是事物的話，就是「感受/感覺」該事物的觸感、質感的意思。

2　**All she could do was (to) smile at him.** 她只能對他微笑。
　〈all . . . can do is (to) . . .〉是「……能做的，就只是……而已」的意思，這時加不加to都可以。

3　**I used to sing much better than that.** 我以前唱得比那還要好聽。
　〈used to＋原形動詞〉是「以前做……」的意思，含有「現在已經不再做了」的意思。

「妳是誰？妳從哪裡來？」王子問。

但是小美人魚不能説話 **cannot speak**，她只是用她哀傷的藍眼睛 **with her sad blue eyes** 深深地望著王子 **look deeply into his eyes**，那一刻，王子對她產生強烈的情感 **have strong feelings**。

「我會帶妳回城堡 **take you to the castle**，照顧妳 **look after you**。」他説。王子把小美人魚帶回他的城堡。每走一步 **every step** 都像鋭利的刀 **feel like sharp knives** 在刺她，但她跟王子在一起 **be with the prince**，所以她很快樂 **be happy**。

接下來的日子 **in the days that followed**，小美人魚開始過新的生活 **start a new life**。王子給她一間屬於她的房間 **her own room**，也給她穿戴漂亮的衣服和珠寶 **beautiful clothes and jewelry**。她是王國裡 **in the kingdom** 最漂亮的女孩 **the most beautiful girl**，但小美人魚沒辦法跟王子説話 **cannot say anything to the prince**，她只能 **all she can do** 對他微笑 **smile at him**。

王子舉辦了很多宴會 **hold many parties**。有一晚 **one night**，一些女孩 **some girls** 為王子獻唱 **sing for the prince**，她們唱得很好聽 **sing well**，但小美人魚很傷心 **be sad**。她想，「我以前唱得比她們還好聽 **sing much better than that**，但願王子能聽到我的歌聲 **hear my singing voice**。」

女孩們開始跳舞，小美人魚現在也能為王子跳舞 **dance for the prince** 了，她跳啊跳 **dance and dance**，全身 **throughout her body** 承受劇烈的痛苦 **suffer terrible pain**，但是她卻跳得很美 **dance beautifully**，大家 **everyone** 都對小美人魚的舞姿感到很訝異 **be amazed**。王子目不轉睛地盯著她看 **cannot stop watching her**。

宴會結束後 **after the party**，小美人魚和王子形影不離 **do everything together**，一起在沙灘上 **on the beach** 野餐 **have picnics**，一起騎馬 **go riding**，一起在平靜的海邊散步 **walk beside the calm ocean**。小美人魚的腳很痛 **ache**，但她不在乎 **do not care**，她跟王子在一起很快樂。

有時夜裡 **sometimes at night**，她會到海邊 **go to the ocean**，把腳放在涼涼的海水裡 **put her feet into the cool water**，這讓她覺得很舒服 **feel so good**。在那獨處的時刻裡 **at those times**，她會想起她的家人 **think of her family**，她很想念他們 **miss them so much**。「我希望他們過得很好 **be well**，我希望他們諒解我 **understand me**。」她想。

GRAMMAR POINT

I wish . . . (假設語氣) ：能……的話就好了、但願……

⇨ I wish 後接的從屬子句，若使用過去式動詞的話，就是表示和現在的事實相反的期望。

- **I wish** the prince **could hear** my singing voice. 但願王子能聽到我的歌聲。
- **I wish** I **had** two legs and **walked** on the beach every day.
  但願我有一雙腳，可以每天在海灘上散步。
- **I wish** I **were** a human. 但願我是人類。（在與現在事實相反的假設中，be動詞用過去式 were，不用was。）

Day by day, / the prince loved the Little Mermaid / more and more. But he loved her / like a sister. He did not think of / marrying her.

One day, / the prince told the Little Mermaid, "You are the sweetest girl / I know. You remind me of a girl. This girl saved my life / when my ship sank. I almost drowned. I only saw her once, / but I cannot forget her. She is the only girl / I can ever love."

"I wish / I could tell him / it was me!" the Little Mermaid thought. "I saved you. But you don't know me." She felt so sad.

One day, / the king ordered the prince / to visit the next kingdom. The king wanted the prince / to marry the princess of the kingdom.

"I must go there / because my father ordered me," said the prince, "but no one can make me / marry this princess. You remind me / more of my lost love. If I must get married, / I will marry you." He kissed the Little Mermaid. "Will you come with me? I want you / to sail with me," he asked.

The prince, the Little Mermaid, and many others / got on a ship / and sailed across the sea. At last, / they arrived at a beautiful town. Many people came to the ship / and welcomed the prince. And there was / the princess. She had deep blue eyes, / just like the Little Mermaid.

"It is you," cried the prince. "My true love! You are the girl / who saved my life. Let us get married / tonight."

The prince / turned to the Little Mermaid. He said, "My wish has come true. I am so happy. I have found my true love. And I know / you will be happy for me / because you love me."

The Little Mermaid's heart / was broken. She would never marry the prince now. His wedding / meant one thing. She must die.

- **day by day** 日子一天天地過去　・**sweetest** 最甜美的　・**remind** 提醒
- **save one's life** 救某人的命　・**drown** 溺死　・**forget** 忘記
- **I wish I could . . .** 但願我能……　・**order** 命令　・**lost** 失去的　・**sail** 航行
- **get on a ship** 上船　・**welcome** 迎接　・**turn to** 轉向　・**come true** 實現
- **be broken** 心碎　・**wedding** 婚禮

CLOSE UP

1　**You remind me of a girl.** 妳讓我想起一個女孩。/
　You remind me more of my lost love. 妳更讓我想起我失去的愛人。
　〈. . . remind me of . . .〉是「看到……讓我想起……」的意思。

2　**ordered the prince to visit the next kingdom** 國王下令要王子去拜訪鄰國
　〈order . . . to . . .〉是「命令……去做……」的意思。

3　**make me marry this princess** 逼我娶那個公主 /
　If I must get married, I will marry you. 如果我一定要結婚，我會娶妳。/
　Let us get married tonight. 我們今晚結婚吧。
　一般來說，若表示「結婚」的狀態時，就要用 get married；若表示「和誰結婚」時，就要用 marry。
　這時 marry 後不要接介系詞 with，這點要注意。

日子一天天地過去 day by day。王子愈來愈 more and more 喜愛小美人魚 love the Little Mermaid，但他把她當妹妹一樣 like a sister 愛她，沒有想過要娶她。

有一天，王子告訴小美人魚：「妳是我認識最甜美的女孩 the sweetest girl，妳讓我想起一個女孩 remind me of a girl，船沉的時候，我差點溺死 almost drown，是這個女孩救了我的命 save my life，我只見過她一次 see her once，但我忘不了她 cannot forget her，她是我唯一所愛的女孩 the only girl I can ever love。」

「但願我能告訴他 I wish I could，」小美人魚想，「是我 it is me 救了你 save you，但你卻不知道是我 don't know me。」她很傷心 feel so sad。

有一天，國王下令 order 要王子去拜訪鄰國 visit the next kingdom，國王要王子娶鄰國的公主 marry the princess of the kingdom。

「我父親命令我 order me 去那裡 go there，所以我必須去，」王子說，「但是沒有人 no one 可以逼我娶那個公主 make me marry this princess，妳讓我想起我失去的愛人 my lost love。如果我一定要結婚 must get married，我會娶妳 will marry you。」他親了小美人魚 kiss the Little Mermaid。「妳願意跟我一起去 come with me 嗎？我希望妳和我一起乘船航行 sail with me。」他問。

王子、小美人魚和其他人上了船，橫渡大海。最後，他們到了一座美麗的小鎮，很多人來他們的船迎接王子。有一位公主也來了，她有一雙深藍色的眼睛，就跟小美人魚一樣。

「是妳 it is you，」王子大叫，「我的真愛 my true love！妳是那個救我的女孩，我們今晚結婚吧 let us get married tonight。」

王子轉向小美人魚 turn to the Little Mermaid，說：「我的願望 my wish 成真 come true 了，我很高興，我找到了我的真愛 find my true love，我知道妳也會為我感到高興的，因為妳愛我。」

小美人魚的心 the Little Mermaid's heart 碎了 be broken，她再也不能嫁給王子了，他的婚禮 his wedding 只意味一件事 mean one thing，她必定會死 must die。

GRAMMAR POINT

who / whom (關係代名詞)

⇨ 代替前面出現的人名（先行詞），由 who 或 whom 引導的關係子句，是用來修飾該先行詞的，當受格的 whom 可以省略。

- You are *the girl* **who** saved my life. 妳是那個救我的女孩。
- You are *the sweetest girl* **(whom)** I know. 妳是我認識最甜美的女孩。
- She is *the only girl* **(whom)** I can ever love. 她是我唯一所愛的女孩。

That night, / the prince and the princess / got married / on his ship. The wedding was beautiful. There was joyful music / everywhere. But the Little Mermaid / did not hear the music.

"This is / my last night on Earth," she said to herself. "Tomorrow, / I will die / and become foam on the sea."

At the wedding, / the Little Mermaid danced / for the last time. She moved / like an angel. **She danced / more beautifully than ever.** But her feet and heart / were in pain. After that night, / she would not see the prince again.

At midnight, / the music stopped, / and the prince led his bride away. All was silent, / yet **the Little Mermaid stayed awake.** She went out / to look at the water / by herself.

Just then, / the Little Mermaid's sisters / swam up to the ship. They looked different. Their beautiful hair / was gone.

"Little sister!" they cried. "We gave our hair / to the sea witch. In return, / she gave us a knife. Before the sun rises, / you must kill the prince. When his blood splashes on you, / your tail will return. You will become a mermaid again. Hurry up / and do it. You must kill him / before the sun rises, / or it will be too late."

The Little Mermaid **took the knife / from her sisters.** It was very sharp. She sneaked into the prince's room. The prince and the princess / were sleeping peacefully. The Little Mermaid / **took the knife out.** She looked at the knife. Then, / she looked at the prince. No, / she could not do it. She loved him. She threw the knife / into the sea. Then, / she jumped into the sea. The sun was rising.

- **come down** 下來　• **put** 放　• **walk into** 走進鞋店　• **enough** 足夠的
- **go out** 出門　• **even more** 更多　• **a while later** 過了一會兒　• **customer** 顧客
- **enter** 走進　• **pay for** 買什麼付錢　*pay-paid-paid　• **wonder** 納悶
- **instead** 反而　• **hide** 躲　*hide-hid-hidden　• **wait** 等

1　**She danced more beautifully than ever.** 她跳得比之前更美。
〈比較級＋than ever〉是「比之前任何時候更……」的意思。

2　**the Little Mermaid stayed awake** 小美人魚依然醒著
〈stay＋形容詞〉是「維持/保持著……的狀態」的意思。
例 stay healthy（維持健康）/ stay young（青春永駐）

3　**took the knife from her sisters** 小美人魚從姊姊那裡收下刀子 / **took the knife out** 拿出刀子
這裡take基本的意思是「用手抓著、拿著」的意思。文章中出現的第一個take是從對方手中「收下、接下」的意思，第二個take則是將東西從裡面拿到外面，「拿出、取出」的意思。

那天晚上 **that night**，王子和公主 **the prince and the princess** 在他的船上 **on his ship** 結婚 **get married** 了。婚禮很美妙，到處都是歡樂的音樂 **joyful music**，但小美人魚聽不見這些音樂 **do not hear the music**。

「這是我在這世界上的最後一晚 **my last night on Earth** 了，」她對自己說，「明天 **tomorrow**，我就會死 **die**，化成海上的泡沫 **become foam on the sea**。」

婚禮上 **at the wedding**，小美人魚跳最後一次舞 **dance for the last time**，舞動得像個天使 **move like an angel**，跳得比之前更美 **more beautifully than ever**，但她的雙腳和心 **her feet and heart** 都很痛苦 **be in pain**。那晚之後，她將再也見不到王子。

午夜 **at midnight**，樂聲停止，王子帶著他的新娘離開 **lead his bride away**。一切都變得寂靜無聲 **be silent**，但小美人魚依然醒著 **stay awake**，她走出去 **go out** 獨自 **by herself** 看著海水 **look at the water**。

那時 **just then**，小美人魚的姊姊們 **the Little Mermaid's sisters** 游到船邊 **swim up to the ship**，她們看起來不一樣 **look different** 了，她們美麗的長髮 **their beautiful hair** 不見了 **be gone**。

「小妹 **little sister**！」她們大叫，「我們把頭髮 **our hair** 給 **give** 海巫 **to the sea witch**，跟她交換 **in return** 一把刀 **a knife**。日出前，妳一定要殺了王子 **kill the prince**。當他的血 **his blood** 濺到妳身上 **splash on you**，妳的尾鰭 **your tail** 就會變回來 **return**，妳就可以變回人魚 **become a mermaid again**。快點 **hurry up** 去做 **do it**，妳一定要在日出前殺了他，要不然就太遲 **be too late** 了。」

小美人魚從姊姊那裡 **from her sisters** 拿了刀 **take the knife**，刀非常銳利 **be very sharp**。她偷偷溜進王子的房間裡 **sneak into the prince's room**，王子和公主睡得很安詳 **sleep peacefully**。小美人魚拿出刀子 **take the knife out**，她看看刀 **look at the knife**，然後再看看王子 **look at the prince**。不 **no**，她沒辦法下手 **cannot do it**。她愛王子，她把刀扔到大海裡 **throw the knife into the sea**，然後，跳進海裡 **jump into the sea**，太陽升起了。

The Little Mermaid felt cold water. "I am dying," she thought.

But the Little Mermaid / did not turn into foam. Suddenly, / she felt her body / rising into the air. She saw / other lovely floating children. They were singing / around her.

"Where am I? Who are you?" asked the Little Mermaid. She could speak again! She had a new voice. It was even more beautiful / than before.

"You're with us / in the sky. We are / the fairies of the air," they responded. "You are now / a fairy of the air. There are many ways / to win a soul. We can get souls / by doing good deeds," they continued.

"Mermaids only get souls / if humans love them. But the fairies of the air / can live for three hundred years. If we do good deeds / for three hundred years, / we can earn souls. You tried so hard / to earn a soul. You loved the prince / so much / that you gave your life / for him. We will help you / get a soul. Your soul will live forever."

"I can earn a soul? This is wonderful."

The Little Mermaid / looked down at the ship. She saw / the prince and the bride. The prince was looking sadly / into the ocean. He seemed to have guessed / what had happened to her.

She flew down to them. Of course, / they could not see the Little Mermaid. She moved her body / around them. They felt the cool air / move around them. The Little Mermaid / kissed the prince and his bride. Then, she smiled / and flew up into the sky.

"In three hundred years, / I will have a soul," she said. "And I will see my prince / in heaven."

- **turn into** 變成　• **rise** 升起　• **lovely** 可愛的　• **floating** 飄　• **fairy** 仙子
- **win a soul** 得到靈魂　• **deed** 行為　• **earn a soul** 得到靈魂　• **sadly** 悲傷地
- **guess** 猜到　• **fly down** 飛下來　• **fly up** 飛上　• **heaven** 天堂

CLOSE UP

1　**It was even more beautiful than before.** 甚至比以前更美。
比較級前的even是「……得多」的意思，用來修飾比較級，除此之外，much、far、still、a lot等，也可以修飾比較級。

2　**We can get souls by doing good deeds.** 我們可以由行善得到靈魂。
〈by＋V-ing〉是「藉由做……」的意思，表手段及方法。

3　**We will help you (to) get a soul.** 我們會幫妳得到靈魂的。
〈help＋受詞＋（to）原形動詞〉是「幫……去做……」的意思，這裡加不加to都可以。
例 I'll help you (to) find it.（我們會幫你找到它的。）

4　**He seemed to have guessed what had happened to her.**
他似乎猜到小美人魚發生了什麼事。
〈seem to have p.p.〉是「看起來像是已經……了」的意思。
名詞子句 what had happened to her是過去完成式，表示這個事件比主要子句的事件還要早發生。

小美人魚感覺到海水的冰冷 **feel cold water**。「我快要死 **be dying** 了。」她想。

但是小美人魚沒有變成泡沫 **do not turn into foam**，突然間，她覺得她的身體升到空中 **rise into the air**，她看到可愛的孩子們在空中飄著 **other lovely floating children**，在她身邊唱歌 **sing around her**。

「我在哪裡？你們是誰？」小美人魚問。她又可以說話 **can speak again** 了！她有新的聲音 **have a new voice**，甚至比以前的聲音更好聽 **even more beautiful than before**。

「妳跟我們 **with us** 在天上 **in the sky**，我們是天上的仙子 **the fairies of the air**，」他們回答。「妳現在是天上的仙子 **a fairy of the air**。有很多方式 **many ways** 可以得到靈魂 **win a soul**，我們可以靠行善 **do good deeds** 得到靈魂 **get souls**。」他們繼續說。

「只有人類愛上人魚，人魚才能得到靈魂。天上的仙子可以活300年 **live for three hundred years**。如果這300年不斷行善，我們就能得到靈魂 **earn souls**。妳這麼努力 **try so hard** 想得到靈魂，為了王子 **for him** 願意獻上自己的性命 **give your life**，我們會幫妳得到靈魂的，妳的靈魂 **your soul** 將永恆不朽 **live forever**。」

「我可以得到靈魂？這真是太棒了。」

小美人魚往下看著船 **look down at the ship**，看到王子和新娘 **see the prince and the bride**。王子很悲傷地看著大海 **look sadly into the ocean**，似乎猜到 **seem to guess** 小美人魚發生了什麼事 **what happens to her**。

她飛下來，飛到他們身邊 **fly down to them**。當然，他們看不到小美人魚，她在他們身邊飛來飛去 **move her body around them**，他們感受到一股涼涼的氣流 **the cool air** 在他們四周流動 **move around them**。小美人魚親 **kiss** 了王子和他的新娘，然後微笑 **smile**、飛上天空 **fly up into the sky**。

「再過300年 **in three hundred years**，我就會擁有靈魂 **have a soul** 了，」她說，「到時我會在天堂 **in heaven** 見到我的王子 **see my prince**。」

Super
Reading
Story
Training
Book

Beauty and the Beast

Once, / there was / a rich merchant / who had many ships. He bought and sold / things from around the world. He lived in a big house / by the sea. He had three daughters. The daughters were all very beautiful, / but the youngest was the most beautiful / of all. In fact, / she was so beautiful / that everyone called her "Beauty."

Beauty was not only pretty / but also kind and smart. She loved reading. Her two sisters / were not very nice / though. They were selfish and greedy. They liked to go to parties / and to wear nice dresses. They were always mean to Beauty. They laughed at her / when she read books. They only thought about / marrying rich men.

One day, / there was a terrible storm / at sea. All the merchant's ships sank, / so he lost everything. The man had to sell his big house / and move into a small house / in the countryside.

"I'm sorry, my children. All my ships sank," said the man. "We have no money, / so we have to work / to earn money."

"But, Father," said the eldest daughter, "we have never worked / in our lives. We don't know / how to work."

"We can't work. No rich man / will want to marry us!" the middle daughter cried.

The family moved / to the small country house.

"This house is so tiny," said the eldest daughter.

"How are we supposed to live here?" the middle daughter cried.

- **rich** 有錢的，富有的 ≠ **poor**　• **merchant** 商人　• **youngest** 最年幼的
- **in fact** 事實上　• **not only . . . but also . . .** 不僅……而且……　• **kind** 善良的
- **smart** 聰明的　• **though** 儘管　• **selfish** 自私的　• **greedy** 貪心的
- **go to a party** 參加宴會　• **mean** 壞心的　• **laugh at** 嘲笑　• **marry** 結婚
- **terrible** 可怕的　• **storm** 暴風雨　• **sink** 沉　• **lose** 失去　• **countryside** 鄉間
- **earn money** 賺錢　• **eldest** 最年長的　• **cry** 大叫；大聲說　• **tiny** 極小的
- **be supposed to** 應該

CLOSE UP

1　**she was so beautiful that everyone called her "Beauty"** 她美到所有人都叫她「美麗」
〈so . . . that . . .〉意「如此……所以……」。
〈call A B〉意「把A叫作B」。

2　**The man had to sell his big house** 商人必須把大房子賣掉 /
we have to work to earn money 我們得工作賺錢
〈have to . . .〉意「必須去做……」，過去式要用（had to）。

3　**How are we supposed to live here?** 我們怎麼可以住在這裡？
〈be supposed to . . .〉意「應該」、「必須要」。

美女與野獸

　　從前 once，有一個很富有的商人 a rich merchant，他有很多艘船 have many ships，他在世界各地 around the world 買賣貨物 buy and sell things，住在海邊 live by the sea 的一棟大房子 a big house 裡，有三個女兒 have three daughters，女兒們都很美麗，但最小的 the youngest 女兒最美麗 be the most beautiful。事實上 in fact，她美到所有人都叫她「美麗」call her "Beauty"。

　　美麗不僅漂亮 be pretty，她還很善良、聰明 be kind and smart，她喜歡閱讀 love reading。她的兩個姊姊 her two sisters 不善良 be not very nice，她們又自私又貪心 be selfish and greedy，喜歡參加宴會 go to parties，穿好的衣服 wear nice dresses，總是對美麗很壞 be mean to Beauty，嘲笑她 laugh at her 看書。她們一心只想嫁給有錢人。

　　有一天 one day，海上 at sea 掀起可怕的暴風雨 a terrible storm，商人所有的船隻 all the merchant's ships 都沉 sink 了，失去了一切 lose everything。商人必須把大房子賣掉 sell his big house，搬到 move 鄉下 countryside 的小房子 a small house。

　　「對不起，我的孩子們 my children，我所有的船 all my ships 都沉 sink 了。」商人說，「我們沒有錢 have no money 了，得工作 have to work 賺錢 earn money。」

　　「爸爸，」大女兒說，「我們這輩子 in our lives 從來沒工作過 never work，不知道怎麼工作 don't know how to work。」

　　「我們不能工作 can't work，沒有一個有錢人 no rich man 會想娶我們 marry us 的！」二女兒大聲地說。

　　一家人搬到鄉下的小房子 move to the small country house。

　　「這房子太小 be so tiny 了。」大女兒說。

　　「我們怎麼能住這裡？」二女兒大聲地說。

GRAMMAR POINT

not only . . . but also . . . : 不僅……還……

- Beauty was **not only** pretty **but also** kind and smart. 美麗不僅漂亮，她還很善良、聰明。
- She loved **not only** reading **but also** cooking. 她不僅喜歡閱讀，還喜歡下廚。

Beauty and the Beast　**59**

[pp. 60–61]

The two sisters / did not stop complaining. But Beauty did not complain / at all. Instead, / she tried to be happy / and to make everyone else happy.

"I will clean the house, / Father," she said. "This house is small, / but we can be happy here."

Beauty worked hard / every day. She woke up / early in the morning / and cleaned the house. She cooked / breakfast, lunch, and dinner / for her family. But her sisters / never did any work. They sat around / and complained / all the time.

One day, / Beauty's father / received a letter. He read the letter / and instantly cheered up.

"Children, / I just heard some good news," he said. "One of my ships / did not sink. It is bringing back / lots of gold and silver / for us. We are rich again. I must go to the port now."

Beauty's sisters / jumped for joy. "We are rich! We are rich!" they cried.

"Oh, Father, / you must buy us / some new dresses," said the two older sisters.

"Yes, my dears, / I will," said their father.

"And you, Beauty, / what would you like me / to get you?" asked her father.

Beauty did not want anything. She was happy / just because she could see her father happy. "Please bring me a rose, / Father," said Beauty. "There are no roses / in our garden."

Beauty's father / hurried to the port. When he arrived there, / he heard some bad news.

"The gold and silver / are gone," his friend told him. "Pirates stole it. There is your ship. It has many holes in it, / so you must fix the holes / before the ship can sail again."

Beauty's father / fell to the ground.

"Without any gold or silver, / I cannot afford / to fix my ship," said Beauty's father sadly. "I will leave the ship there / for now / and return to the countryside."

- **complain** 抱怨　　• **wake up** 醒來　　• **sit around** 什麼也不做，只是坐著
- **receive** 收到　　• **instantly** 很快地　　• **cheer up** 開心起來　　• **bring back** 帶回來
- **port** 港口　　• **jump for joy** 高興地跳了起來　　• **garden** 花園　　• **hurry** 趕去
- **be gone** 消失　　• **pirate** 海盜　　• **steal** 偷　　• **fix** 修理　　• **fall to the ground** 跌坐在地
- **afford to** 付得起；買得起

CLOSE UP

1　**she tried to be happy and to make everyone else happy** 她試著讓自己、讓別人快樂
〈try to . . .〉意「試著要去……」，這裡的 to be 和 to make 是 tried 的受詞。

2　**I cannot afford to fix my ship.** 我付不起修船的錢。
〈cannot afford to . . .〉指「沒有足夠的時間或金錢去做……」。

兩個姊姊不停地抱怨 do not stop complaining，但美麗一點也沒有抱怨 do not complain，她反而試著讓自己、讓別人快樂 make everyone else happy。

「我會打掃房子 clean the house，爸爸，」她說，「雖然這房子很小 be small，但我們在這裡會很快樂的 be happy here。」

美麗每天 every day 辛勤地工作 work hard，一大早就起床 wake up early in the morning，打掃家裡，為家人做早餐、午餐和晚餐 cook breakfast, lunch, and dinner，但兩個姊姊什麼也不做 never do any work，始終 all the time 坐著 sit around 抱怨。

有一天，美麗的爸爸 Beauty's father 收到一封信 receive a letter，讀完信 read the letter 以後，立刻開心起來 cheer up。

「孩子們，我剛剛收到一些好消息 hear some good news，」他說，「我的其中一艘船 one of my ships 沒有沉 do not sink，帶回 bring back 了很多金銀 lots of gold and silver，我們又可以很有錢 be rich again 了，我現在得去港口 go to the port。」

美麗的姊姊高興地跳了起來 jump for joy。「我們有錢了！我們有錢了！」她們大聲說。

「喔！爸爸，你一定要為我們買一些漂亮的新衣服 buy us some new dresses。」兩個姊姊說。

「好的，我親愛的，我會的。」爸爸說。

「妳呢？美麗，妳想要我帶什麼給妳？」爸爸問。

美麗什麼也不想要 do not want anything，她因看到父親開心 see her father happy，而感到開心。「請為我帶一朵玫瑰 bring me a rose，爸爸，」美麗說，「我們的花園 our garden 裡沒有玫瑰 no roses。」

美麗的父親趕到港口 hurry to the port，當他到那裡 arrive there，他聽到一些壞消息 hear some bad news。

「金銀 the gold and silver 都不見 be gone 了，」他的朋友告訴他：「被海盜 pirates 偷走 steal it 了，那是你的船，船裡都是破洞 have many holes in it，你得在下次出航 sail again 前把洞補好 fix the holes。」

美麗的父親跌坐在地上 fall to the ground。

「沒有金銀 without any gold or silver，我付不起 cannot afford to fix 修船的費用。」美麗的父親哀傷地說：「我現在 for now 只能把船留在那兒 leave the ship there，回鄉下去 return to the countryside。」

would like . . . to . . . ：想要……去做…… ⇨ would like 一般都用縮寫 'd like。

- What **would** you **like** me **to** get you? 你想要我帶什麼回來給你？

- I **would like** you **to** buy me some new dresses. 我想要你買一些新衣服給我。
  (= I'**d like** you **to** . . .)

Then he remembered his daughters. He looked in his pockets / and found only a few coins. "I don't have enough money / to buy any dresses." Sadly, / he started to walk back home.

Suddenly, / the weather became terribly cold. It began to snow, / and the wind blew heavily. Soon, / he was lost / in a forest.

"This is very strange," he said to himself. "I have never seen this forest / before. I must be lost."

He heard wolves / howling loudly. He began to feel very afraid. "I must find some shelter. There is no way / I will get home tonight," he said.

He looked around / and saw a light / at some distance. "What is that? Is there a house / there?"

Beauty's father / followed the light. After a few minutes, / he found a castle.

"I wonder / who lives here," he said. He went to the door of the castle.

"Hello?" he called. But there was no answer. The door was open, / so he walked inside. He saw no one. It was cold, / and he was tired. He entered a large hall. It was a dining room. A huge fire was burning / in the fireplace. And the dining table / was full of food. There was a single plate / on the table / with a knife and fork beside it.

"This must be / someone's dinner," he thought. He waited / for the person to arrive, / but no one came. Finally, / after he had waited / for a couple of hours, / he sat down at the table / and ate the food. Because he was starving, / he ate all of the food. Then, / he found a bedroom / and fell asleep immediately.

• **remember** 想起；記起　• **coin** 錢幣　• **terribly** 非常地　• **heavily** 猛烈地
• **be lost** 迷路　• **wolf** 狼　• **howl** 嚎叫　• **shelter** 躲避處
• **look around** 環視；四處看　• **at some distance** 不遠處　• **wonder** 納悶；好奇
• **dining room** 飯廳　• **burn** 燃燒　• **fireplace** 壁爐　• **dining table** 餐桌
• **be full of** 充滿　• **plate** 盤子　• **dinner** 晚餐　• **a couple of** 一些
• **starving** 飢餓的　• **fall asleep** 睡著　• **immediately** 馬上；立刻

CLOSE UP

1 **found only a few coins** 只找到幾枚硬幣
   a few 意「一些、幾個」，後接複數名詞；only a few 意「只有幾個」、「只有一些」。

2 **I must be lost.** 我一定是迷路了。/ **I must find some shelter.** 我得找到一個躲避處。/
   This must be someone's dinner. 這一定是某人的晚餐。
   must 意「（因義務、需要）必須⋯⋯」或「（推測）必定是⋯⋯」，依句意選出最合適的意思來使用。

3 **There is no way (that) I will get home tonight.** 我今晚不可能到得了家。
   〈there is no way (that) . . .〉意「絕對不可能」。

4 **waited for the person to arrive** 等候那人的到來
   〈wait for . . . to . . .〉意「等⋯⋯去做⋯⋯」。

他想起他的女兒們 remember his daughters，他看看口袋 look in his pockets，只有幾枚錢幣 only a few coins。「我不夠錢買衣服。」他傷心地 sadly 走回家 walk back home。

突然間，天氣 the weather 變得非常冷 become terribly cold，開始下雪 snow，風 the wind 狂吹 blow heavily。不久，他在森林裡 in a forest 迷路 be lost 了。

「真奇怪 be very strange。」他告訴自己，「我以前沒看過這座森林 never see this forest before，我一定是迷路了。」

他聽到狼 wolves 嚎叫得很大聲 howl loudly，開始覺得很害怕 feel very afraid。「我一定要找一個躲避處 find some shelter，今晚不可能 no way 到得了家 get home。」他說。

他環顧四周 look around，看到 see 不遠處 at some distance 有燈光 a light。「那是什麼？那是一棟房子 a house 嗎？」

美麗的父親跟著光走 follow the light，幾分鐘後 after a few minutes，他發現一座城堡 find a castle。

「我很好奇 I wonder 誰住在這裡。」他說。他往城堡的門 the door of the castle 走去。

「哈囉 hello？」他大聲說，但沒有人回應 no answer。門是開著的，於是他走進去 walk inside，沒有看到任何人 see no one。天氣很冷，他很累。他走進大廳 enter a large hall，是一間飯廳 a dining room。壁爐裡 in the fireplace 燃著 burn 熊熊火焰 a huge fire。飯桌 the dining table 上滿桌的食物 be full of food，桌上 on the table 卻只有一個盤子 a single plate，旁邊 beside 放了刀叉 a knife and fork。

「這一定是某人的晚餐 someone's dinner」他想。他等候那個人出現 wait for the person to arrive，但沒有人 no one 來 come，最後 finally，他等了幾個小時，他坐下來 sit down 吃那些食物 eat the food，因為他實在是太餓了 be starving，他吃完所有的食物 eat all of the food，然後他找到一間臥室 find a bedroom，就立刻睡著 fall asleep 了。

have/has + p.p.（現在完成式：表經驗）⇨ 可以用來表到目前為止的經驗

- I **have** never **seen** this forest before. 我從未見過這座森林。

- We can't work. We **have** never **worked** in our lives.
我們不能工作，我們這輩子從來沒有工作過。

- You look familiar. I'm sure we **have met** before. 你看起來很面熟，我確定我們以前見過面。

In the morning, / Beauty's father woke up. He looked around the room. He saw some breakfast / on the table. But he did not see anybody. He sat down at the table / and enjoyed breakfast. While he ate, / he looked outside. He saw a beautiful garden / full of flowers.

"That's strange," he thought. "Last night, / there was a huge snowstorm, / but the sun is shining now, / and the flowers are blooming."

Just then, / he remembered the promise / that he had made to Beauty.

"A rose!" he said aloud. "I promised Beauty / I would bring her a rose." He went out to the garden / and found a rose bush. It was full of / beautiful red roses. He picked one. But as soon as he picked the rose, / he heard a loud roar. And he saw a frightful, angry beast / coming toward him.

"You dirty thief!" cried the Beast.

"I saved your life / and gave you food and a bed. But, in return, / you are stealing my flowers. Now you're going to / pay for it. I'm going to / kill you."

Beauty's father fell to the ground / and cried out, "Forgive me. I only wanted a single rose / for my daughter. I promised to bring a rose / to my youngest daughter, Beauty. Please do not kill me."

The Beast looked down at him angrily / and said, "All right. You may go home. But you have to / send me your daughter. She must come here / and live in this castle / with me. If not, / then you must return here / and die. Go back to your bedroom. There is a box of gold / there. Take it and go."

- **huge** 巨大的　• **snowstorm** 暴風雪　• **shine** 發光　• **bloom**（花朵）綻放
- **promise** 答應　• **rose bush** 玫瑰花叢　• **pick** 摘（花）
- **as soon as** 一……就……　• **roar** 吼叫　• **frightful** 可怕的　• **dirty** 髒的；卑鄙的
- **thief** 小偷　• **save one's life** 救某人的命　• **in return** 作為回報　• **steal** 偷
- **pay for** 為……付出代價　• **forgive** 原諒　• **angrily** 生氣地

1 **a beautiful garden full of flowers** 一座種滿鮮花的美麗花園
It was full of beautiful red roses. 它充滿了美麗的紅玫瑰。
〈full of . . .〉意「充滿了……」。

2 **as soon as he picked the rose** 他一摘玫瑰
〈as soon as＋主詞＋動詞〉意「一當……的時候」。

3 **Now you're going to pay for it.** 現在你將為此付出代價。/
I'm going to kill you. 我要把你殺掉。
〈be going to . . .〉意「將要……」，看到現在的狀況而決定未來一定要去做什麼事，或通常是說出已經決定或計畫好要去做的事。

到了早上 in the morning，美麗的父親醒來 wake up，他環視房間 look around the room，看到 see 桌上 on the table 有一些早餐 some breakfast，但他沒有看到任何人 do not see anybody，他坐在桌子前，享用早餐 enjoy breakfast，吃早餐的時候，他看見外面 look outside，有一座美麗的花園 a beautiful garden 種滿了花 full of flowers。

「真奇怪，」他想，「昨晚 last night 有一場大暴風雪 a huge snowstorm，但是現在太陽 the sun 光芒四射 shine，花朵 the flowers 綻放 bloom。」

就在此時 just then，他想起 remember 他對美麗的承諾 the promise。

「一朵玫瑰 a rose！」他大聲說：「我答應美麗要帶一朵玫瑰給她 bring her a rose。」他走到花園 go out to the garden，找到一片玫瑰花叢 find a rose bush，上面開滿美麗的紅玫瑰，他摘了一朵 pick one。可是他一摘玫瑰，就聽見一聲狂吼 hear a loud roar，他看到一頭可怕、生氣的野獸 a frightful, angry beast 走向他 come toward him。

「你這卑鄙的小偷 you dirty thief！」野獸大聲說。

「我救了你的性命 save your life，給你食物和床 give you food and a bed，但你卻偷我的花 steal my flowers，作為回報 in return。現在你將為此付出代價 pay for it，我要殺了你 kill you。」

美麗的父親跌坐在地 fall to the ground，大叫：「原諒我 forgive me，我只想摘一朵玫瑰花 want a single rose 給我女兒。我答應帶一朵玫瑰花給我最小的女兒 my youngest daughter 美麗，請你不要殺我 do not kill me。」

野獸憤怒地 angrily 低頭看著他 look down at him，說：「好吧 all right，你可以回家 go home，但你得把你女兒送來 send me your daughter，她必須來 come 跟我 with me 住在城堡裡 live in this castle。不然的話 if not，你就必須回到這裡 return here，葬身於此 die。回你的房間去 go back to your bedroom，那裡有一箱金子 a box of gold，拿去 take it，離開吧！」

promise 的用法

- I **promised** Beauty **(that)** I would bring her a rose. 我答應美麗要帶一朵玫瑰給她。
- I **promised to** bring a rose to my youngest daughter, Beauty.
  我答應要帶一朵玫瑰給我最小的女兒美麗。

- -

- I **promised** my daughter Beauty **to** bring her a rose. 我答應我女兒美麗要帶一朵玫瑰給她。

Beauty's father / hurried away from the castle / as fast as he could. When he got home, / he told his children / what had happened.

"I must return to the castle," he said. "I just wanted to say goodbye / to all of you."

Beauty's sisters / suddenly became angry at her.

"Beauty, / what have you done?" they shouted. "It's your fault. You wanted the rose, / and now Father must die. You stupid girl!"

"Father, / I'll go to the Beast. I'm not afraid. I will go / and live with the Beast," Beauty said quietly.

"No, Beauty, no."

"There is no choice," she said. "The Beast will kill you and our family / if I do not go."

Beauty's father was very sad. He went to his bedroom. Beauty followed him there.

"What is the Beast like, / Father? Is he very ugly?" she asked.

"Yes, the Beast is ugly, / but he can also be kind. Look. He gave me / this box of gold. But do not tell your sisters / about it. They will only want / to spend it on new dresses."

"Father, / please give the money / to them," Beauty told her father. "While you were away, / two men came here. My sisters are going to marry them, / so they will have to / buy many things. They need that money."

The next morning, / Beauty said goodbye to her family / and left for the castle. She was very sad, / but she did not cry. Late in the evening, / she finally arrived at the Beast's castle. The door was open, / so she walked up to it. She saw nobody. "Hello?" she yelled, / but no one answered.

"What a weird place!" thought Beauty. But she was very brave. She walked around the castle / and found the dining room. There was a table / with lots of food on it. All her favorite foods / were on the table. There were / two plates, two glasses, two forks, and two knives. Beauty sat down / and ate the food.

- **say goodbye** 道別　• **angry at** 對……生氣　• **fault** 錯誤　• **stupid** 愚笨的
- **afraid** 害怕的　• **quietly** 安靜地；輕聲地　• **ugly** 醜陋的　• **spend** 花錢
- **be away** 不在的　• **cry** 哭　• **arrive at** 到達某地　• **walk up to** 走上前去　• **yell** 大叫
- **weird** 奇怪的　• **brave** 勇敢的　• **favorite** 最愛的　• **sit down** 坐下

CLOSE UP

1 **as fast as he could** 盡他所能地快
〈as . . . as one can/could〉意「盡某人所能／盡可能的……」，也可以換成〈as . . . as possible〉來使用。

2 **What is the Beast like?** 野獸是什麼樣的人？
〈What is . . . like?〉指「……是怎樣的人？」。

3 **spend it on new dresses** 把錢花在新衣服上
spend指「花（錢）」、「花（時間）」。〈spend＋錢＋on . . .〉指「在……上面花多少錢」。

美麗的父親盡他所能地快 as fast as he can，急忙離開城堡 hurry away from the castle。到家 get home 以後，他告訴女兒們發生了什麼事 what happens。

「我一定要回到那個城堡 return to the castle，」他說，「我只想跟妳們每一個 to all of you 道別 say goodbye。」

美麗的姊姊突然對美麗發火 become angry at her。

「美麗，看妳做了什麼好事？」她們大叫：「都是妳的錯 your fault，妳想要玫瑰 want the rose。現在父親得死 must die 了，妳這個笨女孩 you stupid girl！」

「父親，我會去找野獸 go to the Beast，我不怕，我會去跟他一起住 live with the Beast。」美麗輕聲說。

「不，美麗，不。」

「沒有別的選擇 no choice 了。」她說，「如果我不去，野獸會殺了你和我們家的人 kill you and our family。」

美麗的父親很傷心 be very sad，他回到房間 go to his bedroom，美麗跟著他進去 follow him。

「野獸是什麼樣的人，父親？他很醜 be ugly 嗎？」她問。

「是的，野獸很醜，但他也可以很善良 can also be kind。你看 look，他給我這箱黃金 this box of gold，但是不要告訴 do not tell 妳姊姊，她們只想把錢花在新衣服上面 spend it on new dresses。」

「父親，請把錢給她們。」美麗跟父親說。「你不在的時候 be away，有兩個人 two men 來家裡 come here，姊姊要跟他們結婚 marry them，所以她們得買很多東西 buy many things，她們需要那筆錢 need that money。」

隔天一早 the next morning，美麗跟家人道別 say goodbye，前往城堡 leave for the castle，她很傷心，但沒有哭，深夜 late in the evening，她終於到了野獸的城堡 arrive at the Beast's castle，大門 the door 開著 be open，所以她走上前去 walk up to it，沒看到人 see nobody。「哈囉 hello？」她大叫。但沒有人 no one 回應 answer。

「多麼詭異的地方 a weird place！」美麗想。但她很勇敢 be very brave，在城堡裡四處走 walk around the castle，找到飯廳 find the dining room。桌上擺滿了食物 a table with lots of food on it，桌上都是她愛吃的食物 her favorite foods，有兩個盤子 two plates、兩個杯子 two glasses、兩隻叉子 two forks 和兩隻刀子 two knives。美麗坐下來 sit down 享用食物 eat the food。

---

had + p.p.（過去完成式：比過去更早）

⇨ 提到「比過去某一個時間點更早發生的事」時使用。

- When he got home, he told his children what **had happened**.
  他回家以後，告訴孩子們發生什麼事。（「回家跟孩子說」早於「發生了什麼事」）

- He remembered the promise that he **had made** to Beauty.
  他想起他先前答應過美麗的事。（「回想起約定」早於「和美麗訂下約定」）

After supper, / Beauty started / to look around the castle. It was a beautiful castle / with many fine rooms. When Beauty got to one room, / she looked at the door. There was a sign / on the door. It read "Beauty's Room."

"Is this my room? Well, if he gives me a special room, / maybe he will not kill me," she thought.

Beauty opened the door / and went inside. It was the most beautiful room / she had ever seen. It was full of / flowers, books, and beautiful clothes. She picked up one book / and opened it. Inside, / there was a note. It read:

Welcome, Beauty.
Do not be afraid.
You will be safe and happy / here.
I will do anything / you want.
You may have all of this.

"He must be very kind," Beauty thought. Beauty was very tired. She went to bed / and fell asleep instantly.

Beauty spent the next day / alone. In the evening, / Beauty put on the most beautiful dress / and went to the dining room. All of her favorite foods / were on the table. Beauty sat down. Suddenly, / she heard a gentle growl, / and the Beast came in. He was wearing fine clothes, / but he had as much hair as a lion.

Beauty said, "Thank you for my present, / sir."

"Call me Beast," said the Beast.

"Tell me, / Beauty. Am I very ugly? Are you afraid of me?"

"Yes, Beast, / you are ugly," said Beauty slowly. "But you seem to be very gentle. I'm not afraid of you / because you're nice to me."

"Thank you for saying that," said the Beast.

That evening, / Beauty and the Beast / sat down and ate together. They talked about many topics. By the end of the dinner, / Beauty thought / that the Beast was not so frightening.

• **supper** 晚餐　• **look around** 四處看　• **fine** 華貴精美的　• **sign** 標示　• **read** 上面寫著
• **kill** 殺　• **pick up** 拿起　• **safe** 安全的　• **alone** 獨自　• **put on** 穿上衣服
• **gentle** 溫柔的　• **growl** 咆哮　• **topic** 話題　• **frightening** 可怕的

CLOSE UP

1　**It read "Beauty's Room."** 上面寫著「美麗的房間」。
　　read 的主詞如果是信、告示牌、標示板等，是指「上面寫著……」。

2　**Are you afraid of me?** 你怕我嗎？/ **I'm not afraid of you** 我不怕你。
　　〈be afraid of . . .〉意「害怕……」、「擔心／煩惱……」。

3　**you seem to be very gentle** 你看起來很溫柔
　　〈seem to . . .〉意「看起來、似乎是……」。

晚餐後after supper，美麗開始環視城堡look around the castle。這是座美麗的城堡a beautiful castle，而且有很多很棒的房間with many fine rooms，當美麗走到一間房間get to one room外面，她看著門look at the door。門上on the door有一個標示a sign，上面寫著「美麗的房間Beauty's Room」。

「這是我的房間my room嗎？好吧，如果他給我一間特別的房間a special room，也許maybe他不會殺我。」她想。

美麗開了門open the door，走進房間go inside，這真是她所見過最漂亮的房間the most beautiful room了，充滿了鮮花、書本和漂亮的衣服flowers, books, and beautiful clothes。她拿起一本書pick up one book，打開看，裡面inside有一張小紙條a note，寫著：

> 美麗，歡迎妳welcome。
> 不要害怕do not be afraid。
> 妳在這裡會很安全、很快樂be safe and happy。
> 妳想要什麼anything you want，我都會為妳做到。
> 妳可以擁有這裡所有的一切have all of this。

「他一定非常善良。」美麗想，她很累be very tired，於是上床go to bed 後，就立刻睡著fall asleep了。

隔天美麗獨自一人spend the next day alone。到了傍晚in the evening美麗穿上最美麗的衣服put on the most beautiful dress走到飯廳go to the dining room，桌上全都是她最愛的食物，美麗坐下來，突然間，她聽見一聲很溫柔的吼叫聲hear a gentle growl，野獸走了進來come in，他穿著很好的衣服wear fine clothes，但有像獅子一樣多的毛have as much hair as a lion。

美麗說：「謝謝您的禮物thank you for my present，先生sir。」

「叫我野獸call me Beast」，野獸說。

「告訴我tell me，美麗，我是不是真的很醜陋？妳怕不怕我？」

「是的，野獸，你很醜陋，」美麗緩慢地說，「但是你似乎很溫柔seem to be gentle，我不怕你，因為你對我很好be nice to me。」「謝謝妳這麼說thank you for saying that。」

那天晚上，美麗和野獸Beauty and the Beast坐下來共進晚餐sat down and ate together，他們聊了很多話題talk about many topics。晚餐快結束時by the end of the dinner，美麗覺得野獸也沒這麼可怕be not so frightening。

GRAMMAR POINT

as much/many . . . as . . . ：像……一樣多的……

⇨ 不可數名詞前用much，可數名詞前用many。

- He had **as much** hair **as** a lion. 他的毛像獅子一樣多。

- The garden had **as many** flowers **as** I had expected. 花園裡的花和我期待的一樣多。

The next day, / Beauty went downstairs. There, / she saw the Beast / waiting for her.

"There is a mirror / in your bedroom," the Beast said. "It is a magic mirror. When you want to see your father, / look into that mirror."

"That is very generous / of you. Thank you," replied Beauty.

"Beauty, / I know / that I am ugly," said the Beast. "I must be stupid / as well / because I cannot think of / anything smart / to say to you."

Beauty felt bad. "I know many people / who look beautiful / but have ugly hearts," she said. "I like you better / than those people, / Beast."

"Then will you marry me?" asked the Beast.

"Marry you? Oh, no. I'm sorry, / but I cannot do that," she said.

Beauty lived in the castle / with the Beast, / and they were very happy. Every night / at nine o'clock, / Beauty and the Beast / had dinner together / and chatted. At the end of every dinner, / the Beast always proposed, "Will you marry me?" And Beauty always answered, "I like you, / but I cannot marry you."

For three months, / Beauty lived at the castle. She was happy there. She read books / and walked through the garden / every day. But, one day, / she looked into the magic mirror. She saw her father. He was sick in bed / and was all by himself.

"I must go / and see my father. I must talk to the Beast / at dinner," Beauty thought.

At nine o'clock, / Beauty and the Beast / had dinner together. The Beast said, "If you will not marry me, / then will you be my friend? I want you / to stay with me / forever."

"Of course I will," Beauty answered. "You are kind to me. I will stay here with you, / but there is a problem. I looked into the magic mirror / and saw my father. He is sick in bed / and all by himself. Will you please / let me go to visit him?"

• **go downstairs** 下樓　　• **mirror** 鏡子　　• **look into** 朝……裡面看　　• **generous** 慷慨的
• **feel bad** 覺得很糟或很難過　　• **chat** 聊天　　• **propose** 求婚　　• **sick** 生病的
• **sick in bed** 臥病在床　　• **all by oneself** 獨自一人　　• **stay** 留　　• **forever** 永遠

1　**I know many people who look beautiful but have ugly hearts.**
　　我認識許多外表美麗但內心醜陋的人。
　　〈who . . . hearts〉的部分，是修飾 many people 的關係子句。

2　**all by himself** 他自己一個人
　　all by oneself 意「獨自一人」。
　　例 all by myself（我獨自一人）/ all by herself（她獨自一人）

隔天，美麗下樓 go downstairs，她看到野獸正在等她 wait for her。

「在妳的房間 in your bedroom 有一面鏡子 a mirror。」野獸説：「那是一面魔鏡 a magic mirror。當妳想見妳父親 see your father，就看一看鏡子 look into that mirror。」

「你真是太慷慨 be generous 了，謝謝。」美麗回答。

「美麗，我知道我很醜陋。」野獸説，「我一定也很笨 be stupid 因為我想不到 cannot think of 什麼聰明的話 anything smart 可以跟妳説。」

美麗覺得很難過 feel bad。「我認識很多外表漂亮 look beautiful 的人內心很醜陋 have ugly hearts，」她説，「比起他們，我更喜歡你 like you better，野獸。」

「那麼妳願意嫁給我 marry me 嗎？」野獸問。

「嫁給你？喔，不 oh, no，對不起，但我不能這麼做 cannot do that」她説。

美麗跟野獸 with the Beast 住在城堡裡 live in the castle，他們過得很快樂。每天晚上 every night 九點 at nine o'clock 美麗和野獸共進晚餐 have dinner together，聊天 chat。每次晚餐結束時 at the end of every dinner，野獸總是向她求婚 always propose。「妳願意嫁給我嗎？」美麗總是回答 always answer：「我喜歡你 like you，但我不能嫁給你 cannot marry you。」

美麗住在城堡裡 live at the castle 已經三個月 for three months 了，她很快樂，每天 every day 看書 read books，在花園裡散步 walk through the garden，但是有一天，她看魔鏡 look into the magic mirror，看到父親 see her father 獨自一人 all by himself 臥病在床 be sick in bed。

「我一定要去探望我父親 go and see my father，我得在晚餐時 at dinner 和野獸説 talk to the Beast 這件事。」美麗想。

九點鐘，美麗和野獸一起吃晚餐，野獸説「如果妳不願意嫁給我，可以當我的朋友 be my friend 嗎？我希望妳永遠 forever 留在我身邊 stay with me。」

「當然 of course，我願意。」美麗回答，「你對我這麼好，我願意留在這裡陪你 stay here with you，但有一個問題 a problem，我看魔鏡的時候，看到我父親，他一個人臥病在床，請你讓我去看看他 go to visit him 好嗎？」

GRAMMAR POINT

want ＋ 受詞 ＋ to 不定詞：希望……去做……

let ＋ 受詞 ＋ 原形動詞：允許……去做……

➡ want 後接 to 不定詞，let 後接原形動詞，這點要注意。

• I **want** you **to stay** with me forever. 我希望你永遠留在我身邊。

• Will you please **let** me **go** to visit him? 請你讓我去看看他，好嗎？

"If you leave, / you will not come back," the Beast said.

"I promise to come back," said Beauty. "But let me go there / for one week."

The Beast thought for a moment / and then said, "Okay. You may go."

He gave Beauty a ring / and said, "Take this. Put on this ring / and go to bed. Tomorrow, / you will wake up / in your father's home. After seven days, / take the ring off / and put the ring by your bed. You'll wake up / in this castle."

"Goodbye, Beauty. Don't forget your promise. Come back / in seven days."

Beauty thanked the Beast. She put the ring on / and went to sleep. In the morning, / when she woke up, / she was in her father's home. She got up / and ran to her father.

"Father, / I'm home," she said.

"Oh, Beauty," he cried, "you have returned. I thought / the Beast ate you. I'm so ill, / and I am all alone. Your sisters are married, / and they never visit me."

"Father, / I am only here / for one week, / but I will take good care of you. You will feel better soon," Beauty responded.

Beauty's father looked at her. "You look beautiful," he said. "Your dress looks very nice. Is the Beast good to you?"

"Yes, he is very kind to me. I like him very much. Perhaps I almost love him," Beauty said.

Her older sisters heard / that Beauty was back. They came to visit her / with their husbands. Both sisters were unhappy. One had a very handsome husband, / but he was unkind. The other had a very smart husband, / but he talked too much. When they saw Beauty / in her beautiful dress, / they both became angry.

"Why is she always happy?" said one.

"I can't stand this. Let's keep Beauty here / longer than a week. Then, / the Beast will become angry with her. Maybe the Beast will eat her / then." The other sister agreed.

- **for a moment** 過了一會兒　•**ring** 戒指　•**put on** 穿上；戴上　•**ill** 生病的
- **take care of** 照顧　•**feel better** 感覺好些　•**respond** 回答　•**be good to** 對某人好
- **perhaps** 也許　•**almost** 幾乎　•**unhappy** 不開心　•**handsome** 英俊的
- **unkind** 不善良　•**can't stand** 受不了　•**keep** 留　•**agree** 同意

CLOSE UP

1 **put on this ring** 戴上戒指 / **take the ring off** 脫掉戒指
穿衣服或將其他裝飾用品戴在身上要用 put on，脫掉這些就要用 take off。

2 **Beauty in her beautiful dress** 美麗穿著她漂亮的衣服
in 之後出現衣物等名詞，是指「穿著／帶著／戴著……」。

「如果妳離開 leave，妳就不會回來了 will not come back。」野獸說。

「我向你保證，我會回來 promise to come back，」美麗說，「但給我一個星期 for one week 讓我回家 let me go there。」

野獸想了一會兒 think for a moment，然後說：「好吧 okay，妳可以去 you may go。」

他給美麗一個戒指 give Beauty a ring，說：「拿著這個 take this，戴著這個戒指 put on this ring，上床睡覺 go to bed，明天 tomorrow 妳會在妳父親的家中 in your father's home 醒來 wake up，七天後 after seven days 摘下戒指 take the ring off，把它放在床邊 by your bed，妳就會在城堡裡醒來 wake up in this castle。」

「再見 goodbye，美麗，不要忘了妳的諾言 don't forget your promise，七天內 in seven days 回來 come back。」

美麗向野獸道謝 thank the Beast，戴上戒指 put the ring on，去睡覺 go to sleep，隔天早上 in the morning，她在父親家中 in her father's home 醒來，她起床 get up 跑去找父親 run to her father。

「父親，我回來了 I'm home。」她說。

「喔！美麗，」他大叫，「妳回來了 return，我以為野獸把妳吃掉了，我病得很重，獨自在家，妳姊姊 your sisters 結婚了，她們從來沒回來看我 never visit me。」

「父親，我只能回來一個星期，但是我會好好照顧你的 take good care of you，你很快就會好起來的 feel better soon。」美麗回答。

美麗的父親看著她 look at her。「妳看起來很美 look beautiful，」他說，「妳的衣服看起來很華貴 look very nice，野獸對妳好嗎？」

「是的，他對我非常好 be very kind，我很喜歡他 like him very much，或許我快要愛上他了 almost love him。」美麗說。

她的姊姊聽到美麗回來了，便帶著丈夫 with their husbands 來探望她 come to visit her，兩個姊姊很不高興 be unhappy，一個 one 嫁給一個英俊的丈夫 a handsome husband，但是他心地不好 be unkind，另一個 the other 嫁給一個聰明的丈夫 a smart husband，但是他話太多了 talk too much。當她們看到美麗穿著華麗的衣服，她們都很生氣 become angry。

「她為什麼總是這麼快樂？」一個姊姊說。

「我受不了這種事 can't stand this。我們讓美麗留在這裡 keep Beauty here 超過一個星期 longer than a week，然後野獸會很生她的氣 become angry with her，就會把她吃掉 eat her。」另一個姊姊也同意這麼做。

one / the other ⇨ 兩個中的一個用 one，剩下的那一個用 the other。

- **One** had a very handsome husband. **The other** had a very smart husband.
  一個的丈夫很英俊，另一個的丈夫很聰明。

- There are two roses. **One** is red, and **the other** is pink.
  有兩朵玫瑰花，一朵是紅色的，另一朵是粉紅色的。

So they said to Beauty, "Oh, Beauty, / we are so happy / to see you. Please stay here / for a few more days."

Beauty disliked / seeing them sad. So a week passed, / but Beauty did not go back to the castle.

Then, one night, / Beauty had a dream. In her dream, / she saw the Beast. The Beast was lying / on the grass. He was very sick and sad. He seemed to be dying. Beauty heard the Beast saying, "Oh, Beauty! Beauty, / why haven't you come back yet? I am dying."

Beauty woke up / and jumped out of bed. It was the middle of the night.

"I'm coming back, / Beast!" she said. She removed the ring quickly / and put it beside her bed. Then, / she went back to sleep.

Beauty woke up / in the castle. She jumped up / and went looking for the Beast. She tried every room / in the castle, / but she could not find the Beast / anywhere.

Then, / she remembered her dream. She ran into the garden / and saw the Beast.

"Wake up, / Beast. Wake up," she cried. "I'm back. I'm so sorry."

The beast slowly lifted his head. "I waited for you, / Beauty. But you didn't come. Now it is too late. I'm going to die soon."

"No, Beast, / you cannot die. I need you," said Beauty.

"I love you, / Beast. Please don't die. I want to marry you." Beauty kissed his ugly face.

- **dislike** 不喜歡　• **pass** 過去　• **have a dream** 做了一個夢　• **lie** 躺下
- **seem to** 看起來好像　• **die** 死了　• **jump out of bed** 跳下床
- **the middle of the night** 午夜　• **remove** 拿下　• **go looking for** 去找
- **be back** 回來　• **lift** 抬起　• **wait for** 等待

CLOSE UP

1　**I am dying.** 我快要死了。/ **I'm coming back, Beast!** 我快回來了，野獸！
現在進行式（be V-ing）依句意可以用來表示正在進行的事（正在做……），也可以用來表示未來即將發生的事（將會……）。

2　**She tried every room.** 她每間房間都找過了。
〈try＋名詞〉意「試著對……做什麼看看」，隨著後面出現不同的名詞，會有不同的意思。
例 Try this soup.（嚐嚐這湯。）/ Try these shoes.（試穿這鞋。）

於是她們告訴美麗：「喔！美麗，看到妳真開心，請多留幾天 stay here for a few more days。」

　　美麗不喜歡 dislike 看到她們傷心 see them sad，所以一星期 a week 過了 pass，美麗還沒回城堡 do not go back to the castle。

　　有一天晚上 one night，美麗做了一個夢 have a dream，在她的夢裡 in her dream 她看到野獸 see the Beast，他躺在草地上 lie on the grass，病得很重，而且很傷心 be sick and sad，看起來快要死了 seem to be dying。美麗聽到野獸說：「喔！美麗！美麗，為什麼妳還不回來？我快死了！」

　　美麗醒來，跳下床 jump out of bed，那時是午夜 the middle of the night。

　　「我快回來了，野獸！」她說。她摘下戒指 remove the ring，放在床邊 put it beside her bed，然後她回去睡覺 go back to sleep。

　　美麗在城堡裡醒來 wake up in the castle，跳起來 jump up，去找野獸 go looking for the Beast，她每間房間都找遍了 try every room，但四處 anywhere 找不著野獸 cannot find the Beast。

　　然後，她想起她的夢 remember her dream，跑到花園去 run into the garden 看到了野獸。

　　「醒醒 wake up，野獸，醒醒，」她大叫，「我回來了 I'm back，我很抱歉。」

　　野獸慢慢地 slowly 抬起他的頭 lift his head。「我等妳很久了 wait for you，美麗，但妳沒回來，現在一切都太遲了 it is too late，我即將死去 die soon。」

　　「不，野獸，你不能死 cannot die，我需要你 need you。」美麗說。

　　「我愛你 love you，野獸，請不要死，我願意嫁給你 want to marry you。」美麗親了他醜陋的臉 kiss his ugly face。

GRAMMAR POINT

dislike V-ing：不喜歡做……　　**go V-ing**：要去做……

- Beauty **disliked** see**ing** them sad. 美麗不喜歡看到她們傷心。
- She jumped up and **went** look**ing** for the Beast. 她跳起來，去找野獸。

Beauty and the Beast　**75**

At that moment, / something magical / happened. The sky was filled with bright light. In a moment, / Beauty found herself / inside the castle. The room was filled with flowers. But the Beast was not there. Next to Beauty / was a very handsome young man. He was dressed / like a prince.

"What's going on here? Where is Beast?" Beauty asked.

"I am here, / Beauty," said the prince, "I am the Beast. Well, I was the Beast."

"A long time ago," said the prince, "I was selfish and unkind. A fairy touched me / with her magic wand / and put a spell on me. She turned me / into a beast. She cursed me / to be a beast forever / until someone loved me. You broke the spell, / Beauty. I became a man again / because you love me."

Then, / the fairy suddenly appeared / and said, "Yes, Beauty, / you understand / that kindness is more important / than looks. Your sisters don't understand that. So now they are unhappy / with their husbands. But you will be happy / with your prince. You are the most beautiful couple / in the world. I will marry you / and give you happiness / for the rest of your lives. And I will grant you / many beautiful children, / too."

Beauty and the prince / married soon. They had a wonderful wedding. Beauty invited her father / to live in the castle / with her. Beauty and the prince / lived happily / ever after.

- **at that moment** 在那一刻　• **magical** 魔法的　• **happen** 發生　• **be filled with** 充滿
- **bright** 明亮的　• **be dressed like** 穿得像　• **prince** 王子　• **fairy** 仙子
- **put a spell on** 對我施魔法　• **turn . . . into . . .** 把……變成……　• **curse** 詛咒
- **break a spell** 打破魔咒　• **appear** 出現　• **kindness** 善良　• **looks** 容貌
- **grant** 賜予　• **wonderful** 美好的　• **invite** 邀請

CLOSE UP

1 **Beauty found herself inside the castle.** 美麗發現她在城堡裡。
〈find oneself . . .〉意「發現自己處在……的狀況下」。

2 **I will grant you many beautiful children.** 我將賜給你們許多美麗的孩子。
〈grant A B〉是「答應給A，B這個東西」的意思。

3 **invited her father to live in the castle with her** 邀她父親到城堡裡一塊住
〈invite . . . to . . .〉意「（慎重地）邀請……去……」。

在那一刻 at that moment，有件神奇的事 something magical 發生了 happen。天空充滿了亮光 be filled with bright light，一瞬間 in a moment，美麗發現她自己在城堡裡 find herself inside the castle，房間裡都是鮮花 be filled with flowers，但野獸不在那裡。美麗身邊 next to Beauty 站了一個英俊的年輕人 a handsome young man，穿得像一個王子 be dressed like a prince。

「發生了什麼事 what's going on？野獸在哪裡？」美麗問。

「我在這裡，美麗，」王子説，「我就是野獸，好吧，應該説我曾經是野獸。」

「很久以前 a long time ago，」王子説，「我很自私又壞心 be selfish and unkind，有一個仙子 a fairy 用她的魔杖 with her magic wand 碰了我一下 touch me，對我下了魔咒 put a spell on me，把我變成一隻野獸 turn me into a beast，詛咒我 curse me 永遠變成野獸，直到有人愛上我。妳破除了魔咒 break the spell，美麗，因為妳的愛，我又變回人了 become a man again。」

這時，仙子突然出現 suddenly appear，説：「是的，美麗，妳了解善良 kindness 比外表更重要 more important than looks，妳姊姊不懂這些，所以現在她們跟丈夫在一起很不快樂，但妳跟王子將來會很幸福 be happy with your prince。你們是世上最美麗的一對 the most beautiful couple，我會為你們主婚，讓你們下半輩子 for the rest of your lives 幸福快樂 give you happiness，而且我也會賜予你們許多美麗的孩子 many beautiful children。」

美麗和王子 Beauty and the prince 不久就結婚了 marry soon，舉行了一個很棒的結婚典禮 a wonderful wedding。美麗邀請父親一起住在城堡裡，美麗和王子從此 ever after 過著幸福快樂的日子 live happily。

GRAMMAR POINT

-thing ＋ 形容詞 ⇨ 修飾 -thing 的形容詞，要放在 -thing 的後面。

• At that moment, **something magical** happened. 在那一刻，有件神奇的事發生了。

• I cannot think of **anything smart** to say to you. 我想不出什麼聰明的話好跟妳說。

• There was **nothing interesting** in the castle. 城堡裡沒有什麼有趣的事。

The Stars

I used to be a shepherd / in the Luberon region / of France. It was a very isolated place, / so I was often all alone / in the pasture. Sometimes, / I did not see many people / for weeks. During those weeks, / I only had my dog / and the flocks of sheep / to accompany me.

From time to time, / I saw a loner / who lived on Mount Lure. He would come down / to hear some news / of the outside world. Also, / I sometimes saw coal miners. They worked in the coal mines / near my field, / so I spoke with them / as they went back and forth / to the coal mines.

Once every two weeks, / I got a visitor / from the farm. This person was usually the farm boy / or an old woman / who worked at the farm. They were sent / to bring me supplies / on a mule. I was always happy / to see them. They would tell me / all of the news / from the lowlands.

However, / the news that interested me the most / was about my master's daughter. Her name was Stephanette, / and she was the most beautiful girl / in the surrounding area. Without seeming to take too much interest, / I would ask / how Stephanette was doing. I asked / if there were any young men / who wanted to marry her.

Of course, / I was just a lowly shepherd / who worked for her father. I had to remind myself / that there was no way / that Stephanette would be interested in me. After all, / there were / many wealthy and handsome young men / in the area.

One Sunday, / I was waiting / for the delivery boy / to arrive. It had been two weeks / since my last delivery, / so I was running out of supplies. By ten o'clock, / no one had arrived yet.

- **used to be** 曾經是　　• **shepherd** 牧羊人　　• **isolated** 偏遠的　　• **pasture** 放牧場
- **flock** 羊群　　• **accompany** 伴隨　　• **loner** 獨居者　　• **coal miner** 煤礦工
- **coal mine** 煤礦　　• **go back and forth** 往返　　• **visitor** 訪客　　• **farm** 農場
- **supply** 補給品；生活用品　　• **mule** 騾子　　• **lowlands** 低地　　• **master** 主人
- **surrounding area** 鄰近地區　　• **take much interest** 很感興趣　　• **lowly** 卑微地
- **remind oneself** 提醒某人自己　　• **be interested in** 對……感興趣　　• **wealthy** 有錢的
- **delivery boy** 送貨男孩　　• **run out of** 用完了

CLOSE UP

1 **once every two weeks** 每隔兩週一次
every 是「每個……」、「每……」的意思，是用來表現頻率的。例 every seven years（每隔七年）

2 **without seeming to take too much interest** 看起來不感興趣的樣子
〈without＋V-ing〉是「沒有……地」的意思。〈seem to . . .〉是「似乎要……」的意思。
所以 without seeming to 是「似乎沒有……地」、「不太……地」的意思。

3 **there was no way that Stephanette would be interested in me**
史達芬妮葉特不可能會對我有意思
〈there is no way (that) . . .〉是「……是絕對不會的」、「……是絕對不行的」的意思。

繁星

我曾經在法國的呂貝宏地區 in the Luberon region 當牧羊人 be a shepherd，那是一個與世隔絕的地方 a very isolated place。因此我常常獨自一人 all alone 在牧場上 in the pasture。有時，我好幾個星期 for weeks 都看不到什麼人 do not see many people。那幾個星期裡，只有我的狗 my dog 和羊群 the flocks of sheep 陪著我 accompany me 。

我經常 from time to time 看見一個孤獨的人 see a loner，他住在盧耳山，他會下山來 would come down 聽聽 hear 外面世界的消息 some news of the outside world。有時，我也會看到煤礦工 see coal miners，他們在我的草原附近 near my field 的礦坑裡工作 work in the coal mines。他們往返 go back and forth 礦坑時，我會和他們說話 speak with them。

每隔兩週 once every two weeks，有訪客 get a visitor 從農場 from the farm 來看我。這個訪客通常是農場的男孩 the farm boy，或是在農場裡工作的老婦人 an old woman。他們用騾子 on a mule 為我帶來一些補給品 bring me supplies。我總是很高興 be always happy 見到他們 see them，他們常告訴我 would tell me 低地 the lowlands 所發生的事。

然而，最讓我感興趣的事 interest me the most 是我主人的女兒 my master's daughter，她的名字 her name 是史達芬妮葉特 Stephanette，她是這一帶 in the surrounding area 最美的女孩 the most beautiful girl。我會裝作 without seeming to 不怎麼感興趣，問 ask 她過得好不好 how Stephanette is doing，我會問有沒有年輕男子想要娶她。

當然 of course，我只是一個為她父親工作 work for her father，卑微的牧羊人 a lowly shepherd。我必須提醒自己 remind myself，史達芬妮葉特不可能 no way 對我有興趣 be interested in me，畢竟 after all，這一帶 in the area 有許多 many 又有錢又英俊 wealthy and handsome 的年輕男子 young men。

某個星期天 one Sunday，我在等 wait for 送貨男孩的到來 the delivery boy。距離我上次的補給 since my last delivery 已經過了兩週 two weeks，我的補給品快要用光 run out of supplies。大約十點鐘 by ten o'clock，還沒有人來 no one arrives。

GRAMMAR POINT

would：將會…… ⇨ 表過去時常重複做的事或習慣。

- He **would** come down to hear some news of the outside world.
  他常下來聽外面世界的消息。
- They **would** tell me all of the news from the lowlands.
  他們常把低地發生的一切事情說給我聽。
- I **would** ask how Stephanette was doing. 我總會問史達芬妮葉特過得好不好。

"That's odd," I thought. "There must be a problem / at my master's house."

I continued to wait, / but no one came / by noon. "They must have forgotten / to send my supplies," I said to myself.

Around noon, / I noticed / that a big storm was coming. In the distance, / some dark clouds / were gathering. Soon, / heavy rain / began to pour down. "Now I understand," I said to myself. "The bad weather / has delayed the delivery person. The roads must be muddy / by now. I should not expect him / to arrive yet."

A few hours later, / the storm was over. The sun shone / high in the sky, / and its warm rays / spread bright light / all over the fields.

All of a sudden, / I heard the familiar sound / of the mule's bells. I eagerly looked / to see if it was the farmhand / or the old woman. However, / it was neither the farmhand / nor the old woman. It was the beautiful Stephanette! Oh, / what a wonderful surprise / that was!

She got off the mule, / and then she said to me, "I got lost / on my way up the hill."

"Are you all right, / mistress?" I asked.

She smiled / and nodded at me.

"The farmhand is sick," said Stephanette, "and the old woman is visiting her children / to spend the holiday with them. So my father sent me instead."

I could not take my eyes off her. She looked so beautiful / in that fresh afternoon air. In fact, / I had never seen her so close / before. And I had never spoken to her. I had only ever seen her / from a distance.

When I returned to the lowlands / in the winter, / her father would invite me to dinner / at his farm. At those times, / she would walk silently / across the room / and not say a word / to any of the servants. She had always looked very proud / during those times. And now / she was standing / in front of me.

- **odd** 奇怪的　**notice** 注意　**gather** 聚集　**pour down** 傾盆而下　**delay** 延誤
- **muddy** 泥濘的　**shine** 發光　**ray** 光芒　**spread** 散布　**all of a sudden** 突然間
- **familiar** 熟悉的　**eagerly** 熱切地　**farmhand** 農場工人　**get off** 下來
- **get lost** 迷路　**mistress** 小姐　**nod** 點頭　**instead** 反而　**from a distance** 從遠處
- **invite** 邀請　**silently** 安靜地　**servant** 僕人　**proud** 高傲的

CLOSE UP

1 **They must have forgotten to send my supplies.** 他們一定是忘了送我的補給品來。
〈must have p.p.〉是「一定已經……了」的意思，用在對過去的事做很有把握的推測時。

2 **I should not expect him to arrive yet.** 我不該期望他會來。
〈expect ... to ...〉是「期望……去做……」的意思。

3 **I could not take my eyes off her.** 我無法將視線從她身上移開。
〈take one's eyes off ...〉是「將視線離開……」的意思，一般和cannot一起使用，表感嘆某物相當有魅力，無法將視線轉移。

4 **I had never seen her so close before** 我以前從未這麼近距離地看著她 /
I had never spoken to her 我還沒跟她說過話
〈had never p.p.〉是「（過去、之前）不曾做過……」的意思，表過去已經完成的經歷。

「太奇怪了，」我想，「我主人家裡 at my master's house 一定出了什麼問題 a problem。」

我繼續等 continue to wait，但是到了中午 by noon 還沒有人來。「他們一定是忘了 forget 送生活用品給我 send my supplies。」我告訴自己。

將近中午 around noon 我注意到有一場暴風雨 a big storm 快來了，不遠處 in the distance 有些烏雲 some dark clouds 正在聚集 gather。不久，下起了 pour down 傾盆大雨 heavy rain。「現在我懂了，」我跟自己說，「是壞天氣 the bad weather 耽擱了送貨的人 delay the delivery person，現在 by now 路上 the roads 一定滿是泥濘 be muddy，我不該期待他會來。」

幾個小時以後 a few hours later，暴風雨 the storm 停了 be over，太陽 the sun 在高空 high in the sky 照耀 shine，溫暖的陽光 its warm rays 將亮光 bright light 灑在整片草原上 spread all over the fields。

突然間 all of a sudden，我聽到熟悉的聲音，騾子鈴噹的聲音 the familiar sound of the mule's bells，我急忙看是不是農場工人或老婦人，結果，不是農場工人 neither the farmhand 也不是老婦人 nor the old woman，而是美麗的史達芬妮葉特 the beautiful Stephanette。喔，這真是個美妙的驚喜 what a wonderful surprise！

她從騾子上下來 get off the mule，然後她跟我說：「上山來的路上 on my way up the hill，我迷路了 get lost。」

「妳還好嗎 are you all right，小姐 mistress？」我問。

她微笑 smile，對我點點頭 nod at me。

「農場工人病了 be sick，」史達芬妮葉特說，「老婦人去看她的孩子 visit her children，跟他們過節，所以我父親差我來 send me instead。」

我的視線離不開她 cannot take my eyes off her，在那午後清新的空氣中 in that fresh afternoon air 她看起來很美 look so beautiful。事實上 in fact，我以前從來沒有靠她這麼近過 never see her so close，我也從來沒有和她說過話 never speak to her，我只從遠處看過她 from a distance。

冬天 in the winter 我回到低地 return to the lowlands 時，她父親會邀我到他的農場吃晚餐 would invite me to dinner at his farm，那時候 at those times，她會靜靜地 silently 走過房間 walk across the room，不和任何僕人 to any of the servants 說話 not say a word。那時候 during those times 她看起來很高傲 look very proud，但是現在她站在我面前 stand in front of me。

GRAMMAR POINT

neither ... nor ... ：不是……也不是……

• It was **neither** the farmhand **nor** the old woman. 來的既非農場工人，也非老婦人。

• **Neither** he **nor** I will be there. 他不在那，我也不在那。

After she took my supplies off the mule, / Stephanette looked around the area. She seemed curious / about the pasture and the small barn.

"So this is / where you live, / shepherd?" she asked. She noticed my bed / in the barn. It was a simple bed / made of straw and sheepskin. There were / a cape and a stick / hanging on the wall / above my bed.

"You must be lonely and bored / because you are always alone," she continued. "What do you do / all day long?"

I wanted to answer, "I only think about you, / Stephanette," but I did not. As a matter of fact, / I could not say a single word / to her. How embarrassed / I was.

Stephanette must have noticed / my embarrassment. She started to tease me.

"Do the fairies come to see you / sometimes?" She was laughing / with a twinkle in her eyes. I thought / she was like a fairy, / but I did not say those words. Instead, / I said nothing.

"Well, I must leave now," she said. Stephanette got back on the mule / and said goodbye to me. Then, / the mule led her back / toward the farm. I watched her / as she disappeared down the hill. The sound of the mule's footsteps / continued for a while. The sound of those footsteps / remained with me / for a long time.

Later in the evening, / I brought the flock of sheep back in / from the fields. As I was completing my chores, / I heard a voice / calling my name. It was Stephanette. She had returned. But she was not smiling anymore. Now, / she was soaking wet / and shivering from the cold.

"At the bottom of the mountain, / there is a river / as you know. The rain from the storm / caused the river / to flood. The water has risen very high. I tried to cross the river, / but I almost drowned / in the water. I was so scared / and didn't know what to do. So I just returned here," she said / in a trembling voice.

- take . . . off . . . 把……從……拿下　• curious 好奇的　• barn 穀倉　• notice 注意
- straw 乾草　• sheepskin 羊皮　• cape 斗篷　• hang 掛　• lonely 孤單的
- bored 無聊的　• alone 獨自　• as a matter of fact 事實上　• embarrassed 尷尬的
- embarrassment 尷尬　• tease 逗　• with a twinkle in one's eyes 眼中閃爍著光芒
- disappear 消失　• footstep 足跡　• remain 維持；留下　• complete 完全的
- chore 例行工作；雜務　• soaking 濕透的　• shiver 顫抖　• cause 導致　• flood 淹水
- rise 升；漲　• cross 越過　• drown 淹死　• be scared 害怕　• tremble 顫抖

CLOSE UP

1 **The rain from the storm caused the river to flood.** 暴風雨導致河水氾濫。
cause 是表原因，若是〈 . . . cause A to . . . 〉的話，則是「因為……使得A去做……」的意思。

2 **I almost drowned in the water.** 我差點溺水。
動詞前有almost或nearly的話，則是「幾乎、差一點就……」的意思。

她把我的補給品從騾子上面拿下來 take my supplies off the mule 時，史達芬妮葉特環視這一帶 look around the area，她似乎 seem 對草場 the pasture 和小穀倉 the small barn 感到很好奇 curious。

　　「這裡就是你住的地方 where you live 嗎？牧羊人。」她問。她注意到我穀倉裡的床 notice my bed。這是一張簡陋的床 a simple bed，上面舖滿了稻草和羊毛皮 straw and sheepskin，牆上 on the wall 掛了 hang 一件斗蓬和一根手杖 a cape and a stick。

　　「你總是一個人 always alone，一定很寂寞、很無聊 be lonely and bored 吧。」她繼續說，「你整天 all day long 都做些什麼呢？」

　　我想回答她，「我都在想妳 only think about you，史達芬妮葉特。」但我沒有。事實上 as a matter of fact，我一個字 a single word 也說不出口 cannot say，我真的很糗 how embarrassed。

　　史達芬妮葉特一定是注意到我的尷尬 notice my embarrassment，她開始逗我 tease me。

　　「有時仙子 the fairies 會來看你 come to see you 嗎？」她笑起來的時候，雙眼璀璨如星 with a twinkle in her eyes，我想她就像仙女一樣 be like a fairy，但我沒有這麼說，我什麼也沒說 say nothing。

　　「好吧，我得走了 must leave。」她說。史達芬妮葉特騎上騾子 get back on the mule，跟我道別 say goodbye to me，然後騾子就載著她朝農場走去 lead her back toward the farm，我看著她消失在山下 disappear down the hill。騾子的腳步聲 the sound of the mule's footsteps 持續 continue 了一會兒 for a while，腳步聲在我耳邊繚繞 remain with me 很久 for a long time。

　　那天傍晚 later in the evening 我帶著羊群 bring the flock of sheep 從草地 from the fields 回來 back in，做完我的工作 complete my chores 時，我聽到有聲音 hear a voice 在叫我的名字 call my name，是史達芬妮葉特。她回來了，但是她不再微笑，現在她全身濕透 soaking wet 了，冷得發抖 shiver from the cold。

　　「如你所知 as you know，山腳下 at the bottom of the mountain 有一條河 a river，暴風雨帶來的雨 the rain from the storm 讓河水氾濫 cause the river to flood 了，水 the water 漲得很高 rise high。我試著過河 cross the river，但我差點就溺水了 almost drown。我很害怕 be so scared，不知道怎麼辦 don't know what to do，所以我只好回來這裡 return here。」她說話聲音顫抖 in a trembling voice。

V－ing 現在分詞 ⇨ 和 be 動詞一起形成進行式，或引導分詞片語來修飾名詞或補充名詞。

- She was <u>laughing</u> with a twinkle in her eyes. 她笑的時候眼中閃爍如星。（進行式）
- There were a cape and a stick **hanging** on the wall above my bed.
  我床上的牆上掛了一件斗蓬和一根柺杖。（現在分詞片語）
- As I was **completing** my chores, I heard a voice **calling** my name.
  我做完事的時候，聽見有一個聲音在呼喚我的名字。（進行式）（現在分詞片語）

I was not sure / what to do. It was not right / for her / to spend the night on the mountain. I also could not leave / the flock of sheep / to take her home. But then I thought, "The nights in July / are short. It's only one night."

I immediately made a fire / so that she could dry / her feet and clothes. Then, / I gave her / some milk and cheese, / but Stephanette was not interested in eating. She burst into tears. And I almost felt like crying, / too. It was completely dark / outside. I took her to the barn, / and I prepared a bed for her. I laid out a new sheepskin / on the fresh straw / so that she could rest. I said goodnight / and went outside.

I sat down / in front of the door. I tried not to think of the young lady / who was resting in my house. But all that I could think of / was her. I was proud / because I had assisted her. Tonight, / it was my responsibility / to keep her safe. In happiness, / I looked up in the sky. The stars shone / more beautifully than ever / that night.

A while later, / the barn door opened, / and Stephanette came out.

"I cannot sleep," she said. "Do you mind / if I sit next to the fire?"

She sat down / by the fire. I gave her a goatskin / to wrap around herself. We sat by the fire / in silence. That night, / every creature / seemed to come alive. The frogs in the pond / croaked louder / than normal. The insects sang loudly / as well. The fire made a brilliant bright light / as it burned through the night. Even the night air / seemed to be fresher / than normal.

Some noises in the night / frightened her. She moved / closer to me. Just then, / a shooting star / passed in the sky / above us. It was the most beautiful shooting star / I had ever seen.

• leave 離開　• dry 弄乾　• burst into tears 突然哭了起來　• completely 完全地
• prepare 準備　• lay out 展開　• rest 休息　• be proud 驕傲的　• assist 幫助
• responsibility 責任　• keep . . . safe 讓某人安全　• in happiness 沉浸於快樂之中
• Do you mind if . . . ? 你介意我……？　• wrap around oneself 裹住某人
• in silence 安靜　• creature 生物　• croak 鳴叫　• normal 正常的
• brilliant 明亮的　• noise 聲響　• frighten 害怕　• shooting star 流星

CLOSE UP

1 **so that she could dry her feet and clothes** 以便她能把腳和衣服弄乾 / **so that she could rest** 以便她能休息
〈so that . . .〉是「這樣就能……」、「以便……」的意思。

2 **I almost felt like crying, too.** 我差一點也哭出來。
〈feel like＋V-ing〉是「想要……、感覺要……」的意思。

3 **seemed to come alive** 彷彿活了起來 / **seemed to be fresher** 似乎更清新
〈seem to . . .〉是「看起來……的」的意思。

4 **It was the most beautiful shooting star I had ever seen.** 那是我所見過最美的流星。
〈最高級＋名詞＋主詞＋have/had ever seen〉是「到目前為止所見過最……的」的意思。

我不確定該怎麼辦，她留在山上 on the mountain 過夜 spend the night，是不對的 be not right。我也不能丟下羊群 leave the flock of sheep 送她回家 take her home，但後來我想，「七月的夜晚 the nights in July 很短 be short，反正只有一晚 only one night。」

我立刻升火 make a fire，好讓她烘腳和衣服 dry her feet and clothes，然後我給她一些牛奶和起司 some milk and cheese，但史達芬妮葉特不想吃，她突然哭了起來 burst into tears。我差一點也要哭出來 feel like crying。天色很暗。我帶她到穀倉裡 take her to the barn 為她舖床 prepare a bed for her，我在新的乾草上 on the fresh straw 舖了新的羊毛皮 lay out a new sheepskin 讓她可以休息。我向她道晚安 say goodnight，然後就出去了 go outside。

我在門前 in front of the door 坐下 sit down，試著不去想 think of 正在我屋裡休息的少女 the young lady，但我所想的全都是她 all that I can think of。幫助她 assist her 讓我覺得很驕傲 be proud，今晚，保護她的安全 keep her safe 是我的責任 my responsibility。我沉浸在快樂裡 in happiness，抬頭望著天空 look up in the sky。那晚繁星 the stars 比以往閃耀得更加美麗 shine more beautifully than ever。

過了一會 a while later，穀倉的門開了，史達芬妮葉特出來了 come out。

「我睡不著 cannot sleep，」她說：「你介意我坐在火堆旁邊 sit next to the fire 嗎？」

她在火堆旁坐下 sit down by the fire，我給她一件山羊皮 a goatskin，讓她裹著身體 wrap around herself。我們沉默地 in silence 坐在火堆旁 sit by the fire。那晚，所有生物 every creature 似乎都生機勃勃 come alive，池塘裡的青蛙 the frogs in the pond 叫得 croak 比平常 than normal 大聲 louder；昆蟲 the insects 也大聲鳴叫 sing loudly。火帶來了明亮的光 make a brilliant bright light，在漫漫長夜中燃燒 burn 了一夜 through the night；連夜晚的空氣 the night air 似乎也比平常更清新 be fresher。

夜裡的一些聲音 some noises 嚇壞了她 frighten her，她更靠近我 move closer to me。就在此時，一道流星 a shooting star 劃過 pass 我們上方 above us 的天空 in the sky。那是我見過 see 最美的流星 the most beautiful shooting star。

虛主詞 it；真主詞 to 不定詞

⇨ to 不定詞是句子的真主詞時，幾乎都會把虛主詞 it 放在句首，將 to 不定詞片語放到主要動詞後。

- Tonight, **it** was my responsibility **to keep** her safe. 今晚我的責任是保護她的安危。
- **It** was not right **for her to spend** the night on the mountain.
  讓她在山上過夜是不對的。
  （這裡的 for her 是 to spend ... 意思上的主詞，故要以〈for＋受格〉這種形式放在 to 不定詞之前。）

"What is that?" asked Stephanette.

"A soul / that has entered Heaven," I responded.

Stephanette looked at me / and said, "You are not like / the other young men / I know."

I answered, "I am probably like / most other men, / but my life in the field / is very different from theirs. Here, / I live close to the stars. I know / what happens up there / better than people from the plains."

Stephanette looked up into the sky / and said, "Look! There is / another shooting star." She pointed to a shooting star / streaking across the sky.

"It's so beautiful. I have never seen / so many beautiful stars / in my life. Do you know / the names of the stars?"

"Of course, mistress, / I do," I answered. "Look up there. Do you see / the streak of light / that travels across the sky? That is the Milky Way. The Milky Way / stretches all across France / and goes into Spain. Soldiers often use / the Milky Way / to find their way home."

I continued to point out / some of the stars / to her. I explained constellations / to her.

"Many stars combine / to form constellations. They are like / pictures in the sky. Can you see / that group of stars? That is the Big Dipper. The three stars in front / are the Three Animals. And there is / Orion the Hunter / up there."

"Did you know / that we shepherds / are able to use the sky / like a clock? I can tell the time / by looking at the stars. For instance, / right now, / it is almost midnight." I kept talking.

- **soul** 靈魂　• **probably** 或許　• **plains** 平原　• **streak** 閃現
- **a streak of light** 一道光束　• **the Milky Way** 銀河　• **stretch** 延伸
- **find one's way home** 找到回家的路　• **point out** 指出　• **constellation** 星座
- **combine** 結合　• **form** 形成　• **tell the time** 判斷時間

CLOSE UP

1 **You are not like the other young men.** 你不像其他年輕男子。/
  I am probably like most other men. 我或許和大部分男子一樣。/
  They are like pictures in the sky. 它們很像空中的畫作。
  〈be like ...〉是「像……」、「和……相似」的意思。

2 **my life in the field is very different from theirs** 我在牧場裡的生活和別人非常不一樣
  〈be different from ...〉是「和……不同」的意思。這裡的 theirs 是 their lives 的意思。

3 **I can tell the time by looking at the stars.** 我能藉由觀星判斷時間。
  〈can tell the time〉是「知道現在是幾點」、「會看手錶」的意思。
  〈by＋V-ing〉是「藉由……」的意思，表手段或方法。

「那是什麼？」史達芬妮葉特問。

「上天堂 enter Heaven 的靈魂 a soul。」我回答。

史達芬妮葉特看著我說：「你一點也不像其他我所認識的年輕男子。」

我回答：「我或許和大部分的男人一樣 be like most other men，但我在牧場裡的生活 my life in the field 和他們很不一樣 be different from theirs，在這裡我住得離繁星很近 live close to the stars，我知道上面 up there 發生了什麼事 what happens，比平地的人還要了解 know better。」

史達芬妮葉特望著天空 look up into the sky 說：「你看 look！又有一顆流星 another shooting star 劃過天空 streak across the sky。」她指著流星 point to a shooting star。

「這真美，我這輩子 in my life 從沒見過 never see 這麼多美麗的星星 so many beautiful stars。你知道星星的名字 the names of the stars 嗎？」

「當然，小姐，我知道，」我回答，「妳看上面那裡 look up there，妳看到那道光束 the streak of light 橫跨天際 travel across the sky 嗎？那是銀河 the Milky Way，銀河跨越法國 stretch all across France 延伸到西班牙 go into Spain。士兵 soldiers 常利用銀河 use the Milky Way 找到回家的路 find their way home。」

我繼續把一些星星指給她看 point out some of the stars，解釋星座 explain constellations 給她聽。

「許多星星 many stars 連在一起 combine 形成星座 form constellations，就像天上的畫作 pictures in the sky 一樣，妳看到那群星星 that group of stars 了嗎？那是北斗七星 the Big Dipper，前面的三顆星 the three stars 是三隻動物 the Three Animals；上面那裡 up there 是獵戶座 Orion the Hunter。」

「妳知道我們牧羊人 we shepherds 會把天空當成時鐘 use the sky like a clock 嗎？我可以靠觀星 look at the stars 知道現在幾點 can tell the time，例如 for instance，現在 right now 將近午夜 almost midnight。」我繼續說。

to 不定詞：達到……（表目的）

- Soldiers often use the Milky Way **to find** their way home.
  士兵常靠銀河找到回家的路。

- Many stars combine **to form** constellations.
  許多星星聯合在一起形成星座。

"All of the stars / are beautiful. But the most beautiful star of all / is the Evening Star. It comes out first / every night. It is the shepherd's friend. She lights our way / at dawn / when we take our flocks out to the fields / and also in the evening / when we return. We call her Maguelonne. Maguelonne chases Saturn in the sky / and marries him / every seven years."

"What? The stars can marry?" she exclaimed.

"Oh, sure. The stars can get married," I told her.

I was just about to explain / how the stars get married. Then, / I felt / as Stephanette laid her head / on my shoulder / and fell asleep. In the cool breeze, / the ribbons in her hair / danced, / and I felt the touch of her curls / against my neck. It was the most enchanting feeling.

We stayed like that / until the stars began to fade / and the first rays of dawn / appeared. I wanted that night / to last forever.

All above us, / the stars continued their march / across the night sky. I imagined / that one of the stars, / the finest and the most brilliant, / had lost her way / and was resting her head / on my shoulder.

- **the Evening Star** 黃昏之星 •**dawn** 黎明 •**take out** 帶出 •**chase** 追逐
- •**exclaim** 驚呼 •**be just about to** 正要 •**lay** 放 •**shoulder** 肩膀 •**fall asleep** 睡著
- •**breeze** 微風 •**ribbon** 緞帶 •**curls** 捲髮 •**enchanting** 迷人的
- •**march** 行進 •**imagine** 想像 •**finest** 最美好的 •**rest** 休息

CLOSE UP

1 **I was just about to explain** 我正要解釋
〈be about to . . .〉是「正要去做……」的意思。

2 **the touch of her curls against my neck** 她的卷髮輕觸我的脖子
這裡的〈against . . .〉是「靠著……」、「貼著……」的意思。

「所有星星 all of the stars 都好美麗 be beautiful，但最美的星星 the most beautiful star 是黃昏之星 the Evening Star。它每天晚上 every night 第一個出現 come out first，它是牧羊人的朋友 the shepherd's friend。在黎明時 at dawn 我們趕著羊群到牧場 take our flocks out to the fields，它照亮我們的路；傍晚 in the evening 回家途中也照亮我們的路 light our way。我們稱她瑪格龍 call her Maguelonne，她追逐空中的土星 chase Saturn，每隔七年 every seven years 就跟他結一次婚 marry him。」

「什麼 what？星星可以結婚？」她驚呼。

「喔，當然，星星可以結婚。」我告訴她。

就在我正要解釋 be about to explain 星星如何結婚，這時，我發覺史達芬妮葉特的頭靠在我的肩上 lay her head on my shoulder 睡著 fall asleep 了，涼爽的微風中 in the cool breeze 她髮上的絲帶 the ribbons in her hair 飄舞 dance 著。我感覺到 feel 她的卷髮 her curls 輕觸 the touch 我的脖子 against my neck。這是最令人著迷的感覺 the most enchanting feeling 了。

我們維持這樣的姿勢 stay like that 直到星星 the stars 開始消逝 fade，第一道曙光 the first rays of dawn 出現 appear，我希望那一夜永遠長存 last forever。

我們頭上，繁星持續行進 continue their march 跨越夜空 across the night sky。我想像 imagine 最美好的 the finest、最明亮的 the most brilliant 那一顆星迷了路 lose her way，正將她的頭靠在我的肩上 rest her head on my shoulder。

Super Reading Story Training Book

Answers
and
Translations

The Magic Cooking Pot

Stop & Think

- **Why did the little girl begin to cry?** 小女孩為什麼開始哭呢？
  ⇨ She could not find anything to eat. 她找不到任何東西吃。 /
  She was hungry but had no food. 她餓了，可是沒有食物吃。

- **What did the old woman have?** 老婆婆有什麼？
  ⇨ She had a magic cooking pot. 她有一個魔法鍋子。

CHECK UP

1 The little girl lived   **a.** a magic cooking pot.
2 The little girl searched for food   **b.** with her mother.
3 The old woman had   **c.** in the forest.
4 The pot started   **d.** cooking porridge.

1 小女孩跟媽媽一起住。
2 小女孩到森林裡找食物。
3 老婆婆有一個魔法鍋子。
4 鍋子開始煮麥片粥。

Stop & Think

- **What should the little girl do to stop the pot from cooking?** 小女孩要做什麼才能讓鍋子不再繼續煮東西？
  ⇨ She should say, "Stop, little pot, stop." 她應該說：「停止，小鍋子，停止。」

- **Why did the mother decide to eat without her daughter?** 為什麼女孩的媽媽決定不等女兒就吃飯呢？
  ⇨ Her daughter went out for a long time, and she became hungry.
  她女兒出門很久沒回來，她餓了。

CHECK UP

1 The little girl took the pot and <u>ran back</u> to her home.
2 Soon, the pot was <u>full</u> of porridge.
3 The pot <u>immediately</u> stopped cooking.
4 The little girl and her mother ate <u>porridge</u> every day.

1 小女孩拿了鍋子，跑回她的家。
2 不久，鍋子盛滿了麥片粥。
3 鍋子立刻停止煮東西。
4 小女孩和媽媽每天都吃麥片粥。

Stop & Think

- **Why did the pot keep making porridge?** 為什麼鍋子一直煮出麥片粥？
  ⇨ The little girl's mother forgot the magic words. 小女孩的媽媽忘了咒語。

CHECK UP

1 The mother did not remember <u>how to</u> make it stop.
2 The porridge <u>spilled</u> onto the floor.
3 Every house in the village had <u>porridge</u> in it.

1 媽媽忘記怎麼讓它停下來。
2 麥片粥溢出來流到街上。
3 村裡的每一間屋子裡都有麥片粥。

The Shoemaker and the Elves

Stop & Think

- **Were there many customers in the shop?** 小店裡有許多顧客嗎？
  ⇨ No, few people visited the shop. 不，很少人光顧小店。

- **Who made the beautiful shoes?** 誰做了這麼美麗的鞋？
  ⇨ We don't know. 我們不知道。 /
    Somebody made the shoes for the shoemaker. 有人替鞋匠做了鞋子。

CHECK UP

1 The shoemaker was very poor.   <u>T</u>
2 The shoemaker finished his last pair of shoes.   <u>F</u>
3 The lady gave the shoemaker three gold coins for the shoes.   <u>T</u>
4 The next morning, the shoemaker made two more pairs of shoes.   <u>F</u>

1 鞋匠很窮。
2 鞋匠做完了他最後一雙鞋。
3 女士付了三枚金幣給鞋匠，買下鞋子。
4 隔天早上鞋匠又做了兩雙鞋。

Stop & Think

- **Why did the shoemaker and his wife hide downstairs?** 為什麼鞋匠和他的妻子要躲在樓下？
  ⇨ To find out who was making the shoes. 為了找出鞋子是誰做的。

CHECK UP

1 The next morning, the shoemaker and his wife <u>came down</u>.
2 They saw two beautiful <u>pairs of</u> shoes on the table.
3 The two customers paid <u>twelve</u> gold coins for the four pairs of shoes.
4 The shoemaker and his wife <u>hid</u> downstairs.

1 隔天早上鞋匠和妻子下樓。
2 他們看到桌上有兩雙漂亮的鞋子。
3 兩名顧客付了十二枚金幣買那四雙鞋。
4 鞋匠和妻子躲在樓下。

Stop & Think

• **Who made the beautiful shoes?** 誰做了美麗的鞋子？
  ⇨ Two elves made the shoes. 兩個精靈做了鞋子。

• **Why did the elves leave?** 精靈為什麼要離開？
  ⇨ The shoemaker and his wife knew about them. 鞋匠和他的妻子已經知道他們的存在。

CHECK UP

1 Two <u>elves</u> made the shoes at night.
2 The shoemaker and his wife made tiny <u>clothes</u>.
3 The <u>elves</u> left and never came back.
4 The shoemaker and his wife became <u>rich</u>.

1 兩個精靈夜裡做了鞋子。
2 鞋匠和妻子做了很小件的衣服。
3 精靈走了，再也沒回來過。
4 鞋匠和妻子變有錢了。

Jack and the Beanstalk

Stop & Think

• **What did the strange old man offer Jack?** 奇怪的老人給傑克什麼東西？
  ⇨ He offered Jack some magic beans. 他要給傑克一些魔豆。

CHECK UP

1 What did Jack sell the strange old man? (c)
  a. magic beans　　**b.** some food　　**c.** a cow
2 What did Jack's mother do with the beans? (b)
  a. She ate them.　　**b.** She threw them out the window.　　**c.** She planted them.

1 傑克把什麼東西賣給奇怪的老人？
  a. 魔豆　　**b.** 一些食物　　**c.** 一頭牛
2 傑克的媽媽怎麼處理魔豆？
  a. 把它們吃了。　　**b.** 把它們丟到窗外。　　**c.** 把它們種在土裡。

Stop & Think

• **Who lived in the castle?** 誰住在城堡裡？
  ⇨ The giant and his wife lived in the castle. 巨人和妻子住在城堡裡。

- Why did Jack climb the beanstalk again? 傑克為什麼又爬上豌豆莖？
  ⇨ He ran out of gold. 他把金子花光了。

CHECK UP

1 The giant's wife   **a.** the giant's gold.
2 The giant's huge bag   **b.** was kindhearted.
3 Jack stole   **c.** was filled with gold.

1 巨人的妻子很善良。
2 巨人的大袋子裝滿了金子。
3 傑克偷了巨人的金子。

pp. 18–19

Stop & Think

- Why did Jack cut down the beanstalk? 為什麼傑克把豌豆莖砍斷？
  ⇨ The giant was chasing him. 巨人在追他。 /
  To stop the giant from coming down. 阻止巨人下來。

CHECK UP

1 The hen laid golden eggs.
2 The harp played beautiful music.
3 Jack stole the harp and ran out of the castle.
4 Jack cut down the beanstalk with an axe.

1 母雞下金蛋。
2 豎琴奏出美妙的音樂。
3 傑克偷了豎琴，逃離城堡。
4 傑克用斧頭砍斷豌豆莖。

The Ugly Duckling

pp. 20–21

Stop & Think

- How did the seventh egg look? 第七顆蛋長得怎麼樣？
  ⇨ It was bigger than the other ones. 它比其他的蛋還要大。
- How did the ugly duckling look? 醜小鴨長得怎麼樣？
  ⇨ He was big, gray, ugly, and strange looking. 他又大、又灰、又醜，長相奇特。

CHECK UP

1 Mother Duck did not remember the seventh egg.   T
2 The last baby duckling looked strange.   T
3 The ugly duckling looked like the old duck.   F

1 鴨媽媽不記得這第七顆蛋。
2 最後一隻鴨寶寶看起來很奇怪。
3 醜小鴨看起來像一隻老鴨子。

Stop & Think

• **Why was the ugly duckling sad?** 為什麼醜小鴨很傷心？
  ⇨ Nobody loved him. 沒人愛他。

• **Who killed the two geese?** 誰殺了兩隻鵝？
  ⇨ Hunters killed the geese. 獵人殺了鵝。

CHECK UP

1 The ugly duckling was a <u>good</u> swimmer.
2 The farm girl <u>disliked</u> the ugly duckling.
3 The ugly duckling <u>ran away from</u> the farm.
4 Hunters with <u>rifles</u> killed the two geese.

1 醜小鴨很會游泳。
2 農場女孩不喜歡醜小鴨。
3 醜小鴨逃離農場。
4 拿槍的獵人殺了兩隻鵝。

Stop & Think

• **What did the ugly duckling see in the sky?** 醜小鴨看到天上有什麼？
  ⇨ He saw three swans. 他看到三隻天鵝。

• **How did the ugly duckling survive the winter?** 醜小鴨是怎麼熬過冬天的？
  ⇨ A farmer took the ugly duckling to his home. 有個農夫帶醜小鴨回家。

CHECK UP

1 Why couldn't the ugly duckling swim in the lake? (c)
  a. There was no water. **b.** He was a bad swimmer. **c.** The water froze.
2 When did the farmer set the ugly duckling free? (b)
  a. in the winter **b.** in the spring **c.** in the summer

1 醜小鴨為什麼不能在湖裡游泳？
  a. 湖裡沒有水。 b. 他游得不好。 c. 湖結冰了。
2 農夫什麼時候放醜小鴨走？
  a. 冬天 b. 春天 c. 夏天

Stop & Think

• **What was the ugly duckling?** 醜小鴨是什麼？
  ⇨ He was a swan. 他是一隻天鵝。

CHECK UP

1 The ugly duckling <u>flew</u> into the sky.
2 The ugly duckling saw his <u>reflection</u> in the water.
3 He was not an <u>ugly</u> duckling anymore.
4 The ugly duckling was <u>the most</u> beautiful of all the swans.

1 醜小鴨飛上天空。
2 醜小鴨看到自己的水中倒影。
3 他不再是隻醜小鴨了。
4 醜小鴨是所有天鵝中最美的一隻。

The Ant and the Grasshopper

pp. 28–29

Stop & Think

- **Why** *does the ant work hard every day?* 螞蟻為什麼每天都辛勤地工作？
  ⇨ To save food for the winter. 為冬天存糧。

- **What** *does the grasshopper do every day?* 蚱蜢每天都在做什麼？
  ⇨ He plays and sings every day. 他每天都在玩耍和唱歌。

CHECK UP

1 The ant gathers a lot of food for the winter.
2 In winter, the grasshopper has no food to eat.
3 The grasshopper realizes how foolish he was.
4 Is the grasshopper in the field in the next spring? (No)

1 螞蟻為過冬收集了很多食物。
2 冬天時，蚱蜢沒有食物可以吃。
3 蚱蜢明白自己有多愚蠢。
4 隔年春天蚱蜢還在田野裡嗎？（不）

The Hare and the Tortoise

pp. 30–31

Stop & Think

- **Why** *did the tortoise and the hare race?* 為什麼烏龜和兔子要賽跑？
  ⇨ To find out who the faster animal was. 找出誰是跑得最快的動物。

CHECK UP

1 The hare bragged — b. about how fast he could run.
2 The tortoise bet — d. he could beat the hare.
3 The tortoise — a. kept walking to the finish line.
4 The hare woke up — c. too late.

1 兔子誇口他可以跑很快。
2 烏龜打賭他可以打敗兔子。
3 烏龜繼續走向終點線。
4 兔子醒來發現來不及了。

The Sick Lion

pp. 32–33

Stop & Think

- **What did the lion do?** 獅子做了什麼？
  ⇨ He ate the animals that entered his cave. 他把所有進到他洞穴裡的動物都吃掉了。
- **Why did the fox refuse to enter the cave?** 狐狸為什麼不肯進入洞穴？
  ⇨ He only saw footprints entering the cave. 他只看到進入洞穴的腳印。

CHECK UP

1 The lion could not <u>hunt</u> animals anymore.
2 The animals felt <u>sorry</u> for the lion.
3 The lion <u>pretended</u> to be sick.
4 The fox looked at the <u>footprints</u> outside the cave.

1 獅子再也不能捕捉動物。
2 動物為獅子感到難過。
3 獅子假裝生病了。
4 狐狸看著洞穴外的腳印。

The Boy Who Cried Wolf

pp. 34–35

Stop & Think

- **Why did the shepherd boy yell, "Wolf!" the first time?** 牧童開始大叫「狼來了」是為了什麼？
  ⇨ He was bored watching the sheep by himself. 他一個人看守羊群很無聊。
- **Why did the villagers not go to help the shepherd boy?** 為什麼村民後來都不幫牧童？
  ⇨ They thought he was tricking them again. 他們認為他又在捉弄他們了。

CHECK UP

1 The shepherd boy tricked the villagers by crying out, "Wolf!"   T
2 A wolf attacked the shepherd boy's sheep.   T
3 The shepherd boy killed the wolf.   F

1 牧童大喊「狼來了！」捉弄村民。
2 有一隻狼來攻擊牧童的羊。
3 牧童把狼殺了。

The Little Mermaid

pp. 38–39

CHECK UP

1 The Little Mermaid had a <u>beautiful</u> singing voice.
2 All mermaids have a <u>tail</u> instead of legs.
3 The Little Mermaid dreamed of the <u>land</u> above the water.

1 小美人魚的歌聲很動聽。
2 人魚只有尾鰭，沒有腿。
3 小美人魚幻想水上的陸地。

pp. 40–41

Stop & Think

• **Who did the Little Mermaid see inside the ship?** 小美人魚看到誰在船裡面？
⇨ She saw many handsome gentlemen and a prince. 她看到很多英俊的紳士和王子。

CHECK UP

1 The Little Mermaid thought the prince was handsome.　　T
2 The prince could breathe underwater.　　F
3 The Little Mermaid saved the prince's life.　　T

1 小美人魚認為王子很英俊。
2 王子可以在水底下呼吸。
3 小美人魚救了王子的性命。

pp. 42–43

Stop & Think

• **Who found the prince on the beach?** 誰在海灘上發現王子？
⇨ A pretty girl found the prince. 一個美麗的女孩發現王子。

• **What did the Little Mermaid wish?** 小美人魚想要什麼？
⇨ She wished to become a human. 她想要變成人類。

CHECK UP

1 The Little Mermaid hid behind some <u>rocks</u>.
2 The Little Mermaid only thought about the <u>prince</u>.
3 <u>Mermaids</u> live for three hundred years.
4 Humans have <u>souls</u>, but mermaids do not.

1 小美人魚躲在岩石後面。
2 小美人魚只想著王子。
3 人魚可以活300年。
4 人類有靈魂，但人魚沒有。

Stop & Think

- **How can a mermaid *get a soul*?** 人魚要怎麼做才能擁有靈魂？
  ⇨ A man must love her and marry her. 有個男人愛她，願意娶她。

- **How can the Little Mermaid *become a human*?** 小美人魚要怎麼變成人類？
  ⇨ She has to drink the magic drink before sunrise. 她得在日落前喝下魔藥。

CHECK UP

1 Humans think   a. wanted a pair of human legs.
2 The sea witch's house   b. was made from bones.
3 The Little Mermaid   c. will split in two.
4 The Little Mermaid's tail   d. tails are ugly.

1 人類認為尾鰭很醜。
2 海巫的家是用骨頭建造而成的。
3 小美人魚想要一雙人類的腿。
4 小美人魚的尾鰭會裂成兩半。

Stop & Think

- **What did the *sea witch* take from the Little Mermaid?** 海巫從小美人魚身上奪走什麼？
  ⇨ She took the Little Mermaid's voice. 她奪走小美人魚的聲音。

CHECK UP

1 What will happen to the Little Mermaid if the prince marries someone else? (b)
  a. She will lose her voice.   **b.** She will turn into foam.   **c.** She will get a soul.

2 What happened right after the Little Mermaid drank the magic drink? (c)
  a. She became a human.   **b.** She found the prince.   **c.** She passed out.

1 如果王子娶了別人，小美人魚會怎麼樣？
  a. 她會失去她的聲音。   **b.** 她會化成泡沫。   **c.** 她會得到靈魂。
2 小美人魚一喝下魔藥之後，就發生了什麼事？
  a. 她變成人類。   **b.** 她發現王子。   **c.** 她昏倒了。

Stop & Think

- **Where did the prince take the Little Mermaid?** 王子帶小美人魚去哪？
  ⇨ He took her inside his castle. 他帶她回城堡。

- **What did the Little Mermaid do at the *prince's party*?** 在王子的宴會上，小美人魚做了什麼？
  ⇨ She danced beautifully. 她跳舞跳得很美。

CHECK UP

1 Some girls sang for the prince at the party.
2 The Little Mermaid and the prince did everything together.
3 The Little Mermaid missed her family.

1 某些女孩在宴會上為王子獻唱。
2 小美人魚和王子形影不離。
3 小美人魚想念她的家人。

pp. 50–51

Stop & Think

• **How did the prince feel about the Little Mermaid?** 王子覺得小美人魚怎麼樣？
⇨ He loved her like a sister. 他把她當妹妹一樣地愛她。

CHECK UP

1 The prince did not think of marrying the Little Mermaid.   T
2 The king ordered the prince to marry the Little Mermaid.   F
3 The prince met the girl he had been looking for.   T
4 The princess of the next kingdom saved the prince's life.   F

1 王子沒想過要娶小美人魚為妻。
2 國王命令王子娶小美人魚。
3 王子遇到他一直在尋找的女孩。
4 鄰國的公主救了王子的性命。

pp. 52–53

Stop & Think

• **What did the Little Mermaid do at the wedding?** 小美人魚在婚禮上做了什麼？
⇨ She danced more beautifully than ever. 她跳舞跳得比之前更美。

CHECK UP

1 The prince and the princess —— a. got married on the ship.
2 The Little Mermaid's sisters —— b. couldn't kill the prince.
3 The Little Mermaid had to kill —— c. gave their hair to the sea witch.
4 The Little Mermaid —— d. the prince before the sun rose.

1 王子和公主在船上結婚。
2 小美人魚的姊姊把她們的頭髮給海巫。
3 小美人魚得在日出前把王子殺掉。
4 小美人魚下不了手，殺死王子。

pp. 54–55

Stop & Think

• **What did the Little Mermaid become?** 小美人魚變成什麼了？
⇨ She became a fairy of the air. 她變成天上的仙子。

• **Why did the prince look sad?** 為什麼王子看起來很傷心？
⇨ The Little Mermaid was gone. 小美人魚不見了。

CHECK UP

1 The Little Mermaid became a fairy of the air.

2 The Little Mermaid can get a <u>soul</u>.

3 The prince <u>guessed</u> what had happened to the Little Mermaid.

4 The Little Mermaid <u>kissed</u> the prince and princess.

1 小美人魚變成天上的仙子。

2 小美人魚可以得到靈魂。

3 王子猜到小美人魚發生了什麼事。

4 小美人魚親了王子和公主。

Beauty and the Beast

pp. 58–59

Stop & Think

- **What kind of a person was Beauty?** 美麗是什麼樣的人？

  ⇨ She was pretty, kind, and smart. 她很漂亮、既很善良，又聰明。

- **What happened to the merchant's ships?** 商人的船怎麼了？

  ⇨ They sank in a storm at sea. 它們在暴風雨中沉入大海裡了。

CHECK UP

1 Beauty's sisters were <u>selfish</u> and greedy.

2 Beauty was beautiful and <u>enjoyed</u> reading.

3 The merchant sold his house and moved to the <u>countryside</u>.

4 Their new house was very <u>tiny</u>.

1 美麗的姊姊又自私又貪心。

2 美麗很漂亮，喜歡看書。

3 商人把房子賣了，搬到鄉下。

4 他們的新家非常小。

pp. 60–61

Stop & Think

- **How did Beauty's sisters like their new house?** 美麗的姊姊喜歡他們的新家嗎？

  ⇨ They disliked it and complained a lot. 她們不喜歡，諸多抱怨。

- **What happened to Beauty's father's ship?** 美麗父親的船怎麼了？

  ⇨ Pirates stole all the ship's gold and silver, and the ship had many holes in it.
  海盜把船上的金銀搶走了，船破了很多洞。

1 Beauty worked hard and   **a.** cleaned every day.
2 One of Beauty's father's ships   **b.** afford to fix the ship.
3 Some pirates stole   **c.** did not sink.
4 Beauty's father could not   **d.** the gold and silver.

1 美麗辛勤地工作,每天打掃家裡。
2 美麗父親有一艘船沒有沉。
3 有些海盜掠奪了金銀。
4 美麗的父親負擔不起修船的費用。

pp. 62–63

Stop & Think

• **What did Beauty's father see in the dining room?** 美麗的父親在飯廳看到什麼?

⇨ There were a table full of food and a plate with a knife and fork beside it.
滿桌的食物,還有一個盤子旁邊放了刀叉。

CHECK UP

1 The weather suddenly became very cold.
2 Beauty's father saw a light in the forest.
3 There was no one in the castle.
4 Beauty's father sat down at the table and ate the food.

1 天氣突然變得很冷。
2 美麗的父親看到森林裡有光。
3 城堡裡沒有人。
4 美麗的父親在餐桌前坐下,吃桌上的食物。

pp. 64–65

Stop & Think

• **Why did Beauty's father go to the garden?** 美麗的父親為什麼要去花園?

⇨ To pick a rose for Beauty. 要摘一朵玫瑰花給美麗。

• **What did the Beast want Beauty's father to do in return for sending him home?**
野獸把美麗的父親送回家,要求什麼作為回報?

⇨ The Beast wanted Beauty's father to send his daughter to live in his castle with him.
野獸希望美麗的父親把女兒送到城堡裡跟他一塊住。

CHECK UP

1 The garden had many yellow roses.   F
2 The Beast wanted to eat Beauty's father.   F
3 The Beast gave Beauty's father a box of gold.   T

1 花園裡有許多黃玫瑰。
2 野獸想把美麗的父親吃掉。
3 野獸給美麗的父親一箱黃金。

pp. 66–67

Stop & Think

- **What did Beauty ask her father about the Beast?** 美麗問父親野獸怎麼樣？
  ⇨ She asked if the Beast was ugly. 她問野獸是不是很醜。
- **Who met Beauty at the castle?** 誰在城堡迎接美麗呢？
  ⇨ No one met her. 沒人迎接她。

CHECK UP

1 What did Beauty's father show her? (a)
   a. a box of gold   **b.** a picture of the Beast   **c.** a red rose

2 What was on the dining table? (b)
   a. nothing   **b.** Beauty's favorite foods   **c.** some cakes and pies

1 美麗的父親給她看什麼？
   a. 一箱黃金   **b.** 野獸的畫像   **c.** 紅玫瑰

2 飯桌上有什麼？
   a. 什麼都沒有   **b.** 美麗最愛吃的食物   **c.** 一些蛋糕和派

pp. 68–69

Stop & Think

- **What did Beauty find in the book?** 美麗在書裡找到什麼？
  ⇨ She found a note from the Beast. 她找到野獸寫給她的紙條。

CHECK UP

1 The <u>sign</u> on the door read "Beauty's Room."
2 The Beast had hair like a <u>lion</u>.
3 Beauty told the Beast that he was <u>ugly</u>.
4 Beauty thought the Beast was not so <u>frightening</u>.

1 門上的標示寫著「美麗的房間」。
2 野獸有像獅子一樣的毛髮。
3 美麗跟野獸說，他很醜。
4 美麗認為野獸沒有這麼可怕。

pp. 70–71

Stop & Think

- **What did the Beast ask Beauty to do?** 野獸要求美麗做什麼？
  ⇨ He asked Beauty to marry him. 他希望美麗嫁給他。
- **Why did Beauty want to go home?** 為什麼美麗想要回家？
  ⇨ Her father was sick in bed and all by himself. 她父親一個人生病臥床。

1 The Beast gave Beauty   a. had dinner together every night.
2 Beauty and the Beast   b. sick in bed.
3 Beauty saw her father   c. a magic mirror.

1 野獸給美麗一面魔鏡。
2 美麗和野獸每天一起共進晚餐。
3 美麗看見父親生病臥床。

pp. 72–73

Stop & Think

• **Why did the Beast give Beauty a ring?** 野獸為什麼要給美麗一枚戒指？
⇨ So Beauty could go to see her father and come back to the castle.
這樣美麗才可以去看她父親，也可以回到城堡。

• **How did Beauty feel about the Beast?** 美麗覺得野獸怎麼樣？
⇨ She liked him and almost loved him. 她喜歡他，幾乎愛上他了。

CHECK UP

1 Beauty <u>put on</u> the ring and went to bed.
2 In the morning, Beauty was in <u>her father's house</u>.
3 Beauty's sisters were very <u>unhappy</u>.

1 美麗戴上戒指，上床睡覺。
2 早上，美麗回到父親的家。
3 美麗的姊姊很不高興。

pp. 74–75

Stop & Think

• **Where did Beauty see the Beast?** 美麗在哪裡看見野獸？
⇨ She saw the Beast in her dream. 她在夢中看到野獸。

• **What did Beauty tell the Beast?** 美麗跟野獸說了什麼？
⇨ She loved him and wanted to marry him. 她愛上他，願意嫁給他。

CHECK UP

1 The Beast was dying in Beauty's dream.   T
2 Beauty woke up from the dream and removed the ring.   T
3 Beauty found the Beast in the dining room.   F

1 在美麗的夢裡野獸快死了。
2 美麗夢醒之後，摘下戒指。
3 美麗在飯廳找到野獸。

pp. 76–77

Stop & Think

• **What did the fairy do to the prince?** 仙子對王子做了什麼？
⇨ The fairy cursed the prince and turned him into the Beast. 仙子對王子下咒，把他變成野獸。

1 How did Beauty break the spell? (c)
   a. She kissed the Beast.   **b.** She married the Beast.   **c.** She loved the Beast.

2 What did the fairy promise Beauty and the prince? (a)
   a. many children   **b.** long lives   **c.** lots of money

1 美麗是怎麼破除魔咒的？
   a. 她親了野獸。   **b.** 她嫁給野獸。   **c.** 她愛野獸。
2 仙子答應要給美麗和野獸什麼？
   a. 許多孩子   **b.** 很長的壽命   **c.** 許多錢

The Stars

pp. 78–79

Stop & Think

• **Who did the shepherd sometimes see?** 牧羊人有時會看到什麼？
   ⇨ A loner and some coal miners. 獨居者和幾名煤礦工。

• **What news interested the shepherd the most?** 牧羊人最感興趣的消息是什麼？
   ⇨ News about Stephanette. 有關史達芬妮葉特的消息。

CHECK UP

1 The shepherd spent most of his time alone.   T
2 A person delivered supplies to the shepherd every week.   F
3 The shepherd often spoke with Stephanette.   F
4 One Sunday, the delivery boy arrived at ten o'clock.   F

1 牧羊人大部分的時間都獨自一人。
2 每週都有一個人幫牧羊人送補給品。
3 牧羊人常跟史達芬妮葉特說話。
4 某個週日，送貨的男孩十點才到達。

pp. 80–81

Stop & Think

• **Why did Stephanette come to the field?** 史達芬妮葉特為什麼到牧場來？
   ⇨ The farmhand was sick, and the old woman was visiting her children.
   農場工人生病了，老婦人去看她的小孩。

CHECK UP

1 The heavy rain delayed the delivery person.
2 The person on the mule was Stephanette.
3 Stephanette got lost on her way to the field.
4 Had the shepherd ever spoken to Stephanette before? (No)

1 下大雨讓送貨的人耽擱了。
2 騾子上的人是史達芬妮葉特。
3 史達芬妮葉特到牧場的路上迷路了。
4 牧羊人以前跟史達芬妮葉特說過話嗎？（不）

Stop & Think

- **What did the shepherd say to Stephanette?** 牧羊人跟史達芬妮葉特說了什麼？
  ⇨ He said nothing to her. 他什麼也沒跟她說。

- **Why did Stephanette return to the shepherd?** 為什麼史達芬妮葉特又回到牧羊人那裡？
  ⇨ She could not cross the river. 她過不了河。

CHECK UP

1 The shepherd's bed was   **a.** embarrassed in front of Stephanette.
2 The shepherd was   **b.** had risen too high.
3 Stephanette left to go   **c.** made of straw and sheepskin.
4 The water in the river   **d.** back to the farm.

1 牧羊人的床是用乾草和羊毛皮鋪成的。
2 牧羊人在史達芬妮葉特面前很害羞。
3 史達芬妮葉特離開，要回農場去。
4 河水漲得太高。

Stop & Think

- **How did the shepherd feel about taking care of Stephanette?**
  牧羊人覺得照顧史達芬妮葉特怎麼樣？
  ⇨ He felt proud of his responsibility. 他覺得為他的責任感到驕傲。

- **What did Stephanette suddenly do?** 史達芬妮葉特突然做了什麼？
  ⇨ She came out of the barn and sat by the fire. 她走出穀倉，坐在火堆旁。

CHECK UP

1 Where did the shepherd make a bed for Stephanette? (b)
   a. by the fire   **b.** in the barn   **c.** in the pasture

2 How did the noises make Stephanette feel? (b)
   a. warm   **b.** frightened   **c.** angry

1 牧羊人在哪裡為史達芬妮葉特鋪床？
   a. 火堆旁   **b.** 穀倉裡   **c.** 草場上
2 聲響讓史達芬妮葉特覺得怎麼樣？
   a. 溫暖   **b.** 害怕   **c.** 生氣

Stop & Think

- **What did the shepherd show Stephanette in the sky?** 牧羊人指著天上的什麼東西指給史達芬妮葉特看？
  ⇨ He showed her the Milky Way and the constellations. 他把銀河和星座指給她看。

CHECK UP

1 Stephanette pointed to a shooting star in the sky.
2 The Milky Way stretches across all of France.

3 Shepherds can <u>tell</u> time by looking at stars.

1 史達芬妮葉特指著天上的一顆流星。

2 銀河跨越了整個法國。

3 牧羊人可以靠觀星判斷時間。

pp. 88−89

Stop & Think

• **How did Stephanette fall asleep?** 史達芬妮葉特是怎麼睡著的？

  ⇨ With her head on the shepherd's shoulder. 頭靠在牧羊人的肩上。

CHECK UP

1 The <u>Evening Star</u> is the most beautiful star of all.

2 Stephanette <u>fell asleep</u> in front of the fire.

3 Stephanette <u>laid</u> her head on the shepherd's shoulder.

1 黃昏之星是所有星星中最美的一顆。

2 史達芬妮葉特在火堆前睡著了。

3 史達芬妮葉特把頭靠在牧羊人的肩上。

Michael A. Putlack
專攻歷史與英文，擁有美國麻州 Tufts University 碩士學位

e-Creative Contents
專為非母語英語學習者研發教材的創意團隊

國家圖書館出版品預行編目 (CIP) 資料

FUN學英語故事閱讀訓練(合訂本) / Michael A. Putlack, e-Creative
Contents著；陳怡靜、彭尊聖譯. -- 初版. -- [臺北市] :寂天文化,
2020.03
　　面；　公分
ISBN 978-986-318-902-2 （16K平裝附光碟片）

1.英語　2.讀本

805.18　　　　　　　　　　　　　　　　　　109002273

作　　　者	Michael A. Putlack & e-Creative Contents
譯　　　者	陳怡靜／彭尊聖
校　　　對	黃詩韻
編　　　輯	陳怡靜
封 面 設 計	郭瀞暄
內 文 排 版	郭瀞暄／執筆者
製 程 管 理	洪巧玲
出　版　者	寂天文化事業股份有限公司
電　　　話	+886-(0)2-2365-9739
傳　　　真	+886-(0)2-2365-9835
網　　　址	www.icosmos.com.tw
讀 者 服 務	onlineservice@icosmos.com.tw
出 版 日 期	2020 年 03 月 初版一刷

劃 撥 帳 號	1998620-0　寂天文化事業股份有限公司
	訂購金額 600（含）元以上郵資免費
	訂購金額 600 元以下者，請外加郵資 65 元
	【若有破損，請寄回更換，謝謝】

以名著閱讀法，打造閱讀原文書的實力
不用頻查字典就能品嚐最原味的感動

本書是廣受讀者喜愛的《超級英語閱讀訓練》的續集，內容由兩大部分構成，第一部分為全英文的課文，第二部分為拆解英文語句的解析文，精心設計名著閱讀法，從15篇世界經典童話故事和短篇小說中，堅實打造直接閱讀原文小說的實力。學會如何閱讀，就能在閱讀中學習知識。

本書由易至難共有六個學習階段（6 steps），依文章難易度分為兩冊：

Book 1 Step 1 ~ Step 3，適合初學者　　　**Book 2** Step 4 ~ Step 6，適合進階學習者

1 經典文學名著
佐彩繪插圖
> 本書共收錄15篇世界經典名著改編故事，搭配彩繪插圖賞心悅目，增添學習樂趣。故事內容類型豐富，包含童話故事、寓言及發人深省的短篇小說，品味文學芬芳，提升人文素養。

2 全英文課本
不需字典也能讀懂
> ◆ 英文單字搭配彩圖，圖像學習超 easy。
> ◆ 關鍵字彙與片語英英解釋，搭配上下文，熟練字彙運用。
> ◆ 課文行間穿插英文單字注釋，快速擴充字彙量，培養閱讀原文書實力。

3 訓練書英文語句、
文法結構大解密
> ◆ 透過「斷句法」（Chunking）掌握句子結構，達到「即讀即解」的成效。
> ◆ 中文翻譯與重要片語中英對照（Translations and Expressions）體會中英表達大不同。
> ◆ 用法特寫（Close Up）、文法解析（Grammar Point）解析片語、句型及文法等重要觀念，精心編寫超有料。

4 綜合測驗即時檢驗
學習成果
> ◆ 引導式問題（Stop & Think）➡ 抓出文章主旨及細節，以及培養獨立思考的能力。
> ◆ 英語檢定常見題型（Check Up）➡ 是非題、字彙選填、選擇題及配合題，為參加考試作準備。

5 生動故事朗讀MP3
> 由專業母語人士以正確、清晰的發音朗讀精采故事，加強聽力，同時練習發音及朗誦。

寂天　文化事業股份有限公司
Cosmos Culture Ltd.
www.icosmos.com.tw

FUN 學
英語故事閱讀訓練 2

Michael A. Putlack & e-Creative Contents_著

陳怡靜、彭尊聖_譯

Super
Reading
Story
Training
Book

MAIN
BOOK

以名著閱讀法，
打造閱讀原文書的實力

　　一旦掌握英語閱讀的技能，就能藉由閱讀拓展國際視野，因此閱讀訓練非常重要，是一定要打好基礎的入門功夫，《Fun學英語故事閱讀訓練》要把閱讀訓練法中最有效的「名著閱讀法」傳授給你，幫助讀者培養閱讀原文書的實力，體驗不用頻查字典就能品味原文小說的感動。

1 本套書精選15篇世界經典文學名著及改編童話故事，如丹麥安徒生童話之中的《小美人魚》、英國大文豪狄更斯的《聖誕頌歌》、俄國寫實作家托爾斯泰的《人靠什麼活著》等大作，帶你品味文學芬芳，提升人文素養；搭配彩繪插圖，賞心悅目，增添學習樂趣。

2 本書共有六個學習階段（6 steps），依文章難易度分為兩冊：
- Book 1　包含Step 1~Step 3，適合初學者
- Book 2　包含Step 4~Step 6，適合進階學習者

3 每一冊各分兩大部分，精心設計各種實用學習幫手，讓你更有效率、更輕鬆地學會閱讀原文書：
- 課本 Main Book：全英語呈現，藉由學習幫手不需字典也能讀懂
- 訓練書 Training Book：英文語句、文法結構大解密

4 讀完一段課文後，隨即有Stop & Think測驗掌握主旨及細節的能力，以及有Check Up練習各種常見的閱讀測驗題型，如字彙選填、是非題及配合題等5種題型變化，不僅驗收閱讀理解成效，也為日後參加英語檢定作準備。

強力推薦給這些人！

- 想把英語根基扎得又深又牢的人。
- 想順暢閱讀《時代》雜誌推薦小說原著的人。
- 想在多益、托福等各種英文考試中得高分的人。
- 想上全英語教學或雙語教學課程的人。
- 正準備出國留學的人。

培養不用字典就能讀原文小說的實力，現在，就讓它變成你的競爭力吧。

How to Use This Book

《Fun學英語故事閱讀訓練》共兩冊，每冊各分兩大部分，第一部分為全英文的課本，第二部分為拆解英文語句的訓練書，訓練書是為提升「即讀即解」的能力和「理解英語句子結構」的能力而編寫的。

Main Book | 課本 | 六個學習階段（6 steps），共15篇故事。

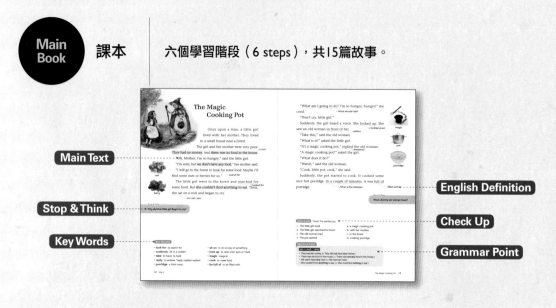

Main Text
Stop & Think
Key Words
English Definition
Check Up
Grammar Point

1 讀課文（Main Text）

首先，只看全英文的課文，不懂的單字或用語，可以透過精心設計的學習幫手了解字義，因此不需字典也能讀懂課文：

- 彩圖字彙解說，圖像學習超easy。
- 英英單字注釋（Key Words），快速擴充字彙量。
- 課文中附註英文釋義（English Definition），搭配上下文，熟練字彙運用。
- 文法解析（Grammar Point）學習常見句型。

2 試做練習題（Stop & Think / Check Up）

讀完課文後，立即透過5種測驗題型，檢核字彙能力及文章理解程度。

Stop & Think ➡ 引導式問題，訓練你抓出文章主旨（main idea）及細節（details），以及培養獨立思考的能力。

Check Up ➡ 英語檢定常見題型，是非題、字彙選填、選擇題及配合題，為參加考試作準備。

訓練書提供了即讀即解的課文，以意義為單位來斷句，以斜線（／）標示句子的結構，還設計了**用法特寫**（Close Up）和**文法解析**（Grammar Point），加強英文句型及文法能力。書末附有課本的正確答案和翻譯。

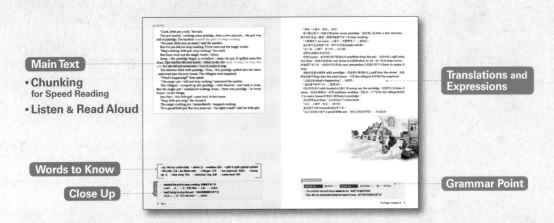

Main Text
• **Chunking** for Speed Reading
• **Listen & Read Aloud**

Words to Know

Close Up

Translations and Expressions

Grammar Point

3 查看訓練書
首先將單字學習（Words to Know）裡重要關鍵英單的中文釋義瀏覽一遍，接著讀斷句課文（Chunking），藉由清楚劃分句子的結構，可達到「即讀即解」的成效。再對照中文翻譯與重要片語中英對照（Translations and Expressions），以意義為單位來理解英文課文，同時亦作為中英翻譯練習參考，還可透過學習幫手Close Up，和Grammar Point學習片語、句型及文法。

4 挑戰看斷句課文自行翻譯
現在不看翻譯，參考活用斷句標示（／），試著自己翻譯英文課文。若有不明之處，就再確認中文釋義和英文用法，反覆查看，直到完全理解為止。

5 聽MP3朗讀並複誦
背英文時，一面看一面讀出聲音，記得更牢。本書隨書附贈MP3，課文皆由英語母語人士以正確、清晰的發音朗讀。聽課文時，要注意斜線（／）斷句的地方，並注意聽母語人士的發音、語調及連音等。最好自己在課文上把語調和連音標示出來，然後大聲地跟著MP3朗誦，盡量跟上英語母語人士的速度。

6 不聽MP3，自己朗讀課文
接著，不聽MP3，自己唸課文，並盡量唸得與母語人士一樣。若有發音或語調不順的地方，就再聽一次MP3，反覆練習。

7 重新閱讀英文課文
現在再回來看課本，再讀一次英文課文，並試著解題，如果讀得很順，練習題也都答對，訓練就成功了。

★ 正確答案請見訓練書書末的〈Answers & Translations〉。

The Introduction of Training Book

訓練書
特色説明

透過「斷句」掌握「即讀即解」的竅門

　　為了能更快、更正確地閱讀英文，就需要能夠掌握英文的句子結構。而要培養英文句子結構的敏銳度，最好的方法就是以各「意義單元組」來理解句子，也就是將英文句子的「意義單元組」（具一個完整意義的片語或詞組），用斷句（chunk）的方式分開，然後再來理解句子。只要能理解各個「意義單元組」，那麼再長的句子，都能被拆解與理解。

　　聽力也是一樣，要區分「意義單元組」，這樣能幫助很快聽懂英文。例如下面這個句子可以拆解成兩個部分：

> I am angry at you.
> I am angry / at you
> **我生氣　　　　對你**

　　我們會發現，這個句子由兩個「意義單元組」所組成。不管句子多長多複雜，都是由最簡單的基本句型（主詞＋動詞）發展而成，然後再在這個主要句子上，依照需求，添加上許多片語，以表現各式各樣的句意。

　　在面對英文時，腦子裡能立刻自動快速分離基本句型和片語，就能迅速讀懂或聽懂英文。在讀誦英文時，從一個人的斷句，大致就能看出個人的英文能力。現在再來看稍微長一點的句子。經過斷句以後，整個句子變得更清楚易懂，閱讀理解就沒問題了：

> Beauty was not only pretty / but also kind and smart.
> **美麗不僅漂亮　　　　　　　還很善良、聰明**

一個句子有幾個斷句？

一個句子有幾個斷句？有幾個「意義單元組」？這是依句子的情況和個人的英語能力，而有不同的。一般來説，以下這些地方通常就是斷句的地方：

★ 在「主詞＋動詞」之後
★ 在 and、but、or 等連接詞之前
★ 在 that、who 等關係詞之前
★ 在副詞、不定詞 to 等的前後

另外，主詞很長時，時常為了要區分出主詞，在主詞後也會斷句。例如：

A man / who wants to learn / can learn anything.
人　　　願意學習　　　　　就能學會任何事

對初學者來説，一個句子裡可能會有很多斷句的斜線，而當閱讀能力越來越強之後，你需要斷句的地方就會越來越少，到後來甚至能一眼就看懂句子，不需要用斷句的方式來幫助理解。

本訓練書因為考慮到初學者，所以盡可能細分可斷句處，只要是能分為一個「意義單元組」的地方，訓練書上就標示出斷句。等你的英文實力逐漸提升，到了覺得斷句變成是一種累贅，能夠不用再做任何標記就能讀懂課文時，就是你的英文能力更進一階的時候了。透過斷句的練習，熟悉英語的排列順序和結構，你會驚訝地發現到，自己的閱讀能力突飛猛進！

Table of
Contents

BOOK 2

BOOK 1

Super
Reading
Story
Training
Book

4

What Men Live By

— Leo Tolstoy

•

How Much Land Does a Man Need?

— Leo Tolstoy

What Men Live By

shoemaker

hut

fret

naked

There was once a poor shoemaker named Simon. He had no house or land. He lived in a hut with his wife → *small house, cottage* and children. One morning, he went to the village to buy some sheepskins for a winter coat. He had only three rubles, but he planned to visit some of his → *was going to* customers on the way. They owed him five rubles for → *had to pay* work he had already done. ← *while going there*

Simon visited several customers' houses, but he could not collect any money. He went to the store and → *gather, receive* asked if he could buy the sheepskins on credit. But the → *whether* → *without cash* shopkeeper refused to give them to Simon. → *turned down ≠ accepted*

Simon felt downhearted and started walking → *was sad* homeward. "Though I have no sheepskin coat, I don't care. I can live without a coat. Yet my wife will surely → *Still, Nevertheless* fret," he thought. → *get upset*

While he was walking home, he passed by a church → *went by*

Stop & Think

Why couldn't Simon pay for the sheepskins?

KEY WORDS

- **on the way** while going somewhere
- **refuse** to turn down; to reject
- **homeward** toward home
- **robber** a thief
- **look back** to look behind oneself
- **owe** to have to pay money to
- **feel downhearted** to be sad; to be depressed
- **naked** having no clothes on
- **interfere** to get involved
- **frightened** scared

at the bend in the road. Simon saw something white behind the church. He did not know what it was. He came closer, and, to his surprise, it was a naked man. He was sitting against the church without any clothes on.

→ *not wearing any clothes*

Suddenly, Simon felt afraid. "Robbers must have killed him and stolen his clothes. If I interfere, I will have a big problem," Simon thought.

Thieves ←
steal-stole-stolen ←
→ *get involved*

Simon continued walking, but when he looked back, he saw the man was moving. Simon felt more frightened.

→ *scared*

"If I go there, he might kill me for my clothes. Even if he doesn't attack me, what can I do for him?" thought Simon.

Even though ←

He ran down the road. But he suddenly stopped.

→ *≠ defend*

robber

Stop & Think
What did Simon see behind the church?

CHECK UP True or false?

1 Simon had five rubles. _____
2 Simon wanted to buy some sheepskins. _____
3 There was a robber next to the church. _____
4 Simon was afraid of the naked man. _____

GRAMMAR POINT

though / if / even if

- **Though** I have no sheepskin coat, I don't care.
- **If** I interfere, I will have a big problem.
- **Even if** he doesn't attack me, what can I do for him? (**even if = even though**)

stick

surprised

felt boots

"What am I doing? The man could be dying!" He felt guilty, so he turned around and went back to the church. ⤳ felt bad   ⤳ turned back

When Simon went behind the church, he saw that the stranger was a young man. He was freezing and frightened. Simon immediately took off his coat and put it around the man. Then, he put boots on the man. Simon had an extra pair of boots. ⤳ very cold   ⤳ removed ≠ put on   ⤳ ≠ took off   ⤳ additional

"Can you walk?" asked Simon. "It's too cold to stay here. I will take you to my home. Here is a stick for you to lean on while you walk." ⤳ rest on   ⤳ got up *stand–stood–stood

The man stood up and looked kindly at Simon. But he did not speak. As they walked to Simon's home, Simon asked him where he was from and how he got to the church. The man replied with a calm voice, "I'm not from around here. God has punished me." ⤳ quiet

Simon was surprised by the response. But he said, "Well, God rules all men. Come home with me and at ⤳ controls

---

Stop & Think

What did Simon give the man?

KEY WORDS

- **feel guilty** to feel bad
- **freezing** very cold
- **punish** to penalize a person for doing something wrong
- **disappointment** the state of being disappointed; displeasure
- **drunk** a person who is drunk
- **drunkard** a drunk
- **go back** to return
- **lean on** to lean against; to rest on
- **supper** a light dinner

least make yourself warm." As Simon walked with the stranger, he felt glad to help another person.

Simon's wife was preparing dinner when Simon and the man came into the house. Matryna noticed that the man had no hat and was wearing felt boots. And he was wearing her husband's coat. Simon had no sheepskins. Her heart was ready to break with disappointment. "He has been out drinking, and now he has brought another drunk home with him," she thought.

saw, became aware ⟵ (noticed)
was about to (was ready to)
≠ satisfaction (disappointment)
bring–brought–brought (brought)

drunk = drunkard

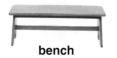
bench

vodka

Simon took off his hat and sat down on the bench as if things were all right. Then, he said, "Have a seat, my friend, and let us have some dinner."

Matryna became very angry and said, "I cooked dinner, but not for you. You went out to buy some sheepskins but bring a strange man home instead. He doesn't even have any clothes of his own. You must have spent all our money on vodka. I have no supper for drunkards like you."

drunks (drunkards)

Stop & Think
What did Simon's wife think about her husband?

CHECK UP Finish the sentences.

1 The man said that
2 Simon felt glad
3 Matryna was
4 Matryna thought that Simon

a. very disappointed with Simon.
b. to help another person.
c. was a drunkard.
d. God had punished him.

GRAMMAR POINT

what/where/how . . . + S + V (indirect question)

* Simon asked him **where he was** from and **how he got** to the church.

curious

anger

be folded

in pain

Simon tried to explain to his wife how he had met the man, but she did not listen. She angrily walked out the door, but then she stopped undecidedly; she wanted to work off her anger, but she also wanted to learn what sort of a man the stranger was. She was curious about the man.

not decided, not determined

release

"If he were a good man, he would not be naked. Where is he from?" she asked.

"That's just what I'm trying to tell you," answered Simon. "When I passed the church, I saw him sitting there naked and frozen. God made me go to help him, or he would have died. What should I have done? So I helped him get up, gave him my coat, and brought him here. Don't be so angry with me. Anger is a sin."

went by

ice cold

Being mad or angry

As Matryna listened to her husband, she looked closely at the man. He sat on the bench without moving. His hands were folded on his knees, and he looked down at the floor. His eyes were closed as if he were in pain.

fold–folded–folded

hurting, pained

Stop & Think

What did Simon say to make Matryna calm down?

KEY WORDS

- **undecidedly** unable to make up one's mind
- **sin** something one does that is against the laws of God
- **be in pain** to hurt   • **soften** to become less hard (≠ harden)
- **feel pity for** to feel bad for someone (= take pity on)   • **feed** to give food to someone
- **reward** to give something to someone for doing a good deed

"Matryna, don't you love God?" asked Simon.

Suddenly, her heart softened toward the stranger. She
went back into the kitchen. She set the table and served
→ became soft
dinner. While they were eating, Matryna felt pity for
felt sorry ←
the stranger. She did not feel angry anymore. She even
began to like him. At that moment, the man looked
at Matryna and smiled at her. A light seemed to come
from his face.
→ appeared to

set the table

When they had finished supper, she asked the man
where he was from. But the man said he did not know.
All he said was, "God punished
me. I was naked and freezing
cold. Then, Simon saw
→ felt pity for, pitied
me, took pity on me, and
brought me here. You have
→ feed–fed–fed
fed me and pitied me, too.
→ pity–pitied–pitied
God will reward you."

repay ≠ punish

CHECK UP Answer the questions.

1 What did Matryna feel for the stranger?
   a. concern   **b.** love   **c.** pity
2 What happened after the man smiled?
   a. A light came from his face.   **b.** Simon felt pity for him.   **c.** Matryna's heart softened.

GRAMMAR POINT

if . . . (subjunctive)

* If he **were** a good man, he **would** not **be** naked.
* God made me go to help him, or he **would have died**.
  (= **If** God **had** not **made** me go to help him, he **would have died**.)

grieved

wake up

Matryna gave the man some clothes, and he went to get some sleep. Then, she and Simon went to bed, too, but Matryna could not sleep. She could not get the stranger out of her mind. Then, she suddenly remembered that they had eaten their last piece of bread, so there was nothing left for tomorrow. She felt grieved.

> forgot
> felt sad, felt very bad

"Simon, what will we do tomorrow?"

"As long as we are alive, we will find something to eat," Simon answered.

The next morning, Simon and Matryna woke up and saw that the stranger was already awake. He looked much better than the day before.

> not sleeping ≠ asleep

Simon said, "Well, friend, we have to work for a living. What work do you know?"

"I do not know anything," answered the man.

Surprised, Simon said, "A man who wants to learn can learn anything."

> Shocked

"Then I will learn how to work."

"What is your name?" asked Simon.

Stop & Think

What work did Michael know?

KEY WORDS

- **get . . . out of one's mind** to forget about something
- **feel grieved** to feel very bad
- **wake up** ≠ fall asleep
- **awake** ≠ asleep
- **carriage** a wagon drawn by horses
- **servant** a person who works for another
- **stride into** to walk into *stride–strode–stridden
- **master** a skilled person; a person in charge

"Michael."

"Well, Michael, if you work with me, I will give you food and shelter," offered Simon.

shelter ---> a safe place, a home

"May God reward you," answered Michael. "Show me what to do."

Simon showed Michael how to make boots. Michael learned quickly and was very skilled. He ate little food and almost never went anywhere.

skilled ---> skillful

carriage

servant

He made boots so well that many people came to Simon's shop. Soon, Simon began to make a lot of money.

make a lot of money ---> earn money

A year passed. Michael lived and worked with Simon. One day, Simon and Michael were working hard when a carriage drawn by three horses drove up to the hut. A servant opened the door, and a gentleman wearing a fur coat got out. He strode into the hut and asked, "Which of you is the master bootmaker?"

drawn ---> pulled by *draw-drew-drawn
drove up ---> went up to *drive-drove-driven
got out ---> got off ≠ got on
strode into ---> walked into
bootmaker ---> shoemaker

fur coat

Stop & Think

Who was in the carriage?

CHECK UP Put the right words.

| Michael | skilled | bread | shelter |

1 Simon and Matryna had no more of _____.
2 The stranger's name was _____.
3 Simon offered Michael food and _____ in return for work.
4 Michael became a very _____ bootmaker.

GRAMMAR POINT

"–ing" form (present participle) / "–ed" form (past participle)

• A gentleman **wearing** a fur coat got out. (**active meaning**)

• A carriage **drawn** by three horses drove up to the hut. (**passive meaning**)

leather

lose one's shape

"I am, sir," Simon answered.

Then the gentleman said, "Do you see this leather here?"

"Yes, it is good leather, sir."

"You fool," laughed the gentleman. "It is the finest [*best, nicest*] leather. It comes from Germany and is extremely [*very, really*] expensive. I want you to make me a pair of boots that will last for years. [*remain in a good condition*] If they lose their shape [*change shape*] or fall apart, [*break*] I will throw you into prison. [*send*] [*jail*] After one year, if the boots are still good, I will pay you ten rubles for them," said the rich man.

Simon was terrified, [*very scared*] but Michael advised him to make the boots. So Simon agreed, and then he measured the gentleman's feet. While he was doing that, Simon saw Michael was gazing behind the rich man as if someone were there. [*looking, staring*]

Suddenly, Michael smiled, and his face turned bright.
→ became

"What are you grinning at, you fool?" shouted the
→ smiling at

man. "You had better make these boots on time. I will

come back in two days."
→ not late

prison

"They will be ready," answered Michael.

After he left, Simon looked at Michael and said,

"Michael, we must be cautious with this expensive

leather. We cannot make a single mistake."
→ careful

measure

Michael started cutting the leather, but he did not

cut it for boots. Instead, he started to make soft slippers.

Simon saw what Michael was doing, and he was

shocked.
→ surprised

slippers

"What are you doing, Michael? The gentleman

ordered boots, not slippers. You've ruined that leather.

What's going to happen to me now?"
→ spoiled, destroyed

Stop & Think
**What did Michael do when he looked
behind the gentleman?**

CHECK UP Choose the right words.

1 The gentleman showed Simon some _____ leather. (expensive | cheap)
2 The gentleman _____ Simon. (angered | terrified)
3 The gentleman wanted his boots in _____. (two weeks | two days)
4 Michael made _____ for the gentleman. (boots | slippers)

GRAMMAR POINT

as if . . . (subjunctive)

• Michael was gazing behind the rich man **as if** someone **were** there.

rush

corpse

crippled

At that very moment, the gentleman's servant rushed into the hut.   *hurried into, ran into* ←

"My master does not need boots anymore," he announced. "He is dead. He did not even make it home alive as he died in the carriage. My master's wife sent me here to cancel the order for boots. Instead, she wants you to quickly make a pair of soft slippers for his corpse."   *dead body*   → *shocked, stunned*

→ *stated, said*

→ *because, since*

→ *stop*

Simon was amazed. Michael took the pair of soft slippers he made and handed them to the servant.   → *gave to*

More time passed, and Michael had now lived with Simon for six years. He never went anywhere, and he was always quiet. He had only smiled two times in six years: once when Matryna gave him food and a second time when the rich man was in their hut. Simon adored Michael and was afraid that Michael would leave him.   → *didn't go anywhere*   → *for*   *liked very much, loved* ←

One day, one of Simon's sons came running to Michael. "Uncle Michael," he cried, "Look! A lady with two little girls is coming, and one of the girls is lame."   *unable to walk properly* ←

Stop & Think

What happened to the gentleman?

KEY WORDS

- **corpse** a dead body
- **hand . . . to** to give something to someone
- **lame** unable to walk properly
- **be a master at** to be very skilled at doing something
- **confused** puzzled; not understanding
- **give birth to** to bear; to produce a baby
- **amazed** shocked; stunned
- **adore** to like very much (≠ hate)
- **crippled** disabled
- **crush one's leg** to break one's leg

12 *Step 4*

Michael immediately stopped work and looked out the window. Simon was surprised since Michael never looked outside. Simon also looked out and saw that a well–dressed woman with two little girls was coming to his hut. One of the girls was crippled in her left leg.

⌐⤳ disabled

twins

The woman came in and said, "I want leather shoes for these two girls for spring."

Simon answered, "I have never made such small shoes, but my assistant Michael is a master at making shoes, so he can do it."

⤳ helper   ⤳ is very skilled at

give birth to

Michael was staring at the girls as if he had known

looking at, gazing at ⤙⋯   ⋯⤳ like

them before. Simon was confused, but he began to

⋯⤳ puzzled

measure the girls' feet. The woman mentioned that the

⤳ said, told

girls were twins.

Simon asked, "How did it happen to her? Was she born this way?"

broke, squashed ⤙⋯

"No," the woman answered. "Her mother crushed her leg. Their father died one week before they were

⌐⤳ die-died-died

born. And their mother died right after she gave birth

bore ⤙⋯

to them."

CHECK UP True or false?

1 Michael smiled two times in six years.   _____
2 A woman with two girls came to Simon's hut.   _____
3 The two girls were cousins.   _____
4 The woman was the girls' mother.   _____

GRAMMAR POINT

tense agreement

• Simon **was** afraid that Michael **would** leave him.

nurse

sigh

wipe tears

She continued, "My husband and I were their neighbors. When I visited their hut, I found that the mother, when dying, had rolled on this child and crushed her leg. The babies were left alone. What could I do? I was the only woman in the village with a baby, so I took both girls and nursed them as well.

people who live near another

rolled over onto

broke

"I thought the crippled one would die, so I did not feed her at first. But I had so much milk that I could feed my son and both girls. Then, my own son died when he was two." She sighed.

"I thank God for giving me these two girls. I would be very lonely without them. They are precious to me."

lonesome, feeling alone

She wiped some tears from her face as she told the story.

wipe–wiped–wiped

very dear, valuable

a wise saying

Then, Matryna said, "The old proverb is true. 'One may live without father or mother, but one cannot live without God.'"

Stop & Think

How did the girl's leg get injured?

KEY WORDS

- **roll on** to roll over onto
- **nurse** to provide milk for a baby; to feed
- **lonely** feeling alone
- **proverb** a wise saying
- **forgive** to pardon *forgive–forgave–forgiven

- **crush** to break; to squash
- **sigh** to exhale loudly
- **precious** dear; valuable
- **bow** to bend over in a sign of respect
- **gloomy** sad; depressing

As they talked, suddenly a bright light filled the room. They looked at Michael, who was the source of this light. He was smiling and looking up at the heavens.

origin ⤙
the sky ⤏

heavens

After the woman left with the girls, Michael bowed low to Simon and Matryna. "Farewell," he said. "God has forgiven me. I ask your forgiveness, too, for anything I have done wrong."

Goodbye ⤏
pardoned ⤏
beg forgiveness ⤏

bow

They saw a light was shining from Michael. Simon bowed to Michael and said, "I see that you are not an ordinary man. But please tell me. When I first met you and brought you home, you were quite gloomy. But you smiled at my wife after she gave you some food. Then, when the rich man came and ordered boots, you smiled again. Finally, when the woman brought the girls, you smiled a third time. And now you have become as bright as day. Why is your face shining like that, and why did you smile those three times?"

normal ⤏
sad, depressing ⤏

shine

Stop & Think

What happened as everyone was talking?

CHECK UP Finish the sentences.

1 The woman said the girls
2 Michael asked Simon and Matryna
3 Simon realized that Michael

a. was not an ordinary man.
b. were precious to her.
c. to forgive him.

GRAMMAR POINT

may

• One **may** live without father or mother. (**possibility**)

angel

breast

pray

Michael answered, "Light is shining from me because I was punished, but now God has forgiven me. I smiled three times because God sent me here to learn three truths, and I have learned them. I learned the first

----→ facts

when your wife pitied me, so I smiled then. I learned

----→ at that time

the second when the rich man ordered the boots, so I smiled again. And I learned the third when I saw the little girls, so I smiled for the third time."

Simon asked, "Michael, why did God punish you? And what are the three truths? I would like to learn them for myself."

Michael answered, "God punished me because I disobeyed him. I was an angel in Heaven, but I

----→ ≠ obey

disobeyed God. God sent me to take the soul of a

make the person die ←----

woman. I came down to Earth and saw a sick woman lying alone. She had just given birth to twin girls. The woman saw me and said, 'Angel of God, my husband has just died, and there is no one to look after my girls.

----→ nurse, take care of

Stop & Think

Why did God punish Michael?

KEY WORDS

- **disobey** to not follow a command or order
- **care for** to take care of
- **pray** to make a prayer
- **dwell** to live

- **lie alone** to be by oneself
- **breast** a woman's chest
- **stay alive** to not die
- **live by** to be supported by

16 *Step 4*

Do not take my soul. Let me live to care for my babies. Children cannot live without father or mother.'"

take care of

Michael continued, "I put one child at her breast and put the other in her arms. Then, I returned to Heaven. I told God, 'I could not take the mother's soul. Her husband died, and the woman has twins and prays to stay alive.'"

live, not to die

"But God said, 'Go back and take the woman's soul, and learn three truths: Learn what dwells in man. Learn what is not given to man. And learn what men live by. When you learn all three things, you may return to Heaven.'"

lives

be supported by

Stop & Think

What did God order Michael to learn about?

CHECK UP Answer the questions.

1 Why did Michael smile three times?
   a. He learned three truths. **b.** He saw God. **c.** He knew the little girls.

2 Whose soul was Michael supposed to take?
   a. Simon's soul **b.** the mother's soul **c.** the girls' souls

GRAMMAR POINT

be + p.p. (passive)
- I **was punished** (by God), but now God has forgiven me.
- Learn what **is** not **given** to man.

wings

crawl

frown

"So I flew back to Earth and took the mother's soul. The babies fell from her breast. Her body rolled over on

fall–fell–fallen

the bed and crushed one of the baby's legs. I tried to fly up to Heaven with the mother's soul, but my wings suddenly dropped off. Then, I fell to Earth. That is how you found me, Simon."

> fell off

Simon and Matryna now understood who had been living with them, so they began to cry for joy. ⟶ happiness

The angel Michael said, "I was alone in the field and naked. I had never known cold or hunger until I became a man. I crawled to a church. Then, I saw a man coming down the road.

"He frowned as he passed me, but he came back a few minutes later. He gave me some clothes and brought me to his house. When I entered the house, his wife

looked ⟵ seemed very angry. She wanted to send me back into the cold, but her husband mentioned God to her. The woman changed at once. When she brought me some

⟶ instantly

Stop & Think

What did Michael do when he returned to Earth?

KEY WORDS

- **drop off** to fall off
- **frown** ≠ smile
- **mention** to say about something

- **crawl** to walk on one's hands and feet
- **stand** ≠ sit
- **last** to continue in time; to remain in useful condition

food, I looked at her. I noticed she had changed. She had become alive, and God was in her." → teaching

"Then, I remembered the first lesson God had sent me. God told me, 'Learn what dwells in man.' I understood. It was love. Love lives in men. God had shown me the first truth, so I smiled." → show–showed–shown

"After a year, a rich gentleman came to order some boots. I looked at him and saw the Angel of Death standing behind him. Only I could see the Angel of Death, so I knew that he would die soon. The man was about to die, yet he wanted boots that would last for years." → was going to

"Then, I remembered God's second order: → command 'Learn what is not given to man.' I learned that men are not given the knowledge to know what they need. So I smiled for a second time."

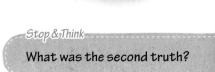

Stop & Think

What was the second truth?

CHECK UP Choose the right words.

1 Michael could return to _____ after he learned all three truths. (Heaven | Earth)
2 Michael learned the _____ truth from Matryna. (first | second)
3 Michael learned another truth from the _____. (rich man | poor man)

GRAMMAR POINT

not/never . . . until . . .

• I had **never** known cold or hunger **until** I became a man.

roof

ray of light

"I still did not know the third truth, so I have waited for God to reveal it.

⟶ show ≠ hide

"In my sixth year here, the woman and the two girls came. I recognized the girls and listened to how the

⟶ knew

woman had kept them alive. After she told the story, I

⟶ living ≠ dead

realized that the woman had loved two children who were not her own. I saw the living God in her, and then I learned the last lesson: I learned what men live by. I knew God had revealed it to me and had forgiven me, so I smiled for a third time."

⟶ was enclosed by

Just then, Michael's body was surrounded by a bright light. He said, "I have learned that all men live not by care for themselves but by love. I did not die because a man and his wife took pity on me and loved me. The

Stop & Think

What was the third truth?

→ children with no parents

orphans stayed alive because of the love of a woman who was not their mother. And all men live because love is in them. A person who has love is in God, and God is in that person because God is love."

Then, the roof opened, and a ray of light fell down

spread–spread–spread ←

from Heaven. Michael spread his wings and flew up in the light.
→ went up

Simon stood there, gazing after him. After a while, the roof was closed. No one but Simon and his family remained.

→ were left

CHECK UP   Choose the right words.

1 Michael learned the _____ truth from the woman. (third | second)
2 A _____ light surrounded Michael's body. (dim | bright)
3 Did Michael fly away from Simon's house? (Yes | No)

GRAMMAR POINT

because + S + V / because of + noun

- I did not die **because** a man and his wife took pity on me and loved me.
- The orphans stayed alive **because of** the love of a woman.
- All men live **because** love is in them.

How Much Land Does a Man Need?

An elder sister went to visit her younger sister in the country. The elder sister was married to a tradesman in town and the younger sister to a peasant in the village.

> peasant → poor farmer

As the sisters sat over their tea talking, the elder began

> sat over their tea talking → talking over a cup of tea

to boast about the advantages of town life. She talked

> boast → brag
> advantages → benefit ≠ disadvantages

about how comfortably they lived there, how well

> comfortably → easily

they dressed, what good things they ate and drank, and how she went to the theater and other types of entertainment.

> entertainment → something fun

peasant

theater

The younger sister was annoyed and in turn mocked

> annoyed → bothered
> mocked → laughed at

the life of a tradesman. She stood up for the life of a

> stood up for → defended

peasant.

"I would not change my way of life for yours," she said. "We may live roughly, but at least we are free

> roughly → toughly

from anxiety. You live in a better style than we do, but

> anxiety → worry

though you often earn more than you need, you are very likely to lose all you have."

> likely → seem to, look like

Stop & Think

Why was the younger sister annoyed?

KEY WORDS

- **peasant** a poor farmer
- **in turn** one after another; as a result of something
- **stand up for** to defend
- **chatter** talking; gossip

- **annoyed** bothered
- **mock** to make fun of; to laugh at
- **lie on** to recline on
- **the Devil** Satan; Lucifer

She continued, "We know the proverb 'Loss and gain are brothers twain.' It often happens that people who are wealthy one day are begging for their bread the next. Our way is safer. Though a peasant's life is not a fat one, it is long."

saying → proverb
two → twain
asking for → begging
not a rich life → not a fat one

beg

Pahom, the master of the house, was lying on the top of the stove, and he listened to the women's chatter.

the head of the household → the master of the house
talking, gossip → chatter

"It is perfectly true," he said. "Busy as we are from childhood farming Mother Earth, we peasants have no time to let any nonsense settle in our heads. Our only trouble is that we haven't got enough land. If I had plenty of land, I wouldn't fear the Devil himself!"

the earth → Mother Earth
live in → settle in
be afraid of → fear

The women finished their tea, chatted a while about dresses, and then cleared away the tea things and lay down to sleep. But the Devil had been sitting behind the stove and had heard all that was said.

cleaned up → cleared away

Stop & Think

How would Pahom feel if he had plenty of land?

CHECK UP Answer the questions.

1 How did the younger sister feel about her way of life?
   a. She felt anxious.　**b.** She liked it.　**c.** She wanted to change it.

2 Where was the Devil sitting?
   a. on the stove　**b.** behind the stove　**c.** under the stove

GRAMMAR POINT

that + S + V (that–clause)

- **It** often happens **that** people who are wealthy one day are begging for their bread the next.
- Our only trouble is **that** we haven't got enough land.

How Much Land Does a Man Need?　**23**

seed

sow

harvest

plow

He was pleased to hear that the man had boasted that if he had plenty of land, he would not fear the Devil himself.

"All right," thought the Devil. "We will have a contest. I'll give you enough land, and by means of that land, I will get you into my power."

⌐⟶ compete, bet   ⌐⟶ through

One day, Pahom heard that a neighbor was going to buy fifty acres of land, so he felt envious. Pahom and his wife sold some of their property and borrowed some money. Then, they bought a farm of forty acres.

⌐⟶ sell–sold–sold   ⌐⟶ was jealous   ⌐⟶ ≠ lent

So now Pahom had land of his own. He borrowed seed and sowed it on the land he had bought. The harvest was a good one, and within a year, he had managed to pay off his debts. So he became a landowner. When he went out to plow his fields or to look at his growing corn, his heart would fill with joy.

⌐⟶ planted   ⌐⟶ pay back the money   ⌐⟶ be filled with

- **property** land or buildings
- **trespass** to go onto land that is not one's own
- **district court** regional court
- **be taught a lesson** to be punished
- **sneak onto** to go somewhere without being seen

- **manage to** to be able to do; to deal with
- **lose patience** to become impatient
- **overlook** to ignore; to forget about
- **upset with** angry at
- **take someone to court** to sue a person

However, over time, some of the peasants in the neighborhood began to trespass across Pahom's land with their cows and horses. For a long time, Pahom forgave the owners. But at last he lost patience and complained to the district court. He thought, "I cannot go on overlooking it, or they will destroy all I have. They must be taught a lesson."

as time goes by
became impatient
forgiving
*be punished *teach–taught–taught*

Pahom began to fine his neighbors for trespassing on his land. This made them very upset with him, so they started to trespass on his land on purpose. Sometimes, they even sneaked onto his land at night and chopped down his trees. Pahom was furious.

charge money
angry at
intentionally
cut down
very angry

He tried to figure out who was doing it, and he decided that it was probably Simon. He took Simon to court, but Pahom had no evidence against Simon. The judges let Simon go, so Pahom got angry at them and quarreled with the judges and with his neighbors. Threats to burn his building began to be uttered.

find out
sued
proof
Warnings
said

sneak

furious

judge

Stop & Think

Why did Pahom fine his neighbors?

CHECK UP Finish the sentences.

1. The Devil decided to
2. Pahom bought a farm
3. Pahom's neighbors began to
4. Pahom took Simon

a. and became a landowner.
b. trespass on his land on purpose.
c. have a contest with Pahom.
d. to court for trespassing.

GRAMMAR POINT

if . . . (subjunctive)

• If he **had** plenty of land, he **would** not **fear** the Devil himself.

rumor

estate

About this time, there was a rumor that many people were moving to a new place. "There's no need for me to leave my land," thought Pahom. "But some of the others might leave our village, and then there would be more room for us. I would take over their land myself and make my estate a bit bigger."

gossip

space
land
get control of

One day, Pahom was sitting at home when a peasant passing through the village happened to call on him. The peasant was allowed to stay the night, and supper was given to him. Pahom had a talk with this peasant and asked him where he had come from. The stranger answered that he had come from beyond the Volga River, where he had been working. He said that many people were moving there. Anyone who moved to the village was given twenty–five acres of land for free.

going through
visit
past
for nothing

"The land there is very good," said the peasant. "One peasant moved to the village with nothing at all, but now he is very wealthy."

Pahom's heart was filled with desire. He thought, "Why should I suffer in this narrow hole if one can live

experience pain

Stop & Think

What did the stranger tell Pahom about the village?

KEY WORDS

- **rumor** gossip or information which may not be true
- **pass through** to go through
- **for free** without having to pay money for
- **find out** to learn about
- **grow tired of** to get tired of; to dislike

- **estate** a large amount of land
- **call on** to visit a person
- **suffer** to experience pain
- **better off** richer; wealthier
- **rush for** to hurry after; to run to

so well elsewhere? I will sell my land here, and with the money I get, I will start all over again with more land. But I must first go and find out all about it myself."

ten times

So Pahom went down to the land beyond the Volga. It was just as the stranger had said. The peasants owned plenty of land. The village gave each person twenty–five acres of land, and people could also buy as much land as they could afford. Pahom moved with his family to the new settlement.

→ once again, from beginning

had ←

→ be able to pay

→ place to live

argue

Pahom had much more land than before. In fact, he was ten times better off than he had been. This made Pahom very happy. But after he got used to it, he began to think that even here he did not have enough land. He grew tired of having to rent other people's land every year. Wherever there was good land to be had, the peasants would rush for it and argue about the land.

→ richer, wealthier

→ was adapted to

→ got tired of   → lease

→ run to

Stop & Think

Why was Pahom not happy in the village?

CHECK UP   True or false?

1 The peasant came from a land beyond the Volga River.   _____
2 The village beyond the Volga gave everyone 250 acres of land for free.   _____
3 Pahom visited the village to find out about the land.   _____
4 Pahom was ten times better off than before.   _____

GRAMMAR POINT

where / wherever (relative adverb)

• He went to *a place* **where** they had pitched their tents.

• He had come from *beyond the Volga River*, **where** he had been working.

• **Wherever** there was good land to be had, the peasants would rush for it.

chief

prairie

gift

"If it were my own land," thought Pahom, "I would be independent, and there would not be all this unpleasantness."

> free ≠ dependent

So Pahom began looking out for land which he could buy. One day, a peddler went by his house. He said that he was just returning from the land of the Bashkirs, which was far away. There, he had bought thirteen thousand acres of land for one thousand rubles.

> searching for, hunting for
> tradesman, merchant

"That area has so much land that you could walk for a year and still be in the land of the Bashkirs. They sell their land for very cheap prices. All one has to do is make friends with the chief. The land lies near a river, and the whole prairie is virgin soil."

> undeveloped land

Pahom was curious, so he made up his mind to visit the land of the Bashkirs. Before he went there, he bought some gifts. The peddler had told him that it was their custom to give gifts.

> decided
> traditional habit

On the seventh day of his travels, he came to a place where the Bashkirs had pitched their tents. It was all just as the peddler had said. The people lived by a river on the steppes in felt–covered tents.

> put up, built

Stop & Think

How much land did the peddler buy?

KEY WORDS

- **unpleasantness** ugliness; a bad situation
- **pitch** to put up a tent
- **felt–covered tent** a tent that has felt on it
- **uneducated** having no schooling
- **make up one's mind** to decide
- **steppe** a plain; a grassland
- **despite** in spite of

They were a simple people. They did not farm at all.
The men merely sat around, drank tea, ate lamb, and
played their pipes to make music. Still, despite being

only, just

in spite of

uneducated and knowing no Russian, they were good–

not educated

natured enough.

warm–hearted, kind–hearted

lamb

cart

As soon as they saw Pahom, they came out of their
tents and gathered around their visitor. An interpreter
was found, and Pahom told them he had come about

translator

some land. They took Pahom and led him into one of
the best tents. Pahom took some presents out
of his cart and distributed

gave, passed out

them among the Bashkirs.

The Bashkirs were

delighted.

very happy, pleased

CHECK UP Put the right words.

| tents | peddler | visit | interpreter |

1 The _____ said that the Bashkirs sold their land for cheap prices.

2 Pahom decided to _____ the land of the Bashkirs.

3 The Bashkirs pitched their _____ beside a river.

4 Pahom told the _____ that he had come about some land.

GRAMMAR POINT

which (relative pronoun)

- So Pahom began looking out for *land* **which** he could buy.

- He was just returning from *the land of the Bashkirs*, **which** was far away.

present

crowded

exhausted

point out

The Bashkirs talked for a while and then told the interpreter to translate. "They wish to tell you," said the interpreter, "that they like you, and that it is our custom to do all we can to please a guest and to repay him for his gifts. You have given us presents. Now tell us which of the things we possess please you best so that we may present them to you."

interpret ←
→ want to
pay back ←
→ have, own
→ give, award

"What pleases me best here," answered Pahom, "is your land. Our land is crowded, and the soil is exhausted; but you have plenty of land, and it is good land." The interpreter translated.

→ full of people
→ used up, old

The Bashkirs talked among themselves for a while. Then, they were silent and looked at Pahom while the interpreter said, "They wish me to tell you that in return for your presents, they will gladly give you as much land as you want. You have only to point it out with your hand, and it is yours."

→ quiet
→ as payment for

Stop & Think

What did Pahom say about the Bashkirs' land?

KEY WORDS

- **translate** to interpret
- **possess** to have; to own
- **crowded** full of people (≠ empty)
- **in return for** as payment for something
- **have a dispute** to argue
- **rise to one's feet** to stand up

- **repay** to pay a person back for something
- **present** to give; to award
- **exhausted** used up; spent; old
- **point out** to show
- **in one's absence** while one is not around
- **address** to speak to

The Bashkirs talked again for a while and began to have a dispute. Pahom asked what they were arguing about. The interpreter told him that some of them thought they ought to ask their chief about the land and ought not to act in his absence.

> argue
> should
> while he is not around

dispute

While the Bashkirs were arguing, a man in a large fox–fur cap appeared on the scene. They all became silent and rose to their feet. The interpreter said, "This is our chief himself."

> on the spot
> stood up *rise-rose-risen

dressing gown

Pahom immediately took out the best dressing gown and five pounds of tea, and he offered these to the chief. The chief accepted them and seated himself in the place of honor. The Bashkirs at once began telling him something. The chief listened for a while and addressed himself to Pahom. Speaking in Russian, he said, "Well, let it be so. Choose whatever piece of land you like. We have plenty of it."

> gave
> at the top seat
> spoke to

Stop & Think

What did Pahom give to the chief?

CHECK UP Choose the right words.

1 The Bashkirs wanted to _____ Pahom for his gifts. (repay | replay)
2 The Bashkirs told Pahom to _____ the land he wanted. (point out | purchase)
3 The _____ arrived while the Bashkirs were arguing. (interpreter | chief)
4 Did the chief speak to Pahom in Russian? (Yes | No)

GRAMMAR POINT

ought to / ought not to

• They **ought to** ask their chief about the land and **ought not to** act in his absence.

deed

"How can I take as much as I like?" thought Pahom. "I must get a deed to make it secure, or else they may say, 'It is yours,' and afterward they may take it away again."

certain, safe ←- - - - - - - - - -→ *if not, otherwise*

←- - -→ *later*   ←- - -→ *take back, steal*

To the chief, he said, "I must get a deed as a guarantee, or else you may take the land away from me in the future."

promise ←- - -

The chief said, "We will go to the town with you and make a deed for the land."

"And what will be the price?" asked Pahom.

The chief answered, "Our price is always the same: one thousand rubles a day."

calculation
↑

Pahom did not understand. "A day? What measure is that? How many acres would that be?"

- -→ *calculate*

The chief said, "We don't know how to figure out the acres, so we sell land by the day. As much as you can go round on your feet in a day is yours, and the price is one thousand rubles a day."

Stop & Think

How much was the land Pahom wanted to buy?

KEY WORDS

- **deed** a paper that gives a person ownership of property
- **take away** to take back; to steal
- **guarantee** a promise
- **measure** a calculation
- **figure out** to calculate
- **tract** an area of land
- **condition** a requirement
- **spot** a place
- **set** to go down
- **enormous** huge; very large
- **imagine** to think about; to picture

Pahom said, "But you can walk around a large <u>tract of</u>
<u>land</u> in a single day." $\dashrightarrow$ *one day*

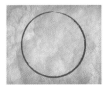

circle

$\dashleftarrow$ *area*

The chief laughed and then answered, "It will all be
yours. But there is one <u>condition</u>: If you don't return
$\dashrightarrow$ *requirement*
to the <u>spot</u> where you started on the same day, your
$\dashrightarrow$ *place*
money is lost. You must make a circle. You may make as
large a circle as you wish, but you must return to your
starting point before the sun <u>sets</u>. Then, all of the land
$\dashrightarrow$ *goes down*
that you walked around will be yours."

imagine

Pahom agreed to the chief's conditions, and they
decided to start the next morning.

That night, Pahom lay in bed thinking about the
land. He thought, "I can cover an <u>enormous</u> amount
$\dashrightarrow$ *huge*
of land. I can easily walk thirty–five miles in one day.
<u>Imagine</u> how much land that will be."
$\dashrightarrow$ *Think, Suppose*

Stop & Think
What was the condition the chief gave Pahom?

CHECK UP   Answer the questions.

1 What did Pahom want the chief to give him with the land?
   a. a deed   **b.** some money   **c.** some servants

2 How far did Pahom think he could walk in one day?
   a. 20 miles   **b.** 35 miles   **c.** 50 miles

GRAMMAR POINT

as . . . as . . .

- How can I take **as much as** I like?
- **As much as** you can go round on your feet in a day is yours.
- You may make **as large** a circle **as** you wish.

lie awake

doze off

hoof

horn

Pahom <u>lay awake</u> all night and <u>dozed off</u> only just before dawn. <u>Hardly</u> were his eyes closed when he had a dream. In his dream, the chief of the Bashkirs was sitting in front of a tent and laughing. "What are you laughing at?" he asked the chief. But the chief was no longer there. Instead, it was the peddler who had stopped at his house and told him about the Bashkirs. Then, the peddler <u>disappeared</u>, and the peasant who had told him about the land beyond the Volga River suddenly <u>appeared</u>. Then, he saw that it was not the peasant either, but the Devil himself with hoofs and horns, sitting there and <u>chuckling</u>. There was a man lying dead in front of the Devil, and it was Pahom himself. He awoke <u>horror-struck</u>.

did not sleep *lie–lay–lain

fell asleep for a short time

Scarcely

vanished

came into sight

laughing

very shocked and afraid

Looking round, he saw through the open door that the dawn was breaking. "It's time to wake them up," he thought. "We ought to be starting."

Pahom, the chief, and the other Bashkirs met on the land early in the morning. The chief <u>stretched</u> his arms out and said, "All of this land—as far as you can see—belongs to us. You may have any part of it you like."

extended

Stop & Think

What happened to Pahom in his dream?

KEY WORDS

- **lie awake** to lie in bed but not to sleep
- **appear** ≠ disappear
- **stretch out** to extend
- **dawn** the time when the sun rises
- **horror-struck** extremely shocked and afraid
- **spade** a shovel

The chief took off his fox–fur cap, placed it on the ground, and said, "This will be the mark. Start from here and return here again. All the land you go around shall be yours." Pahom took out his money and put it on the cap.

Pahom stood ready to start with a spade in his hand. He considered for some moments which way he had better go. Then, he concluded, "I will go toward the rising sun."

mark

spade

Stop & Think

What did the chief put down to mark the starting spot?

CHECK UP Finish the sentences.

1 Pahom had a dream   **a.** on the fox–fur cap.
2 The Devil was   **b.** the night before the contest.
3 Pahom put his money   **c.** laughing in Pahom's dream.

GRAMMAR POINT

hardly . . . when . . .

- **Hardly** were his eyes closed **when** he had a dream.
  (= His eyes were **hardly** closed **when** he had a dream.)

How Much Land Does a Man Need?   **35**

girdle

ant

noon

lie down

Pahom started walking neither slowly nor quickly. After having gone a thousand yards, he stopped, dug a hole, and placed pieces of turf one on another to make it more visible. Then, he went on. Now that he had
> can be seen ≠ invisible

walked off his stiffness, he quickened his pace. After a
> walked enough to soften
> moved faster

while, he dug another hole.

The weather was getting warmer. He looked at the sun. It was time to think of breakfast. "It is too soon yet to turn. I will just take off my boots," he said to himself. He sat down, took off his boots, stuck them
> put, pushed *stick–stuck–stuck

into his girdle, and went on. It was easy to walk now.
> belt
> kept walking

"I will go on for another three miles," he thought, "and then turn to the left. This land here is so nice that it would be a pity to lose it."
> shame

He went straight on for a while, and then he looked
> went right ahead ≠ went backward

back. The people on the hill where he had started were as small as ants. "Ah, I have gone far enough in this direction," he thought. "It's time to turn and go another direction. Besides, I'm getting tired and need something to drink."

KEY WORDS

- **turf** grass; sod
- **quicken one's pace** to move faster (≠ slow down)
- **go straight** to go right ahead of oneself
- **lie down** to get down on the ground
- **damp** wet

- **stiffness** a feeling of inflexibility
- **a pity** a shame; a sad situation
- **look back** to look behind (≠ look ahead)
- **perceive** to notice
- **hollow** a valley

He looked at the sun and saw that it was noon. He
sat down, ate some bread, and drank some water. But
he did not lie down as he thought that if he did, he
might fall asleep. After sitting for a little while, he went
on again. It had become terribly hot, and he felt sleepy.
Still, he went on, thinking, "An hour to suffer, a lifetime
to live."

knew, noticed → saw
because → as
extremely → terribly
endure pain → suffer

hollow

horizon

He went a long way in this direction also and was
about to turn to the left again when he perceived a
damp hollow. "It would be a pity to leave that out," he
thought. So he went on past the hollow and dug a hole
on the other side of it.

noticed → perceived
wet → damp
valley → hollow
not include, omit → leave that out

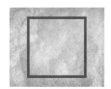

square

"Ah!" thought Pahom, "I have made the sides too
long; I must make this one shorter." And he went along
the third side as he moved faster. He looked at the sun.
It was nearly halfway to the horizon, and he had not
yet done two miles of the third side of the square. He
was still ten miles from his goal.

almost → nearly

> **Stop & Think**
>
> Why did Pahom not lie down at lunch?

CHECK UP True or false?

1 Pahom walked for 100 yards on the first side of the square. _____
2 Pahom did not stop to have lunch. _____
3 Pahom made the first side and the second side of the square too long. _____

GRAMMAR POINT

it would be a pity to . . .

- This land here is so nice that **it would be a pity to** lose it.
- **It would be a pity to** leave that out.

straight line

bare feet

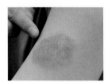
bruised

flask

> *rush to get back*

"I've got to <u>hurry back</u> in a straight line now. I shouldn't go too far," he thought. "Besides, I already have a huge amount of land." So Pahom turned and hurried toward the hill that he had started from.

> *was defeated by*

But he now walked with difficulty. He was <u>done in by</u> the heat, his bare feet were cut and <u>bruised</u>, and his legs began to <u>fail</u>. He <u>longed to</u> rest, but it was impossible if he meant to get back before sunset. The sun waits for no man, and it was <u>sinking</u> lower and lower.

> *give out, not to work any longer* — *injured, black and blue*
> *wanted to*
> *going down ≠ rising*

"Oh dear," he thought, "if only I had not <u>blundered</u> by trying for too much. What if I am too late?" *made a mistake*

He looked toward the hill and at the sun. He was still far from his goal, and the sun was already near the <u>rim</u>.

> *edge*

Pahom walked on and on. It was very hard to walk, but he went quicker and quicker. He began running. He <u>threw</u> away his coat, his boots, his <u>flask</u>, and his cap and kept only the spade which he used as a support.

> *discarded, got rid of* *throw–threw–thrown*

Stop & Think

What did Pahom throw away while he was returning to the hill?

KEY WORDS

- **hurry back** to rush to get back
- **bruised** injured; black and blue
- **blunder** to make an error
- **soaking** very wet
- **give way** to fail

- **be done in by** to lose to; to be defeated by
- **long to** to desire; to want to
- **breathless** unable to breathe
- **parched** very dry

"What shall I do?" he thought again. "I have grasped too much and ruined the whole affair. I can't get there before the sun sets." This fear made him still more breathless.

grabbed, seized

destroyed

event

unable to breathe

Pahom went on running. His soaking shirt and trousers stuck to him, and his mouth was parched. His chest was working like a blacksmith's bellows, his heart was beating like a hammer, and his legs were giving way as if they did not belong to him. Though afraid of death, he could not stop. He gathered the rest of his strength and ran on.

very wet

attached *stick–stuck–stuck

very dry

hitting

failing

trousers

blacksmith

hammer

Stop & Think

What was Pahom afraid of as he returned to the hill?

CHECK UP Put the right words.

support	land	heart

1 Pahom thought he had tried for too much _____.
2 Pahom kept his spade and used it as a _____.
3 Pahom's _____ was beating like a hammer.

GRAMMAR POINT

–er and –er (double comparatives)

- The sun waits for no man, and it was sinking **lower and lower**.
- It was very hard to walk, but he went **quicker and quicker**.

How Much Land Does a Man Need? **39**

hold one's sides

was near to

The sun was close to the rim. Now, yes now, it was about to set. The sun was quite low, but he was also near his aim. Pahom could already see the people on the hill waving their arms to hurry him up. He could see the fox–fur cap on the ground and the money on it, and the chief sitting on the ground holding his sides. And Pahom remembered his dream.

goal

"There is plenty of land," he thought, "but will God let me live on it? I have lost my life. I shall never reach that spot."

died

Pahom looked at the sun, which had reached the earth. With all his remaining strength, he rushed on.

KEY WORDS

- **hold one's sides** to laugh badly
- **labor** work
- **take a long breath** to breathe deeply
- **flow** to come from
- **bury** to put a dead person into the ground
- **lose one's life** to die
- **in vain** for no use; without gain
- **fellow** a person; a guy
- **click one's tongue** to make a clicking noise
- **six feet** about two meters; the depth at which a person is buried

became dark *grow–grew–grown ⤶

Just as he reached the hill, it suddenly grew dark. He looked up—the sun had already set. He gave a cry. "All my labor has been in vain," he thought.

> work ⤵   > for no use ⤵

He was about to stop, but he heard the Bashkirs still shouting. He realized that the sun seemed to have set, but the Bashkirs on the hill could still see it. He took a long breath and ran up the hill. It was still light there.

> was going to ⤵   > appeared to ⤵   > took a deep breath ⤵

He reached the top and saw the cap. He fell forward and reached the cap with his hands.

"Ah, that's a fine fellow!" exclaimed the chief. "He has gained much land."

> nice guy ⤵

Pahom's servant came running up and tried to raise him, but he saw that blood was flowing from his mouth. Pahom was dead.

> coming from ⤵

The Bashkirs clicked their tongues to show their pity.

His servant picked up the spade and dug a grave long enough for Pahom to lie in and buried him in it. Six feet from his head to his heels was all he needed.

> lifted ⤵   > dig–dug–dug ⤵   > rest in ⤵   > 1.8 meters ⤵

blood

grave

Stop & Think

How much land did Pahom need?

CHECK UP   Choose the right words.

1 The sun set at the bottom of the hill _____ than at the top. (slower | faster)
2 The _____ said that Pahom had gained much land. (chief | interpreter)
3 Pahom's servant saw that he was _____. (alive | dead)
4 Did the Devil win his contest with Pahom? (Yes | No)

GRAMMAR POINT

enough . . . to . . .

• His servant dug a grave long **enough** for Pahom **to** lie in.

Super
Reading
Story
Training
Book

Step

5

A Christmas Carol

— Charles Dickens

A Christmas Carol

One Christmas Eve, Scrooge sat busy in his office. It was cold and foggy weather. The city clocks had just rung three times, but it was already quite dark.
> ring-rang-rung

foggy

Scrooge was an old man. He was known by everyone
> not nice ≠ kind   a person who sins ←
to be mean, miserly, and cold. He was a greedy sinner.
> stingy
No warmth could warm him, and no cold could chill
make cold ←
him. Nobody ever stopped Scrooge on the street to say, "My dear Scrooge, how are you?" No beggars implored
begged ←
him to give them some money. Even the dogs seemed to know him, and they avoided him, too. But Scrooge
> kept away from
did not care at all. He liked it that way. People avoided him, and he avoided people.

greedy

beggar

He had worked in the same dark office for many years. Once it had been the office of *Scrooge and Marley*. Scrooge and Marley had been partners for many years. And even now, seven years after Marley had died, those names were still on the door.

It was a very small room with a very small fire. The only other person in the office was Bob Cratchit,

Stop & Think

How did people feel about Scrooge?

KEY WORDS

- **miserly** acting like a miser; refusing to spend money
- **greedy** wanting more money
- **implore** to beg; to plead
- **sinner** a person who sins; a bad person
- **bah, humbug** an expression of unhappiness or disgust

Scrooge's clerk. Bob was very cold. Scrooge did not give Bob much wood for his fire because he did not like to spend money. So the clerk put on his coat and tried to warm himself by the light of a candle.

merry

Scrooge did not like anything. He especially hated Christmas.

"Merry Christmas, Uncle," cried a cheerful voice. It was the voice of Scrooge's nephew Fred.

---> happy, pleasant

"Bah, humbug," said Scrooge.

---> ≠ niece

"Oh, come on, Uncle," said Fred. "I'm sure you don't mean it."

you don't intend to do it <---

"I do," said Scrooge. "Why are you merry? You're a poor man."

---> happy

"Well, why aren't you merry? You're a very rich man. And it's Christmas!"

"Bah, humbug," said Scrooge again. "You keep Christmas in your own way, and let me keep it in mine."

as you like <---

CHECK UP True or false?

1 Scrooge was a greedy man. _____
2 Scrooge and Marley still worked together. _____
3 Bob Cratchit was Scrooge's boss. _____

GRAMMAR POINT

no + noun (emphasis)

- **No warmth** could warm him, and **no cold** could chill him.
- **No beggars** implored him to give them some money.

portly

books

bow

"Don't be so angry, Uncle. Come and have dinner with us tomorrow."

Scrooge merely answered, "Goodbye."
> only, simply

"I don't want to be angry with you, Uncle," said Fred. "So a Merry Christmas, Uncle."

"Goodbye," Scrooge only said.

After Scrooge's nephew left, the clerk let two other people in. They were portly gentlemen. They had books
> rather fat

and papers in their hands and bowed to Scrooge.

"Excuse us. May I ask, are you Mr. Scrooge or Mr. Marley?" said one of the gentlemen.

"Mr. Marley has been dead these seven years. He died seven years ago this very night," answered Scrooge.

"Mr. Scrooge then," said the man. "At this festive season of the year, it is nice for everyone to give something to

Christmas season ← people who have nothing–no homes, no food."

"Are there no prisons? Any orphanages?" said Scrooge.

jails ← "There are. But they always need a little more. So a → places where orphans live

few of us are raising funds to buy the poor some meat,
> raising money

drink, and means of warmth. What shall I put you

down for?" → tools, equipments

write down, record

Stop & Think

What did Scrooge's nephew ask him to do?

KEY WORDS

- **portly** overweight; rather fat
- **raise funds** to raise money
- **anonymous** of unknown name (≠ signed)
- **excuse** a reason
- **orphanage** a place where orphans live
- **put down** to write down; to note
- **all day off** not having to work for an entire day
- **pick a man's pocket** to steal money from a man

"Nothing!" answered Scrooge. ⟶ a gift without a name

"You wish to give an <u>anonymous gift</u>?"

lazy

"No. I wish to be left alone. I don't make merry at Christmas, and I can't afford to make lazy fools merry. I <u>have my work to worry about</u>." ⟶ don't have money to

After the men left, Scrooge turned to his clerk. "You'll want <u>all day off</u> tomorrow, I <u>suppose</u>?" he asked.

⟶ do not go to work   ⟶ guess, think

"If that's <u>convenient</u>, sir," the clerk responded.

⟶ suitable, okay

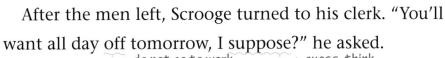
empty

"It's not convenient, and it's <u>not fair</u>. Yet you'll still expect me to pay you a day's <u>wages</u> for no work, won't you?"

⟶ unfair

⟶ money that is paid for work

"It's only once a year, sir."

"That's a <u>poor excuse</u> for <u>picking a man's pocket</u> every twenty–fifth of December. But I suppose you must have the whole day. Be here early the next morning."

bad reason   ⟶ stealing money from a man

The clerk promised that he would arrive early. Scrooge walked out of the office and went back to his <u>empty</u> home.

⟶ ≠ full

Stop & Think

What did Scrooge give Bob Cratchit for Christmas?

CHECK UP Put the right words.

money	wages	died	early

1 Scrooge said that Marley _____ seven years ago.
2 The men asked Scrooge to give them some _____.
3 Scrooge paid Bob Cratchit his day's _____ for Christmas.
4 Bob Cratchit promised to arrive _____ the day after Christmas.

GRAMMAR POINT

dead (adjective) / die (verb)

• Mr. Marley has **been dead** these seven years.
• He **died** seven years ago this very night.

knocker

dressing gown

nightcap

drag

cask

When Scrooge got to his building, he put the key into the lock of the door. But when he looked at the knocker, he did not see a knocker but Marley's face. Scrooge stared for a moment, and then it was a knocker again. He said, "Pooh, pooh!" and closed the door with a bang.

> *looked at*

> *with a very loud sound*

Scrooge went up to his room, and carefully locked the door. He checked twice to see if the door was locked and then made a little fire in the fireplace. He put on his dressing gown, slippers, and nightcap, and sat down before the very low fire. As he threw his head back in his chair, he heard something in the house. It was far away, but it was coming closer. It sounded as if some person were dragging a heavy chain over the casks in the wine merchant's cellar. Then, he heard the noise much louder on the floors below. Then, it came up the stairs, and then it came straight toward his door. It came right through the heavy door, and a ghost passed into the room before his eyes. The face! He recognized it right away as Marley's. It was Marley's ghost.

> *whether*

> *started a fire*

> *leaned his head back*

> *distant ≠ near*

> *like*

> *spirit*

> *knew*

> *immediately*

Stop & Think

What went into Scrooge's room?

- **knocker** an old–fashioned doorbell
- **drag** to pull something on the ground
- **caustic** sarcastic
- **dreadful** frightening; scary
- **linger** to remain in one place
- **low fire** a fire that is not hot
- **straight toward** directly at something
- **as ever** as usual
- **apparition** a ghost
- **stay away from** to keep away from; to avoid

"How now," said Scrooge,
caustic and cold as ever.
→ sarcastic
as usual ←
"What do you want with
me?"

"Much." Marley's voice,
no doubt about it.

"Who are you?"

"Ask me who I was."

"Who were you then?" said Scrooge, raising his voice.

"In life, I was your partner, Jacob Marley."

"Mercy! Dreadful apparition, why do you trouble me?
→ ghost
What do you want?" Scrooge's voice trembled as he spoke.
→ shook

"I have been traveling since I died. Though I am
dead, I must walk through the world of the living. I
cannot rest. I cannot stay. I cannot linger anywhere."
→ stay, remain

dreadful

"Why?" asked Scrooge.

"Because I'm unhappy. I was very bad to people when I
→ keeps away from, avoids
was alive. If a man stays away from other people while he
is alive, that man becomes like me," said Marley's ghost.

CHECK UP Answer the questions.

1 What kind of noise did Scrooge hear?
   a. a screaming man   **b.** a dragging chain   **c.** a laughing woman

2 What could Marley not do?
   a. rest   **b.** speak   **c.** move

GRAMMAR POINT

as if . . . (subjunctive)

• It sounded **as if** some person **were dragging** a heavy chain over the casks.

escape

chain

bell

wide open

"I am here tonight to warn you that you have yet a chance and hope of escaping my fate," said Marley's ghost.
→ destiny

"This is the chain I made during my lifetime. Every time I refused to help those in need, the chain became
→ rejected   → poor, needy
longer and heavier. When I died, our chains were about the same, Scrooge, but now, after seven years, yours is much longer than mine. I want to help you not to be unhappy like me when you die."

"How?" asked Scrooge.

"You will be visited by three more ghosts," answered Marley's ghost. "Expect the first tonight when the bell
→ Anticipate
tolls one. Expect the second tomorrow night at the
→ rings
same hour. The third will come the next night, when the last stroke of twelve has rung."
→ beat   → ring-rang-rung

The ghost began floating out the window.
→ flying out

"But wait. Will I see you again? Can't you tell me more?"
→ will not

"No, Scrooge, you won't see me again. Remember what I told you, for your own sake, or you will soon see your own heavy chain."   → for your own good

The ghost disappeared out the window, which was wide open.   → vanished

Stop & Think

How many ghosts will visit Scrooge?

KEY WORDS

- **escape** to avoid; to get away from
- **in need** poor; needy
- **float out** to fly out by being carried by the wind
- **be drawn aside** to be opened

- **fate** destiny
- **stroke** a knock; a beat
- **troubled sleep** a restless sleep
- **figure** a form or shape; the human form

As Scrooge went to the window to see where Marley had gone, he suddenly heard some crying down below. Again, Scrooge's heart froze. The voices came not from people, but from ghosts. He quickly closed the window. He tried to say, "Humbug," but he stopped at the first syllable.

> freeze-froze-frozen
> a part of a word

flash up

"This couldn't have happened. I will go to sleep, and tomorrow everything will be fine," he thought. Then, he went to bed and fell into a troubled sleep.

> can't be true, can't be possible
> restless sleep

figure

When Scrooge awoke, it was still so dark. "Was it all a dream?" he wondered. Just then, the clock tolled a deep, dull, hollow one.

> woke up *awake-awoke-awoken
> instantly, at once
> rang
> ≠ sharp   empty

green holly

Light flashed up in the room in an instant, and the curtains of his bed were drawn aside by a strange figure. The ghost was an old man with long white hair. He held a branch of fresh green holly in his hand. From the top of his head, a bright clear jet of light sprang.

> opened
> appeared *spring-sprang-sprung

"I am the Ghost of Christmas Past," he said.

"Whose past?"

> a ray of light

"Your past," answered the ghost.

"What do you want?"

Stop & Think
What was the first ghost to visit Scrooge?

"Rise and walk with me."

> Stand up

CHECK UP Choose the right words.

1 Marley said that Scrooge's _____ was longer than his own. (life | chain)
2 The first ghost was going to come at _____ in the morning. (one | three)
3 The first ghost looked like _____. (an old man | a young man)

GRAMMAR POINT

be + p.p. (passive)

- You will **be visited by** three more ghosts.
- The curtains of his bed **were drawn** aside **by** a strange figure.

> hold–held–held

hold one's hand

decoration

tears

Scrooge got up from his bed. He held the ghost's hand, and they passed through the wall together. Suddenly, > went through
they were standing in the country where he had lived as a boy. It was clear enough by the decorations in the shops that there, too, it was Christmastime.

They saw many boys and girls going home across the fields, happily shouting "Merry Christmas" to each other. Scrooge remembered the happiness and joy when he was a child. He could feel tears on his cheek.

"Are you sad?" asked the ghost.

"No, no, I am . . . happy," said Scrooge.

"They are not real. They are only spirits from Christmas past. They cannot see us."
> ghosts

But Scrooge knew the spirits, just as he knew the streets, the houses, and the townspeople. Then, they > alone, by himself
saw Scrooge as a boy, reading on his own in an empty classroom. Seeing himself as he had once been, Scrooge sat down at a desk next to him and began to cry.

"It's me. Once when I was a boy, I was left alone here on Christmas. My father and mother weren't at home. Now,

Stop & Think

What time of year did the ghost take Scrooge to?

KEY WORDS

- **get up** to rise; to stand up
- **on one's own** alone (≠ together)
- **grow quiet** to become quiet
- **prepare** to get ready; to make something ready
- **decoration** an ornament
- **be left alone** to be by oneself
- **get angry** to become upset
- **apprentice** a person who is learning a skill

suddenly, I wish I would . . ." Scrooge's voice grew quiet.

apprentice

- - -> became quiet

"What do you wish?" the ghost asked.

"Last night, a young boy came to my office window and sang me a Christmas carol. I just got angry and told him to leave. I wish I'd given some money to that poor boy," said Scrooge with heavy sadness.

- - - -> became upset

The ghost smiled. "Let's see another Christmas," he said.

This time, Scrooge saw the office where he had first worked. He saw Mr. Fezziwig, the man whom he had worked for. Young Scrooge was helping them prepare the office for a Christmas party. Soon, there were many young people there. They were his fellow apprentices. They were enjoying themselves and dancing. Even he, Scrooge himself, was dancing and enjoying himself.

- - - -> get ready

companion <- - - -

- - - -> learners

CHECK UP Finish the sentences.

1 Scrooge and the ghost
2 The images Scrooge saw
3 Scrooge once worked

a. were not real.
b. in an office for Mr. Fezziwig.
c. passed through the wall together.

GRAMMAR POINT

where (relative adverb)

- Suddenly, they were standing in *the country* **where** he had lived as a boy.

- This time, Scrooge saw *the office* **where** he had first worked.

in pain

shadow

At the end of the party, Mr. and Mrs. Fezziwig said "Merry Christmas" to everybody.

"It's old Mr. Fezziwig's office. He was such a happy, kind boss." → supervisor, head

The ghost looked at Scrooge and asked, "What's the matter?"

"I was thinking of my clerk, Bob Cratchit. I wish I'd said something to him yesterday," said Scrooge.

The ghost smiled again. "Come, my time grows short," said the ghost. "Another Christmas," he said. → becomes

The scene changed. Scrooge again saw himself. He → view
was older now–a man in the prime of life. He was sitting with a young woman. She had once been his girlfriend. She was crying. → the best years of life

"No, it's too late. You have another love now," she said.

"What? What other love?" Scrooge asked.

"Money. You love only money now, not me. Goodbye."

"No more! Ghost! Please remove me from this place," Scrooge cried in pain. → take me away from

"No, Scrooge. I told you that these were shadows of the things that have been," said the ghost. "There is one more scene."

Stop & Think

Who did Scrooge see with himself?

KEY WORDS

- **the prime of life** the best years of one's life
- **bear** to stand
- **struggle with** to fight with
- **be interested in** to like; to care about
- **haunt** to follow around
- **drowsiness** sleepiness

Years had passed since the last scene. Scrooge saw a beautiful woman smiling with her children in a warm house. The door opened, and the father came in. His arms were full of Christmas presents. He gave one to
→ were filled with
each of his children. The children laughed and shouted as they opened the presents.

haunt

Scrooge looked at the mother. She was the woman from Scrooge's past. She had left him because he had been more interested in money than in her. Looking at
→ liked, cared about
the happy family, Scrooge realized what he had lost.

exhausted

"No more! Leave me, ghost," shouted Scrooge.

"This was your life. These things happened and cannot be changed. Only the future can be changed," the ghost said.

drowsiness

stand
"Please, ghost, I cannot bear it. Haunt me no longer!"
→ Follow around
Scrooge shouted sadly.
→ fought with
As Scrooge struggled with the spirit, he suddenly became exhausted. He was overcome by drowsiness and
→ got tired   → defeated by   → sleepiness
sank into a heavy sleep.
→ fell into *sink–sank–sunk

Stop & Think
What did Scrooge tell the ghost?

CHECK UP   True or false?

1 Scrooge never had a girlfriend in his entire life.   _____
2 Scrooge loved money more than people.   _____
3 The beautiful woman Scrooge saw was his mother.   _____
4 Scrooge asked the ghost to show him some more scenes. _____

GRAMMAR POINT

I wish . . . (subjunctive)
• **I wish I'd said** something to him yesterday.

bowl of punch

couch

torch

robe

Scrooge awoke in his bedroom. It was one in the morning again—time for the second ghost. He looked around his bedroom. There was nobody there. He went to the door of his living room.

"Come in, Ebenezer Scrooge," said a voice.

He opened the door and saw something very surprising. The room looked so different. The walls were covered with Christmas trees. Heaped upon the floor [Piled] [filled with] were turkeys, geese, pigs, sausages, plum puddings, chestnuts, apples, and great bowls of punch. Upon the couch in the center of the room sat a happy giant, holding a glowing torch which lit the room. [burning] [light–lit–lit]

"Come in. Come in. I am the Ghost of Christmas Present," said the giant.

"Ghost, I learned a lot from the ghost last night. Tonight, if you have something to teach me, take me anywhere you want," said Scrooge.

"Touch my robe," said the giant.

Stop & Think

Who was the second ghost?

KEY WORDS

- **heaped upon** piled on
- **light** to make light
- **crutch** a stick one uses to help one walk
- **gather** to get together

- **couch** a long sofa
- **bless** to say something good about
- **complain** to grumble; to criticize
- **propose** to offer

Scrooge did as he was told. Scrooge found they were walking in a London street on Christmas morning. The ghost took him to the Cratchits' house. At the door, the ghost smiled and stopped to bless Bob Cratchit's dwelling.

find–found–found

the Cratchit family's

≠ curse

crutch

Mrs. Cratchit, Bob's wife, was preparing their Christmas dinner. Just then Bob Cratchit was coming back from church with the youngest son, Tiny Tim. Tiny Tim was ill and used a crutch to walk.

gather

The family sat down to eat their meal. They had only one goose, some potatoes, and a small Christmas pudding. It seemed very small for such a large family, but nobody complained. Though it was a very simple Christmas meal, they were still as happy as if they had eaten a king's meal. After dinner, all the Cratchit family gathered around the fire. Bob proposed, "A Merry Christmas to us all, my dears. God bless us!"

grumbled

got together

offered

Stop & Think

What did Bob Cratchit's family have to eat?

CHECK UP Put the right words.

giant   Tiny Tim   touch   enjoyed

1 There was a _____ sitting in the middle of Scrooge's living room.
2 The ghost told Scrooge to _____ his robe.
3 _____ needed to use a crutch to walk.
4 The Cratchits had a simple meal, but they _____ it.

GRAMMAR POINT

such a/an + adjective + noun (high degree)

• It seemed very small for **such a large family**.

"God bless us everyone!" said Tiny Tim. Tiny Tim sat very close to his father's side upon his little stool. He was very sick. Bob held his withered little hand in his
> thin and dry, shrunken

as if he loved the child and wished to keep him by his side, but he dreaded that Tiny
> feared, was afraid

Tim might be taken from him.
> be taken away from

stool

"Will he be here next Christmas?" Scrooge asked.

"With help," replied the ghost.

Scrooge raised his head when he heard his name spoken.

"Let's drink to Mr. Scrooge," said Bob.
> turned red

"To Scrooge?" Mrs. Cratchit's face reddened, and she said, "Why should we drink to that old, stingy, unfeeling man?"
miserly < > unkind

"My dear," was Bob's mild answer, "it's Christmas Day."

"Well, you are right. I'll drink to him. But nothing we do could make that mean old man feel happy or merry," said Mrs. Cratchit.

Stop & Think

Who did Bob Cratchit propose a toast to?

KEY WORDS

- **withered** shrunken
- **stingy** greedy; miserly
- **cast a shadow** to darken; to make dark
- **dig up** to unearth
- **dread** to fear; to be afraid of
- **unfeeling** having no emotions; unkind
- **take away** to remove
- **vanish** to disappear

The mention of his name cast a dark shadow on the
party, which lasted for a full five minutes. After some

→ made dark

time, the Cratchits became cheerful again. They were
not a handsome family. They were not well dressed.

→ happy, pleasant

But they were happy, grateful, and pleased with one
another.

wearing nice clothes ←

→ thankful   → happy with

cheerful

The ghost took Scrooge away from the Cratchits'
house. The two of them walked through the streets of
London. People were going to parties with their friends
and families. Suddenly, they were in a cold, dark, empty
place. They looked through the window of a small

→ looked into

look through

house. Inside, there was a big family in a very small
room. Yet they were happy and were singing Christmas
carols together.

Scrooge asked, "Who are they?"

miner

"They are poor miners," answered the ghost. "They
have hard lives working inside the Earth to dig up coal."

Slowly, the scene vanished, and Scrooge suddenly

→ disappeared

dig up

heard a hearty laugh. It was his nephew Fred's house.

→ cheerful laugh

Fred was telling everyone about his visit to his uncle.

hearty laugh

CHECK UP   Answer the questions.

1 How did Mrs. Cratchit feel about drinking to Scrooge?
   a. pleased   **b.** nervous   **c.** unhappy

GRAMMAR POINT

which (relative pronoun) : referring to a previous clause

• The mention of his name cast a dark shadow on the party, **which** lasted for a full five minutes.

phantom

mist

**bend down
upon one's knee**

"So when I said 'Merry Christmas' to him, he replied 'Bah, humbug!'" said Fred. Everyone laughed.

"He's a strange old man," said Fred. "He is rich, but he doesn't do anything good with his money. He even lives like he's poor. I invite him to have Christmas dinner with us every year, but he never comes. Someday, perhaps he will change his mind. And someday perhaps he will pay poor Bob Cratchit more money as well."

as if
maybe, possibly
think differently

For the rest of the evening, Scrooge and the ghost watched his nephew and friends enjoy their Christmas party. Then, the clock struck twelve. Scrooge looked around for the ghost, but he saw the ghost no more. Then, he remembered Marley's prediction, and he lifted his eyes.

*rang *strike-struck-struck*
a guess about the future

Scrooge saw a solemn phantom coming like a mist along the ground toward him. Unlike the others, he could not see this one's face or body. It was covered from head to toe in a long black garment. The only visible part of the phantom was one outstretched hand.

quiet and serious
fog
not like
a piece of clothing
extended

The phantom moved slowly and silently. As it came near him, Scrooge bent down upon his knee, for the ghost seemed to scatter gloom and mystery as it moved. The ghost did not speak at all.

kneeled
spread
unhappiness

KEY WORDS

- **prediction** a guess about the future
- **phantom** a ghost
- **garment** a piece of clothing
- **scatter** to spread
- **yet to come** the future
- **solemn** quiet and serious
- **mist** fog
- **outstretched** extended
- **gloom** unhappiness; sadness
- **funeral** a ceremony held for a dead person

"I am in the presence of the Ghost of Christmas Yet
to Come," said Scrooge. "You are about to show me the
things which have not happened yet, but will happen
in the time before us," Scrooge said, looking at the
strange ghost. "Is that so, Spirit?"

→ in front of, nearby

→ future

**point with one's
hand**

The ghost silently moved its head a little and pointed
with its hand. Scrooge suddenly found himself in the
middle of the city. The ghost stopped beside a group of
businessmen. Scrooge could hear some of them talking.

funeral

"I don't know much about it. I only know he's dead,"
said one great fat man.

"When did he die?" inquired another.

→ asked

"Last night, I believe."

"What has he done with his money?" asked a red-
faced gentleman.

"I haven't heard," responded the first man. "He
didn't leave it to me though. That's all I know."

"At least his funeral will be very cheap," said one man.

Stop & Think

Who was the third ghost?

CHECK UP Choose the right words.

1 Fred wanted Scrooge to give Bob Cratchit more _____. (money | food)
2 The third ghost wore _____ clothes. (black | white)
3 The third ghost said _____. (many things | nothing)
4 Were the people the ghost showed Scrooge talking about a marriage? (Yes | No)

GRAMMAR POINT

for + S + V (reason) : given as an afterthought

• Scrooge bent down upon his knee, **for** the ghost seemed to scatter gloom and mystery.

old rag

shopkeeper

"That's true. He had no friends. No one liked him, so nobody will go to his funeral."

Scrooge did not understand why the ghost wanted him to listen to this conversation, but he knew the ghost would not answer him, so he did not ask.

> little known

They left the busy scene and went to an obscure part of the town. The streets were dark and small. They visited a dirty shop full of horrible old things you can

> awful, terrible

imagine—iron, old rags, bottles, clothes, and bones. It was a place where people came to sell their things when they needed money.

Scrooge watched as three people brought things to sell to the shopkeeper. They were from the same dead man's house.

"What have you got to sell?" asked the shopkeeper.

One woman took out some towels, silver teaspoons, and other small things, and said, "He doesn't need these now."

"No indeed, ma'am," answered the shopkeeper.

> certainly, surely

Stop & Think

Where did the three people get the items they were selling?

KEY WORDS

- **obscure** little known
- **in horror** in fear; in disgust
- **pale light** a dim light
- **uncared for** not taken care of
- **tenderness** kindness; mercy

- **be not likely to** be unlikely to
- **bare** having nothing; empty
- **unwept** not mourned
- **as silent as ever** quiet like usual
- **connected with** related to; concerning

"Take a look at these," said the other woman. "Bed curtains and blankets. He isn't likely to catch a cold without them now."
→ doesn't seem to, is unlikely to

blanket

Scrooge listened to this dialogue in horror. "Ghost, I
→ in fear
see. The case of this unhappy man might be my own."
→ situation, condition

catch a cold

The scene had suddenly changed, and Scrooge found himself in another terrible room. There was a bare bed
having nothing, empty →
with no blankets or curtains around it. A pale light from
dim light →
outside fell straight upon the bed. On it, unwatched,
not watched →
unwept, and uncared for, was the dead body of the
→ not mourned   → not taken care of
unknown man. He was covered by a thin sheet.

sheet

The ghost, as silent as ever, merely pointed at the
→ quiet like usual
body. Scrooge realized that the ghost wanted him to look at the face of the dead man, but he could not do it.

chamber

"I cannot look at his face," cried Scrooge. "Let me see
→ kindness, mercy
some tenderness connected with this death, or this dark
→ related to
chamber will be forever in my memory."
→ large room
The scene changed to another home. A woman stood
→ got up
up as her husband entered the room. "Have you gotten
any news?" she asked.
→ Have you heard

CHECK UP Finish the sentences.

1 The shopkeeper asked the women
2 One woman was selling
3 The ghost pointed at

a. what they had to sell.
b. bed curtains and blankets.
c. a dead body covered by a sheet.

GRAMMAR POINT

be likely to . . . / it is likely that . . .

- He **isn't likely to** catch a cold without them now.
  = It **isn't likely that** he will catch a cold without them now.

A Christmas Carol **63**

flow down

churchyard

grave

⤳ discover, learn

"When I visited him to find out if we could pay the money one week later," he answered, "an old woman told me he was dead."

"That's great news," she said. "I'm sorry for saying that. I mean that now we have time to get the money that we have to pay."

⤳ feel bad about

"No, ghost! Show me someone who's sorry about a death, not someone who's happy because of a death," shouted Scrooge.

The ghost took him to poor Bob Cratchit's house. Scrooge saw the family sitting quietly around the fire. They were talking about Tiny Tim.

"I met Fred, Mr. Scrooge's nephew," said Bob. "And he said that he was very sorry to hear about Tiny Tim."

Bob turned to his family and said, "We must never forget what a good boy Tiny Tim was."

"No, never father," shouted all the children.

Then, Bob Cratchit broke down all at once. He couldn't help it as the tears flowed down his face.

started to cry ⟵ ⟶ *suddenly*

was unable to stop doing it ⟵

"Ghost," said Scrooge, "something informs me that

⤳ tells

Stop & Think

Why was the Cratchit family sad?

KEY WORDS

• **be sorry about** to regret; to feel bad about
• **all at once** immediately; suddenly
• **neglected** ignored
• **but for** if not; without

• **break down** to suddenly start crying a lot
• **churchyard** the land around a church
• **lie upon** to rest on
• **assure** to promise; to tell

our parting moment is at hand. Tell me. Who was the dead man we saw?"

> *the time to leave* (our parting moment)
> *near, close* (at hand)

The Ghost of Christmas Yet to Come took Scrooge to a churchyard. The ghost stood among the graves and pointed down to one. Scrooge crept toward it, trembling as he went, and followed the finger to read the name on the neglected grave: EBENEZER SCROOGE.

> *move slowly *creep-crept-crept* (crept)
> *ignored, uncared for* (neglected)

"Am I that man who lay upon the bed? No, ghost! Oh no, no. I am not the man I was. I will not be the man I must have been but for this evening. Why show me this if I am past all hope? Assure me that I may yet change these shadows."

> *lie–lay–lain* (lay)
> *if not, without* (but for)
> *if I cannot be saved* (if I am past all hope)
> *Promise, Tell* (Assure) *still* (yet)

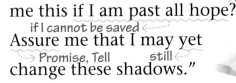

CHECK UP True or false?

1 The Ghost of Christmas Yet to Come took Scrooge to a churchyard. _____
2 Scrooge wanted to know who the dead man was. _____
3 The name on the grave was Scrooge's. _____

GRAMMAR POINT

relative pronoun

- Now we have time to get *the money* **that** we have to pay.
- Show me *someone* **who**'s sorry about a death, not *someone* **who**'s happy because of a death.
- Who was *the dead man* **(whom)** we saw?
- Am I *that man* **who** lay upon the bed?

butcher's shop

butcher

Scrooge continued, "I will honor Christmas in my heart and try to keep it all the year. I will live in the past, present, and future. I will never forget the lessons that I have been taught."

> keep, remember

> teach–taught–taught

Then, the phantom began to disappear, and Scrooge realized that he was back in his own bedroom. Best and happiest of all, time was before him. He had time to make amends.

> make up for the mistakes

Scrooge heard the church bells ringing loudly. Running to the window, he opened it and put out his head. It was a clear, bright, stirring, golden day.

> exciting, thrilling

"What day is it today?" cried Scrooge to a boy down on the street.

"Today? It's Christmas Day, sir," answered the boy.

"Christmas!" Scrooge was surprised. All of the visits from the ghosts had taken place in one night.

> occurred, happened

"Do you know the butcher's shop down the street?" Scrooge asked. "Please go and tell the butcher I'll buy a big goose. Come back with the man, and I'll give you a nice tip." The boy ran off quickly.

"I'll send it to Bob Cratchit's. He won't know who

Stop & Think

What did Scrooge tell the boy to do?

KEY WORDS

- **honor** to keep; to remember
- **stirring** exciting, thrilling
- **dress oneself** to put on one's clothes
- **a dozen times** 12 times
- **make amends** to make up for a past mistake
- **butcher's shop** a store that sells meat
- **one's Sunday best** one's finest clothes
- **courage** bravery

is sending it. It's twice the size of Tiny Tim," Scrooge thought to himself.

> put on his finest clothes

Scrooge then <u>dressed</u> himself in his <u>Sunday best</u> and went out onto the streets. Many people were on the streets, and Scrooge gave each of them a <u>delighted</u> smile. He said, "Good morning, sir," or "A Merry Christmas to you," to everyone he passed.

pleased

delighted

knock

Later in the afternoon, he walked toward his nephew's house. He passed the door <u>a dozen times</u> before he had the <u>courage</u> to go up and knock. But he finally did.

> 12 times; many times

> bravery

Fred was very surprised to see his <u>uncle</u>. "Uncle, why are you here?" he asked.

> ↔ aunt

"I have come to dinner. Will you let me in, Fred?" Scrooge asked.

"Of course you may!" cried out Fred.

Fred was very happy, and so were his wife and all their friends. They had a wonderful party together.

CHECK UP Put the right words.

the goose	one night	have dinner

1 Scrooge realized that all three ghosts had visited him in _____.
2 Scrooge sent _____ to Bob Cratchit's house.
3 Scrooge went to his nephew's house to _____.

GRAMMAR POINT

So am I.

- You are happy. <u>So am</u> I. (= I <u>am also happy</u>.)
- Fred was very happy, and <u>so were</u> his wife and all their friends.
  = Fred was very happy, and **his wife and all their friends <u>were also very happy</u>**.

salary

assist

The next day, Scrooge went to the office early in the morning. He wanted to be there before Bob got there. Bob was eighteen minutes late. As Bob walked in, Scrooge said, "Hello. What do you mean by coming here at this time of day?"

arrived

"I'm very sorry, sir. I'm late," replied Bob.

"Yes, I think you are," said Scrooge.

"Now, I'll tell you what, my friend," said Scrooge. "I'm not going to stand this sort of thing any longer. And therefore . . . therefore, I am going to pay you more money!"

this kind of thing

Scrooge continued, "I'll raise your salary and assist your struggling family. We will discuss your affairs this very afternoon," Scrooge said with a nice smile.

increase *help, aid* *having a hard time* *personal or business interests*

That afternoon, Scrooge took Bob out for a drink and explained how he was going to help him.

Stop & Think
What did Scrooge tell Bob Cratchit he was going to do?

KEY WORDS

- **raise salary** to give more money for working
- **struggling** having a hard time
- **this very afternoon** today; now
- **do not mind** to not care
- **ever afterward** forever

- **assist** to aid; to help
- **affairs** personal or business interests
- **laugh at** to make fun of; to tease
- **dealing with** a relationship with

Scrooge was better than his word. He did everything he said he was going to do and more. He became a friend of the Cratchit family, and to Tiny Tim, who did not die, he was like a second father. He became as good a friend, as good a master, and as good a man as the city ever knew.

a person who acts like a father

laugh at

Some people laughed at him because he had changed. Scrooge did not mind. Scrooge's own heart laughed, and that was quite enough for him. He had no further dealings with ghosts, but he lived happily ever afterward.

did not care

spirit

relationship with

forever

Stop & Think

How did Scrooge act toward Tiny Tim?

CHECK UP Answer the questions.

1 What did Scrooge promise Bob Cratchit?
  a. a bigger house   **b.** a healthy family   **c.** a higher salary

2 What kind of man did Scrooge become?
  a. a greedy man   **b.** a good man   **c.** a silly man

GRAMMAR POINT

as . . . as . . . ever . . .

• He became **as good** a friend, **as good** a master, and **as good a man** **as** the city **ever** knew.

Super
Reading
Story
Training
Book

Step

6

The Last Leaf

— O. Henry

The Last Leaf

♪ 10

In a little district west of Washington Square, the streets have run crazy and broken themselves into small strips called "places." These "places" make strange angles and curves. One street crosses itself a time or two. An artist once discovered a valuable possibility on this street. Suppose a collector with a bill for paints, paper, and canvas should, in taking this route, suddenly meet himself coming back, without a cent having been paid on account.

region (→ district)
split into (→ broken themselves into)
Imagine (→ Suppose)
following this way (→ taking this route)

So, to quaint old Greenwich Village, the art people soon came prowling, hunting for north windows and eighteenth-century gables and Dutch attics and low rents. Then, they imported pewter mugs and a dish or two from Sixth Avenue and became a "colony."

old-fashioned (→ quaint)
gathered around (→ came prowling)
brought in (→ imported)
village (→ colony)

angle

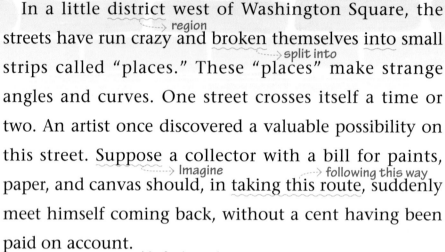

gable

attic

Stop & Think

What kind of people went to old Greenwich Village?

KEY WORDS

- **run crazy** to move in a strange way
- **quaint** old-fashioned
- **colony** an area where a group of similar-minded people live
- **pneumonia** an inflammation of the lungs
- **boldly** bravely
- **victim** someone who has been hurt or killed

- **possibility** a chance; an opportunity
- **prowl** to move around looking for something
- **stride** to walk with quick, long steps
- **scores of** large numbers of (1 score = 20)
- **tread** to walk slowly

At the top of an ugly, three–story brick house, Sue and Johnsy had their studio. "Johnsy" was a nickname for Joanna. One was from Maine; the other from California. They had met at the restaurant Delmonico's on Eighth Street and had found that their tastes in art, food, and clothes were so similar that the joint studio resulted.

> having three floors

> workroom

three–story

That was in May. In November, a cold, unseen stranger, whom the doctors called Pneumonia, visited the colony, touching one here and there with his icy fingers. Over on the east side, this ravager strode boldly, claiming scores of victims, but his feet trod slowly through the maze of the narrow and moss–grown "places."

> very cold fingers

> stride–strode–stridden

> many

> tread–trod–trodden

> labyrinth

fingers

maze

Mr. Pneumonia was not what you would call a gentleman. A small woman with blood thinned by the warm California zephyrs was no match for the tough and deadly illness.

> a pale complexion

> breeze, gentle wind

> not able to compete against

moss–grown

Stop & Think
What happened in the colony in November?

CHECK UP   Choose the right words.

1   There were "_____" in Washington Square. (places | attics)
2   People went to old Greenwich Village looking for low _____. (rents | houses)
3   Sue and _____ lived together. (Delmonico | Johnsy)
4   Did many people get pneumonia in May? (Yes | No)

GRAMMAR POINT

one / the other

• **One** was from Maine; **the other** from California.

But he attacked Johnsy, and she lay, scarcely moving, on her painted iron bedstead, looking through the small Dutch windowpanes at the blank side of the next brick house.

> empty

One morning, the busy doctor invited Sue into the hallway.

> a ten-percent chance; 10%

"She has one chance in–let us say, ten," he said, as he shook down the mercury in his clinical thermometer.

> shake-shook-shaken

"And that chance is for her to want to live. Sometimes when people give up trying to live, it doesn't matter what medicines I give. Your friend has made up her mind that she's not going to get well.

> quit, stop

> decided, determined

> get better

Has she anything on her mind?"

> Is there anything she cares about?

"She . . . she wanted to paint the Bay of Naples some day," said Sue.

> nonsense

"Paint? Bosh! Does she have anything on her mind worth thinking about twice, like a man, for instance?"

> important, valuable

"A man?" said Sue, with a hard sound in her voice.

windowpane

Stop & Think

What did the doctor say Johnsy needed to do?

KEY WORDS

- **deadly** causing death; lethal
- **one chance in ten** a ten-percent chance, 1/10
- **have on one's mind** to think about something
- **weakness** a weak point; problem (≠ strength)
- **subtract** to take away; to remove
- **swagger** to walk; to stride

- **windowpane** the glass part of a window
- **make up one's mind** to decide
- **bosh** nonsense; pshaw
- **accomplish** to do; to complete
- **one-in-five chance** a twenty-percent chance, 1/5
- **popular tune** a well-known song

"Is a man worth–but, no, Doctor. There is nothing of the kind."

"Well, it is the weakness then," said the doctor. "I will do all that science, so far as it may be employed by me, can accomplish. But whenever my patient begins to count the carriages in her funeral procession, I subtract fifty percent from the power of medicine to cure. If you can get her to ask one question about the new winter styles in cloak sleeves, I will promise you a one–in–five chance for her instead of one in ten."

weak point, problem

as much as what I can do

do

take away ←

heal ←

a twenty–percent chance; 20% ←

rather than

After the doctor left, Sue went into the workroom and cried a napkin to a pulp. Then, she swaggered into Johnsy's room with her drawing board, whistling a popular tune.

cried very hard

strode

popular song

without moving

Johnsy lay, scarcely making a move under the bedclothes, with her face toward the window. Sue stopped whistling, thinking she was asleep.

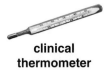

clinical thermometer

carriage

drawing board

Stop & Think

What did the doctor want Sue to do?

CHECK UP Put the right words.

medicine   cried   live

1 The doctor said Johnsy had one chance in ten to _____.
2 _____ is less effective when patients think about death.
3 Sue _____ very hard after the doctor left.

GRAMMAR POINT

participle clause

* she lay, scarcely **moving**, . . . **looking** through the small Dutch windowpanes . . .
* Johnsy lay, scarcely **making** a move under the bedclothes, . . .
* Sue stopped whistling, **thinking** she was asleep.

count backwards

ivy vine

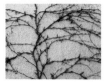

skeleton branch

→ set up

She arranged her board and began a pen-and-ink drawing to illustrate a magazine story. Young artists *→ draw a picture* must pave their way to art by drawing pictures for the *→ make a path* magazine stories that young authors must write to pave their way to literature.

As Sue was sketching a pair of elegant horseshow riding trousers and a monocle on the figure of the hero, an Idaho cowboy, she heard a low sound, several times repeated. She quickly went to the bedside. *→ said again*

Johnsy's eyes were open wide. She was looking out the *→ were wide awake* window and counting backwards. "Twelve," she said, *→ ≠ forwards* and a little later, "eleven"; and then "ten," and "nine"; and then "eight" and "seven" almost together.

Sue looked out the window. What was there to count? There was only a bare, dreary yard to be seen, *having nothing ←   → dull, dark, gloomy* and the blank side of the brick house twenty feet away. An old, old ivy vine, twisted and decayed at the roots, *→ rotten* climbed halfway up the brick wall. The cold breath of autumn had taken most of its leaves from the vine until *the cold autumn wind ←* its skeleton branches clung, almost bare, to the bricks.

"What is it, dear?" asked Sue. *→ cling-clung-clung*

KEY WORDS

- **pave one's way** to make a path
- **bare** having nothing
- **blank** bare; empty
- **cling to** to hold on to
- **ten to one** a ninety-percent chance
- **eyes be open wide** to be wide awake
- **dreary** dark; gloomy
- **skeleton branches** branches that have no leaves
- **have to do with** to be concerned with
- **as good a chance as** very good odds

"Six," said Johnsy, in almost a whisper. "They're falling faster now. Three days ago, there were almost a hundred. It made my head ache to count them. But
> gave me a headache

now it's easy. There goes another one. There are only five left now."

"Five what, dear. Tell your Sudie."

"Leaves. On the ivy vine. When the last one falls, I must go, too. I've known that for three days. Didn't the doctor tell you?"

> silliness

"Oh, I have never heard of such nonsense," complained Sue, with magnificent scorn. "What have old ivy leaves to do with your getting well? And you
> be concerned with

used to love that vine so, you naughty girl. Don't be like that. Why, the doctor told me this morning that
> Well, You know

your chances for getting well real soon were—let's see exactly what he said—he said the chances were ten to
> ninety percent; 90%

one. Why, that's almost as good a chance as we have in New York when we ride on the streetcars or walk past a new building."

streetcar

Stop & Think

What was Johnsy counting?

CHECK UP   True or false?

1 Johnsy was counting backward. _____
2 Johnsy said she would die when the last leaf fell. _____
3 Sue said Johnsy's chances of living were ten to one. _____

GRAMMAR POINT

the subject of gerund

• What have old ivy leaves to do with **your/you** getting well?

broth

pork chop

"Try to have some broth now, and let Sudie go back to her drawing, so she can sell it to the editor. Then, I'll buy port wine for her sick child and pork chops for her greedy self."

"You don't need to get any more wine," said Johnsy, keeping her eyes fixed out the window.

attached to, set on

"There goes another. No, I don't want any broth. That leaves just four. I want to see the last one fall before it gets dark. Then, I'll go, too."

becomes dark

leaning over

"Johnsy, dear," said Sue, bending over her, "will you promise to keep your eyes closed and not to look out the window until I am done working? I must hand my drawings in by tomorrow. I need the light, or I would pull the shade down."

turn in, submit

curtain

"Couldn't you draw in the other room?" Johnsy asked coldly.

I would prefer to

"I'd rather be here beside you," said Sue. "Besides, I don't want you to keep looking at those silly ivy leaves."

foolish, ridiculous

Stop & Think

What did Sue ask Johnsy to do?

KEY WORDS

- **port wine** a type of wine
- **bend over** to lean over
- **be tired of** to be sick of
- **beard** facial hair on a man's chin and cheeks
- **except for** not including
- **fixed** attached to; set on
- **hand in** to turn in; to submit
- **hermit** a man who lives by himself
- **noteworthy** important; remarkable
- **minor** ≠ major

"Tell me as soon as you have finished," said Johnsy, closing her eyes, and lying white and still as a fallen statue, "because I want to see the last one fall. I'm tired of waiting. I'm tired of thinking. I want to turn loose my hold on everything and go sailing down, down, just like one of those poor, tired leaves."

> not moving
> sick of
> let go

statue

"Try to sleep," said Sue. "I must call Behrman up to be my model for the old hermit–miner. I'll just be gone for a minute. Don't try to move until I come back."

> contact
> a person who lives alone

miner

Old Behrman was a painter who lived on the ground floor beneath them. He was past sixty and had a long beard like Michelangelo's Moses curling down from his wide head. Behrman was a failure in art. He had been painting for forty years, but he had never produced anything noteworthy. He had always been about to paint a masterpiece, but he had never yet begun it. For several years, he had painted nothing except for minor advertisements here and there.

> loser
> remarkable, significant
> a great work
> small ≠ major

beard

Moses

Stop & Think

Who was Behrman?

CHECK UP   Answer the questions.

1 What did Johnsy ask Sue to do?
   a. draw in another room   **b.** give her some broth   **c.** pull the shade down

2 What kind of an artist was Behrman?
   a. a successful one   **b.** an average one   **c.** a failed one

GRAMMAR POINT

not to + V

• Will you promise to keep your eyes closed and **not to look** out the window?

juniper berry

canvas

easel

He earned a little by serving as a model for those young artists in the colony who could not pay for a professional. He drank gin to excess and still talked about his coming masterpiece. For the rest, he was a fierce little old man, who made fun of anyone who was soft and who regarded himself as a bulldog ready to protect the two young artists living in the studio above him.

too much →
Also →
very aggressive →
laughed at →
thought of himself as

Sue found Behrman smelling strongly of juniper berries in his dimly lit den below. In one corner was a blank canvas on an easel that had been waiting there for twenty–five years to receive the first line of the masterpiece. She told him about Johnsy's fancy and how she feared she would, indeed, light and fragile as a leaf herself, float away when her slight hold upon the world grew weaker.

not bright ←
a small quiet room →
imagination ←
was afraid →
easily breakable ←
small, weak ←

Old Behrman, with his red eyes plainly streaming, shouted about how silly Johnsy's idea was.

clearly ←
flowing →

"What!" he cried. "Are there people in this world so foolish to believe that they will die when a leaf falls off

drops ←

Stop & Think

What did Behrman drink too much of?

KEY WORDS

- **to excess** too much (≠ in moderation)
- **regard oneself as** to think of oneself as
- **den** a small quiet room
- **float away** to be carried away by the wind
- **stream** to flow
- **horrid** awful; horrible

- **fierce** ≠ meek
- **dimly lit** not bright; dark
- **fragile** easily breakable
- **plainly** clearly; obviously
- **pose as a model** to sit for someone to use as a model
- **lie sick** to be sick in bed

80 *Step 6*

a vine? I have never heard of such a thing. No, I will not pose as a model for you. Why did you allow such a silly thought to enter her head? Oh, that poor little Miss Johnsy."

"She is very ill and weak," said Sue, "and the fever has ~~has~~ ⟶ has allowed left her mind filled with thoughts of death and other horrible things. Very well, Mr. Behrman, if you do not care to pose for me, you don't have to. ⟶ you don't need to But I think you are a horrid old man." ⟶ awful, very bad

"You are just like a woman!" yelled Behrman. "Who said I will not pose? Go on. I will go with you. For half an hour, I have been trying to say that I am ready to pose. God, this is not a place in which someone as pretty as Miss Johnsy should lie sick. ⟶ be sick in bed Someday, I will paint a masterpiece, and we shall all go away. God, yes."
leave ⟵

pose as a model

CHECK UP Finish the sentences.

1 Behrman worked as
2 There was a blank canvas
3 Behrman thought Johnsy's idea
4 Behrman decided to

a. in one corner of Berhman's den.
b. pose as a model for Sue.
c. a model for artists in the colony.
d. was silly.

GRAMMAR POINT

relative pronoun : separating a noun from its relative pronoun

- . . . for *those young artists* in the colony **who** could not pay for a professional
- . . . *a blank canvas* on an easel **that** had been waiting there for twenty–five years . . .

windowsill

peer out

serrated

decay

♪ 12

Johnsy was sleeping when they went upstairs. Sue pulled the shade down to the windowsill and motioned [drew down] [gave a signal →] Behrman to go into the other room. In there, they fearfully peered out the window at the ivy vine. Then, [looked out →] they looked at each other for a moment without speaking. A persistent, cold rain was falling along with [constant →] some snow. Behrman, in his old blue shirt, took his seat [sat down ←] as the hermit–miner on an upturned kettle for a rock. [upside–down →]

When Sue awoke from an hour's sleep the next morning, she found Johnsy with dull, wide–open eyes staring at the drawn green shade. [draw–drew–drawn →]

"Pull it up. I want to see," she ordered in a whisper. [Open it. / Raise it. →]

Wearily, Sue obeyed. [followed →] [≠ Energetically] But, incredibly, despite the beating rain and fierce [amazingly ←] [in spite of →] gusts of wind that had lasted throughout the entire [strong winds →] night, there still remained one ivy leaf against the wall. It was the last one on the vine. Still dark green near its stem, but, with its serrated edges tinted yellow as it was [colored →]

Stop & Think

What did Johnsy tell Sue to do when she woke up?

KEY WORDS

- **motion** to give a signal; to make a motion
- **peer out** to look out at something
- **upturned** upside–down; turned over
- **gusts of wind** strong winds
- **hang** to hold on to; to cling

- **fearfully** in a scared manner; with fear
- **persistent** constant; continual
- **incredibly** amazingly
- **decay** to rot
- **lean . . . down** to bend down; to bend over

rot →

beginning to decay, it hung bravely from a branch some

twenty feet above the ground.   clung *hang–hung–hung

"It is the last one," said Johnsy. "I thought it would

surely fall during the night. I heard the wind. It will fall

today, and I shall die at the same time."

→ weary

"Dear, dear!" said Sue, leaning her worn face down to

bending ←

the pillow. "Think of me, if you won't think of yourself.

What would I do?"

worn face

Stop & Think

What did Johnsy and Sue see outside?

CHECK UP   Choose the right words.

1   Sue and Behrman looked out the _____ at the ivy vine. (window | door)

2   There was still _____ left on the vine. (one leaf | two leaves)

3   Johnsy thought the last leaf would fall during the _____. (day | night)

4   Was Johnsy ready to die? (Yes | No)

GRAMMAR POINT

despite (= in spite of)

• **Despite** the beating rain and fierce gusts of wind . . . , there still remained one ivy leaf against the wall.

tie

twilight

eave

stir

But Johnsy did not answer. The most lonesome thing →lonely

in the entire world is a soul when it is making ready to

go on its mysterious, far journey. The fancy seemed to

possess her more strongly as, one by one, the ties that →distant ≠ near →connections

bound her to friendship and to Earth were loosed. →take up →were freed

The day passed, and even in the twilight, they could →tied *bind-bound-bound

see the lone ivy leaf clinging to its stem against the →hanging

wall. And then, with the coming of the night, the

north wind again began to blow while the rain still beat

against the windows and ran down the eaves. hit

When it was light enough, Johnsy, the merciless,

commanded that the shade be raised. →ordered without mercy, cruel

The ivy leaf was still there. →pulled up

Johnsy lay for a long time looking at it. And then she

called to Sue, who was stirring her chicken broth over

the gas stove. →mixing, blending

"I've been a bad girl, Sudie," said Johnsy. "Something

has made that last leaf stay there to show me how

Stop & Think

What did Sue and Johnsy see the next morning?

KEY WORDS

- **mysterious** strange; unknown
- **twilight** the period of time when the sun goes down
- **command** to order
- **wicked** evil; very bad
- **sit up** to sit while one is in bed
- **be loosed** to be let go; to be freed
- **merciless** without mercy; cruel
- **stir** to mix; to blend
- **sin** a bad deed; a wrong act
- **even chances** a fifty-percent chance

wicked I was. It is a sin to want to die. You may bring
→ evil, bad   → bad deed, wrong act
me a little broth now and some milk with a little port in
                                        port wine ←
it, and . . . No, bring me a hand—mirror first, and then

pack some pillows about me, and I will sit up and watch
→ set
you cook."

hand—mirror

An hour later, she said, "Sudie, someday I hope to
paint the Bay of Naples."

pillow

The doctor came in the afternoon, and Sue had an
excuse to go into the hallway as he left.   made an excuse

"Even chances," said the doctor, taking Sue's thin,
→ a fifty—percent chance; 50%
shaking hand in his. "With good nursing, you'll win.
→ trembling   → care
And now I must see another case I have downstairs.
Behrman, his name is—some kind of an artist, I believe.
Pneumonia, too. He is an old, weak man, and the attack
is acute. There is no hope for him, but he goes to the
→ ≠ chronic
hospital today to be made more comfortable."

CHECK UP Put the right words.

| the last leaf | nutrition | pneumonia | wicked |

1 Johnsy looked at _____ for a long time.
2 Johnsy said it was _____ for her to want to die.
3 The doctor told Sue that Behrman had _____.
4 The doctor said that Johnsy needed _____ and care.

GRAMMAR POINT

command that + S (+ should) + V

• Johnsy, the merciless, **commanded** that the shade **(should) be raised**.

knit

janitor

The next day, the doctor said to Sue, "She's out of danger. You've won. Nutrition and care now—that's all she needs."

> safe
> healthy food
> nursing

That afternoon, Sue went to the bed where Johnsy lay, contentedly knitting a very blue and very useless woolen shoulder scarf, and she put one arm around her, pillows and all.

> happily

"I have something to tell you, my dear," she said. "Mr. Behrman died of pneumonia in the hospital today. He was ill for only two days. The janitor found him on the morning of the first day in his room downstairs helpless

> caretaker

Stop & Think

What happened to Behrman?

KEY WORDS

- **out of danger** safe
- **contentedly** happily
- **janitor** a person who looks after a building; a cleaning man
- **helpless** unable to help oneself
- **be soaked** to be very wet
- **dreadful** awful; horrible
- **scattered** spread out
- **flutter** to move, often because of the wind

with pain. His shoes and clothing were soaked and icy

→ were very wet

cold. They couldn't imagine where he had been on such

a dreadful night. And then they found a lantern, still

→ awful, horrible

lit, a ladder that had been dragged from its place, some

→ drawn

scattered brushes, and a palette with green and yellow

→ spread out

colors mixed on it, and–look out the window, dear, at

the last ivy leaf on the wall. Didn't you wonder why

it never fluttered or moved when the wind blew? Ah,

→ moved by wind

darling, it's Behrman's masterpiece. He painted it there

the night that the last leaf fell."

lantern

ladder

palette

CHECK UP True or false?

1 The janitor saw Behrman painting outside. _____
2 Behrman was found with his shoes and clothes soaking wet. _____
3 Behrman painted the last leaf. _____
4 The last leaf was Behrman's masterpiece. _____

GRAMMAR POINT

die of / die from

- Mr. Behrman **died of** pneumonia in the hospital today.
- She **died from** injuries after the car accident.

Super
Reading
Story
Training
Book

TRAINing
BOOK

Table of
Contents

BOOK 2

BOOK 1

Super
Reading
Story
Training
Book

4

What Men Live By

— Leo Tolstoy

•

How Much Land Does a Man Need?

— Leo Tolstoy

What Men Live By

There was once / a poor shoemaker / named Simon. He had no house or land. He lived in a hut / with his wife and children. One morning, / he went to the village / to buy some sheepskins / for a winter coat. He had only three rubles, / but he planned / to visit some of his customers / on the way. They owed him five rubles / for work / he had already done.

Simon visited several customers' houses, / but he could not collect any money. He went to the store / and asked if he could buy the sheepskins / on credit. But the shopkeeper refused / to give them to Simon.

Simon felt downhearted / and started walking homeward. "Though I have no sheepskin coat, / I don't care. I can live / without a coat. Yet my wife will surely fret," he thought.

While he was walking home, / he passed by a church / at the bend in the road. Simon saw something white / behind the church. He did not know / what it was. He came closer, / and, to his surprise, / it was a naked man. He was sitting against the church / without any clothes on.

Suddenly, / Simon felt afraid. "Robbers must have killed him / and stolen his clothes. If I interfere, / I will have a big problem," Simon thought.

Simon continued walking, / but when he looked back, / he saw / the man was moving. Simon felt more frightened.

"If I go there, / he might kill me / for my clothes. Even if he doesn't attack me, / what can I do for him?" thought Simon.

He ran down the road. But he suddenly stopped.

·**hut** 木屋　·**sheepskin** 羊皮　·**ruble** 盧布（俄國的錢幣單位）·**customer** 客人
·**on the way** 在路上　·**owe** 欠　·**collect** 收帳　·**on credit** 賒帳　·**refuse** 拒絕
·**feel downhearted** 覺得沮喪　·**pass by** 經過　·**naked** 光著身子　·**robber** 強盜
·**interfere** 介入　·**have a big problem** 惹上大麻煩　·**look back** 回頭看
·**frightened** 受驚的　·**attack** 攻擊

CLOSE UP

1　**owed him five rubles** 欠他五盧布
〈owe＋人＋錢〉是「向某人借多少錢」、「欠某人多少錢」的意思。

2　**to his surprise** 出乎他所料
to one's surprise 是「出乎某人意料之外」、「令人訝異的是」的意思。
例 To my surprise, he was alive.（出乎我所料，他竟還活著。）

3　**must have killed him and (must have) stolen his clothes** 一定殺了他、搶了他的衣服
〈must have p.p.〉是「一定已經……了」的意思，用於對過去的事作很有把握的推測時。

人靠什麼存活

　　從前 once 有一個貧窮的鞋匠 a poor shoemaker 叫西門 named Simon，他沒有房子，也沒有土地 have no house or land，他和妻子、孩子 with his wife and children 住在一棟小木屋裡 live in a hut。有天早晨 one morning，他到村莊裡 go to the village 買些羊皮 buy some sheepskins 想作一件冬天的大衣。他只有三個盧布 only three rubles，他計劃 plan 在路上 on the way 拜訪 visit 他的幾個顧客 some of his customers，他幫他們做鞋 for work he does，他們還欠他五個盧布 owe him five rubles。

　　西門拜訪了幾個客戶的家，但收不到半毛錢 cannot collect any money。他到商店裡 go to the store 問能不能賒帳 on credit 買羊皮，但店主 the shopkeeper 拒絕把羊皮賣給西門 refuse to give them to Simon。

　　西門覺得很沮喪 feel downhearted，於是往回家路上走 walk homeward。「儘管我沒有羊皮大衣 have no sheepskin coat，我不在乎 don't care，我沒有大衣 without a coat 也活得下去 can live，但我太太 my wife 一定會很憂愁 will surely fret。」他想。

　　當他走回家的時候，在路上的轉彎處 at the bend 經過一間教堂 pass by a church，西門看到有個白白的東西 something white 在教堂後面 behind the church，他不知道那是什麼，他走近 come closer 一看，很訝異 to his surprise。那是一個光著身子的男子 a naked man，一絲不掛地 without any clothes on 背靠著教堂坐著 sit against the church。

　　突然間 suddenly，西門很害怕 feel afraid。「強盜 robbers 一定殺了他 kill him，搶了他的衣服 steal his clothes。如果我插手 interfere，我會惹上大麻煩 have a big problem。」西門想。

　　西門繼續走 continue walking，但他回頭 look back 一看，他看到那個人動了，西門更害怕 feel more frightened 了。

　　「如果我去那裡 go there，他可能會為了我的衣服 for my clothes 把我殺掉 kill me。即使他沒有攻擊我 attack me，我又能為他做什麼呢？」他想。

　　他往前跑 run down the road，但他突然停下來 suddenly stop。

though：即使……也……　　**if**：如果……的話　　**even if**：即使……也……

- **Though** I have no sheepskin coat, I don't care. 即使我沒有羊皮大衣，我也不在乎。
- **If** I interfere, I will have a big problem. 如果我插手，我會惹上大麻煩。
- **Even if** he doesn't attack me, what can I do for him? (**even if = even though**)
  即使他不攻擊我，我又能為他做什麼呢？

"What am I doing? The man could be dying!" He felt guilty, / so he turned around / and went back to the church.

When Simon went behind the church, / he saw / that the stranger was a young man. He was freezing and frightened. Simon immediately took off his coat / and put it around the man. Then, / he put boots on the man. Simon had / an extra pair of boots.

"Can you walk?" asked Simon. "It's too cold / to stay here. I will take you / to my home. Here is a stick for you / to lean on / while you walk."

The man stood up / and looked kindly at Simon. But he did not speak. As they walked to Simon's home, / Simon asked him / where he was from / and how he got to the church. The man replied / with a calm voice, "I'm not from around here. God has punished me."

Simon was surprised by the response. But he said, "Well, God rules all men. Come home with me / and at least / make yourself warm." As Simon walked with the stranger, / he felt glad / to help another person.

Simon's wife was preparing dinner / when Simon and the man / came into the house. Matryna noticed / that the man had no hat / and was wearing felt boots. And he was wearing her husband's coat. Simon had no sheepskins. **Her heart was ready to break** / with disappointment. "He has been out drinking, / and now he has brought another drunk home / with him," she thought.

Simon took off his hat / and sat down on the bench / **as if things were all right**. Then, he said, "Have a seat, my friend, / and let us have some dinner."

Matryna became very angry / and said, "I cooked dinner, / but not for you. You went out / to buy some sheepskins / but bring a strange man home / instead. He doesn't even have / **any clothes of his own**. You must have spent / all our money / on vodka. I have no supper / for drunkards like you."

- **feel guilty** 覺得愧疚 · **turn around** 轉身   · **go back** 回去 · **stranger** 陌生人
- **freezing** 凍死人的 · **take off** 脫下 · **extra** 多的 · **stick** 枴杖 · **lean on** 靠著
- **stand up** 站起來 · **calm** 平靜的 · **punish** 懲罰 · **be surprised by** 對……感到驚訝
- **response** 回應 · **at least** 至少 · **notice** 注意 · **felt boots** 毛氈靴子
- **disappointment** 失望 · **bring** 帶 · **drunk** 喝醉的 · **supper** 晚餐
- **drunkard** 醉漢

CLOSE UP

1. **her heart was ready to break** 她的心要碎了
   〈be ready to . . .〉是「快要……」的意思。

2. **as if things were all right** 好像一切都很好的樣子
   〈as if . . .〉是「有如……」的意思。

3. **any clothes of his own** 任何屬於他自己的衣服
   of one's own是「屬於某人的」的意思。例 a shop of my own（屬於我的店）

「我在做什麼？那個人快死 be dying 了！」他感到愧疚 feel guilty，於是轉身 turn around 走回教堂 go back to the church。

當西門走到教堂後面 go behind the church，他看到那個陌生人 the stranger 是個年輕男子 a young man，他凍僵了 freezing，而且很害怕 frightened。西門立刻脫下他的大衣 take off his coat，把它披在男子的身上 put it around the man，然後，西門多帶了一雙靴子 have an extra pair of boots，他幫男人穿上了靴子 put boots on the man。

「你能走嗎？」西門問：「留在這裡太冷了，我帶你回我家 take you to my home，這裡有一根枴杖 a stick 你可以撐著走 lean on。」

那人站了起來 stand up 和藹地看著西門 look kindly at Simon，一語不發 do not speak。他們往西門的家走去 walk to Simon's home。西門問他從哪裡來 where he was from，又是怎麼到教堂的 how he got to the church。那人用平靜的聲音 with a calm voice 回答：「我不是附近這一帶 from around here 的人，神 God 懲罰了我 punish me。」

他的回答 by the response 讓西門很驚訝 be surprised，但他說：「好吧，神掌管所有人 rule all men，跟我回家吧 come home with me，至少 at least 能讓你溫暖 make yourself warm。」西門和陌生人一起走 walk with the stranger，幫助別人 help another person 讓他覺得很開心 feel glad。

西門和那人走進屋裡 come into the house 的時候，西門的妻子 Simon's wife 正在準備晚餐 prepare dinner。瑪琪娜 Matryna 注意到那人沒戴帽子 have no hat，腳上穿著毛氈靴子 wear felt boots，身上穿著他丈夫的大衣 wear her husband's coat。西門沒有羊皮 have no sheepskins。她的心 her heart 因失望 with disappointment 快要碎了 be ready to break。「他一定是去喝酒 be out drinking 了，現在他帶了一個醉漢 another drunk 回來。」她想。

西門脫下帽子 take off his hat，坐在板凳上 sit down on the bench，好像一切都很好的樣子，然後他說：「請坐 have a seat，我的朋友，我們一起吃晚餐 have some dinner 吧！」

瑪琪娜生氣 become angry 了，她說：「我煮了晚餐 cook dinner，但不是給你吃的 not for you，你去買羊皮，卻帶了一個陌生人回來 bring a strange man home。他甚至連一件自己的衣服 any clothes of his own 都沒有。你一定把我們所有的錢拿去買伏特加 spend all our money on vodka 了。我不把晚餐 have no supper 給像你們這樣的酒鬼 drunkards like you 吃。」

假設疑問句 ⇨ 〈疑問詞＋主詞＋動詞〉

- Simon asked him **where he was** from and **how he got** to the church.
  西門問他從哪裡來，又是怎麼到教堂的。

- He saw something white. He did not know **what it was**.
  他看到白白的東西，不知道那是什麼。

Simon tried to explain / to his wife / how he had met the man, / but she did not listen. She angrily walked out the door, / but then she stopped undecidedly; she wanted to work off her anger, / but she also wanted to learn / what sort of a man / the stranger was. **She was curious about the man.**

"If he were a good man, / he would not be naked. Where is he from?" she asked.

"That's just / what I'm trying to tell you," answered Simon. "When I passed the church, / I saw him sitting there / naked and frozen. God made me / go to help him, / or he would have died. What should I have done? So I helped him get up, / gave him my coat, / and brought him here. Don't be so angry with me. Anger is a sin."

As Matryna listened to her husband, / she looked closely at the man. He sat on the bench / without moving. His hands were folded / on his knees, / and he looked down at the floor. His eyes were closed / as if he were in pain.

"Matryna, / don't you love God?" asked Simon.

Suddenly, / her heart softened / toward the stranger. She went back into the kitchen. She set the table / and served dinner. While they were eating, / Matryna felt pity for the stranger. She did not feel angry / anymore. She even began to like him. At that moment, / the man looked at Matryna / and smiled at her. A light seemed to / come from his face.

When they had finished supper, / she asked the man / where he was from. But the man said / he did not know. All he said / was, "God punished me. I was naked and freezing cold. Then, Simon saw me, / took pity on me, / and brought me here. You have fed me / and pitied me, too. God will reward you."

· **undecidedly** 猶豫地　·**work off** 消除　·**anger** 憤怒　·**frozen** 冰凍的　·**sin** 罪
· **be folded** 交疊　·**be in pain** 很痛苦　·**soften** 軟化　·**serve** 送上
· **feel pity for** 為……感到同情　·**seem to** 似乎　·**take pity on** 憐憫……　·**feed** 餵
· **reward** 回報

1 **She was curious about the man.** 她對那人感到好奇。
〈be curious about . . .〉是「對……感到好奇」的意思。

2 **felt pity for the stranger** 同情陌生人 / **took pity on me** 憐憫我 / **pitied me** 憐憫我
〈feel pity for . . .〉、〈take pity on . . .〉、〈pity . . .〉全都是「對……感到同情/憐憫」的意思。

西門想把他怎麼遇到那個人的經過解釋 **try to explain** 給她太太聽，但她不想聽 **do not listen**，她很生氣地 **angrily** 走出門 **walk out of the door**，但她猶豫不決地 **undecidedly** 停了下來 **stop**，她想要平息她的憤怒 **work off her anger**，但又想了解那個陌生人到底是什麼樣的人 **what sort of a man**。她對那人感到好奇 **be curious about the man**。

　「如果他是一個好人，他不該光著身子，他從哪兒來？」她問。

　「這正是我想跟妳說的事 **what I'm trying to tell you**，」西門回答，「我經過教堂的時候，我看到他坐在那裡光著身子 **naked**，凍僵了 **frozen**。神讓我去幫助他 **go to help him**，不然他可能會死，我應該怎麼做？所以我扶他站起來 **help him get up**，把我的大衣給他穿 **give him my coat**，把他帶回來 **bring him here**。不要這麼生我的氣 **don't be so angry with me**。怒氣 **anger** 是一種罪 **a sin**。」

　瑪琪娜趁丈夫 **listen to her husband** 說話的時候，仔細地看著那人 **look closely at the man**。他坐在板凳上 **sit on the bench** 一動也不動 **without moving**，他的雙手 **his hands** 疊 **be folded** 在膝蓋上 **on his knees**，然後低頭看著地板 **look down at the floor**。他的雙眼 **his eyes** 閉著 **be closed**，好像很痛苦 **be in pain** 的樣子。

　「瑪琪娜，難道妳不愛神嗎？」西門問。

　突然間，她心軟了 **soften**，回到廚房 **go back into the kitchen**，擺好桌子 **set the table**，端上晚餐 **serve dinner**。他們正在吃飯的時候，瑪琪娜對陌生人起了憐憫之情 **feel pity for the stranger**，她不再生氣，她甚至開始喜歡他 **like him**。那一刻 **at that moment**，那人看著瑪琪娜 **look at Matryna** 對著她笑 **smile at her**，他的臉上 **from his face** 似乎散發著一抹光芒 **a light**。

　他們用完晚餐以後，她問那人他從哪裡來，但那人說他不知道，他只是一直說：「神處罰我，我光著身子，快凍僵 **freezing cold** 了，然後，西門看到我、同情我 **take pity on me**，把我帶來這裡 **bring me here**。妳給我食物 **feed me**，憐憫我 **pity me**，神會回報你的 **reward you**。」

GRAMMAR POINT

if . . . （假設語氣）⇨ 有「過去式」和「過去完成式」。

- **If** he **were** a good man, he **would** not **be** naked. 如果他是好人，他不可能赤身露體。
  （過去式：和現在事實相反的假設，if子句的be動詞要用were，不用was。）

- God made me go to help him, or he **would have died**.
  (= **If** God **had** not **made** me go to help him, he **would have died**.)
  如果神沒有讓我去幫助他，他就會死去。
  （過去完成式：和過去事實相反的假設）

Matryna gave the man some clothes, / and he went to get some sleep. Then, / she and Simon went to bed, too, / but Matryna could not sleep. She could not get the stranger / out of her mind. Then, / she suddenly remembered / that they had eaten / their last piece of bread, / so there was nothing left / for tomorrow. She felt grieved.

"Simon, / what will we do tomorrow?"

"As long as we are alive, / we will find something to eat," Simon answered.

The next morning, / Simon and Matryna woke up / and saw / that the stranger was already awake. He looked much better / than the day before.

Simon said, "Well, friend, / we have to work / for a living. What work do you know?"

"I do not know anything," answered the man.

Surprised, / Simon said, "A man / who wants to learn / can learn anything."

"Then I will learn / how to work."

"What is your name?" asked Simon.

"Michael."

"Well, Michael, / if you work with me, / I will give you food and shelter," offered Simon.

"May God reward you," answered Michael. "Show me / what to do."

Simon showed Michael / how to make boots. Michael learned quickly / and was very skilled. He ate little food / and almost never went anywhere. He made boots so well / that many people came to Simon's shop. Soon, / Simon began to make a lot of money.

A year passed. Michael lived and worked / with Simon. One day, / Simon and Michael / were working hard / when a carriage / drawn by three horses / drove up to the hut. A servant opened the door, / and a gentleman / wearing a fur coat / got out. He strode into the hut / and asked, "Which of you / is the master bootmaker?"

- get . . . out of one's mind 將……趕出腦海中   · feel grieved 感到哀傷
- wake up 醒來   · awake 醒著的   · surprised 驚訝的   · shelter 住處
- skilled 技術良好的   · carriage 馬車   · drawn by 被……拉著   · drive up to 驅車往
- servant 僕人   · stride into 大步走   · master bootmaker 製靴大師

CLOSE UP

1 **how to work** 怎麼工作 / **what to do** 做什麼 / **how to make boots** 如何製靴
〈how to . . .〉是「如何去……（的方法）」的意思。〈what to . . .〉是「要去……」的意思。

2 **May God reward you.** 願神獎賞你。
〈May＋主詞＋動詞原形〉是「願某人怎麼樣」的意思。 例 May God be with you.（願神與你同在。）

3 **He made boots so well that many people came to Simon's shop.**
他做靴子做得非常好以致大家都來西門的店裡光顧。
〈so . . . that . . .〉是「如此……以致於……」的意思。

瑪琪娜拿了一些衣服給那人 give the man some clothes，他睡覺 get some sleep 去了，然後她和西門也上床睡覺 go to bed，但瑪琪娜睡不著 cannot sleep，陌生人在她腦中揮之不去 cannot get the stranger out of her mind，然後她突然想起，他們吃了最後一塊麵包 their last piece of bread，明天沒有半點食物 nothing left 可以吃，她覺得很哀傷 feel grieved。

　　「西門，我們明天該怎麼辦？」

　　「只要我們還活著 be alive，我們會找到東西吃的 find something to eat。」西門回答。

　　隔天一早 the next morning，西門和瑪琪娜醒來 wake up，看到陌生人已經醒了 be awake，他看起來比前一天好很多 look much better than the day before。

　　西門說：「好吧，朋友，我們得工作 have to work 賺錢過活 for a living，你會做什麼工作？」

　　「我什麼也不會 do not know anything。」那人回答。

　　西門很驚訝地 surprised 說：「願意學習 want to learn 的人就能學會任何事 can learn anything。」

　　「那麼我願意學習怎麼工作 how to work。」

　　「你叫什麼名字 your name？」西門問。

　　「麥可 Michael。」

　　「好吧，麥可，如果你跟我一起工作 work with me，我會給你食物和住宿的地方 food and shelter。」西門提議 offer。

　　「願神獎賞你 may God reward you，」麥可回答，「請教我 show me 怎麼做 what to do。」

　　西門教麥可怎麼做靴子 how to make boots，麥可學得很快 learn quickly，而且手藝很好 be very skilled，他吃得很少 eat little food，且哪也不去 never go anywhere。

　　他做的靴子很棒 make boots so well，許多人 many people 來光顧西門的店 come to Simon's shop。不久，西門開始賺很多錢 make a lot of money。

　　一年 a year 過去了 pass，麥可和西門一同生活、工作 live and work with Simon。有一天 one day，正當西門和麥可認真工作 work hard 的時候，一輛有三匹馬拉著 drawn by three horses 的馬車 a carriage 向小木屋駛來 drive up to the hut。一個僕人 a servant 打開車門 open the door，一個紳士 a gentleman 身穿毛皮大衣 wearing a fur coat 走了出來 get out，大步走進小木屋 stride into the hut，他問：「你們哪一個 which of you 是靴子師傅 the master bootmaker？」

GRAMMAR POINT

主動的現在分詞（V-ing）/ 被動的過去分詞（V-en）

⇨ 分詞可以修飾名詞。現在分詞（V-ing）含有主動的含意，過去分詞（V-en）含有被動的含意。

- *A gentleman* **wearing** a fur coat got out. 一個穿著毛皮大衣的紳士走了出來。

- *A carriage* **drawn** by three horses drove up to the hut.

　　一輛由三匹馬拉著的馬車驅車前往　小木屋。

"I am, sir," Simon answered.

Then the gentleman said, "Do you see this leather here?"

"Yes, it is good leather, sir."

"You fool," laughed the gentleman. "It is the finest leather. It comes from Germany / and is extremely expensive. I want you to make me / a pair of boots / that will last for years. If they lose their shape / or fall apart, / I will throw you into prison. After one year, / if the boots are still good, / I will pay you ten rubles / for them," said the rich man.

Simon was terrified, / but Michael advised him / to make the boots. So Simon agreed, / and then he measured the gentleman's feet. While he was doing that, / Simon saw / Michael was gazing behind the rich man / as if someone were there. Suddenly, / Michael smiled, / and his face turned bright.

"What are you grinning at, / you fool?" shouted the man. "You had better make these boots / on time. I will come back / in two days."

"They will be ready," answered Michael.

After he left, / Simon looked at Michael / and said, "Michael, / we must be cautious / with this expensive leather. We cannot make a single mistake."

Michael started cutting the leather, / but he did not cut it / for boots. Instead, / he started to make soft slippers. Simon saw / what Michael was doing, / and he was shocked.

"What are you doing, / Michael? The gentleman ordered boots, / not slippers. You've ruined that leather. What's going to happen to me now?"

·fool 傻瓜　·extremely 非常地　·last 持續　·lose one's shape 變形
·fall apart 裂開　·throw . . . into prison 把……丟進大牢　·terrified 嚇人的
·advise 建議　·measure 測量　·gaze 盯　·grin at 對……微笑　·on time 準時
·cautious 謹慎的　·make a mistake 犯錯　·ruin 毀掉

1　**a pair of boots that will last for years**　一雙可以穿好幾年的靴子
這裡的 last 是動詞「夠用」、「（功能）持續」的意思，that will last for years 是修飾 a pair of boots 的關係子句。

2　**advised him to make the boots**　建議他做靴子
〈advise . . . to . . . 〉是「建議……去……」的意思。

3　**You had better make these boots on time.**　你最好準時做完這雙靴子。
〈had better ＋動詞原形〉是「最好……」的意思，表警告，意指如果不這樣做的話，可能會有不好的事發生。
〈on time〉是「準時地」、「沒有耽誤時間地」的意思。

「我是，先生。」西門回答。

紳士說：「你看到這些皮 see this leather 了嗎？」

「是的，這是很好的皮 good leather。」

「你這個傻子 you fool，」紳士笑，「這是最好的皮 the finest leather，從德國來的 come from Germany，非常地昂貴 be extremely expensive。我要你幫我做一雙可以穿上好幾年 last for years 的靴子 make a pair of boots。如果它們變形 lose their shape 或裂開 fall apart，我就把你關進大牢 throw you into prison。一年後 after one year，如果這靴子還完好如初 be still good，我會付你10個盧布 pay you ten rubles。」富人說。

西門嚇壞了 be terrified，但麥可建議他做這雙靴子，於是西門同意了 agree，然後他量了那個人的雙腳 measure the gentleman's feet。西門做這些事的時候，他看到麥可盯著富人的身後 gaze behind the rich man 看，好像有人 someone 在那裡 be there 似的。忽然間，麥可笑了，他的臉 his face 變亮了 turn bright。

「你在對誰笑 grin at？你這個傻子，」富人大叫，「你最好準時 on time 完成，我過兩天 in two days 再來 come back。」

「我們會把靴子準備好 be ready。」麥可回答。

他走了以後，西門看看麥可，說：「麥可，我們用這麼貴的皮 with this expensive leather，一定要謹慎處理 be cautious，不能出半點差錯 cannot make a single mistake。」

麥可開始裁切皮革 cut the leather，但不是拿來做靴子，相反地，他開始做一雙柔軟的拖鞋 make soft slippers。西門看到麥可正在做的事 what Michael is doing，非常震驚 be shocked。

「你在做什麼，麥可？那個紳士訂製的是靴子 order boots，不是拖鞋 not slippers。你已經毀了那塊皮 ruin that leather。我會出什麼事呢？」

GRAMMAR POINT

as if . . .（假設語氣）：就像……一樣 ⇨ 好像是那樣，但事實上並不是。

- Michael was gazing behind the rich man **as if** someone **were** there.
  麥可盯著那有錢人的後面，好像有人在那裡一樣。（過去式：表與現在事實相反的假設）

- Michael was staring at the girls **as if** he **had known** them before.
  麥可盯著女孩們，好像他曾經認識她們一樣。（過去完成式：表與過去事實相反的假設）

[pp. 12–13]

At that very moment, / the gentleman's servant / rushed into the hut.

"My master does not need boots anymore," he announced. "He is dead. He did not even make it home alive / as he died in the carriage. My master's wife / sent me here / to cancel the order for boots. Instead, / she wants you to quickly make / a pair of soft slippers / for his corpse."

Simon was amazed. Michael took / the pair of soft slippers / he made / and handed them to the servant.

More time passed, / and Michael had now lived with Simon / for six years. He never went anywhere, / and he was always quiet. He had only smiled / two times in six years: / once / when Matryna gave him food / and a second time / when the rich man was in their hut. Simon adored Michael / and was afraid / that Michael would leave him.

One day, / one of Simon's sons / came running to Michael. "Uncle Michael," he cried, "Look! A lady / with two little girls / is coming, / and one of the girls / is lame."

Michael immediately stopped work / and looked out the window. Simon was surprised / since Michael never looked outside. Simon also looked out / and saw / that a well-dressed woman / with two little girls / was coming to his hut. One of the girls / was crippled / in her left leg.

The woman came in / and said, "I want leather shoes / for these two girls / for spring."

Simon answered, "I have never made / such small shoes, / but my assistant Michael / is a master at making shoes, / so he can do it."

Michael was staring at the girls / as if he had known them before. Simon was confused, / but he began to measure the girls' feet. The woman mentioned / that the girls were twins.

Simon asked, "How did it happen to her? Was she born this way?"

"No," the woman answered. "Her mother crushed her leg. Their father died / one week before they were born. And their mother died / right after she gave birth to them."

·**rush** 趕去　·**cancel** 取消　·**corpse** 屍體　·**amazed** 驚訝的　·**hand . . . to** 把……交給
·**adore** 很喜歡　·**be afraid** 很害怕　·**lame** 跛腳的　·**crippled** 跛腳的
·**assistant** 助理　·**master** 大師　·**stare at** 盯著　·**confused** 困惑的　·**mention** 提到
·**twins** 雙胞胎　·**crush** 壓壞

CLOSE UP

1　**did not even make it home alive** 甚至沒有活著回到家
〈make it to . . .〉是「到……地方」、「（勉強地）在時間內到……」的意思，這裡的 home 是副詞，所以不加 to。

2　**is a master at making shoes** 是做鞋子的大師
master 是對某事相當通達的「達人、大師」的意思。
〈be a master at＋V–ing〉是「擅長做……」、「做……的達人」的意思。

3　**Was she born this way?** 她生來如此嗎？ / **she gave birth to them** 她生下她們
〈be born〉是「被生出來」的意思。〈give birth to . . .〉是「生孩子」的意思。

那一刻 at that very moment，紳士的僕人 the gentleman's servant 飛奔進小木屋 rush into the hut。

「我的主人 my master 不再需要靴子 do not need boots 了。」他宣布，「他死了 be dead，他甚至沒有活著回家，就死在馬車上了 die in the carriage。我主人的妻子 my master's wife 派我來這裡 send me here，取消訂單 cancel the order。她希望你為他的遺體 for his corpse 趕緊 quickly make 改做一雙軟拖鞋 a pair of soft slippers。」

西門很驚訝 be amazed，麥可把他做的那雙軟拖鞋拿給僕人 hand them to the servant。

日子 more time 又過去了 pass，麥可和西門 with Simon 一起住了六年 for six years，麥可哪裡都不去 never go anywhere，總是很安靜 be quiet。六年之中 in six years 只微笑 smile 了兩次 two times：一次 once 是瑪琪娜給他食物 give him food，第二次是 a second time 富人 the rich man 到他們的木屋 be in their hut 時。西門很喜歡麥可 adore Michael，很怕麥可有天會離開他。

有一天，西門其中一個兒子跑來找麥可，「麥可叔叔 Uncle Michael，」他喊：「你看 look！一位女士 a lady 帶著兩個小女孩 with two little girls 走過來，其中一個女孩 one of the girls 的腿瘸了 be lame。」

麥可立刻停下工作 stop work 往窗外一看 look out the window。西門很驚訝，因為麥可從不看窗外。西門也往外看，看到一個穿得很體面的女人 a well-dressed woman，帶著兩個小女孩，往他的木屋走來 come to his hut，其中一個女孩左腿 in her left leg 瘸了 be crippled。

女人進來以後說：「我想要做皮鞋 want leather shoes 給這兩個女孩春天穿的 for these two girls for spring。」

西門回答：「我從來沒做過這麼小的鞋子，但我的助理 my assistant 麥可是製鞋巧匠 a master at making shoes，他能幫妳做鞋子。」

麥可盯著兩個小女孩 stare at the girls，猶如他之前認識她們 know them before。西門很困惑 be confused，但他開始量女孩們的腳 measure the girls' feet。女人說兩個小女孩是雙胞胎 twins。

西門問：「她發生了什麼事？她生來如此 be born this way 嗎？」

「不，」女人回答，「她母親 her mother 壓壞她的腳 crush her leg，她們的父親在她們出世前一週過世，而母親生下她們 give birth to them 之後也過世了。」

She continued, "My husband and I / were their neighbors. When I visited their hut, / I found / that the mother, / when dying, / had rolled on this child / and crushed her leg. The babies were left alone. What could I do? I was the only woman / in the village / with a baby, / so I took both girls / and nursed them / as well."

"I thought / the crippled one / would die, / so I did not feed her / at first. But I had so much milk / that I could feed my son and both girls. Then, / my own son died / when he was two." She sighed.

"I thank God / for giving me these two girls. I would be very lonely / without them. They are precious to me."

She wiped some tears / from her face / as she told the story.

Then, Matryna said, "The old proverb is true. 'One may live / without father or mother, / but one cannot live / without God.'"

As they talked, / suddenly a bright light / filled the room. They looked at Michael, / who was the source of this light. He was smiling / and looking up at the heavens.

After the woman left / with the girls, / Michael bowed low / to Simon and Matryna. "Farewell," he said. "God has forgiven me. I ask your forgiveness, too, / for anything / I have done wrong."

They saw / a light was shining from Michael. Simon bowed to Michael / and said, "I see / that you are not an ordinary man. But please tell me. When I first met you / and brought you home, / you were quite gloomy. But you smiled at my wife / after she gave you some food. Then, / when the rich man came / and ordered boots, / you smiled again. Finally, / when the woman brought the girls, / you smiled a third time. And now / you have become / as bright as day. Why is your face shining like that, / and why did you smile / those three times?"

·**neighbor** 鄰居 ·**roll on** 翻身 ·**nurse** 養育 ·**sigh** 嘆氣 ·**lonely** 孤單的
·**precious** 珍貴的 ·**wipe tears** 拭淚 ·**proverb** 箴言 ·**source** 來源
·**look up** 向上看 ·**the heavens** 天堂；天上 ·**bow** 鞠躬 ·**farewell** 道別；再見
·**forgive** 原諒 ·**shine** 發光 ·**ordinary** 平凡的 ·**gloomy** 憂鬱的
·**three times** 三次

CLOSE UP

1 **thank God for giving me these two girls** 感謝神給我這兩個女孩
〈thank . . . for . . .〉是「對……因……表示感謝」的意思。

2 **bowed low to Simon and Matryna** 向西門和瑪琪娜深深鞠躬 /
bowed to Michael 向麥可鞠躬
〈bow to . . .〉是「向……（彎腰）鞠躬」、「向……點頭示意」的意思。
bow low：「深深地彎腰一鞠躬」。

3 **have become as bright as day** 變得像白天一樣明亮
〈as bright as day〉是「像白天一樣明亮」的意思。

她繼續說：「我丈夫和我 my husband and I 是他們的鄰居 their neighbors，當我去探視他們的木屋 visit their hut 時，我發現她們的母親快要死了，臨死前她轉身壓在這個孩子的身上，壓壞了她的腳。這一家只留下 be left alone 小嬰兒 the babies。我能怎麼辦？我是村裡 in the village 唯一 the only 有嬰兒 with a baby 的女人 woman，於是我把兩個女孩帶走 take both girls，養育她們 nurse them。」

「我以為瘸腿的女孩 the crippled one 會死，所以我一開始 at first 沒餵她 do not feed her，但我有很多奶水 have so much milk，所以我能餵飽我兒子和兩個女孩 feed my son and both girls。結果，我自己的兒子 my own son 兩歲 be two 時過世了 die。」女人嘆息 sigh。

「我感謝神 thank God 給我這兩個女孩，如果沒有她們 without them 我會很孤單 be very lonely，對我來說她們很寶貝 be precious。」

她一邊敘述 tell the story 一邊擦拭臉上的淚水 wipe some tears from her face。

瑪琪娜說：「一句古老的諺語 the old proverb 說的是真的 be true－『人可以活著 may live 沒有父母 without father or mother，但是不能活著 cannot live 沒有神 without God。』」

他們在聊天時，突然一道白光 a bright light 充滿了整個房間 fill the room，他們看著麥可 look at Michael，因為他是光芒的來源 the source of this light，他正微笑看著天上 look up at the heavens。

女人帶著兩個女孩離開以後，麥可向西門和瑪琪娜深深鞠躬 bow low。「再見 farewell，」他說：「神已經原諒我了 forgive me。如果我曾做錯什麼 do wrong，我也請求你們的原諒 ask your forgiveness。」

他們看到一道光 a light 從麥可身上 from Michael 散發出來 shine。西門向麥可鞠躬 bow to Michael 說：「我知道你不是凡人 an ordinary man，但請告訴我 tell me，我第一次遇見你 first meet you、帶你回家 bring you home 時，你看起來很憂鬱 be quite gloomy，但當我妻子給你食物 give you some food 後，你卻對她微笑 smile at my wife，接著富人 the rich man 來訂靴子 order boots 的時候，你再次微笑 smile again，最後，那婦人 the woman 帶兩個女孩 bring the girls 來的時候，你第三次微笑 smile a third time。現在你如白晝般明亮 as bright as day，為什麼你的臉會這樣發光 shine like that 呢？你為什麼微笑那三次 smile those three times 呢？」

GRAMMAR POINT

may ：能……；可能……（表可能性）；可以……（表允許）

- One **may** live without father or mother. 一個人可以沒有父母而活著。

- When you learn all three things, you **may** return to Heaven.
等你學會這三件事，才可以回到天堂。

Michael answered, "Light is shining from me / because I was punished, / but now God has forgiven me. I smiled three times / because God sent me here / to learn three truths, / and I have learned them. I learned the first / when your wife pitied me, / so I smiled then. I learned the second / when the rich man ordered the boots, / so I smiled again. And I learned the third / when I saw the little girls, / so I smiled for the third time."

Simon asked, "Michael, / why did God punish you? And what are the three truths? I would like to learn them / for myself."

Michael answered, "God punished me / because I disobeyed Him. I was an angel in Heaven, / but I disobeyed God. God sent me / to take the soul of a woman. I came down to Earth / and saw a sick woman / lying alone. She had just given birth to twin girls. The woman saw me / and said, 'Angel of God, / my husband has just died, / and there is no one / to look after my girls. Do not take my soul. Let me live / to care for my babies. Children cannot live / without father or mother.'"

Michael continued, "I put one child at her breast / and put the other in her arms. Then, / I returned to Heaven. I told God, 'I could not take the mother's soul. Her husband died, / and the woman has twins / and prays to stay alive.'"

"But God said, 'Go back / and take the woman's soul, / and learn three truths: Learn / what dwells in man. Learn / what is not given to man. And learn / what men live by. When you learn all three things, / you may return to Heaven.'"

- **be punished** 受罰　· **truth** 真理　· **the third time** 第三次　· **disobey** 違背
- **Heaven** 天堂　· **take a soul** 取走靈魂　· **lie alone** 獨自躺著　· **care for** 照顧
- **breast** 胸部　· **pray** 祈求　· **stay alive** 活下去　· **dwell** 住　· **live by** 靠……活著

CLOSE UP

1　**sent me here to learn three truths** 派我來這學習三件事 /
　sent me to take the soul of a woman 派我帶走女人的靈魂
　〈send . . . to . . .〉是「派……去……」的意思。

2　**I would like to learn them** 我想學它們
　〈I would like to . . .〉是「我想要……」的意思。

3　**look after my girls** 照顧我的女兒 / **care for my babies** 照顧我的寶寶
　〈look after . . .〉和〈care for . . .〉是「照顧/照料……」的意思。

麥可回答：「我之前受神懲罰 be punished，但如今神已經原諒我 forgive me 了，所以光從我身上散發出來，我微笑是因為我已經學會神差我來這裡 send me here 要我學的三項真理 learn three truths。你妻子憐憫我 pity me 的時候，我學會了第一件事 the first，所以我笑了；當富人來訂靴子 order the boots 的時候，我學會了第二件事 the second，所以我又笑了；當我看到兩個小女孩 see the little girls 的時候，我學會了第三件事 the third，所以我笑了第三次。」

　　西門問：「麥可，為什麼神要懲罰你？那三項真理又是什麼呢？我也想學那三件事。」

　　麥可回答：「因為我違背祂 disobey Him，所以受到神的懲罰，我曾是天堂裡的天使 an angel in Heaven，但我沒有順服神。神派我把一個女人的靈魂帶走 take the soul of a woman，於是我來到人間 come down to Earth。我看到一個生病的女人 a sick woman 獨自躺著 lie alone，剛剛生下一對雙生女嬰 just give birth to twin girls。女人看見我 see me，就說：「神的天使 Angel of God，我丈夫 my husband 剛死 just die，沒有人 no one 可以照顧我女兒 look after my girls，請不要帶走我的靈魂，讓我活下來 let me live 照顧我的寶寶 care for my babies。孩子們沒有父母會活不了。」

　　麥可繼續說：「我把一個孩子 one child 放在她的胸部上 at her breast，另一個 the other 放在她的手臂中 in her arms，然後，我便回到天堂 return to Heaven。我告訴神：『我不能帶走那位母親的靈魂，她的丈夫死了，留下一對雙胞胎 have twins，她祈求能繼續活下去 pray to stay alive。』」

　　「但神說：『回去 go back，帶回那個女人的靈魂，學習三項真理 learn three truths：認識什麼住在人裡面 what dwells in man；認識神沒有賜給人什麼 what is not given to man；認識人靠什麼活著 what men live by。當你學會這三件事，你才能回到天堂。』」

GRAMMAR POINT

be + p.p.（被動語態）

⇨ 主詞「承受」動詞的行為時使用，行為者放在 by 之後，從句意就能知道行為者是誰的話，這時一般都會將行為者省略。

• I **was punished** (by God), but now God has forgiven me.
　我被神懲罰，但如今神已經原諒我了。

• Learn what **is** not **given** to man.　認識神沒有賜給人什麼。

"So I flew back to Earth / and took the mother's soul. The babies fell from her breast. Her body rolled over on the bed / and crushed one of the baby's legs. I tried to fly up to Heaven / with the mother's soul, / but my wings suddenly dropped off. Then, / I fell to Earth. That is / how you found me, Simon."

Simon and Matryna now understood / who had been living with them, / so they began to cry for joy.

The angel Michael said, "I was alone in the field / and naked. I had never known / cold or hunger / until I became a man. I crawled to a church. Then, / I saw a man / coming down the road.

"He frowned / as he passed me, / but he came back / a few minutes later. He gave me some clothes / and brought me to his house. When I entered the house, / his wife seemed very angry. She wanted to send me back into the cold, / but her husband mentioned God to her. The woman changed / at once. When she brought me some food, / I looked at her. I noticed / she had changed. She had become alive, / and God was in her.

"Then, / I remembered the first lesson / God had sent me. God told me, 'Learn / what dwells in man.' I understood. It was love. Love lives in men. God had shown me the first truth, / so I smiled."

"After a year, / a rich gentleman came / to order some boots. I looked at him / and saw the Angel of Death / standing behind him. Only I could see the Angel of Death, / so I knew / that he would die soon. The man was about to die, / yet he wanted boots / that would last for years.

"Then, / I remembered God's second order: 'Learn / what is not given to man.' I learned / that men are not given the knowledge / to know / what they need. So I smiled / for a second time."

·**fly back** 飛回去　·**drop off** 脫落　·**joy** 歡樂 ≠ **sadness**　·**crawl** 爬　·**frown** 皺眉
·**alive** 活著　·**stand** 站

1 **that is how you found me** 那就是你找到我的經過
〈that is how . . . 〉是「那就是……的整個經過情形」的意思，表示事件的整個來龍去脈。

2 **the man was about to die** 那人將要死
〈be about to . . . 〉是「即將……」、「很快就會……」的意思。

3 **the knowledge to know what they need** 明白他們需要什麼的能力
knowledge（知識、分析能力）是 know（知道）的名詞。

「於是我飛回人間 **fly back to Earth**，帶走那位母親的靈魂 **take the mother's soul**。小寶寶從她的胸前掉下來 **fall from her breast**，她的身體在床上翻了過去 **roll over on the bed**，壓壞了其中一個寶寶的腳 **crush one of the baby's legs**。我試著帶母親的靈魂 **with the mother's soul** 飛回天堂 **fly up to Heaven**，但我的雙翼 **my wings** 突然掉落 **drop off**，我掉到人間 **fall to Earth**，這就是你發現我 **find me** 的經過，西門。」

西門和瑪琪娜現在明白誰和他們住在一塊，於是他們高興地大叫 **cry for joy**。

天使麥可 **the angel Michael** 說：「我在田裡 **in the field** 孤單一人 **alone** 赤身露體 **naked**。變成人 **become a man** 之前，我從不知道什麼是寒冷或飢餓 **cold or hunger**，我爬到教堂 **crawl to a church**，看到一個人沿途走來。

「他經過我 **pass me** 的時候，皺著眉頭 **frown**，但幾分鐘後 **a few minutes later** 他走回來 **come back**，給了我一些衣服 **give me some clothes**，帶我回到他家 **bring me to his house**。我進到他家 **enter the house** 的時候，他的妻子看起來很生氣 **seem very angry**，她想把我送回寒冷的屋外 **send me back into the cold**，但她丈夫向她提到神 **mention God**。那女人的態度立刻 **at once** 轉變了 **change**，她給我一些食物 **bring me some food** 時，我看著她 **look at her**，我注意到她改變了。她變得生氣勃勃 **become alive**，是神在她裡面 **be in her**。

「然後，我記起神要我學的第一課 **remember the first lesson**，神告訴我『認識住在人裡面的是什麼。』我明白了，是愛 **love**，愛住在人裡面。神將第一項真理啟示給我看，於是我笑了。」

一年過後 **after a year**，一個有錢的紳士 **a rich gentleman** 來訂製靴子 **order some boots**，我看著他，看到他身後站了 **stand behind him** 死亡天使 **the Angel of Death**，只有我能看見死亡天使，於是我知道他不久就要死了。那人都快要死了 **be about to die**，他卻想要一雙可以穿很多年的靴子。

「於是，我想起神的第二個命令 **God's second order**：『認識神沒有賜給人什麼。』我認識人不知道自己所需的是什麼 **not given the knowledge to know what they need**，於是我又笑了。」

not/never . . . until . . . ：直到……才……

- I had **never** known cold or hunger **until** I became a man.
  在變成人之前，我從不知道什麼是寒冷或飢餓。

- I did **not** realize how much I loved him **until** he died.
  直到他死了以後，我才明白我有多麼愛他。

"I still did not know the third truth, / so I have waited / for God to reveal it.

"In my sixth year here, / the woman and the two girls / came. I recognized the girls / and listened to / how the woman had kept them alive. After she told the story, / I realized / that the woman had loved two children / who were not her own. I saw the living God in her, / and then I learned the last lesson: I learned / what men live by. I knew / God had revealed it to me / and had forgiven me, / so I smiled / for a third time."

Just then, / Michael's body / was surrounded by a bright light. He said, "I have learned / that all men live / not by care for themselves / but by love. I did not die / because a man and his wife / took pity on me / and loved me. The orphans stayed alive / because of the love of a woman / who was not their mother. And all men live / because love is in them. A person / who has love / is in God, / and God is in that person / because God is love."

Then, / the roof opened, / and a ray of light / fell down from Heaven. Michael spread his wings / and flew up in the light. Simon stood there, / gazing after him. After a while, / the roof was closed. No one / but Simon and his family / remained.

· **reveal** 啟示；揭示　· **recognize** 認得　· **be surrounded by** 被圍繞　· **orphan** 孤兒
· **ray of light** 光芒　· **spread** 展開　· **fly up** 飛上去　· **remain** 剩下

1 **I have waited for God to reveal it** 我等候神向我啟示它
〈wait . . . to . . .〉是「等候……去……」的意思。

2 **how the woman had kept them alive** 那女人如何讓她們存活下來
〈keep＋受詞＋補語〉是「讓……維持／保持著……的狀態」的意思。

3 **not by care for themselves but by love** 不是靠他們對自己的照顧，而是靠著愛
〈not . . . but . . .〉是「不是……而……」的意思；這裡的 care for themselves 是「自己照顧自己」也就是「愛護自己」的意思。這裡的 love 是照顧、愛護他人的心，也就是「愛心」。

「我還不知道第三項真理是什麼，於是我繼續等候神的啟示 **reveal it**。」

「我在這裡的第六年 **in my sixth year here**，婦人和兩個女孩來了。我認得那兩個女孩 **recognize the girls**，聽婦人說明她如何養活她們 **keep them alive**，她說完事情經過 **tell the story** 以後，我明白那婦人愛這兩個不是她親生的孩子 **love two children who were not her own**，在她裡面 **in her** 我見到永活的神 **the living God**，學會了第三個功課 **learn the last lesson**：我知道人靠什麼而活。我知道神已向我啟示、原諒我，所以我微笑了第三次。」

此時，麥可的身體 **Michael's body** 被亮光圍繞 **be surrounded by a bright light**，他說：「我認識到所有人 **all men** 不是憑著他們的照料 **care for themselves** 而活，而是靠著愛而活 **live by love** 我沒有死是因為一個男人和他的妻子 **a man and his wife** 憐憫我 **take pity on me**，並且愛我 **love me**；那兩個孤兒 **the orphans** 活下來 **stay alive** 是因為一個女人的愛 **the love of a woman**，而她並不是他們的親生母親。人活著是因為愛在他們裡面，有愛 **have love** 的人在神裡面 **be in God**，神也在那個人裡面 **be in that person**，因為神就是愛 **God is love**。」

於是，屋頂 **the roof** 開了 **open**，一道光 **a ray of light** 從天而降 **fall down from Heaven**，麥可展開他的雙翼 **spread his wings** 飛到光中 **fly up in the light**，西門站在那裡 **stand there**，盯著他的身影 **gaze after him**。過了一會兒 **after a while**，屋頂關上 **be closed** 了，只有西門和他的家人 **but Simon and his family** 還留 **remain** 在那裡。

GRAMMAR POINT

because ＋主詞＋動詞：因為……　　**because of** ＋名詞：因為……

⇨ because 後接子句；because of 後接名詞。

- I did not die **because** a man and his wife took pity on me and loved me.
  因為有個人和他的妻子憐憫我、愛我，所以我沒有死。
- The orphans stayed alive **because of** the love of a woman.
  因為一個女人的愛，孤兒活下來了。
- All men live **because** love is in them. 因為人裡面有愛，所以人能存活。

How Much Land Does a Man Need?

An elder sister / went to visit her younger sister / in the country. The elder sister was married / to a tradesman in town / and the younger sister / to a peasant in the village. As the sisters sat over their tea talking, / the elder began to boast about / the advantages of town life. She talked about / how comfortably they lived there, / how well they dressed, / what good things they ate and drank, / and how she went to the theater and other types of entertainment.

The younger sister was annoyed / and in turn / mocked the life of a tradesman. She stood up for / the life of a peasant.

"I would not change my way of life / for yours," she said. "We may live roughly, / but at least / we are free from anxiety. You live in a better style / than we do, / but though you often earn more / than you need, / you are very likely to lose / all you have."

She continued, "We know the proverb / 'Loss and gain are brothers twain.' It often happens / that people / who are wealthy one day / are begging for their bread the next. Our way is safer. Though a peasant's life is not a fat one, / it is long."

Pahom, / the master of the house, / was lying on the top of the stove, / and he listened to the women's chatter.

"It is perfectly true," he said. "Busy as we are from childhood / farming Mother Earth, / we peasants have no time / to let any nonsense settle in our heads. Our only trouble is / that we haven't got enough land. If I had plenty of land, / I wouldn't fear the Devil himself!"

The women finished their tea, / chatted a while about dresses, / and then cleared away the tea things / and lay down to sleep. But the Devil had been sitting behind the stove / and had heard all / that was said.

- be married to 嫁給　• tradesman 商人　• peasant 農夫　• boast 誇口
- advantage 好處；優點　• entertainment 娛樂　• annoyed 煩人的　• in turn 接著
- mock 嘲諷　• stand up for 捍衛……　• one's way of life 人的生活方式
- anxiety 憂慮　• proverb 諺語　• twain 雙生子　• beg for 乞求
- the master of the house 屋主　• lie 躺　• chatter 聊天　• Mother Earth 大地
- settle 停留　• the Devil 撒旦　• clear away 清理

CLOSE UP

1　**we are free from anxiety** 我們免於憂慮
　〈be free from . . .〉是「不再……」的意思，這裡的free指「沒有不愉快或痛苦」、「自由自在」。

2　**you are very likely to lose all you have** 你很可能會失去你所有的一切
　〈be likely to . . .〉是「很可能會……」、「……的可能性很高」的意思，likely前面加very的話，表可能性非常高。〈all you have〉是「你擁有的全部」，也就是「你全部的財產」的意思。

3　**busy as we are from childhood** 如同孩童時期起就很忙碌
　〈形容詞＋as＋主詞＋動詞〉是「如……那麼的……」的意思。

人需要多少土地？

　　有一個姊姊 an elder sister 去拜訪她住在鄉下的妹妹 visit her younger sister。姊姊嫁給鎮上的商人 be married to a tradesman，妹妹嫁給村裡的一個農夫 to a peasant。當姊妹倆坐在一塊喝茶談天 sit over their tea talking，姊姊開始誇耀 boast 鎮上生活的好處 the advantages of town life，說他們在那裡住得 live 有多舒服 how comfortably，穿得 dress 有多好 how well，吃的、喝的 eat and drink 有多好 what good things，還有戲院 the theater 和其他各種娛樂 other types of entertainment。

　　妹妹聽了覺得很煩 be annoyed，接下來 in turn 她嘲諷 mock 商人的生活 the life of a tradesman，捍衛 stand up for 農夫的生活 the life of a peasant。

　　「我才不會改變自己的生活方式 change my way of life，換成你們那樣的 for yours，」她說：「我們可能過得很差 live roughly，但至少 at least 我們無須擔憂 be free from anxiety。你們過得比我們好 live in a better style，賺的錢比所需的還多 earn more than you need，但你們有可能失去 be very likely to lose 所有的一切 all you have。」

　　她繼續說：「我們都知道諺語 know the proverb 說：『失去和獲得 loss and gain 是攣生兄弟 brothers twain』，它通常發生在今天 one day 很有錢 be wealthy，明天 the next 卻要乞討維生 beg for their bread 的人身上。我們的生活方式比較安全，雖然農夫的生活並不優渥 be not fat one，卻比較長久 be long。」

　　房子的主人 the master of the house，帕霍姆 Pahom，躺在爐子上面 lie on the top of the stove，聽見女人們的談話。

　　「這真是完全正確，」他說：「從小 from childhood 忙著耕地 farm Mother Earth，我們農夫沒有時間讓 have no time to let 任何無意義的事 any nonsense 停留在我們腦中 settle in our heads，我們唯一的煩惱 our only trouble 是土地不夠多 haven't got enough land。如果我們有足夠的土地 have plenty of land，我才不怕 wouldn't fear 撒旦本人 the Devil himself！」

　　女人喝完茶 finish their tea，聊了一會衣服 chat about dresses，收拾完 clear away 茶具 the tea things 以後，就躺下睡覺 lie down to sleep。撒旦 the Devil 一直坐在爐子後面 sit behind the stove，聽見 hear 所有的談話 all that is said。

當作主詞、補語、受詞來用的 that 子句

- **It** often happens **that** people who are wealthy one day are begging for their bread the next.
  它通常發生在今天很有錢，明天卻要向人乞討維生的人身上。
  （that 子句當主詞：一般都會用虛主詞 it 放在句首，真主詞 that 子句則出現主要動詞後。）

- Our only trouble is **that** we haven't got enough land.
  我們唯一的煩惱是土地不夠多（that 子句當補語：放在 be 動詞後。）

- Pahom heard (that) a neighbor was going to buy fifty acres of land.
  帕霍姆聽說他的鄰居要買 50 畝地（that 子句當受詞：這時的 that 可以省略。）

He was pleased to hear / that the man had boasted / that if he had plenty of land, / he would not fear the Devil himself.

"All right," thought the Devil. "We will have a contest. I'll give you enough land, / and by means of that land, / I will get you into my power."

One day, / Pahom heard / that a neighbor was going to buy fifty acres of land, / so he felt envious. Pahom and his wife / sold some of their property / and borrowed some money. Then, / they bought a farm of forty acres.

So now / Pahom had land of his own. He borrowed seed / and sowed it on the land / he had bought. The harvest was a good one, / and within a year, / he had managed to pay off his debts. So he became a landowner. When he went out to plow his fields / or to look at his growing corn, / his heart would fill with joy.

However, / over time, / some of the peasants in the neighborhood / began to trespass across Pahom's land / with their cows and horses. For a long time, / Pahom forgave the owners. But at last / he lost patience / and complained to the district court. He thought, "I cannot go on overlooking it, / or they will destroy / all I have. They must be taught a lesson."

Pahom began to fine his neighbors / for trespassing on his land. This made them very upset with him, / so they started to trespass on his land / on purpose. Sometimes, / they even sneaked onto his land at night / and chopped down his trees. Pahom was furious.

He tried to figure out / who was doing it, / and he decided / that it was probably Simon. He took Simon to court, / but Pahom had no evidence / against Simon. The judges let Simon go, / so Pahom got angry at them / and quarreled with the judges / and with his neighbors. Threats to burn his building / began to be uttered.

- have a contest 比賽 · by means of 藉由 · feel envious 覺得嫉妒 · property 財產
- sow 種 · manage to 設法 · pay off one's debts 還清債務 · landowner 地主
- neighborhood 鄰近地區 · trespass 穿過 · lose patience 失去耐性
- district court 地區法院 · overlook 忽視 · be taught a lesson 記取教訓 · fine 罰錢
- upset with 對……很不高興 · on purpose 故意 · sneak 偷溜 · chop down 砍下
- furious 盛怒的 · figure out 找出 · take . . . to court 帶到法庭 · evidence 證據
- judge 法官 · threat 威脅 · utter 說出

---

1. **by means of that land** 靠著那塊土地
   〈by means of . . .〉意「利用……」、「藉由……的幫助」，這裡的 means 指「手段」、「方法」。

2. **he had managed to pay off his debts** 他成功地還清他的債務
   〈manage to . . .〉是「設法去……」、「順利地完成……」、「用任何方法去……」。
   〈pay off〉是「還清」、「償還」債務等的意思。

3. **I cannot go on overlooking it** 我不能繼續坐視不理。
   〈go on + V-ing〉是「繼續／持續去……」的意思。

他很高興 be pleased 聽到那男人誇口自己若有許多土地 plenty of land，便不怕撒旦。

「好吧 all right，」撒旦想，「我們來個比賽 have a contest，我會給你足夠的土地 give you enough land，藉著土地，我會讓你擁有我的力量 get you into my power。」

有天 one day，帕霍姆聽說他的鄰居 neighbor 要買 50 畝地 fifty acres of land，他很嫉妒 feel envious。帕霍姆和妻子把他們一部分的財產賣掉 sell some of their property，借了一些錢 borrow some money，買了一塊 40 畝的農地 a farm of forty acres。

所以現在帕霍姆有自己的土地了 land of his own，他借了一些種子 borrow seed，把它們種 sow 在他買的田地裡。由於田裡的收成 harvest 很好，他在一年內 within a year 便還清了債務，於是他變成地主 become a landowner。當他出去耕田 plow his fields，或是去看他種的玉米 his growing corn，他的心充滿歡喜 fill with joy。

不過，時間一點一滴的過去 over time，附近有些農夫 some of the peasants 開始帶著他們的牛和馬 with their cows and horses 穿越帕霍姆的土地 trespass across Pahom's land。好長一段時間，帕霍姆都原諒了那些牛馬的主人 forgive the owners，但最後 at last，他失去了耐心 lose patience，向地方法庭申訴 complain to the district court。他想「我不能再坐視不理 overlook it，不然他們會毀掉我所有的一切 destroy all I have，他們必須學到教訓 be taught a lesson。」

只要鄰居穿越他的土地 trespass on his land，他就罰他們錢 fine his neighbors。這讓他們很生氣，所以他們故意 on purpose 穿過他的土地。有時候，甚至晚上偷溜到他的土地上 sneak onto his land，砍下他的樹 chop down his trees，帕霍姆氣得火冒三丈 be furious。

他試圖查明 figure out 是誰做的，他判定大概是西門 probably Simon，他帶西門到法院 take Simon to court，控告西門，但是帕霍姆沒有證據 have no evidence。法官 the judges 放了西門 let Simon go，所以帕霍姆很氣他們 get angry at them。他和法官及鄰居起了爭執 quarrel，有人開始恐嚇 threat 要燒毀他的家。

About this time, / there was a rumor / that many people were moving to a new place. "There's no need / for me / to leave my land," thought Pahom. "But some of the others / might leave our village, / and then there would be more room for us. I would take over their land myself / and make my estate a bit bigger."

One day, / Pahom was sitting at home / when a peasant / passing through the village / happened to call on him. The peasant was allowed to stay the night, / and supper was given to him. Pahom had a talk with this peasant / and asked him / where he had come from. The stranger answered / that he had come from beyond the Volga River, / where he had been working. He said / that many people were moving there. Anyone / who moved to the village / was given twenty-five acres of land / for free.

"The land there / is very good," said the peasant. "One peasant moved to the village / with nothing at all, / but now he is very wealthy."

Pahom's heart / was filled with desire. He thought, "Why should I suffer / in this narrow hole / if one can live so well elsewhere? I will sell my land here, / and with the money I get, / I will start all over again / with more land. But I must first go / and find out all about it myself."

So Pahom went down / to the land beyond the Volga. It was / just as the stranger had said. The peasants owned plenty of land. The village gave each person / twenty-five acres of land, / and people could also buy / as much land as they could afford. Pahom moved with his family / to the new settlement.

Pahom had much more land / than before. In fact, / he was ten times better off / than he had been. This made Pahom very happy. But after he got used to it, / he began to think / that even here he did not have enough land. He grew tired of / having to rent other people's land / every year. Wherever there was good land to be had, / the peasants would rush for it / and argue about the land.

- **rumor** 傳言　　·**room** 空間　　·**take over** 接手　　·**estate** 產業　　·**pass through** 經過
- **call on** 拜訪　　·**beyond** 在……的那一邊　　·**for free** 免費　　·**suffer** 受苦
- **start all over again** 重頭來過　　·**find out** 找出　　·**afford** 付得起　　·**settlement** 居住地
- **better off** 更有餘裕的　　·**get used to** 習慣於　　·**grow tired of** 對……厭煩　　·**rush** 搶購

CLOSE UP

1　**There's no need for me to leave my land.** 我不需要離開我的土地。
〈there's no need to . . . 〉是「沒必要去……」的意思，
to不定詞的行為者要用〈for＋受格〉的形式，放在to不定詞前。

2　**could also buy as much land as they could afford** 也可以買很多自己負擔得起的地
〈as much/many . . . as . . . 〉是「像……一樣多的……」的意思。

3　**he was ten times better off than he had been** 他比以前富裕10倍
time 可以用來表倍數，例如three times（三倍）、four times（四倍）；表兩倍的話，twice 比two times 更常用。

這時候 about this time，有傳言 rumor 說許多人 many people 要遷居到一個新的地方 move to a new place。「我不需要 there's no need 離開我的土地 leave my land，」帕霍姆想，「但有些人 some of the others 可能會離開我們的村莊 leave our village，那麼就會有更多地方讓我們耕種，我將親自接手他們的土地 take over their land，讓我的產業更大 make my estate a bit bigger。」

有一天，帕霍姆坐在家裡 sit at home，有一個農夫經過村莊 pass through the village 突然來拜訪他 call on him，帕霍姆讓這個農夫留宿一晚 stay the night，招待他吃晚餐。帕霍姆和這位農夫聊天 have a talk，問他從哪裡來，這個陌生人 the stranger 回答他從伏加河的另一頭來到這裡 come from beyond the Volga River，他曾在那裡工作。許多人都要搬去那裡 move there，任何搬進那座村莊的人 move to the village，就可以免費 for free 獲得25畝地 twenty-five acres of land。

「那裡的土地 the land there 很肥沃 be very good，」那個農夫說：「有一個農夫一開始一貧如洗 with nothing，搬到那個村莊以後，現在很有錢 be very wealthy。」

帕霍姆心裡 Pahom's heart 充滿了慾望 be filled with desire，他想，「如果人可以在其他地方過得這麼好，為什麼我要擠在這個窄洞裡 in this narrow hole 受苦 suffer？我要把我的土地賣掉 sell my land，用我所得到的錢 with the money I get，從頭來過 start all over again，得到更多土地 with more land，但是我得先去，親自打探消息 find out all about it。」

於是帕霍姆來到 go down 伏加河另一邊的土地，如陌生人所說的，那裡的農夫擁有許多田地 own plenty of land，村莊給每個人25畝地，大家也可以買自己能負擔得起的土地 as much land as they can afford。帕霍姆帶著全家 with his family 搬到新的居住地 to the new settlement。

帕霍姆比以前擁有更多地 have much more land，事實上，他比以前富裕10倍 be ten times better off，這讓帕霍姆相當開心，但是等他習慣 get used to it 以後，他又開始覺得他在這裡沒有足夠的田地 do not have enough land。他很厭煩 grow tired of 每年都要跟別人租地 rent other people's land。哪裡有好田地可以買 good land to be had，農夫就會急忙去搶購 rush for it，為土地爭吵 argue about the land。

"If it were my own land," thought Pahom, "I would be independent, / and there would not be all this unpleasantness."

So Pahom began looking out for land / which he could buy. One day, / a peddler went by his house. He said / that he was just returning / from the land of the Bashkirs, / which was far away. There, / he had bought / thirteen thousand acres of land / for one thousand rubles.

"That area has so much land / that you could walk for a year / and still be in the land of the Bashkirs. They sell their land / for very cheap prices. All one has to do / is / make friends with the chief. The land lies near a river, / and the whole prairie is virgin soil."

Pahom was curious, / so he made up his mind / to visit the land of the Bashkirs. Before he went there, / he bought some gifts. The peddler had told him / that it was their custom / to give gifts.

On the seventh day of his travels, / he came to a place / where the Bashkirs had pitched their tents. It was all / just as the peddler had said. The people lived by a river / on the steppes / in felt-covered tents.

They were a simple people. They did not farm at all. The men merely sat around, / drank tea, / ate lamb, / and played their pipes to make music. Still, / despite being uneducated and knowing no Russian, / they were good-natured enough.

As soon as they saw Pahom, / they came out of their tents / and gathered around their visitor. An interpreter was found, / and Pahom told them / he had come about some land. They took Pahom / and led him into one of the best tents. Pahom took some presents out of his cart / and distributed them among the Bashkirs. The Bashkirs were delighted.

· independent 獨立的   · unpleasantness 不愉快   · look out for 向外尋找
· peddler 小販   · virgin soil 處女地   · make up one's mind 下定決心   · custom 習俗
· pitch 紮營   · steppe 大草原   · felt-covered tent 毛氈的帳棚   · farm 耕地
· merely 只是   · despite 除了   · uneducated 沒受過教育的
· good-natured 善良溫厚的   · interpreter 通譯員   · take . . . out of . . . 從……拿出
· distribute 分送   · delighted 高興的

CLOSE UP

1 **All one has to do is (to) make friends with the chief.** 你只須要跟首領交朋友。
〈all . . . have to do is (to) . . . 〉是「……要做的事就只是……」、「……只要做……就可以了」的意思。

2 **he made up his mind to visit the land of the Bashkirs**
他下定決心要探訪巴什基爾人的地
〈make up one's mind to . . . 〉是「決定／下定決心要去……」的意思，也可以換成〈decide to……〉

3 **as soon as they saw Pahom** 他們一看到帕霍姆
〈as soon as . . . 〉是「一當……」的意思。

「如果那是我自己的地 my own land，」帕霍姆想，「我就獨立 be independent 了，這一切的不愉快 all this unpleasantness 就會消失了。」

於是帕霍姆開始到處去找尋他買得起的土地 look out for land。有一天 one day 有一個小販 a peddler 經過他的家 go by his house，他說他剛 just 從巴什基爾人的地 the land of the Bashkirs 回來 return，那在很遠的地方 be far away，他在那裡用 1000 盧布 for one thousand rubles 買下 13000 畝地 thirteen thousand acres of land。

「那個地區 that area 有很多土地 have so much land，你可以走上一年 walk for a year，卻還在巴什基爾人的地上 be in the land of the Bashkirs。他們用很便宜的價錢 for very cheap prices 販賣土地 sell their land。你只需要 all one has to do 跟首領交朋友 make friends with the chief。那片地在河附近 lie near a river，整個草原 the whole prairie 都是處女地 virgin soil。」

帕霍姆很好奇 be curious，於是他下定決心 make up his mind 要去探訪那片土地 visit the land，他出發前買了一些禮物 buy some gifs，小販告訴他送禮 give gifts 是他們的習俗 their custom。

旅途的第七天 on the seventh day，他來到巴什基爾人紮營的地方 pitch their tents，正如小販所說，他們住在河邊 by a river 的大草原上 on the steppes，住在毛氈的帳棚裡 in felt-covered tents。

他們是一群單純的人 simple people，不需要耕地 do not farm，只是坐在一起 sit around，喝茶 drink tea，吃羊肉 eat lamb，吹笛 play their pipes 作樂 make music。除了沒受過教育 be uneducated，不會說俄文 know no Russian，他們相當善良溫厚 good-natured enough。

他們一看到帕霍姆 see Pahom 就走出帳棚 come out of their tents 圍在這位訪客旁邊 gather around their visitor。他們找了一名通譯員 an interpreter，帕霍姆告訴他們，他是為了土地而來 come about some land。他們帶帕霍姆 take Pahom 進到其中一個最好的帳棚 into one of the best tents。帕霍姆從他的推車上 out of his cart 拿出了一些禮物 take some presents，分送給他們 distribute them。巴什基爾人很高興 be delighted。

GRAMMAR POINT

which（關係代名詞）

⇨ 代替前面出現的事物（先行詞）。which 引導的關係子句說明一個不可以省略的必要資訊，稱為限定用法；附帶說明和該事物有關的事項，稱為非限定用法。

- So Pahom began looking out for *land* **which** he could buy.

  於是帕霍姆開始到處去找尋他買得起的土地。（限定用法）

- He was just returning from *the land of the Bashkirs*, **which** was far away.

  他剛從巴什基爾人的地回來，那在很遙遠的地方。（非限定用法：which 前要加逗點）

The Bashkirs talked for a while / and then told the interpreter to translate. "They wish to tell you," said the interpreter, "that they like you, / and that it is our custom / to do all we can / to please a guest / and to repay him for his gifts. You have given us presents. Now tell us / which of the things we possess / please you best / so that we may present them to you."

"What pleases me best here," answered Pahom, "is your land. Our land is crowded, / and the soil is exhausted; / but you have plenty of land, / and it is good land." The interpreter translated.

The Bashkirs talked among themselves / for a while. Then, / they were silent / and looked at Pahom / while the interpreter said, "They wish me to tell you / that in return for your presents, / they will gladly give you / as much land as you want. You have only to point it out / with your hand, / and it is yours."

The Bashkirs talked again for a while / and began to have a dispute. Pahom asked / what they were arguing about. The interpreter told him / that some of them thought / they ought to ask their chief about the land / and ought not to act in his absence.

While the Bashkirs were arguing, / a man in a large fox-fur cap / appeared on the scene. They all became silent / and rose to their feet. The interpreter said, "This is our chief himself."

Pahom immediately took out / the best dressing gown and five pounds of tea, / and he offered these to the chief. The chief accepted them / and seated himself in the place of honor. The Bashkirs at once / began telling him something. The chief listened for a while / and addressed himself to Pahom. Speaking in Russian, / he said, "Well, let it be so. Choose / whatever piece of land / you like. We have plenty of it."

· translate 翻譯　·wish to 希望　·repay 回報　·possess 擁有　·present 禮物
·crowded 擁擠的　·exhausted 疲乏的　·in return for 作為回報　·point out 指出
·have a dispute 爭吵　·ought to 應該　·chief 首領　·in one's absence 某人不在時
·fox-fur cap 狐皮帽　·on the scene 出現　·rise to one's feet 起身
·in the place of honor 上席；主位　·at once 立刻　·address 說話

CLOSE UP

1　**so that we may present them to you** 這樣我們就能把它送給你
〈so that . . . 〉是「這樣就能……」、「以便……」的意思。

2　**in return for your presents** 作為你送我們禮物的回報
〈in return for . . . 〉是「作為……的回報」、「作為……代價」的意思。

3　**you have only to point it out** 你只需要用手指出來
〈have only to . . . 〉是「只要做……就可以了」的意思。

4　**addressed himself to Pahom** 開口跟帕霍姆說話
〈address oneself to . . . 〉是「對……說話」的意思。

巴什基爾人談了一會兒 talk for a while，請通譯員翻譯 translate：「他們想告訴你 wish to tell you，」翻譯說：「他們喜歡你 like you。我們的習俗 our custom 是盡我們所能的 all we can 讓賓客高興 please a guest，報答他的禮物 repay him for his gifts。你為我們帶了禮物 give us presents，現在告訴我們，我們哪一樣東西 the things we possess 讓你最滿意 please you best，我們會把它送給你 present them to you。」通譯員如此說。

　　「這裡最讓我滿意 what pleases me best 的是你們的土地 your land。」帕霍姆回答：「我們的土地 our land 很擁擠 be crowded，土壤 the soil 貧乏了 be exhausted，但你們有許多土地 have plenty of land，而且是肥沃的地 good land。」通譯員翻譯道。

　　巴什基爾人之間 talk among themselves 討論了一會兒，然後他們靜默 be silent，看著帕霍姆 look at Pahom。通譯員說：「他們要我告訴你，作為你送禮的回報 in return for your presents，他們樂意給你土地，想要多少都可以 as much land as you want，你只需要用手 with your hand 指出你想要的地 point it out，那就是你的了。」

　　巴什基爾人談了一會兒，開始爭論 have a dispute。帕霍姆問他們在吵什麼，通譯員告訴他，他們其中有些人認為應該要問首領 ought to ask their chief，不應 ought not to 在他不在的時候 in his absence 自作主張 act。

　　當巴什基爾人爭吵的時候，一個男人頭戴狐皮製成的大帽子 in a large fox-fur cap，出現在他們眼前 appear on the scene。他們全都安靜下來 become silent，站起來 rise to their feet。通譯員說：「那是我們的首領 our chief。」

　　帕霍姆立刻拿出 take out 最上等的袍子 the best dressing gown 和五磅茶葉 five pounds of tea，把它們送給首領 offer these to the chief。首領接受這些禮物 accept them，坐在主位 seat himself in the place of honor。巴什基爾人立刻 at once 開始告訴他發生了什麼事 tell him something，首領聽了一會兒 listen for a while 開口跟帕霍姆說話 address himself to Pahom，用俄語說 speak in Russian：「好，就這麼做吧 let it be so，選 choose 一塊你喜歡的地 whatever piece of land you like，我們多的是。」

"How can I take / as much as I like?" thought Pahom. "I must get a deed / to make it secure, / or else they may say, 'It is yours,' / and afterward / they may take it away again."

To the chief, / he said, "I must get a deed / as a guarantee, / or else / you may take the land away from me / in the future."

The chief said, "We will go to the town with you / and make a deed for the land."

"And what will be the price?" asked Pahom.

The chief answered, "Our price is always the same: one thousand rubles a day."

Pahom did not understand. "A day? What measure is that? How many acres would that be?"

The chief said, "We don't know / how to figure out the acres, / so we sell land / by the day. As much as you can go round / on your feet / in a day / is yours, / and the price is / one thousand rubles a day."

Pahom said, "But you can walk around / a large tract of land / in a single day."

The chief laughed / and then answered, "It will all be yours. But there is one condition: If you don't return to the spot / where you started / on the same day, / your money is lost. You must make a circle. You may make as large a circle / as you wish, / but you must return to your starting point / before the sun sets. Then, / all of the land / that you walked around / will be yours."

Pahom agreed to the chief's conditions, / and they decided to start / the next morning.

That night, / Pahom lay in bed / thinking about the land. He thought, "I can cover / an enormous amount of land. I can easily walk / thirty-five miles / in one day. Imagine / how much land / that will be."

· **deed** 契約　· **secure** 安全的　· **or else** 不然　· **afterward** 之後　· **take away** 拿走
· **guarantee** 保證　· **measure** 單位　· **figure out** 計算
· **a large tract of land** 一大片土地　· **condition** 條件　· **spot** 地方；點　· **set** 日落
· **enormous** 廣大的　· **imagine** 想像

CLOSE UP

1　**you may take the land away from me** 你可能從我這裡把土地拿走
〈take . . . away from . . . 〉是「從……拿走……」的意思。

2　**how to figure out the acres** 畝怎麼算
這裡的 figure out 是「計算、算出」數量或費用等的意思。另外，figure out 也常拿來當作經過審慎思考後「理解／知道……」的意思。例 I can't figure out the answer. （我不知道答案。）

3　**we sell land by the day** 我們以日為單位來賣地
by 也能用來表單位。例 by the hour（以小時為單位）/ by the kilo（以公斤為單位）

「怎樣才能得到更多我想要的土地 as much as I like 呢？」帕霍姆想，「我一定要拿到契約 get a deed，這樣才安全 make it secure，不然 or else 他們可能會說：『那是你的』，然後之後 afterward 又把土地拿走 take it away。」

他對首領說：「我想要一份契約作保證 as a guarantee，不然你將來 in the future 可能從我這裡把土地拿走 take the land away from me。」

首領說：「我們會和你一起到鎮上 go to the town，立一份土地的契約 make a deed for the land。」

「那麼價錢 the price 怎麼算？」帕霍姆問。

首領回答：「我們的價錢一直以來都一樣 be always the same，一天1000盧布 one thousand rubles a day。」

帕霍姆不明白，「一天？這是什麼單位 what measure？這樣是多少畝 how many acres？」

首領說：「我們不知道畝怎麼算 figure out the acres，於是我們以日為單位 by the day 來賣地，只要一天之內 in a day 用腳 on your feet 能走多少 as much as you can go round 就都是你的，價錢都是一天1000盧布。」

帕霍姆說：「但光是一天內 in a single day 就可以走 walk around 一大片土地 a large tract of land。」

首領笑了，然後回答：「那麼土地就都是你的，但有一個條件 one condition，如果你同一天內 on the same day 回不到 don't return 你出發的地方 the spot where you start，你的錢 your money 就沒了 be lost。你一定要走一個圓 make a circle，你想要多大的圓都可以 as large a circle as you wish，但一定要在日落前 before the sun sets 回到起點 return to your starting point，那麼你所走完的土地就是你的了。」

帕霍姆同意首領的條件 agree to the chief's conditions，他們決定 decide 明天早上 the next morning 再開始 start。

那天晚上 that night，帕霍姆躺在床上 lie in bed 想著土地 think about the land，他想，「我可以走完 cover 一片廣大的土地 an enormous amount of land，我一天內 in one day 可以輕鬆走完35哩 walk thirty-five miles，想像 imagine 一下那會是多少地 how much land。」

GRAMMAR POINT

as . . . as. . . :像……一樣……

- How can I take **as much as** I like? 怎樣才能得到更多我想要的土地？
- **As much as** you can go round on your feet in a day is yours.
  只要一天之內你用腳能走多少土地，就算你的。
- You may make **as large** a circle **as** you wish. 你想要走多大的圓都可以。
- The people on the hill were **as small as** ants. 山丘上的人看起來像螞蟻一樣小。

Pahom lay awake all night / and dozed off / only just before dawn. Hardly were his eyes closed / when he had a dream. In his dream, / the chief of the Bashkirs / was sitting in front of a tent / and laughing. "What are you laughing at?" he asked the chief. But the chief was no longer there. Instead, / it was the peddler / who had stopped at his house / and told him about the Bashkirs. Then, the peddler disappeared, / and the peasant / who had told him about the land beyond the Volga River / suddenly appeared. Then, / he saw / that it was not the peasant either, / but the Devil himself / with hoofs and horns, / sitting there and chuckling. There was a man / lying dead in front of the Devil, / and it was Pahom himself. He awoke horror-struck.

Looking round, / he saw through the open door / that the dawn was breaking. "It's time / to wake them up," he thought. "We ought to be starting."

Pahom, the chief, and the other Bashkirs / met on the land / early in the morning. The chief stretched his arms out / and said, "All of this land–as far as you can see– / belongs to us. You may have / any part of it / you like."

The chief took off his fox-fur cap, / placed it on the ground, / and said, "This will be the mark. Start from here / and return here again. All the land / you go around / shall be yours." Pahom took out his money / and put it on the cap.

Pahom stood / ready to start / with a spade in his hand. He considered / for some moments / which way he had better go. Then, he concluded, "I will go toward the rising sun."

·lie awake 清醒地躺著　·doze off 打瞌睡　·dawn 黎明　·hardly 幾乎　·appear 出現
·hoof 蹄　·chuckle 咯咯笑　·lying dead 橫屍　·horror-struck 驚恐萬分
·stretch out 伸出　·spade 鏟子

1　**the peddler disappeared** 那位小販消失 / **suddenly appeared** 突然出現
　appear（出現）和disappear（消失不見）是相反的意思。

2　**It's time to wake them up.** 是時候把他們叫醒了
　〈it's time to . . .〉是「該是……的時候了」的意思。

3　**all of this land–as far as you can see** 這裡所有的地，你能看多遠就有多遠
　〈as far as . . .〉是距離、範圍、程度等的「直到……」的意思。

整晚 **all night** 帕霍姆清醒地躺著 **lie awake**，破曉前 **just before dawn** 才打了一會兒瞌睡 **doze off**，剛閉上雙眼，他就做了一個夢 **have a dream**。在夢裡 **in his dream**，巴什基爾人的首領 **the chief of the Bashkirs** 坐在帳棚前 **sit in front of a tent**，大笑 **laugh**。「你在笑什麼？」他問首領，但首領消失不見了 **be no longer there**，而是 **instead**，那個停留在他家 **stop at his house**、告訴他巴什基爾人 **tell him about the Bashkirs** 的那個小販 **the peddler** 出現了，然後小販又消失 **disappear** 了。那個跟他說伏加河另一邊土地 **the land beyond the Volga River** 的農夫 **the peasant** 突然出現了 **suddenly appear**。然後，他看了一下，又不是農夫，而是有蹄有角 **with hoofs and horns** 的撒旦本尊 **the Devil himself**，坐在那裡 **sit there** 咯咯笑 **chuckle**。有一個人橫屍 **lie dead** 在撒旦前面 **in front of the Devil**，是帕霍姆自己 **Pahom himself**。他又驚又怕地醒了 **awake horror–struck**。

他看看四周 **look around**，從半開的門 **through the open door** 看到黎明 **the dawn** 破曉 **break**。「是時候 **it's time** 把他們叫醒了 **wake them up**，」他想，「我們該開始了。」

帕霍姆、首領和其他巴什基爾人一大早在土地上碰面，首領伸出他的雙臂 **stretch his arms out**，說：「這裡所有的土地 **all of this land**，視線所達之處 **as far as you can see**，都屬於我們的 **belong to us**。你可以得到你想要的任何一部分 **have any part of it**。」

首領拿下他的狐皮帽 **take off his fox–fur cap**，放在地上 **place it on the ground**，說：「這個當作記號 **the mark**，從這裡開始 **start from here**，再回到這裡 **return here**，你走完的所有土地將會是你的。」帕霍姆拿出他的錢 **take out his money**，放在帽子上 **put it on the cap**。

帕霍姆站好準備開始 **ready to start**，他手拿一把鏟子 **with a spade in his hand**，他考慮 **consider** 了一會兒 **for some moments** 他應該走哪個方向 **which way**，然後，他決定 **conclude**，「我要朝日出的方向 **toward the rising sun** 走。」

hardly . . . when . . . ：一……就……（倒裝句）

⇨ 有 hardly 的主要子句，時常都是用過去完成式的，也可以用 scarcely 來代替 hardly。

- **Hardly** were his eyes closed **when** he had a dream. 一閉上雙眼，他就做了一個夢。
  (= His eyes were **hardly** closed **when** he had a dream.
  = His eyes had **hardly** been closed **when** he had a dream.)
- **Hardly** had they seen me **when** they ran away. 他們一看到我，就跑走了。
  (= They had **hardly** seen me **when** they ran away.)

Pahom started walking / neither slowly / nor quickly. After having gone a thousand yards, / he stopped, / dug a hole, / and placed pieces of turf one on another / to make it more visible. Then he went on. Now that he had walked off his stiffness, / he quickened his pace. After a while, / he dug another hole.

The weather was getting warmer. He looked at the sun. It was time / to think of breakfast. "It is too soon yet / to turn. I will just take off my boots," he said to himself. He sat down, / took off his boots, / stuck them into his girdle, / and went on. It was easy / to walk now.

"I will go on / for another three miles," he thought, "and then turn to the left. This land here is so nice / that it would be a pity / to lose it."

He went straight on / for a while, / and then he looked back. The people on the hill / where he had started / were as small as ants. "Ah, I have gone far enough / in this direction," he thought. "It's time / to turn and go another direction. Besides, / I'm getting tired / and need something to drink."

He looked at the sun / and saw / that it was noon. He sat down, / ate some bread, / and drank some water. But he did not lie down / as he thought / that if he did, / he might fall asleep. After sitting for a little while, / he went on again. It had become terribly hot, / and he felt sleepy. Still, he went on, / thinking, "An hour to suffer, / a lifetime to live."

He went a long way / in this direction also / and was about to turn to the left again / when he perceived a damp hollow. "It would be a pity / to leave that out," he thought. So he went on past the hollow / and dug a hole / on the other side of it.

"Ah!" thought Pahom, "I have made the sides too long; I must make this one shorter." And he went along the third side / as he moved faster. He looked at the sun. It was nearly halfway to the horizon, / and he had not yet done / two miles of the third side of the square. He was still ten miles from his goal.

· dig a hole 挖個洞   · turf 草皮塊   · walk off 消除   · stiffness 僵硬   · quicken 加快
· take off 脫下   · girdle 皮帶   · stick 塞在   · a pity 可惜   · go straight 直走
· look back 往回看   · lie down 躺下   · fall asleep 睡著   · suffer 痛苦   · lifetime 一輩子
· perceive 看到   · damp 潮濕的   · hollow 山谷   · horizon 地平線   · square 正方形

CLOSE UP

1   **neither slowly nor quickly** 不慢也不快
〈neither . . . nor . . . 〉(不是……也不是……)。

2   **now that he had walked off his stiffness** 因為走路讓身體的僵硬消失了
〈now that . . . 〉(因為……)。

3   **It is too soon yet to turn.** 現在轉彎還太早了。
〈too . . . to . . . 〉(太……以致不能……)。

4   **was about to turn to the left** 是時候左轉了
〈be about to . . . 〉(正要去……的時候)。

帕霍姆不疾不徐地 **neither slowly nor quickly** 開始走 **start walking**，他走了1000碼（900公尺）**go a thousand yards** 以後，停下來 **stop**，挖個洞 **dig a hole**，放了幾塊草皮 **pieces of turf**，一塊疊一塊 **one on another**，讓它更明顯 **make it more visible**，然後他繼續走 **go on**，走到身體不再僵硬 **walk off his stiffness**，他就加快步伐 **quicken his pace**。過一會兒，他又挖了一個洞 **dig another hole**。

天氣變得暖和 **get warmer**，他看著太陽 **look at the sun**，是時候想想早餐了 **think of breakfast**。「現在轉彎還太早了，我要脫下我的靴子。」他跟自己說，他坐下 **sit down**，脫掉他的靴子 **take off his boots** 把它們塞在他的皮帶 **stick them into his girdle** 裡，然後繼續走 **go on**，現在好走多了。

「我要再繼續走三哩（五公里）**another three miles**，」他想，「然後再左轉 **turn to the left**。這裡的土地 **this land here** 太好了 **be so nice**，如果失去它 **lose it** 很可惜 **a pity**。」

過了一陣子 **for a while** 他又繼續往前走 **go straight on**，然後他往回看 **look back**，山丘上的人 **the people on the hill** 看起來像螞蟻一樣小 **as small as ants**。「啊，我往這個方向 **in this direction** 走得已經夠遠了 **go far enough**，」他想，「是時候轉彎，朝另一個方向走了 **go another direction**，而且 **besides**，我也累了 **get tired**，需要喝點水。」

他看看太陽，已經是中午 **noon** 了，他坐下來，吃了一點麵包 **eat some bread**，喝了一點水 **drink some water**，但他沒有躺下 **do not lie down**，因為他覺得如果他躺下，他可能會睡著 **fall asleep**。他坐了一會兒 **sit for a little while**，又繼續走 **go on again**。天氣變得非常地熱 **become terribly hot**，他覺得很睏 **feel sleepy**，但他仍然繼續走，心想「痛苦一小時 **an hour to suffer**，享受一輩子 **a lifetime to live**。」

他往這個方向走了很長一段路 **go a long way**，又該左轉了，然後他看到一個潮濕的山谷 **perceive a damp hollow**。「捨棄這個 **leave that out** 太可惜了 **a pity**。」他想，於是他繼續走過了山谷 **past the hollow**，在山谷的另一邊 **on the other side of it** 挖了一個洞 **dig a hole**。

「啊 ah！」帕霍姆想，「我把邊界弄得太長了 **make the sides too long**，我得把這邊弄短一點 **make this one shorter**。」他走第三邊 **go along the third side** 時加快了腳步 **move faster**，他看太陽，離地平線只剩一半的距離 **nearly halfway to the horizon**，而他還要走兩哩 **have not yet done two miles**（三公里），才走完正方形的第三邊 **the third side of the square**，他離目標還有10哩 **ten miles from his goal**。

"I've got to hurry back / in a straight line / now. I shouldn't go too far," he thought. "Besides, / I already have a huge amount of land." So Pahom turned / and hurried toward the hill / that he had started from.

But he now walked with difficulty. He was done in by the heat, / his bare feet were cut and bruised, / and his legs began to fail. He longed to rest, / but it was impossible / if he meant to get back / before sunset. The sun waits for no man, / and it was sinking lower and lower.

"Oh dear," he thought, "if only I had not blundered / by trying for too much. What if I am too late?"

He looked toward the hill / and at the sun. He was still far from his goal, / and the sun was already near the rim.

Pahom walked on and on. It was very hard to walk, / but he went quicker and quicker. He began running. He threw away / his coat, his boots, his flask, and his cap / and kept only the spade / which he used as a support.

"What shall I do?" he thought again. "I have grasped too much / and ruined the whole affair. I can't get there / before the sun sets." This fear / made him still more breathless.

Pahom went on running. His soaking shirt and trousers / stuck to him, / and his mouth was parched. His chest was working / like a blacksmith's bellows, / his heart was beating / like a hammer, / and his legs were giving way / as if they did not belong to him. Though afraid of death, / he could not stop. He gathered the rest of his strength / and ran on.

·hurry back 趕回去　·be done in by 精疲力竭　·bare feet 赤腳　·bruised 瘀血的
·fail 走不動　·long to 渴望　·sunset 日落　·sink 沉　·blunder 犯錯
·try for 爭取　·rim 邊緣　·throw away 丟掉　·support 支持　·grasp 抓
·ruin 毀　·affair 事情　·fear 恐懼感　·breathless 快要不能呼吸　·soaking 濕淋淋的
·stick 黏　·parched 乾涸的　·blacksmith 鐵匠　·bellows 風箱　·give way 支撐不住

CLOSE UP

1　**I've got to hurry back** 我必須趕回去
〈have got to . . . 〉和〈have to . . . 〉一樣，是「必須……」的意思，表必須和義務。

2　**he longed to rest** 他很想休息
long 當作動詞時，是「懇切地期望」的意思，要注意〈long to ＋原形動詞〉、〈long for ＋名詞〉。
例 He longed for peace.（他渴望和平的到來）

3　**if only I had not blundered** 要是我沒有犯錯
〈if only . . . 〉是「要是……的話，就好了」的意思，表和事實相反的期望。

4　**What if I am too late?** 萬一我來不及怎麼辦？
〈What if . . . ?〉（要是……的話，該怎麼辦？）。

5　**as if they did not belong to him** 好像不屬於他自己的
〈as if . . . 〉（就像……一樣）。

「我最好走直線 in a straight line 趕回去 hurry back，我不該走太遠 shouldn't go too far，」他想，「而且我已經有一大片土地 a huge amount of land 了。」於是帕霍姆轉彎，趕回他出發的山丘 hurry toward the hill。

但是現在他行走困難 walk with difficulty，高溫讓他精疲力竭 be done in by the heat。他赤腳 his bare feet 被割傷又瘀血 be cut and bruised，他的腿 his legs 開始走不動 fail，他很想休息 long to rest，但如果一定要 mean to 在日落前 before sunset 趕回去 get back，就不可能 be impossible 休息。太陽不等人 wait for no man，它愈來愈往下沉 sink lower and lower。

「哎啊 oh, dear」他想，「但願我沒有為了得到更多土地 try for too much 而犯錯 blunder。萬一我來不及 be too late 怎麼辦？」

他往山丘一看 look toward the hill，又看看太陽，離目標還有很遠 still far from his goal，但夕陽已經在邊緣 near the rim。

帕霍姆繼續走 walk on and on，走得很艱辛，但愈走愈快 go quicker and quicker，開始跑了起來 begin running。他把大衣、靴子、水壺、帽子 his coat, his boots, his flask, and his cap 都丟了 throw away，只留 keep only 用來支撐 as a support 他的鏟子 keep only the spade。

「我該怎麼做？」他又想，「我抓奪了太多 grasp too much，把一切都毀了 ruin the whole affair，日落前我到不了終點 can't get there。」這股恐懼感 this fear 讓他更無法呼吸 more breathless。

帕霍姆繼續跑 go on running，他濕淋淋的上衣和褲子 his soaking shirt and trousers 黏在他身上 stick to him。他的嘴巴 his mouth 渴得要命 be parched。他的胸 his chest 運轉 work 得像一個鐵匠的風箱 like a blacksmith's bellows。他的心臟 his heart 跳動 beat 得像鐵鎚 like a hammer 在敲打。他的雙腳 his legs 支撐不住了 give way，好像不屬於他自己的 do not belong to him。儘管很怕死 afraid of death，他也不能停 cannot stop，他凝聚 gather 所有剩餘的殘力 the rest of his strength，繼續跑 run on。

The sun was close to the rim. Now, yes now, / it was about to set. The sun was quite low, / but he was also near his aim. Pahom could already see / the people on the hill / waving their arms / to hurry him up. He could see / the fox-fur cap on the ground / and the money on it, / and the chief / sitting on the ground / holding his sides. And Pahom remembered his dream.

"There is plenty of land," he thought, "but will God let me live on it? I have lost my life. I shall never reach that spot."

Pahom looked at the sun, / which had reached the earth. With all his remaining strength, / he rushed on. Just as he reached the hill, / it suddenly grew dark. He looked up / —the sun had already set. He gave a cry. "All my labor has been in vain," he thought.

He was about to stop, / but he heard the Bashkirs / still shouting. He realized / that the sun seemed to have set, / but the Bashkirs on the hill / could still see it. He took a long breath / and ran up the hill. It was still light there. He reached the top / and saw the cap. He fell forward / and reached the cap / with his hands.

"Ah, that's a fine fellow!" exclaimed the chief. "He has gained much land."

Pahom's servant / came running up / and tried to raise him, / but he saw / that blood was flowing / from his mouth. Pahom was dead.

The Bashkirs clicked their tongues / to show their pity.

His servant picked up the spade / and dug a grave long enough / for Pahom to lie in / and buried him in it. Six feet / from his head to his heels / was all he needed.

· **aim** 目標　· **hold one's sides** 捧腹大笑　· **lose one's life** 失去某人的性命　· **labor** 努力
· **in vain** 白費　· **be about to** 快要　· **seem to** 看起來　· **take a long breath** 深呼吸
· **fellow** 漢子　· **servant** 僕人　· **raise** 拉起　· **flow** 流出
· **click one's tongue** 舌頭發出嘖嘖聲　· **grave** 墳墓　· **lie in** 躺在裡面　· **bury** 埋
· **six feet** 六呎（180公分）

CLOSE UP

1　**had reached the earth** 落到地上 / **reached the hill** 到上丘上 /
reached the top 到山上 / **reached the cap** 摸到帽子
〈reach . . .〉是「到達／延伸到／擴展到……」的意思，也有「（伸出手去）抓住／拿……」的意思，reach 之後不能接 to，要注意。

2　**All my labor has been in vain.** 我一切的努力都白費了。
〈be in vain〉是「變成白費」、「成為泡沫」的意思。

夕陽接近地平線 close to the rim，現在，就是現在，夕陽將要西沉 be about to set。夕陽很低 quite low，但他也接近目標了 near his aim，帕霍姆已經可以見到山丘上 on the hill 的人向他揮手 wave their arms，要他趕快 hurry him up。他看到地上的狐皮帽 the fox-fur cap 和上面的錢 the money on it。首領坐在地上 sit on the ground 捧腹大笑 hold his sides。帕霍姆想起了他的夢 remember his dream。

「那裡有許多地 plenty of land，」他想「但神會讓我住在其上 let me live on it 嗎？我失去了我的性命 lose my life，永遠也到不了終點 never reach that spot。」

帕霍姆看著太陽落到地平線上 reach the earth，用他剩餘的力氣 with all his remaining strength，他趕上了 rush on。他一到上丘上 reach the hill，天突然變黑 grow dark，他抬頭看 look up，太陽已經下山了 already set。他大叫 give a cry：「我一切的努力 all my labor 都白費了 be in vain。」

他快要停下來 about to stop 的時候，他聽到巴什基爾人還在大叫，他明白太陽看起來下山了 seem to have set，但是山丘上的巴什基爾人 the Bashkirs on the hill 還看得到太陽 can still see it。他深呼吸 take a long breath，跑上山丘 run up the hill，還有一點陽光，他到了山上 reach the top，看到帽子 see the cap，他往前倒 fall forward，用手 with his hands 碰到了帽子 reach the cap。

「啊 ah，真是條好漢 a fine fellow！」首領驚呼：「他得到很多土地 gain much land。」

帕霍姆的僕人 Pahom's servant 衝上前來 come running up，試著扶他起來 raise him，但他看到他口裡 from his mouth 流出 flow 鮮血 blood。帕霍姆死了 be dead。

巴什基爾人的舌頭發出嘖嘖聲 click their tongues，表達他們的遺憾 show their pity。

他的僕人撿起鏟子 pick up the spade，挖了一個墳墓 dig a grave，長得足以讓帕霍姆躺在裡面，然後把他埋進去 bury him in it。從頭到腳 from his head to his heels，他只需要 all he needs 六呎 six feet（180公分）。

GRAMMAR POINT

enough . . . to . . . ：有足夠的……可以去……

⇨ 要注意 enough 的位置，要在形容詞後或名詞前。

- His servant dug a grave long **enough** for Pahom **to** lie in.
  他的僕人挖了一個墳墓，長得足以讓帕霍姆躺在裡面。（形容詞後）

- -

- That area has **enough** land for all of them **to** farm.
  這一帶有足夠的土地可以讓所有人耕種。（名詞前）

Super
Reading
Story
Training
Book

Step

5

A Christmas Carol
— Charles Dickens

A Christmas Carol

One Christmas Eve, / Scrooge sat busy / in his office. It was cold and foggy weather. The city clocks / had just rung three times, / but it was already quite dark.

Scrooge was an old man. **He was known / by everyone / to be mean, miserly, and cold.** He was a greedy sinner. No warmth could warm him, / and no cold could chill him. Nobody ever stopped Scrooge / on the street / to say, "My dear Scrooge, how are you?" No beggars implored him / to give them some money. Even the dogs seemed to know him, / and they avoided him, too. But Scrooge did not care / at all. He liked it / that way. People avoided him, / and he avoided people.

He had worked / in the same dark office / for many years. Once / it had been the office / of *Scrooge and Marley*. Scrooge and Marley / had been partners / for many years. And even now, / seven years after Marley had died, / those names were still on the door.

It was a very small room / with a very small fire. The only other person / in the office / was Bob Cratchit, / Scrooge's clerk. Bob was very cold. Scrooge did not give Bob / much wood for his fire / because he did not like to spend money. So the clerk put on his coat / and tried to warm himself / by the light of a candle.

Scrooge did not like anything. He especially hated Christmas.

"Merry Christmas, Uncle," cried a cheerful voice. It was the voice / of Scrooge's nephew Fred.

"Bah, humbug," said Scrooge.

"Oh, come on, Uncle," said Fred. "I'm sure / you don't mean it."

"I do," said Scrooge. "Why are you merry? You're a poor man."

"Well, why aren't you merry? You're a very rich man. And it's Christmas!"

"Bah, humbug," said Scrooge again. "**You keep Christmas / in your own way, / and let me keep it / in mine.**"

·**foggy** 有霧的　·**mean** 小氣的；心地不好的　·**miserly** 吝嗇的　·**greedy** 貪心的
·**sinner** 罪人　·**chill** 變冷　·**beggar** 乞丐　·**implore** 乞求　·**avoid** 躲避
·**do not care** 不關心　·**clerk** 職員　·**cheerful** 歡樂的　·**bah, humbug** 呸！騙人的東西
·**merry** 快樂的

CLOSE UP

1　**He was known by everyone to be mean, miserly, and cold.**
　大家都知道他很小氣、吝嗇、冷酷。
　〈be known to . . .〉是「以……知名」的意思。by everyone 是為了強調所有人都這麼認為而插入的。

2　**You keep Christmas in your own way, and let me keep it in mine.**
　你用你的方式過聖誕節，我用我的方式過。
　〈in one's own way〉是「以……的方式」的意思。這裡的 in mine 是 in my own way 的縮寫。

聖誕頌歌

　　聖誕節前夕 one Christmas Eve，施顧己 Scrooge 在他的辦公室裡 in his office 坐著忙公事 sit busy。外面天氣又冷，霧又大 cold and foggy，市鐘 the city clocks 剛響了三次 ring three times，天色卻已經很暗了 be quite dark。

　　施顧己是一個老人 an old man，大家都知道他很小氣、吝嗇、冷酷 mean, miserly, and cold。他是一個貪心的罪人 a greedy sinner，沒有溫情 no warmth 可以溫暖他 warm him，沒有冷酷 no cold 可以讓他感到寒冷 chill him。沒有人 nobody 會在街上攔下他 stop Scrooge 説：「我親愛的施顧己，你好嗎 how are you？」沒有乞丐 no beggars 向他乞討 implore，求他給他們一點錢 give them some money。連狗 even the dogs 看起來好像認識他，也躲著他 avoid him，但施顧己一點也不在意 do not care at all。他喜歡這樣 like it that way，大家躲著他，他也躲著大家。

　　他在同一間陰暗的辦公室裡 in the same dark office 工作了好幾年 for many years，這間辦公室曾經是「施顧己和馬里 Scrooge and Marley 公司」。施顧己和馬里曾是好多年的合夥人 partners，就算現在馬里已經過世七年了，那些名字依然留在門上。

　　那是一間很小的房間 a very small room，裡面只有很小的火 with a very small fire。辦公室裡面唯一的另一個人 the only other person 是施顧己的職員 Scrooge's clerk。鮑伯‧克萊契 Bob Cratchit 很冷 be cold，施顧己沒有給他很多木頭生火 much wood for his fire，因為他不想花錢 spend money，於是職員穿上大衣 put on his coat，試著用蠟燭的火光 by the light of a candle 讓自己溫暖一點 warm himself。

　　施顧己討厭一切事物 do not like anything，特別是聖誕節 hate Christmas。

　　「聖誕快樂 Merry Christmas，舅舅。」一個興高采烈的聲音説，那是施顧己的外甥佛萊德 Scrooge's nephew, Fred。

　　「呸 bah！騙人的東西 humbug。」施顧己説。

　　「喔，拜託，舅舅，」佛萊德説：「我相信你不是認真的 don't mean it。」

　　「我是認真的，」施顧己説：「你有什麼好高興的 be merry？你是個窮人 a poor man。」

　　「好吧，你為什麼不快樂？你是個很有錢的人 a rich man，而且是聖誕節呀！」

　　「呸！騙人的玩意，」施顧己又説了一次，「你用你的方式 in your own way 過聖誕節 keep Christmas，我用我的方式過我的。」

no + 名詞：任何……也不能…… ⇨ 想強調否定含意時使用。

- **No warmth** could warm him, and **no cold** could chill him.
  沒有溫情可以溫暖他，沒有冷酷可以讓他感到寒冷。

- **No beggars** implored him to give them some money.
  沒有乞丐向他乞討，求他給他們一點錢。

"Don't be so angry, Uncle. Come / and have dinner with us / tomorrow."
Scrooge merely answered, "Goodbye."

"I don't want / to be angry with you, / Uncle," said Fred. "So / a Merry Christmas, / Uncle."

"Goodbye," Scrooge only said.

After Scrooge's nephew left, / the clerk let two other people in. They were portly gentlemen. They had books and papers / in their hands / and bowed to Scrooge.

"Excuse us. May I ask, / are you Mr. Scrooge / or Mr. Marley?" said one of the gentlemen.

"Mr. Marley has been dead / these seven years. He died / seven years ago / this very night," answered Scrooge.

"Mr. Scrooge then," said the man. "At this festive season of the year, / it is nice / for everyone / to give something to people / who have nothing / –no homes, no food."

"Are there no prisons? Any orphanages?" said Scrooge.

"There are. But they always need / a little more. So / a few of us / are raising funds / to buy the poor / some meat, drink, and means of warmth. What shall I put you down for?"

"Nothing!" answered Scrooge.

"You wish / to give an anonymous gift?"

"No. I wish / to be left alone. I don't make merry / at Christmas, / and I can't afford / to make lazy fools merry. I have my work / to worry about."

After the men left, / Scrooge turned to his clerk. "You'll want / all day off / tomorrow, / I suppose?" he asked.

"If that's convenient, / sir," the clerk responded.

"It's not convenient, / and it's not fair. Yet you'll still expect me / to pay you a day's wages / for no work, / won't you?"

"It's only once a year, / sir."

"That's a poor excuse / for picking a man's pocket / every twenty-fifth of December. But I suppose / you must have the whole day. Be here early / the next morning."

The clerk promised / that he would arrive early. Scrooge walked out of the office / and went back to his empty home.

·merely 只是　　·portly 肥胖的　　·books 帳冊　　·bow 鞠躬　　·festive 歡樂的
·prison 監獄　　·orphanage 孤兒院　　·raise funds 募款　　·means of ……的工具
·put down 寫下　　·anonymous 匿名的　　·can't afford to 付不起　　·lazy 懶惰的
·all day off 整天休息　　·convenient 方便的　　·fair 公平的　　·wages 工資　　·poor 窮的
·excuse 藉口　　·pick one's pocket 偷人的錢　　·empty 空的

CLOSE UP

1 **let two other people in** 讓另外兩個人進來
〈let . . . in〉是「讓……進來」的意思。

2 **You'll want all day off** 你要休假一整天
off 是「不工作，休息」的意思。例 I have two days off this week.（我這星期有兩天休息。）

3 **expect me to pay you a day's wages** 期望我付你一天的工資
〈expect . . . to . . .〉是「期望……去……」的意思。〈pay＋人＋錢〉是「付給……多少錢」的意思。

「不要這麼生氣，舅舅，來吧 come，明天和我們一塊吃晚餐 have dinner with us。」

施顧己只是回答：「再見 goodbye。」

「我不生你的氣，舅舅，」佛萊德說：「聖誕快樂，舅舅。」

「再見。」施顧己說。

施顧己的外甥離開了以後，職員讓另外兩個人進來 let two other people in，兩個胖胖的先生 portly gentlemen，手上 in their hands 拿著帳冊和紙 have books and papers，向施顧己鞠躬 bow to him。

「不好意思 excuse us，我可以請教一下 may I ask，你是施顧己先生，還是馬里先生呢？」其中一位先生開口說道。

「馬里先生 Mr. Marley 已經過世了 be dead 七年之久，七年前 seven years ago 的今晚 this very night 死去 die」施顧己回答。

「那麼施顧己先生，」那人說：「在一年最歡樂的季節當中 at this festive season of the year（festive season 指聖誕節及新年期間），能給 give 那些一無所有 have nothing 的人一些東西 something 是一件善舉 be nice——那些人沒有家 no homes、沒有食物 no food。」

「沒有監獄 no prisons 嗎？沒有孤兒院 any orphanages 嗎？」施顧己說。

「當然有，但他們需要更多一點 need a little more 幫助，所以我們幾個 a few of us 正為窮人 the poor 買肉 meat、飲料 drink 和保暖工具 means of warmth 而募款 raise funds，我該為你寫下 put you down 什麼？」

「什麼都不要 nothing！」施顧己回答。

「你想要以無名氏捐贈禮物 give an anonymous gift 嗎？」

「不，我希望你們讓我獨處 be left alone，我不會在聖誕節製造歡樂 make merry，我也沒有錢讓那些懶惰的笨蛋快樂 make lazy fools merry，我有我的工作要擔心。」

男人離開以後，施顧己轉向他的職員 turn to his clerk。「我猜你明天想要休息一整天 want all day off？」他問。

「如果那樣方便的話 if that's convenient，先生 sir。」職員回答。

「那一點也不方便，而且不公平 it's not fair，但你還是希望 expect 我在你不用上班 for no work 這天，付你一天的工資 pay you a day's wages，對吧？」

「一年只有一次 once a year，先生。」

「這對每年 12 月 25 日 every twenty-fifth of December 都從人的口袋裡把錢偷走 pick a man's pocket 來說，是一個很爛的藉口 a poor excuse，但我猜你想要放一整天的假 have the whole day。隔天早上 the next morning 要早一點來 be here early。」

職員答應 promise 他會早點到 arrive early，施顧己走出辦公室 walk out of the office，回到 go back 自己空蕩蕩的家 to his empty home。

GRAMMAR POINT

dead（形容詞）：死的　**die（動詞）**：死

- Mr. Marley has **been dead** these seven years. 馬里先生已經過世七年了。
- He **died** seven years ago this very night. 他七年前的今晚過世了。

When Scrooge got to his building, / he put the key / into the lock of the door. But when he looked at the knocker, / he did not see a knocker / but Marley's face. Scrooge stared for a moment, / and then / it was a knocker again. He said, "Pooh, pooh!" / and closed the door / with a bang.

Scrooge went up to his room, / and carefully locked the door. He checked twice / to see if the door was locked / and then made a little fire / in the fireplace. He put on his dressing gown, slippers, and nightcap, / and sat down / before the very low fire. As he threw his head back in his chair, / he heard something in the house. It was far away, / but it was coming closer. It sounded / as if some person were dragging a heavy chain / over the casks / in the wine merchant's cellar. Then, / he heard the noise much louder / on the floors below. Then, / it came up the stairs, / and then / it came straight toward his door. It came / right through the heavy door, / and a ghost passed into the room / before his eyes. The face! He recognized it / right away / as Marley's. It was Marley's ghost.

"How now," said Scrooge, / caustic and cold / as ever. "What do you want / with me?"

"Much." Marley's voice, / no doubt about it.

"Who are you?"

"Ask me / who I was."

"Who were you then?" said Scrooge, / raising his voice.

"In life, / I was your partner, / Jacob Marley."

"Mercy! Dreadful apparition, / why do you trouble me? What do you want?" Scrooge's voice trembled / as he spoke.

"I have been traveling / since I died. Though I am dead, / I must walk through / the world of the living. I cannot rest. I cannot stay. I cannot linger anywhere."

"Why?" asked Scrooge.

"Because I'm unhappy. I was very bad to people / when I was alive. If a man stays away from other people / while he is alive, / that man becomes like me," said Marley's ghost.

- **knocker** 門上的門環　·**stare** 盯　·**bang** 砰聲　·**make a fire** 升火　·**fireplace** 壁爐
- **dressing gown** 睡袍　·**nightcap** 睡帽　·**low fire** 微弱的火
- **throw one's head back** 頭向後靠　·**far away** 很遠的　·**drag** 拖
- **cask** 裝酒的木桶　·**wine cellar** 酒窖　·**noise** 聲響　·**pass into** 穿越進入某處
- **recognize** 認出　·**ghost** 鬼魂　·**caustic** 苛刻的　·**as ever** 和以前一樣
- **dreadful** 可怕的　·**apparition** 亡靈　·**linger** 逗留；徘徊
- **stay away from** 離……很遠　·**alive** 活著

CLOSE UP

1　**to see if the door was locked** 看看門鎖好了沒
〈see if ...〉是「確認是否……」、「看看有沒有……」的意思。

2　**He recognized it right away as Marley's.** 他馬上認出是馬里的臉。
〈recognize ... as ...〉是「認出……是……」的意思。這裡的 Marley's 是 Marley's face 的意思。

施顧己到了家門口 get to his building，他把鑰匙插進門鎖中 put the key into the lock，但他看著門環 look at the knocker，他看到的不是門環，而是馬里的臉 but Marley's face。施顧己盯 stare 了一會兒 for a moment，然後又變成門環。他説：「呸呸 pooh, pooh！」然後砰一聲 with a bang 關上門 close the door。

施顧己上去他的房間 go up to his room，小心地把門鎖好 lock the door，他檢查了兩次 check twice，看看門鎖好了沒，然後在壁爐裡 in the fireplace 升了一點小火 make a little fire。他換上睡袍 dressing gown、穿上拖鞋 slippers 和戴上睡帽 nightcap，在微火之前 before the very low fire 坐下 sit down。當他把頭靠在椅子上 throw his head back，他聽到屋內有些聲音 hear something，聲音在很遠的地方，但愈來愈近 come closer，聽起來像是某個人 some person 在商人地窖裡的酒桶上 over the casks 拖著很重的鎖鍊 drag a heavy chain。然後，他聽見地板下 on the floors below 發出更大的聲響 the noise much louder，它走上樓梯 come up the stairs，然後走向他的門 come toward his door，它直接穿過很重的門 through the heavy door，一個鬼魂 a ghost 在他眼前 before his eyes 穿進了房間 pass into the room。那張臉 the face！他立刻 right away 認出了是馬里的臉 recognize it as Marley's，那是馬里的鬼魂 Marley's ghost。

「現在如何 how now？」施顧己説，如以往一樣 as ever 苛刻又冷酷 caustic and cold，「你想要我做什麼？」

「很多。」不須懷疑 no doubt about it，是馬里的聲音 Marley's voice。

「你是誰 who are you？」

「問我以前是誰 who I was。」

「你以前是誰 who were you？」施顧己提高了音量。

「活著的時候 in life，我是你的合夥人 your partner 雅各‧馬里 Jacob Marley。」

「可憐我 mercy 吧！可怕的鬼魂 dreadful apparition，你為什麼來為難我 trouble me？你想要什麼？」施顧己説話的時候，聲音 voice 顫抖 tremble。

「我死後一直飄蕩 travel，雖然我死了，但我得走遍陽間 the world of the living，不能休息 cannot rest，不能停留 cannot stay，不能在任何地方逗留 cannot linger。」

「為什麼 why？」施顧己問。

「因為我很不快樂 be unhappy，我活著的時候 be alive，對人很差勁 be bad to people，如果一個人活著的時候，與他人保持距離 stay away from other people，那人就會變得跟我一樣 become like me。」馬里的鬼魂説。

as if . . .（假設語氣）：像是……一樣

⇨ 雖然事實並不是那樣，但好像真的發生了一樣。

- It sounded **as if** some person **were dragging** a heavy chain over the casks.
  聽起來像是有人在地窖裡的酒桶上拖著重重的鎖鍊。（過去式）

- They were as happy **as if** they **had eaten** a king's meal.
  他們很快樂，有如吃了一頓國王的大餐。（過去完成式）

"I am here tonight / to warn you / that you have yet a chance / and hope of escaping my fate," said Marley's ghost.

"This is the chain / I made during my lifetime. **Every time** / **I refused to help** / **those in need,** / the chain became longer and heavier. When I died, / our chains were about the same, Scrooge, / but now, / after seven years, / yours is much longer than mine. I want to help you / not to be unhappy / like me / when you die."

"How?" asked Scrooge.

"You will be visited / by three more ghosts," answered Marley's ghost. "Expect the first / tonight / when the bell tolls one. Expect the second / tomorrow night / at the same hour. The third will come / the next night, / when the last stroke of twelve / has rung."

The ghost began floating out the window.

"But wait. Will I see you again? Can't you tell me more?"

"No, Scrooge, / you won't see me again. Remember / what I told you, / for your own sake, / or you will soon / see your own heavy chain."

The ghost disappeared out the window, / which was wide open.

As Scrooge went to the window / to see / where Marley had gone, / he suddenly heard some crying / down below. Again, / Scrooge's heart froze. The voices **came** / **not from people,** / **but from ghosts.** He quickly closed the window. He tried to say, "Humbug," / but he stopped / at the first syllable.

"**This couldn't have happened.** I will go to sleep, / and tomorrow / everything will be fine," he thought. Then, he went to bed / and fell into a troubled sleep.

When Scrooge awoke, / it was still so dark. "Was it all a dream?" he wondered. Just then, / the clock tolled / a deep, dull, hollow one.

Light flashed up / in the room / in an instant, / and the curtains of his bed / were drawn aside / by a strange figure. The ghost was an old man / with long white hair. He held / a branch of fresh green holly / in his hand. From the top of his head, / a bright clear jet of light / sprang.

"I am / the Ghost of Christmas Past," he said.

"Whose past?" "Your past," answered the ghost.

"What do you want?" "Rise / and walk with me."

· **warn** 警告　· **escape** 逃離　· **fate** 命運　· **toll**（鐘）敲　· **stroke** 鐘敲的動作
· **ring** 響　· **float** 飄　· **for one's own sake** 看在……的份上　· **disappear** 消失
· **freeze** 呆住；僵住　· **syllable** 音節　· **troubled sleep** 睡不安穩　· **awake** 醒來
· **hollow** 空洞的　· **flash up** 閃爍　· **in an instant** 一剎那　· **draw . . . aside** 拉到一邊
· **figure** 身形　· **holly** 冬青　· **a jet of light** 一縷光　· **spring** 光芒出現

CLOSE UP

1　**every time I refused to help those in need** 每次我拒絕幫助那些有需要的人
〈every time . . .〉意「每次都……」;〈refuse to . . .〉意「拒絕去……」;〈in need〉意「處於困境中的、窮困的」。

2　**came not from people, but from ghosts** 不是人發出的,而是鬼魂發出的
〈not . . . but . . .〉是「不是……而是……」的意思。

3　**This couldn't have happened.** 這不可能發生。
〈could have p.p.〉意「可能已經……了」;〈couldn't have p.p.〉意「不可能……的」。

「今晚我是來警告你 warn you，你還有機會和希望 a chance and hope 可以脫離我的命運 escape my fate。」馬里的鬼魂說。

「這是我在世時 during my lifetime 造成的鎖鍊 the chain，每次我拒絕幫助 refuse to help 那些有需要的人 those in need，這些鎖鍊就會變得更長、更重 become longer and heavier。我死的時候，我們的鎖鍊差不多一樣長 be about the same，施顧己，但現在，七年後的現在 after seven years，你的比我還要長 be much longer，我想幫你 help you，等你死的時候不要像我一樣不快樂。」

「怎麼做 how？」施顧己問。

「將有三個鬼魂 three more ghosts 來拜訪你，」馬里的鬼魂回答：「今夜 tonight 當鐘敲第一下 toll one 的時候，第一個 the first 會來。第二個 the second 明晚 tomorrow night 同樣的時間 at the same hour 會來。第三個 the third 隔天晚上 the next night 午夜第 12 聲鐘響 the last stroke of twelve 的時候會來。」

鬼魂開始飄出窗外 float out the window。

「等等 wait，我會再見到你嗎？你不能再告訴我多一點 tell me more 嗎？」

「不，施顧己，你再也見不到我了，記得我跟你說的話。為了你自己好 for your own sake，要不然你很快就會看到你沉重的鎖鍊 your own heavy chain。」

鬼魂在窗外消失 disappear out the window，窗戶大開 be wide open。

施顧己走到窗前 go to the window 看看馬里消失的地方，他突然聽到一些下面 down below 傳來的叫聲 hear some crying，施顧己的心又僵住了 freeze，這些聲音不是人發出的，而是鬼魂發出來的 come from ghosts。他很快地把窗戶關上 close the window。他試著說：「騙人的東西 humbug。」但他講了一個音節就停了。

「這不可能發生 couldn't have happened，我要去睡覺 go to sleep，明天一切都會很好。」他想，然後他上床睡覺 go to bed，睡得很不安穩 fall into a troubled sleep。

當施顧己醒來 awake，外面還是一片漆黑。「是一場夢 a dream 嗎？」他納悶，此時 just then，鐘敲了很深、很鈍、很空洞 deep, dull, hollow 的一聲。

一瞬間 in an instant 有光 light 在房間裡閃爍 flash up。床的帷幔 the curtains of his bed 被一個很奇怪的身形 a strange figure 拉到旁邊 be drawn aside。鬼魂是一個老人 an old man，他有長長的白髮 with long white hair 手裡拿著一枝青翠的冬青枝 hold a branch fresh green holly。他的頭頂上 from the top of his head 散發出 spring 一縷又白又亮的光芒 right clear jet of light。

「我是過去聖誕節的鬼魂 Ghost of Christmas Past。」他說。

「誰的過去 whose past？」「你的過去 your past。」鬼魂回答。

「你想要什麼？」「起身 rise 和我走吧 walk with me。」

be + p.p.（被動語態）

⇨ 主詞「承受或接受」動詞的動作時使用的說法，行為者用 by 標示。

- You will **be visited by** three more ghosts. 還有三個鬼魂會來拜訪你。
- The curtains of his bed **were drawn** aside **by** a strange figure.
  床的帷幔被一個奇怪的身形拉到旁邊。

Scrooge got up from his bed. He held the ghost's hand, / and they passed through the wall together. Suddenly, / they were standing in the country / where he had lived / as a boy. It was clear enough / by the decorations in the shops / that there, too, / it was Christmastime.

They saw / many boys and girls / going home across the fields, / happily shouting "Merry Christmas" / to each other. Scrooge remembered / the happiness and joy / when he was a child. He could feel tears / on his cheek.

"Are you sad?" asked the ghost.

"No, no, I am … happy," said Scrooge.

"They are not real. They are only spirits / from Christmas past. They cannot see us."

But Scrooge knew the spirits, / just as he knew / the streets, the houses, and the townspeople. Then, / they saw Scrooge as a boy, / reading on his own / in an empty classroom. Seeing himself / as he had once been, / Scrooge sat down at a desk / next to him / and began to cry.

"It's me. Once / when I was a boy, / I was left alone here / on Christmas. My father and mother / weren't at home. Now, suddenly, / I wish I would … " Scrooge's voice grew quiet.

"What do you wish?" the ghost asked.

"Last night, / a young boy / came to my office window / and sang me a Christmas carol. I just got angry / and told him to leave. I wish / I'd given some money to that poor boy," said Scrooge / with heavy sadness.

The ghost smiled. "Let's see / another Christmas," he said.

This time, / Scrooge saw the office / where he had first worked. He saw Mr. Fezziwig, / the man whom he had worked for. Young Scrooge was helping them / prepare the office / for a Christmas party. Soon, / there were / many young people / there. They were his fellow apprentices. They were enjoying themselves / and dancing. Even he, / Scrooge himself, / was dancing and enjoying himself.

·**rise** 起身   ·**get up from** 從……起來   ·**hold one's hand** 抓著某人的手
·**pass through** 穿越   ·**decoration** 布置   ·**tear** 眼淚   ·**spirit** 靈魂
·**on one's own** 獨自   ·**sit down** 坐下   ·**be left alone** 被單獨留下   ·**grow quiet** 變小聲
·**get angry** 生氣   ·**prepare** 準備   ·**fellow** 同伴的   ·**apprentice** 學徒

CLOSE UP

1   **seeing himself as he had once been** 看到從前的自己
    如果是〈as he is〉的話，是「像他現在的樣子」的意思；〈as he had once been〉則是「像他以前的樣子」。

2   **They were enjoying themselves** 他們玩得很開心
    〈enjoy oneself〉是「享樂」、「玩樂」、「度過愉快的時光」的意思。

施顧己從床上起來 get up from his bed，他抓著鬼魂的手 hold the ghost's hand。他們一起穿牆 pass through the wall，突然間他們站在鄉下 stand in the country。當他還是小男孩的時候 as a boy 曾經住在那裡。商店裡 in the shops 的布置 by the decorations 清楚地 be clear enough 透露出那是聖誕節期 Christmastime。

他們看到許多男孩女孩 many boys and girls 穿過田野 across the fields 回家 go home，快樂地 happily 互相 to each other 叫嚷 shout「聖誕快樂」。施顧己記得兒時的幸福、快樂 the happiness and joy，他感受到自己臉頰上 on his cheek 的淚水 tears。

「你很難過嗎？」鬼魂問。

「不，不，我是……快樂。」施顧己說。

「他們不是真的 be not real，他們只是過去聖誕節的鬼魂 spirits from Christmas past，他們看不見我們 cannot see us。」

但是施顧己認識那些鬼魂，正如他認得那些街道、房子和鎮上的人，然後，他們看到施顧己還是個小男孩 Scrooge as a boy，獨自一個人 on his own 在空蕩蕩的教室裡 in an empty classroom 讀書，看到他自己 see himself 從前的樣子，施顧己坐在他隔壁的桌上 sit down at a desk，開始哭了起來 begin to cry。

「那是我 it's me，從前當我還是小男孩的時候，聖誕節 on Christmas 我一個人被留在這裡 be left alone here，我父母不在家 be not at home，現在突然間，我希望我可以……」施顧己愈說愈小聲 grow quiet。

「你希望怎麼樣？」鬼魂問。

「昨晚 last night 有個小男孩 a young boy 來我辦公室的窗戶旁邊 come to my office window，對我唱一首聖誕頌歌 sing me a Christmas carol，我只是很生氣 get angry，叫他離開 tell him to leave，但願我給了那可憐的男孩 that poor boy 一點錢 give some money。」施顧己非常悲傷地說 with heavy sadness。

鬼魂微笑，「我們來看另一個聖誕節 see another Christmas。」他說。

這次 this time，施顧己看到他第一次工作的辦公室 see the office，他看見費茲威先生 see Mr. Fezziwig，他以前為他工作過，年輕的施顧己在幫他們為聖誕舞會 Christmas party 布置辦公室 prepare the office，不久，許多年輕人 many young people 來了。他們跟他一起當學徒 his fellow apprentices。他們很快樂 enjoy themselves 地跳舞 dance，就連他，施顧己自己，也在跳舞和玩樂。

GRAMMAR POINT

where（關係副詞）

⇨ 放在表場所的名詞後，where 所引導的關係子句，就是用來修飾該名詞的。

- Suddenly, they were standing in *the country* **where** he had lived as a boy.

  突然間，他們站在鄉下，他兒時住過的地方。

- This time, Scrooge saw *the* office **where** he had first worked.

  這次，施顧己看到他第一次工作的辦公室。

At the end of the party, / Mr. and Mrs. Fezziwig said / "Merry Christmas" / to everybody.

"It's old Mr. Fezziwig's office. He was such a happy, kind boss."

The ghost looked at Scrooge / and asked, "What's the matter?"

"I was thinking of my clerk, / Bob Cratchit. I wish / I'd said something to him / yesterday," said Scrooge.

The ghost smiled again. "Come, / my time grows short," said the ghost. "Another Christmas," he said.

The scene changed. Scrooge again / saw himself. He was older now / –a man in the prime of life. He was sitting / with a young woman. She had once been his girlfriend. She was crying.

"No, it's too late. You have another love now," she said.

"What? What other love?" Scrooge asked.

"Money. / You love only money now, / not me. Goodbye."

"No more! Ghost! Please remove me / from this place," Scrooge cried / in pain.

"No, Scrooge. I told you / that these were shadows / of the things / that have been," said the ghost. "There is / one more scene."

Years had passed / since the last scene. Scrooge saw a beautiful woman / smiling with her children / in a warm house. The door opened, / and the father came in. His arms / were full of Christmas presents. He gave one / to each of his children. The children laughed and shouted / as they opened the presents.

Scrooge looked at the mother. She was the woman / from Scrooge's past. She had left him / because he had been more interested in money / than in her. Looking at the happy family, / Scrooge realized / what he had lost.

"No more! Leave me, ghost," shouted Scrooge.

"This was your life. These things happened / and cannot be changed. Only the future / can be changed," the ghost said.

"Please, ghost, / I cannot bear it. Haunt me / no longer!" Scrooge shouted sadly.

As Scrooge struggled with the spirit, / he suddenly became exhausted. He was overcome by drowsiness / and sank into a heavy sleep.

·boss 老闆　·scene 場景　·the prime of life 人生的黃金時期　·remove 調動
·in pain 很痛苦　·shadow 影子　·be interested in 對……感興趣　·bear 承受
·haunt 被鬼纏住　·struggle with 對抗　·exhausted 精疲力盡的　·overcome by 被……戰勝
·drowsiness 疲倦　·sink into 陷入

CLOSE UP

1 **grows short** 變短 / **became exhausted** 變得精疲力盡
〈grow/become＋形容詞〉是「愈來愈……了」的意思，表狀態的變化；grow表感覺到漸漸地產生變化。

2 **remove me from this place** 把我從這個地方帶走
〈remove . . . from . . . 〉是「把……送出／移出……」的意思。

3 **had been more interested in money than in her** 對錢比對她更感興趣
〈be interested in . . . 〉是「對……有興趣」的意思。這裡的money和her是兩個相互作比較的對象。

4 **was overcome by drowsiness** 屈服於疲倦
〈be overcome by . . . 〉是「沒有勝過……」、「被……擊敗」的意思。

舞會結束時，費茲威夫婦向大家說：「聖誕快樂」。

「那是老費茲威先生的辦公室，他真是一個又快樂又善良的老闆 such a happy, kind boss。」

鬼魂看著施顧己問：「怎麼回事 what's the matter？」

「我想到我的職員鮑伯・克萊契 think of my clerk, Bob Cratchit，但願我昨天和他說點什麼 say something to him。」施顧己說。

鬼魂又微笑了。「來吧 come，我的時間 my time 不多了 grow shorter，」鬼魂說。「另一個聖誕節 another Christmas。」他說。

場景 the scene 變換 change，施顧己又看到他自己 see himself，現在他年紀大了一點 be older，正處於人生的黃金時期 in the prime of life。他和一個年輕女子 with a young woman 坐在一起，她曾是他的女朋友 his girlfriend，她在哭 cry。

「不，一切都太遲了，你現在另有所愛了 have another love。」她說。

「什麼 what？什麼另有所愛 what other love？」施顧己問。

「錢，你現在只愛錢 love only money，不愛我，再見。」

「不要再繼續 no more 了！鬼魂！帶我離開這裡 remove me from this place。」施顧己痛苦地 in pain 大叫。

「不，施顧己，我跟你說過這只是往事 the things that have been 的幻影 shadows，」鬼魂說：「還有一個場景 one more scene。」

距上一個場景之後，又過了很多年。施顧己看到一個美麗的女人 a beautiful woman 在一個溫暖的房子裡 in a warm house 對著她的孩子 with her children 微笑。門開了，父親 the father 走進來 come in，他的雙臂裡 his arms 都是聖誕禮物 be full of Christmas presents，他給每一個孩子 to each of his children 一個禮物。當他們拆禮物 open the presents 時又笑又叫 laugh and shout。

施顧己看著那個母親 look at the mother，她是施顧己過去的女朋友 the woman from Scrooge's past，因施顧己對錢更有興趣 be more interested in money，所以她離開了他 leave him。看著幸福的家庭，施顧己明白自己失去了什麼。

「不要再繼續了！放過我吧 leave me，鬼魂。」施顧己大叫。

「這是你的人生 your life，已經發生的事 these things happened 不能改變 cannot be changed，只有未來 only the future 可以改變 can be changed。」鬼魂說。

「求求你，鬼魂，我受不了了 cannot bear it，不要再 no longer 纏著我 haunt me 了！」施顧己傷心地大叫。

施顧己和鬼魂對抗 struggle with the spirit，他突然感到精疲力盡 become exhausted，他被睡意征服 be overcome by drowsiness，沉沉睡去 sink into a heavy sleep。

GRAMMAR POINT

I wish . . . （假設語氣）

⇨ I wish 後接的從屬子句，若用「過去完成式」，就表示所期望的事與過去的事實相反。

- **I wish I'd said** something to him yesterday. 但願我昨天和他說點什麼。
- **I wish I'd given** some money to that poor boy. 但願我給了那可憐的男孩一點錢。

Scrooge awoke / in his bedroom. It was one in the morning again / –time for the second ghost. He looked around his bedroom. There was nobody / there. He went to the door of his living room.

"Come in, / Ebenezer Scrooge," said a voice.

He opened the door / and saw something very surprising. The room looked so different. The walls **were covered with Christmas trees. Heaped upon the floor** / **were** / **turkeys, geese, pigs, sausages, plum puddings, chestnuts, apples, and great bowls of punch. Upon the couch** / **in the center of the room** / **sat a happy giant,** / holding a glowing torch / which lit the room.

"Come in. Come in. I am / the Ghost of Christmas Present," said the giant.

"Ghost, / I learned a lot / from the ghost / last night. Tonight, / if you have / something to teach me, / take me / anywhere you want," said Scrooge.

"Touch my robe," said the giant.

Scrooge did / as he was told. Scrooge found / they were walking / in a London street / on Christmas morning. The ghost took him / to the Cratchits' house. At the door, / the ghost smiled and stopped / to bless Bob Cratchit's dwelling.

Mrs. Cratchit, Bob's wife, / was preparing their Christmas dinner. Just then / Bob Cratchit was coming back from church / with the youngest son, Tiny Tim. Tiny Tim was ill / and used a crutch / to walk.

The family sat down / to eat their meal. They had only / one goose, some potatoes, and a small Christmas pudding. It seemed very small / for such a large family, / but nobody complained. Though it was a very simple Christmas meal, / they were still as happy / as if they had eaten a king's meal. After dinner, / all the Cratchit family / gathered around the fire. Bob proposed, "A Merry Christmas / to us all, my dears. God bless us!"

· **surprising** 令人驚訝的　· **be covered with** 充滿了　· **be heaped upon** 在……上面堆滿
· **bowl of punch** 一碗雞尾酒　· **couch** 沙發　· **glowing torch** 發光的火把　· **light** 照亮
· **find** 發現　· **the Cratchits** 克萊契一家 (= the Cratchit family)　· **bless** 祝福
· **crutch** 枴杖　· **complain** 抱怨　· **as if** 有如；好像　· **gather** 聚集
· **propose** 提議為……乾杯

CLOSE UP

1　**were covered with Christmas trees** 蓋滿了聖誕樹
〈be covered with . . . 〉是「被……覆蓋」的意思。

2　**Heaped upon the floor were turkeys, geese, pigs, . . .** 地上堆滿了火雞、鵝、豬……
正常的語序是〈Turkeys, geese, pigs, . . . were heaped upon the floor.〉，將 heaped upon the floor 拿到句首的話，主詞 (turkeys, geese, pigs, . . .) 和動詞 (were) 就要倒裝。主詞太長或要用新主詞的話，就會像這樣用倒裝法，是在文學或說明文中常出現的結構。

3　**Upon the couch in the center of the room sat a happy giant.** 房間正中央的沙發上坐著一個快樂的巨人。
也是倒裝句，正常的語序是〈A happy giant sat upon the couch in the center of the room.〉。

施顧己在他房間裡 in his bedroom 醒來 awake，現在是凌晨一點 one in the morning，第二個鬼魂出現的時間到了 time for the second ghost。他看看自己的房間 look around his bedroom，沒有人 nobody 在，他走到客廳的門口 go to the door of his living room。

「請進 come in，艾伯納瑟・施顧己 Ebenezer Scrooge。」一個聲音說。

他打開門 open the door，看到一個令他非常吃驚的東西 something very surprising，房間看起來很不一樣 look so different。牆上 the walls 蓋滿聖誕樹 be covered with Christmas trees。地板上 upon the floor 堆滿了 be heaped 火雞 turkeys、鵝 geese、豬 pigs、香腸 sausages、梅子布丁 plum puddings、栗子 chestnuts、蘋果 apples、很多好喝的雞尾酒 great bowls of punch。房間正中央 in the center of the room 的沙發上 upon the couch 坐了一個很快樂的巨人 a happy giant，拿著 hold 一個發光的火把 a glowing torch 照亮整個房間 light the room。

「請進，請進，我是現在聖誕節的鬼魂 the Ghost of Christmas Present」巨人說。

「鬼魂，我從昨晚的鬼魂那裡學到很多 learn a lot，今晚如果你有什麼要教我的 something to teach me，帶我 take me 到任何你想帶我去的地方 anywhere you want。」施顧己說。

「摸我的袍子 touch my robe。」巨人說。

施顧己照他所說的 as he is told 去做，施顧己發現他們在聖誕節的早晨 on Christmas morning 走在倫敦的街頭 walk in a London street，鬼魂帶他到克萊契的家 take him to the Cratchits' house，到了門口 at the door，鬼魂微笑並停下 smile and stop 來祝福鮑伯・克萊契的住所 bless Bob Cratchit's dwelling。

克萊契太太 Mrs. Cratchit，鮑伯的妻子 Bob's wife 在準備他們的聖誕晚餐 prepare their Christmas dinner。這時候，鮑伯・克萊契帶著他最小的兒子 the youngest son 小提姆 Tiny Tim 從教堂回來 come back from church。小提姆生病了 be ill，得靠柺杖 use a crutch 才能走路。

一家人坐下來吃他們的晚餐 eat their meal，他們只有一隻鵝 one goose，一些馬鈴薯 some potatoes，和一個小小的聖誕布丁 a small Christmas pudding，要給這麼大的家庭 for such a large family 吃，它看來非常小 seem very small，但沒有人抱怨。雖然那是一頓很簡樸的聖誕大餐 a very simple Christmas meal，他們仍然很快樂，好像吃了一頓國王的大餐 eat a king's meal。晚餐後 after dinner 克萊契一家人 all the Cratchit family 圍著爐火 gather around the fire，鮑伯提議大家舉杯說：「祝我們大家 to us all 聖誕快樂，我親愛的家人，神祝福我們 bless us！」

such a/an ＋形容詞＋名詞：這麼一個……的…… ⇨ 表「程度相當高的」的意思。

- It seemed very small for **such a large family**. 它看來對這麼大的家庭來說非常小。
- Mr. Fezziwig was **such a happy, kind boss**. 費茲威先生是這麼一個又快樂、又善良的老闆。

"God bless us everyone!" said Tiny Tim. Tiny Tim sat / very close to his father's side / upon his little stool. He was very sick. Bob held his withered little hand / in his / as if he loved the child / and wished to keep him by his side, / but he dreaded / that Tiny Tim might be taken from him.

"Will he be here / next Christmas?" Scrooge asked.

"With help," replied the ghost.

Scrooge raised his head / when he heard his name spoken.

"Let's drink / to Mr. Scrooge," said Bob.

"To Scrooge?" Mrs. Cratchit's face reddened, / and she said, "Why should we drink / to that old, stingy, unfeeling man?"

"My dear," was Bob's mild answer, "it's Christmas Day."

"Well, you are right. I'll drink to him. But nothing we do / could make that mean old man / feel happy or merry," said Mrs. Cratchit.

The mention of his name / cast a dark shadow / on the party, / which lasted / for a full five minutes. After some time, / the Cratchits became cheerful again. They were not a handsome family. They were not well dressed. But they were happy, grateful, and pleased with one another.

The ghost took Scrooge away / from the Cratchits' house. The two of them / walked through the streets of London. People were going to parties / with their friends and families. Suddenly, / they were in a cold, dark, empty place. They looked through the window / of a small house. Inside, / there was / a big family / in a very small room. Yet they were happy / and were singing Christmas carols together.

Scrooge asked, "Who are they?"

"They are poor miners," answered the ghost. "They have hard lives / working inside the Earth / to dig up coal."

Slowly, / the scene vanished, / and Scrooge suddenly heard / a hearty laugh. It was his nephew Fred's house. Fred was telling everyone / about his visit to his uncle.

· **stool** 凳子　· **withered** 枯萎的　· **dread** 懼怕　· **be taken from** 被帶走　· **redden** 變紅
· **stingy** 小氣的　· **unfeeling** 無情的　· **mention** 提到　· **cast a shadow** 蒙上陰影
· **last** 持續　· **cheerful** 歡樂的　· **well dressed** 穿著體面　· **grateful** 感恩的
· **pleased with** 滿意的　· **take . . . away from . . .** 把……從……帶走
· **look through** 看穿；看出去　· **Christmas carol** 聖誕頌歌　· **miner** 礦工　· **dig up** 挖
· **vanish** 消失

CLOSE UP

1　**Let's drink to Mr. Scrooge.** 我們來敬施顧己先生。
〈drink to . . . 〉是「為……而乾杯」的意思。

2　**nothing we do could make that mean old man feel happy or merry**
我們做什麼都不能讓那吝嗇老頭幸福或快樂。

nothing we do是主詞，could make是動詞，that mean old man是受詞，feel happy or merry是受詞補語，也就是〈make＋受詞＋受詞補語〉的結構，翻譯成「讓某人怎麼樣」就可以了。

「神祝福我們每一位 bless us everyone！」小提姆説，他坐在小凳子上 upon his little stool，離他爸爸很近 close to his father's side。他病得很重，鮑伯握著 hold 他衰弱的小手 his withered little hand，好像他很愛這個孩子 love the child，希望把他留在身邊 keep him by his side。他很害怕 dread 小提姆會被帶走 be taken from him。

「下一個聖誕節 next Christmas 他還會在這裡 be here 嗎？」施顧己問。

「有人幫忙的話 with help。」鬼魂回答。

施顧己聽到有人説他的名字 hear his name spoken，便抬起頭來 raise his head。

「我們來敬施顧己先生 drink to Mr. Scrooge」鮑伯説。

「敬施顧己先生？」克萊契太太氣得面紅耳赤，她説：「為什麼我們要敬那個又老又吝嗇又無情 old, stingy, unfeeling 的傢伙？」

「我的親愛的，」鮑伯溫和地回答：「今天是聖誕節。」

「好吧，你是對的，我會敬他，但我們做什麼都不能讓那個吝嗇的老頭 that mean old man 幸福或快樂 feel happy or merry。」克萊契太太説。

一提到他的名字 the mention of his name 派對上 on the party 就蒙上一層陰影 cast a dark shadow，整整持續 last 了五分鐘 for a full five minutes。過了一陣子 after some time，克萊契一家人 the Cratchits 又開始歡樂 become cheerful。他們不是很富裕的一家人 a handsome family，穿得不體面 be not well dressed，但他們很快樂、很感恩 be grateful，而且相處融洽 be pleased with one another。

鬼魂把施顧己帶離 take Scrooge away 克萊契的家 from the Cratchits' house，他們兩個 the two of them 經過倫敦街頭 walk through the streets of London。路上行人帶著他們的朋友和家人 with their friends and families 正要赴宴 go to parties，突然間，他們身處一個又冷又暗又空曠的地方 a cold, dark, empty place，從一間很小的房子 a small house 的窗戶往裡看 look through the window，裡面有一間很小的房間 in a very small room，那裡有一大家子的人 a big family 擠在一間小房間裡，但他們很開心，一起唱聖誕頌歌 sing Christmas carols。

施顧己問：「他們是誰？」

「他們是很窮的礦工 poor miners。」鬼魂回答：「他們在地底下工作 work inside the Earth，挖煤礦 dig up coal，生活過得很艱辛 have hard lives。」

慢慢地，場景 the scene 消失 vanish 了。施顧己突然聽到開懷大笑的聲音 hear a hearty laugh，那是他外甥佛萊德的家 Fred's house，佛萊德告訴大家他去拜訪他舅舅的事 his visit to his uncle。

GRAMMAR POINT

which（關係代名詞） ⇨ 代替前面出現的整個子句。

- The mention of his name cast a dark shadow on the party, **which** lasted for a full five minutes. 一提到他的名字就讓派對蒙上陰影，這種氣氛整整持續了五分鐘。

- He visited Fred's house, **which** pleased everyone there.
他到佛萊德的家，在場的每個人都很高興。

"So when I said 'Merry Christmas' to him, / he replied 'Bah, humbug!'" said Fred. Everyone laughed.

"He's a strange old man," said Fred. "He is rich, / but he doesn't do anything good / with his money. He even lives / like he's poor. I invite him / to have Christmas dinner with us / every year, / but he never comes. Someday, / perhaps / he will change his mind. And someday / perhaps / he will pay poor Bob Cratchit more money / as well."

For the rest of the evening, / Scrooge and the ghost / watched his nephew and friends / enjoy their Christmas party. Then, / the clock struck twelve. Scrooge looked around for the ghost, / but he saw the ghost / no more. Then, / he remembered Marley's prediction, / and he lifted his eyes.

Scrooge saw a solemn phantom coming / like a mist along the ground / toward him. Unlike the others, / he could not see / this one's face or body. It was covered / from head to toe / in a long black garment. The only visible part / of the phantom / was one outstretched hand.

The phantom moved / slowly and silently. As it came near him, / Scrooge bent down upon his knee, / for the ghost seemed to scatter / gloom and mystery / as it moved. The ghost did not speak at all.

"I am in the presence of / the Ghost of Christmas Yet to Come," said Scrooge. "You are about to show me the things / which have not happened yet, / but will happen / in the time before us," Scrooge said, / looking at the strange ghost. "Is that so, / Spirit?"

The ghost silently moved its head a little / and pointed with its hand. Scrooge suddenly found himself / in the middle of the city. The ghost stopped / beside a group of businessmen. Scrooge could hear / some of them talking.

"I don't know much about it. I only know / he's dead," said one great fat man.

"When did he die?" inquired another.

"Last night, / I believe."

"What has he done / with his money?" asked a red-faced gentleman.

"I haven't heard," responded the first man. "He didn't leave it to me / though. That's / all I know."

"At least / his funeral will be very cheap," said one man.

· **change one's mind** 改變心意　·**strike**（鐘）敲　·**prediction** 預言
·**solemn** 嚴肅的；莊重的 ·**phantom** 幽靈　·**mist** 薄霧　·**unlike** 不像
·**from head to toe** 從頭到腳　·**garment** 衣服　·**visible** 可見的
·**outstretched** 伸出的　·**bend down upon one's knee** 曲膝　·**scatter** 散布
·**gloom** 黑暗；憂鬱　·**mystery** 神秘　·**point** 指向　·**funeral** 葬禮

CLOSE UP

1　**unlike the others** 不像其他人
介系詞 unlike 是 like（像……）反義字；unlike 是「不像……」、「和……不同」的意思。

2　**I am in the presence of the Ghost of Christmas Yet to Come.**
我在未來聖誕節的鬼魂面前。
〈be in the presence of ...〉是「站在……的面前」的意思。
〈yet to come〉是「還沒出現的」、「即將出現的」的意思。在這裡是「未來（future）」的意思。

「當我跟他説『聖誕快樂』，他回答：『呸，騙人的東西！』」佛萊德説完，大家都笑了。

「他是個怪老頭 a strange old man。」佛萊德説：「他很有錢，但他沒有用錢 with his money 做過什麼好事 don't do anything good，甚至自己也過得像窮人一樣。我每年 every year 邀他 invite him 跟我們 with us 一起吃聖誕晚餐 have Christmas dinner，他從來不來 never come。哪天 someday，説不定他會改變心意 change his mind，哪天説不定他也會給可憐的鮑伯‧克萊契加薪 pay more money。」

接下來的夜晚，施顧己和鬼魂看他的外甥和朋友 his nephew and friends 享受他們的聖誕派對 enjoy their Christmas party，那時鐘敲了 12 下 strike twelve。施顧己四處找鬼魂，但看不見它，他想起馬里的預言 remember Marley's prediction，睜開雙眼 lift his eyes。

施顧己看到一個莊嚴的幽靈 a solemn phantom，像地上的迷霧一樣 a mist along the ground 朝他走過來，不像其他鬼魂 unlike the others，他看不見這個鬼魂的臉或身體。它從頭到腳 from head to toe 都被一件又長又黑的衣服 in a long black garment 蓋住 be covered，鬼魂身上唯一看得到的部分 the only visible part 是一隻伸出來的手 one outstretched hand。

鬼魂緩慢、安靜地 slowly and silently 移動，當它靠近他 come near him，施顧己曲膝 bend down upon his knee，因為那鬼魂移動時似乎散發出 scatter 陰鬱和神秘的氣息 gloom and mystery，他一語不發 do not speak。

「未來聖誕節的鬼魂 the Ghost of Christmas Yet to Come 我在你面前。」施顧己説。「你將要讓我看 show me 尚未發生但將要發生 in the time before us 之事，」施顧己看著這個奇怪的鬼魂説：「是這樣嗎，鬼魂？」

鬼魂微微地點了一下頭 move its head a little，用手指了一下 point with its hand。施顧己突然發現他在市中心 in the middle of the city，鬼魂在一群商人 a group of businessmen 旁邊停了下來，施顧己聽見一些人談話。

「我知道的不多 don't know much about it，我只知道他死了。」一個很胖的男人説。

「他什麼時候死的？」另一個人問。

「我相信是昨晚。」

「他的錢他怎麼處置？」一個紅臉的先生問。

「我還沒聽説 haven't heard。」第一個男人回答：「他沒有留給我 don't leave it to me，那是我所知道的 all I know。」

「至少 at least，他的葬禮 his funeral 會草草了事 be very cheap。」一個男人説。

for + 主詞＋動詞：因為……

⇨ 表話講完後，又附帶地説出理由，這時 for 引導的子句要放在句尾，前面還要加逗點。

- Scrooge bent down upon his knee, **for** the ghost seemed to scatter gloom and mystery.
  施顧己曲膝，因為鬼魂似乎散發出陰鬱和神秘的氣息。

- I didn't follow them, **for** something dangerous was likely to happen.
  我沒有跟著他們，因為危險的事似乎就要發生。

"That's true. He had no friends. No one liked him, / so nobody will go to his funeral."

Scrooge did not understand / why the ghost wanted him / to listen to this conversation, / but he knew / the ghost would not answer him, / so he did not ask.

They left the busy scene / and went to an obscure part of the town. The streets were dark and small. They visited a dirty shop / full of horrible old things / you can imagine / –iron, old rags, bottles, clothes, and bones. It was a place / where people came to sell their things / when they needed money.

Scrooge watched / as three people brought things / to sell to the shopkeeper. They were from the same dead man's house.

"What have you got / to sell?" asked the shopkeeper.

One woman took out / some towels, silver teaspoons, and other small things, / and said, "He doesn't need these now."

"No indeed, ma'am," answered the shopkeeper.

"Take a look at these," said the other woman. "Bed curtains and blankets. He isn't likely to catch a cold / without them / now."

Scrooge listened to this dialogue / in horror. "Ghost, I see. The case of this unhappy man / might be my own."

The scene had suddenly changed, / and Scrooge found himself / in another terrible room. There was a bare bed / with no blankets / or curtains around it. A pale light from outside / fell straight upon the bed. On it, / unwatched, unwept, and uncared for, / was the dead body / of the unknown man. He was covered by a thin sheet.

The ghost, / as silent as ever, / merely pointed at the body. Scrooge realized / that the ghost wanted him / to look at the face of the dead man, / but he could not do it.

"I cannot look at his face," cried Scrooge. "Let me see some tenderness / connected with this death, / or this dark chamber / will be forever in my memory."

The scene changed to another home. A woman stood up / as her husband entered the room. "Have you gotten any news?" she asked.

·obscure 默默無名的　·horrible 可怕的　·bone 骨頭　·shopkeeper 店主
·take out 拿出　·indeed 確實　·catch a cold 感冒　·in horror 在恐懼之中
·case 案例　·terrible 可怕的　·bare 光的；空的　·pale light 暗淡的光
·unwatched 無人看守的　·unwept 無人哭泣的　·uncared for 無人關切的
·dead body 死屍　·be covered by 覆蓋著　·sheet 床單　·point at 指著某物
·tenderness 良善　·connected with 有關於　·chamber 房間　·stand up 站起來

CLOSE UP

1　**On it, . . . , was the dead body of the unknown man.** 上面……是一個不明人士的屍體。
副詞片語 on it 出現在句子前的話，主詞（the dead body of the unknown man）和動詞（was）要倒置，變成倒裝句。

2　**as silent as ever** 如以往一樣安靜
〈as . . . as ever〉是「像以前一樣」的意思。例 He is as greedy as ever.（他如以往一樣貪心。）

「這倒是真的，他沒有朋友 have no friends，沒有人 no one 喜歡他 like him，所以沒有人 nobody 會參加他的葬禮 go to his funeral。」

施顧己不懂為什麼鬼魂要讓他聽這一段談話 listen to this conversation，但他知道鬼魂不會回答他，所以他沒問。

他們離開這個忙碌的場景 leave the busy scene，到鎮上某個不知名的地區 an obscure part of the town。街道又黑又小 be dark and small，他們造訪了一間髒髒的小店 visit a dirty shop，裡面充滿你可以想像到的可怕古物 horrible old things——有鐵 iron、舊破布 old rags、瓶子 bottles、衣服 clothes 和骨頭 bones，這是人需要錢 need money 可以賣東西 sell their things 的地方。

施顧己看著三個人 three people 帶了東西 bring things 來賣給店主 sell to the shopkeeper。

「妳有什麼要賣？」店主問。

一個女人拿出 take out 了一些毛巾 some towels、銀茶匙 silver teaspoons 和其他小東西 other small things，然後說：「他現在不需要這些了。」

「確實不需要了，女士。」店主回答。

「看看這些 take a look at these，」另一個女人說：「床簾 bed curtains、毯子 blankets，他現在沒有它們 without them 也不會感冒 catch a cold 了。」

施顧己很驚恐地 in horror 聽這段對話 listen to this dialogue。「鬼魂，我懂了，這個不幸的男人的案例 the case of this unhappy man 可能就是我自己的。」

場景突然變了，施顧己發現他自己在另一個恐怖的房間 in another terrible room。那裡有一張空床 a bare bed 沒有毯子或床簾，暗淡的光線 a pale light 從外面直接照射在床上 fall upon the bed。沒有人看守 unwatched、沒有人哭 unwept、沒有人關心 uncared for，一個不明人士 the unknown man 的死屍 the dead body 躺在那張床上。屍身上蓋了 be covered 一層薄薄的床單 by a thin sheet。

鬼魂一如以往地安靜 as silent as ever，只是指向那個屍體 point at the body。施顧己明白鬼魂要他看一下 look at 死人 the dead man 的臉 the face，但他辦不到。

「我不敢看他的臉，」施顧己大叫，「讓我看 let me see 一些有關他死亡 connected with this death 好的一面 some tenderness，不然 or 這黑暗的房間 this dark chamber 會永遠 forever 存在我的記憶裡 in my memory。」

場景換到另一個家 change to another home。一個女人在她丈夫進來 enter the room 的時候站了起來 stand up。「你有沒有什麼消息 any news 呢？」她問。

"When I visited him / to find out / if we could pay the money / one week later," he answered, "an old woman told me / he was dead."

"That's great news," she said. "I'm sorry for saying that. I mean / that now we have time to get the money / that we have to pay."

"No, ghost! Show me someone / who's sorry about a death, / not someone / who's happy because of a death," shouted Scrooge.

The ghost took him / to poor Bob Cratchit's house. Scrooge saw the family / sitting quietly around the fire. They were talking about Tiny Tim.

"I met Fred, / Mr. Scrooge's nephew," said Bob. "And he said / that he was very sorry / to hear about Tiny Tim."

Bob turned to his family / and said, "We must never forget / what a good boy Tiny Tim was."

"No, never father," shouted all the children.

Then, / Bob Cratchit broke down / all at once. He couldn't help it / as the tears flowed down his face.

"Ghost," said Scrooge, "something informs me / that our parting moment / is at hand. Tell me. Who was the dead man / we saw?"

The Ghost of Christmas Yet to Come / took Scrooge to a churchyard. The ghost stood among the graves / and pointed down to one. Scrooge crept toward it, / trembling as he went, / and followed the finger / to read the name on the neglected grave: EBENEZER SCROOGE.

"Am I that man / who lay upon the bed? No, ghost! Oh no, no. I am not / the man I was. I will not be / the man I must have been / but for this evening. Why show me this / if I am past all hope? Assure me / that I may yet change these shadows."

- **be sorry about** 很遺憾   - **break down** 崩潰   - **all at once** 突然
- **cannot help it** 忍不住   - **inform** 告知   - **parting moment** 離別時刻
- **at hand** 即將到來   - **churchyard** 教堂的墓地   - **grave** 墳墓   - **creep** 緩慢行進
- **neglected** 棄置的   - **lie** 躺   - **be past all hope** 絲毫沒有希望   - **assure** 確保

CLOSE UP

1 **to find out if we could pay the money one week later** 看看我們能不能一週之後再還錢
這裡的 if 是「是否」的意思，要依據上下文，選出最合適的意思來用。

2 **he was very sorry to hear about Tiny Tim** 他聽說小提姆的事，感到很遺憾
sorry 除「對不起」的意思外，「遺憾」、「可惜」、「可憐」等意思也常被使用。

3 **our parting moment is at hand** 我們分開的時刻即將到來
〈 . . . be at hand〉是「……即將到來」的意思。

4 **the man I was** 從前的我 / **the man I must have been** 那個我可能變成的人
因 was 是 be 動詞的過去式，所以前者是「過去是怎樣的人」的意思。been 是 be 動詞的過去分詞，因為〈must have p.p.〉是「（強烈的推測）一定會是……準沒錯」，所以後者是表推測「一定成為那樣的人」的意思。

5 **but for this evening** 若非今晚
〈but for . . .〉是「要不是……的話」的意思。
例 I would have failed but for your help.（若非你的幫助，我一定會失敗。）

「我去找他 visit him 看看 find out 我們是不是可以一個星期以後 one week later 再還錢 pay the money 的時候，」他回答，「一個老婦人告訴他死了 be dead。」

「那真是好消息 great news，」她說：「我很遺憾這麼說，我的意思 mean 是現在我們有時間 have time 湊出我們該還 we have to pay 的錢 get the money。」

「不，鬼魂！讓我看看 show me 為死亡感到難過 be sorry about a death 的人，而不是為死亡感到高興 be happy 的人。」施顧己大叫。

鬼魂帶他 take him 到可憐的鮑伯‧克萊契的家 to poor Bob Cratchit's house。施顧己看到那家人靜靜地坐在火堆旁 sit around the fire，他們在談論小提姆 talk about Tiny Tim。

「我遇見佛萊德 meet Fred，施顧己先生的外甥 Mr. Scrooge's nephew，」鮑伯說：「他說他很難過 be very sorry 聽到小提姆的事 hear about Tiny Tim。」

鮑伯轉向他的家人 turn to his family，說：「我們永遠不要忘記 never forget 小提姆是個多麼好的小男孩 what a good boy。」

「不，永遠不會，父親。」所有的孩子大叫。

然後，鮑伯‧克萊契突然 all at once 崩潰了 break down，淚水 the tears 從臉上滑落時 flow down his face，他再也忍不住了 cannot help it。

「鬼魂，」施顧己說：「某些事告訴我 inform me 我們分開的時刻 our parting moment 就要到了 be at hand，告訴我 tell me，我們看到的死人是誰？」

未來聖誕節的鬼魂帶他到教堂的墓地 a churchyard，鬼魂站在墳墓之間 stand among the graves，指向其中一座墳墓 point down to one。施顧己慢慢地走向它 creep toward it，邊走邊顫抖 tremble，跟著手指 follow the finger 看到被棄置的墳墓 the neglected grave 上面寫著名字 read the name：艾伯納瑟‧施顧己。

「我是那個躺在床上的人 lie upon the bed 嗎？不，鬼魂！喔，不，不，我不是從前的我 the man I was，若非今晚 but for this evening 我一定還是從前的我 the man I must have been。如果我完全無望 be past all hope，為什麼給我看這個 show me this？向我保證 assure me 我還能改變這些幻影 change these shadows。」

關係代名詞 ⇨ 代替前面出現的名詞（先行詞），關係代名詞引導的子句，用來修飾先行詞。

- Now we have time to get *the money* **that** we have to pay.
  現在我們有時間去湊我們該還的錢。

- Show me *someone* **who**'s sorry about a death, not *someone* **who**'s happy because of a death.
  讓我看看為死亡感到難過的人，而不是為死亡感到高興的人。

- Who was *the dead man* **(whom)** we saw? 我們看到的死人是誰？

- Am I *that man* **who** lay upon the bed? 我是那個躺在床上的人嗎？

Scrooge continued, "I will honor Christmas / in my heart / and try to keep it / all the year. I will live / in the past, present, and future. I will never forget the lessons / that I have been taught."

Then, / the phantom began to disappear, / and Scrooge realized / that he was back in his own bedroom. Best and happiest of all, / time was before him. He had time / to make amends.

Scrooge heard the church bells / ringing loudly. Running to the window, / he opened it / and put out his head. It was a clear, bright, stirring, golden day.

"What day is it today?" cried Scrooge / to a boy down on the street.

"Today? It's Christmas Day, sir," answered the boy.

"Christmas!" Scrooge was surprised. All of the visits from the ghosts / had taken place / in one night.

"Do you know / the butcher's shop down the street?" Scrooge asked. "Please go / and tell the butcher / I'll buy a big goose. Come back with the man, / and I'll give you a nice tip." The boy ran off quickly.

"I'll send it to Bob Cratchit's. He won't know / who is sending it. It's twice the size of Tiny Tim," Scrooge thought to himself.

Scrooge then dressed himself / in his Sunday best / and went out onto the streets. Many people were on the streets, / and Scrooge gave each of them / a delighted smile. He said, "Good morning, sir," or "A Merry Christmas to you," to everyone he passed.

Later in the afternoon, / he walked toward his nephew's house. He passed the door / a dozen times / before he had the courage / to go up and knock. But he finally did.

Fred was very surprised / to see his uncle. "Uncle, why are you here?" he asked.

"I have come to dinner. Will you let me in, Fred?" Scrooge asked.

"Of course you may!" cried out Fred.

Fred was very happy, / and so were his wife and all their friends. They had a wonderful party together.

·**honor** 紀念　·**lesson** 教訓　·**make amends** 彌補　·**stirring** 令人興奮的
·**take place** 發生　·**butcher's shop** 肉鋪　·**butcher** 肉販　·**tip** 小費
·**think to oneself** 心中想著　·**dress oneself** 打扮　·**one's Sunday best** 一個人最好的衣服
·**delighted** 愉快的　·**a dozen times** 很多次　·**courage** 勇氣　·**uncle** 舅舅

CLOSE UP

1　**It's twice the size of Tiny Tim.** 它是小提姆的兩倍大。
　　〈倍數＋名詞〉是「幾倍的……」的意思。「兩倍」是twice，從四倍開始用〈數字＋times〉的形式來表現，例如：four times（四倍）。

2　**Scrooge then dressed himself in his Sunday best** 施顧己穿上他最好的衣服。
　　〈dress oneself in . . .〉是「穿上……（服裝）」的意思。

施顧己繼續說：「我會在心裡 in my heart 紀念聖誕節 honor Christmas，一年到頭 all the year 都會試著記住 keep it，我會活在活去、現在和未來 in the past, present, and future，永遠不會忘記我學到的教訓 never forget the lessons。」

幽靈消失了 disappear，施顧己明白他回到 be back 自己的房間裡 in his own bedroom。最棒也最快樂的 best and happiest of all 是時間在他面前，他還有時間 have time 挽救一切 make amends。

施顧己聽到了教堂的鐘聲 the church bells 響得很大聲 ring loudly，跑到窗邊 run to the window，打開窗戶 open it，探出頭來 put out his head，外面是晴朗 clear、明亮 bright、令人興奮 stirring、珍貴的 golden 一天。

「今天是哪一天 what day？」施顧己對著街上的一個男孩大叫。

「今天？今天是聖誕節 Christmas Day 啊，先生。」男孩回答。

「聖誕節！」施顧己很驚訝 be surprised，所有鬼魂的來訪 the visits from the ghosts 都發生 take place 於一夜之間 in one night。

「你知道街上 down the street 肉販的店 the butcher's shop 嗎？」施顧己問，「請幫我去告訴肉販，我要買一隻肥鵝 buy a big goose，跟著肉販 with the man 回來 come back，我會給你豐厚的小費 a nice tip。」男孩很快地跑去 run off。

「我要把它送到鮑伯・克萊契的家，他不會知道是誰送給他的，這比小提姆還大兩倍 twice the size of Tiny Tim。」施顧己心裡想。

施顧己穿上他最好的衣服 dress himself in his Sunday best，走到街上去 go out onto the streets。街上有許多人 many people，施顧己給他們每一個人 each of them 親切的微笑 give a delighted smile。他對每個經過的人說：「早安 good morning，先生。」或「祝你聖誕快樂 Merry Christmas to you。」

傍晚時 later in the afternoon，他朝他外甥的家 toward his nephew's house 走去，他走過他家門 pass the door 很多次 a dozen times，才有上前 go up 敲門 knock 的勇氣 have the courage，最後他做到了。

佛萊德見到自己的舅舅 see his uncle 非常驚訝。「舅舅，你為什麼在這裡 why are you here？」他問。

「我來吃晚餐 come to dinner，佛萊德，你願意讓我進來 let me in 嗎？」施顧己問。

「當然願意！」佛萊德大聲說。

佛萊德非常高興，他太太和他們的朋友也一樣，他們一起過了一個很美妙的 wonderful 聖誕節。

GRAMMAR POINT

So am I.：我也是。

- You are happy. **So am I.** (= I **am also happy.**) 你很快樂。我也是。
- Fred was very happy, and **so were** his wife and all their friends.
  = Fred was very happy, and **his wife and all their friends were also very happy**.
  佛萊德很高興，他太太和他們的朋友也都一樣。

The next day, / Scrooge went to the office / early in the morning. He wanted to be there / before Bob got there. Bob was eighteen minutes late. As Bob walked in, / Scrooge said, "Hello. **What do you mean / by coming here at this time of day?**"

"I'm very sorry, sir. I'm late," replied Bob.

"Yes, I think you are," said Scrooge.

"Now, I'll tell you what, / my friend," said Scrooge. "**I'm not going to stand this sort of thing** / any longer. And therefore . . . therefore, / **I am going to pay you more money!**"

Scrooge continued, "I'll raise your salary / and assist your struggling family. We will discuss your affairs / this very afternoon," Scrooge said / with a nice smile.

That afternoon, / Scrooge took Bob out for a drink / and **explained** / **how he was going to help him.**

Scrooge was better than his word. He did everything / **he said he was going to do** / and more. He became a friend of the Cratchit family, / and to Tiny Tim, / who did not die, / he was like a second father. He became as good a friend, / as good a master, / and as good a man / as the city ever knew.

Some people laughed at him / because he had changed. Scrooge did not mind. Scrooge's own heart laughed, / and that was quite enough for him. He had no further dealings with ghosts, / but he lived happily ever afterward.

- **stand** 忍受　・**this sort of thing** 這種事　・**raise salary** 加薪　・**assist** 幫助
- **struggling** 生存困難的　・**affairs** 事情　・**this very afternoon** 今天下午
- **second father** 像父親一樣的人　・**laugh at** 嘲笑某人　・**do not mind** 不在意
- **dealings with** 跟誰打交道　・**ever afterward** 從此以後

CLOSE UP

1　**What do you mean by coming here at this time of day?**
你這個時間才來上班是什麼意思？
〈What do you mean by＋V-ing . . .？〉是「……到底是什麼意思呢？」。

2　**I'm not going to stand this sort of thing.** 我不會再繼續忍受這種事。/
I am going to pay you more money. 我將要付你更多錢。/
explained how he was going to help him 解釋他將要如何幫他 /
he said he was going to do 他說他將要做
〈be going to . . .〉是「將會去……」的意思，提到「已經計畫好或決定好未來要去做的事」，或是「看到現在的狀況，決定未來一定要去做的事」時使用。這裡用 was going to，因為主要子句的動詞explained和said是過去式，因時式要一致，所以要用過去式。

隔天 the next day 施顧己一大早 early in the morning 就進了辦公室 go to the office，他希望在鮑伯到達之前 get there 先到那裡 be there。鮑伯遲到了 18 分鐘 eighteen minutes late。當鮑伯走進來 walk in，施顧己說：「哈囉 hello，你這個時間 at this time of day 才來上班 come here 是什麼意思？」。

「非常抱歉，先生，我遲到了 be late。」鮑伯回答。

「是的，我想你是。」施顧己說。

「現在，我的朋友，我要跟你說 tell you what，」施顧己說：「我不打算再忍受這種事 this sort of thing，因此 therefore……，我要幫你加薪 pay you more money。」

施顧己繼續說：「我要加你的薪水 raise your salary，幫助 assist 你艱困的家庭 your struggling family，我們今天下午 this very afternoon 來談談你的事 discuss your affairs。」施顧己微笑地說 with a nice smile。

那天下午 that afternoon，施顧己帶鮑伯出去 take Bob out，喝杯飲料 for a drink，解釋 explain 他要如何幫助鮑伯 help him。

施顧己比他說的還要更好 be better than his word，他說到做到，而且還有過之而無不及 everything and more。他成了克萊契一家人的朋友 become a friend，對還活著的小提姆來說，他就像第二個父親一樣 like a second father。他成了眾所皆知的好朋友、好老闆和大善人。

有些人為他的改變而嘲笑他 laugh at him，施顧己並不在意 do not mind，他內心 Scrooge's own heart 在笑 laugh，這對他來說已然足夠 be quite enough。他沒有繼續和鬼魂打交道 dealings with ghosts，從此以後 ever afterward 過著幸福快樂的日子 live happily。

Super
Reading
Story
Training
Book

Step

6

The Last Leaf

— O. Henry

The Last Leaf

In a little district / west of Washington Square, / the streets have run crazy / and broken themselves into small strips / called "places." These "places" / make strange angles and curves. One street crosses itself / a time or two. An artist once discovered / a valuable possibility / on this street. Suppose / a collector with a bill / for paints, paper, and canvas / should, / **in taking this route,** / suddenly meet himself coming back, / **without a cent having been paid** on account.

So, / to quaint old Greenwich Village, / the art people soon came prowling, / hunting for north windows and eighteenth-century gables and Dutch attics and low rents. Then, / they imported pewter mugs and a dish or two / from Sixth Avenue / and became a "colony."

At the top of / an ugly, three-story brick house, / Sue and Johnsy had their studio. "Johnsy" was a nickname for Joanna. One was from Maine; / the other from California. They had met at the restaurant Delmonico's / on Eighth Street / and **had found** / **that their tastes in art, food, and clothes** / **were so similar** / **that the joint studio resulted.**

That was in May. In November, / a cold, unseen stranger, / whom the doctors called Pneumonia, / visited the colony, / touching one here and there / with his icy fingers. Over on the east side, / this ravager strode boldly, / claiming scores of victims, / but his feet trod slowly / through the maze of the narrow and moss-grown "places."

Mr. Pneumonia was not / what you would call a gentleman. A small woman / with blood thinned by the warm California zephyrs / was no match for the tough and deadly illness.

·**district** 地區 ·**run crazy** 錯綜複雜 ·**strip** 條狀物 ·**valuable** 可貴的
·**possibility** 機會 ·**suppose** 假如 ·**collector** 討債者 ·**take a route** 沿著路走
·**on account** 賒帳 ·**quaint** 奇怪的 ·**prowl** 摸索 ·**gable** 三角牆
·**attic** 閣樓 ·**rent** 房租 ·**import** 引進 ·**colony** 藝術區 ·**three-story** 三層樓
·**studio** 工作室 ·**nickname** 暱稱 ·**result** 導致 ·**pneumonia** 肺炎
·**ravager** 掠奪者 ·**stride** 邁步 ·**boldly** 大膽地 ·**scores of** 許多 ·**victim** 受害者
·**tread** 踏 ·**maze** 迷宮 ·**moss-grown** 長滿青苔的 ·**zephyr** 微風；西風
·**deadly** 致命的 ·**be no match for** 不是某人的對手

1 **in taking this route** 沿著這條路走 / **without a cent having been paid** 沒有收到半分錢
〈in＋V−ing〉是「在做……中」的意思。〈without＋V−ing〉是「不用做……」的意思。
這裡的 a cent 是動名詞片語 having been paid 的主詞。

2 **had found that their tastes in art, food, and clothes were so similar that the joint studio resulted** 發現她們對藝術、飲食、衣著的品味十分相似，於是聯合工作室誕生了
〈that their tastes in art, food, and clothes were so similar〉這部分是 had found 的受詞。
整句是〈so…that…〉（如此……以致……）的結構。

最後一葉

華盛頓廣場 Washington Square 西邊的一個小區 in a little district，街道 the streets 縱橫交錯 run crazy，將這一帶分割成一小條一小條 break themselves into small strips 稱為「街道」called "places"。這些「街道」形成了奇特的角度和曲線 make strange angles and curves，一條街 one street 自己本身就交叉 cross itself 一次或兩次 a time or two。曾經 once 有一個藝術家 an artist 在這條街上發現了它的可貴之處 a valuable possibility，如果一個討債者帶著顏料、紙和畫布的帳單 a collector with a bill，走這條路 take this route 收帳，他會突然 suddenly 發現他遇到沒有收到半毛錢的自己 meet himself coming back。

於是藝術家 the art people 很快地摸索到 come prowling 這個奇特有趣、古老的 quaint old 格林威治村 Greenwich Village。他們尋找面北的窗戶 north windows，18 世紀的三角牆 eighteenth-century gables、荷蘭式的閣樓 Dutch attics，以及低廉的房租 low rents，然後，他們又從第六街 from Sixth Avenue 買進 import 了一些白鑞杯子 pewter mugs 和一兩個盤子 a dish or two，組成了一個「藝術區」become a "colony"。

在一棟醜陋的三層樓磚屋 an ugly, three-story brick house 的頂樓 at the top，蘇和瓊西 Sue and Johnsy 設立了他們的工作室 have their studio。瓊西是喬安娜的暱稱 a nickname for Joanna，她倆一個 one 來自緬因州 from Maine，另一個 the other 來自加州 from California。她們是在第八大道的德爾蒙尼戈飯館相遇的，彼此一談，發現她們對藝術、飲食、衣著 in art, food, and clothes 的品味 tastes 十分相似 be so similar，於是聯合工作室 the joint studio 誕生了 result。

那是五月的事 in May，到了十一月 in November，一個冷酷、隱形的陌生人 a cold, unseen stranger，醫生稱之為「肺炎」Pneumonia 造訪了「藝術區」visit the colony。用他冰冷的手指 with his icy fingers 這裡碰一下，那裡碰一下 touch one here and there。在廣場東側 over on the east side，這個掠奪者 this ravager 明目張膽地邁步 stride boldly，奪去了許多受害者的性命 claim scores of victims，但他步伐在經過如迷宮 maze 般，窄小又長滿青苔的「藝術區」時，慢了下來 tread slowly。

肺炎先生 Mr. Pneumonia 可不是一個你會稱之為紳士的人，一個被加州溫暖的西風 the warm California zephyrs 吹得面無血色 with blood thinned 的弱女子 a small woman 更不是這個難纏、可怕疾病 the tough and deadly illness 的對手 match。

But he attacked Johnsy, / and she lay, / scarcely moving, / on her painted iron bedstead, / looking through the small Dutch windowpanes / at the blank side of the next brick house.

One morning, / the busy doctor invited Sue into the hallway.

"She has one chance in– / let us say, ten," he said, / as he shook down the mercury / in his clinical thermometer.

"And that chance is / for her to want to live. Sometimes / when people give up trying to live, / it doesn't matter / what medicines I give. Your friend has made up her mind / that she's not going to get well. Has she anything on her mind?"

"She . . . she wanted to paint the Bay of Naples / some day," said Sue.

"Paint? Bosh! Does she have anything on her mind / worth thinking about twice, / like a man, for instance?"

"A man?" said Sue, / with a hard sound in her voice. "Is a man worth– / but, no, Doctor. There is nothing of the kind."

"Well, it is the weakness then," said the doctor. "I will do all / that science, / so far as it may be employed by me, / can accomplish. But whenever my patient / begins to count the carriages / in her funeral procession, / I subtract fifty percent / from the power of medicine to cure. If you can get her to ask one question / about the new winter styles in cloak sleeves, / I will promise you / a one-in-five chance for her / instead of one in ten."

After the doctor left, / Sue went into the workroom / and cried a napkin to a pulp. Then, / she swaggered into Johnsy's room / with her drawing board, / whistling a popular tune.

Johnsy lay, / scarcely making a move under the bedclothes, / with her face toward the window. Sue stopped whistling, / thinking she was asleep.

- **scarcely** 幾乎不　・**bedstead** 床架　・**windowpane** 窗戶玻璃　・**blank** 空白的
- **shake down** 搖下；甩下　・**mercury** 水銀　・**clinical thermometer** 體溫計
- **give up** 放棄　・**it doesn't matter** 無所謂　・**make up one's mind** 下定決心
- **get well** 好起來　・**weakness** 缺點　・**accomplish** 完成；做到
- **funeral procession** 喪禮隊伍　・**subtract** 扣除　・**cure** 治療
- **get . . . to . . .** 讓某人達到　・**cloak** 披風　・**cry a napkin to a pulp** 把毛巾哭得一團濕
- **swagger** 精神抖擻　・**whistle** 吹口哨　・**popular tune** 流行曲調

CLOSE UP

1　**Has she anything on her mind? / Does she have anything on her mind?**
她有什麼心事嗎？
〈have . . . on one's mind〉是「有……的念頭」、「有……在心裡」、「擔心……」的意思

2　**so far as it may be employed by me** 盡我所知地治病
這是so far as I may employ it的被動語態，it是指science。這裡的employ是「使用、駕馭」的意思，science是「知識」。〈so far as . . .〉（到目前為止）。

可是，他攻擊了瓊西 attack Johnsy。她躺 lie 在漆過的鐵床架上幾乎一動不動 scarcely move，只能透過小小的荷蘭式玻璃窗凝視 look at 隔壁磚屋 the next brick house 的空牆 the blank side。

有一天早晨，忙碌的醫生 the busy doctor 請蘇和他一起到走廊去 invite Sue into the hallway。

「讓我們這麼說吧 let us say，她只有十分之一的機會 one chance in ten。」他一邊說，一邊把診療用溫度計裡 in his clinical thermometer 的水銀 the mercury 甩下去 shake down。

「這一成希望 that chance 在於她求生的意志 want to live。有時候，人不想活 give up trying to live，不管我給什麼藥 what medicines I give 都沒有用 it doesn't matter。妳的朋友已經下定決定 make up her mind，她不想要康復 get well，她有什麼心事 anything on her mind 嗎？」

「她……她希望有一天 some day 能畫那不勒斯的海灣 paint the Bay of Naples。」蘇說。

「畫畫？胡說 bosh！她還有其他值得再次回味的事 worth thinking about 嗎？例如 for instance，男人 like a man？」

「男人？」蘇扯著嗓子說：「有男人值得……，不，醫生，沒有這種人 nothing of the kind。」

「好吧，這是不利之處 the weakness，」醫生說：「我會盡我所知地 do all that science 治好她，盡我所能地 so far as it may be employed by me 治好她，可是當我的病人 my patient 開始算 count 她出殯 in her funeral procession 時會有多少馬車 the carriages 送葬，治療效果 the power of medicine to cure 就降低一半了 subtract fifty percent。如果妳能讓她問一個有關冬季大衣袖子新樣式 styles in cloak sleeves 的問題 ask one question，我保證能讓她痊癒機率從一成 one in ten 提升為兩成 one in five。」

醫生走後，蘇走進工作室 go into the workroom，把小毛巾哭得一團濕 cry a napkin to a pulp，然後她拿著畫板 with her drawing board 精神抖擻地走進瓊西的房間 swagger into Johnsy's room，口裡吹了一首流行曲 whistle a popular tune。

瓊西躺著，被子底下 under the bedclothes 的身體幾乎不動 scarcely make a move，臉向著窗戶。蘇以為瓊西在睡覺 be asleep，就不再吹口哨 stop whistling。

GRAMMAR POINT

分詞片語 ⇨ 省略連接詞和主詞，以分詞引導的子句，就叫作「分詞片語」。

- she lay, scarcely **moving**, . . . **looking** through the small Dutch windowpanes . . .
  她躺著幾乎不動，……透過小小的荷蘭式玻璃窗凝視……
- Johnsy lay, scarcely **making** a move under the bedclothes, . . .
  瓊西躺著，在被子下幾乎完全不動，……
- Sue stopped whistling, **thinking** she was asleep. 蘇以為瓊西在睡覺，就不再吹口哨了。

She arranged her board / and began a pen-and-ink drawing / to illustrate a magazine story. Young artists must pave their way to art / by drawing pictures / for the magazine stories / that young authors must write / to pave their way to literature.

As Sue was sketching / a pair of elegant horseshow riding trousers and a monocle / on the figure of the hero, / an Idaho cowboy, / she heard a low sound, / several times repeated. She quickly went to the bedside.

Johnsy's eyes were open wide. She was looking out the window / and counting backwards. "Twelve," she said, / and a little later, "eleven"; / and then "ten," and "nine"; / and then "eight" and "seven" almost together.

Sue looked out the window. What was there / to count? There was only a bare, dreary yard / to be seen, / and the blank side of the brick house / twenty feet away. An old, old ivy vine, / twisted and decayed at the roots, / climbed halfway up the brick wall. The cold breath of autumn / had taken most of its leaves from the vine / until its skeleton branches clung, / almost bare, / to the bricks.

"What is it, / dear?" asked Sue.

"Six," said Johnsy, / in almost a whisper. "They're falling faster now. Three days ago, / there were almost a hundred. It made my head ache / to count them. But now it's easy. There goes another one. There are only five left now."

"Five what, / dear? Tell your Sudie."

"Leaves. On the ivy vine. When the last one falls, / I must go, too. I've known that / for three days. Didn't the doctor tell you?"

"Oh, I have never heard of such nonsense," complained Sue, / with magnificent scorn. "What have old ivy leaves to do with your getting well? And you used to love that vine so, / you naughty girl. Don't be like that. Why, / the doctor told me this morning / that your chances for getting well real soon / were / —let's see exactly what he said— / he said / the chances were ten to one. Why, / that's almost as good a chance as we have in New York / when we ride on the streetcars / or walk past a new building."

· arrange 架好　· pen-and-ink drawing 鋼筆畫　· illustrate 畫　· literature 文學界
· horseshow 馬術表演　· riding trousers 馬褲　· monocle 單片眼鏡
· count backward 倒數　· bare 荒蕪的　· dreary 陰暗的　· yard 院子
· ivy vine 常春藤　· twisted 盤繞的　· decayed 枯萎的　· skeleton branches 骨幹枝條
· cling to 纏附；抓住　· nonsense 荒唐的話　· with magnificent scorn 非常輕蔑
· have to do with 與……有何關連　· ten to one 九成；百分之九十
· as good a chance as 和……機會一樣大

1　**pave their way to art** 為通往藝術界而鋪路 / **pave their way to literature** 為通往文學界而鋪路
〈pave one's way to . . .〉是「為某人朝……發展作準備」的意思。

2　**It made my head ache to count them.** 讓我數得頭都疼了。
〈make 受詞＋原形動詞〉是「使某人怎麼樣」的意思，這裡的 It 是虛主詞，to count them 是真主詞。

3　**There goes another one.** 又掉了一個。
〈there goes . . .〉是「走了」、「沒有了」、「(機會等)溜走了」的意思。

她架好畫板 **arrange her board**，開始為雜誌裡的故事 **illustrate a magazine story** 畫鋼筆插畫 **a pen-and-ink drawing**，年輕畫家 **young artists** 不得不為雜誌裡的故事畫插畫，為通往藝術界而舖路 **pave their way to art**，而年輕作家 **young authors** 不得不為雜誌寫故事，為通往文學界而舖路 **pave their way to literature**。

蘇正在幫故事中的英雄 **the hero**，一個愛達荷州牛仔 **an Idaho cowboy** 的身上描繪 **sketch** 一件馬術表演穿的精緻馬褲和一片單片眼鏡時，她聽見了一個低沉的聲音 **a low sound**，重複了好幾次 **several times repeated**，她趕忙走到床邊 **go to the bedside**。

瓊西眼睛睜得大大的 **be open wide**，望著窗外 **look out the window**，倒數 **count backward**，「十二 **twelve**」她說，過了一會兒 **a little later**，「十一 **eleven**」，然後 **and then**「十 **ten**」、「九 **nine**」，接著幾乎同時 **almost together** 數「八 **eight**」、「七 **seven**」。

蘇看看窗外，窗戶外面有什麼可以數呢？只看見 **to be seen** 一片荒蕪陰暗的院子 **a bare, dreary yard**，20 英呎外 **twenty feet away** 還有一面磚屋的空牆 **the blank side**。一棵很老很老的常春藤 **an old, old ivy vine**，枯萎 **decayed** 的根盤繞 **twisted** 在一塊，蔓延至磚牆的半腰處 **climb halfway up the brick wall**。秋天的寒風 **the cold breath of autumn** 將藤葉幾乎全數吹落 **take most of its leaves from the vine**，只有光禿的 **bare** 枝條 **its skeleton branches** 還纏附在磚塊上 **cling to the bricks**。

「什麼，親愛的？」蘇問道。

「六 **six**」瓊西低聲說：「現在它們掉得更快 **fall faster** 了。三天前 **three days ago**，還有將近一百個 **almost a hundred**，讓我數 **count** 得頭都疼 **make my head ache** 了，但現在很好數。又掉了一個 **another one**，只剩下五個了 **only five left**。」

「五個什麼 **five what**，親愛的？告訴妳的小蘇。」

「葉子 **leaves**，那棵常春藤上的 **on the ivy vine**，等最後一葉 **the last one** 落下 **fall**，我也要走了 **must go**。我三天前就已經知道了，難道醫生沒告訴妳嗎？」

「喔，我從來沒聽過這麼荒唐的話 **such nonsense**，」蘇輕蔑地 **with magnificent scorn** 抱怨 **complain** 道，「老常春藤的葉子 **old ivy leaves** 跟妳康復 **your getting well** 有什麼關係？妳這個淘氣的女孩 **you naughty girl**，妳以前很喜歡那棵常春藤 **love that vine so**。別這樣嘛 **don't be like that**，醫生今天早上告訴我，妳康復的機會 **your chances for getting well**，讓我想想他怎麼說的 **what he said**，他說機會有九成 **ten to one**，那就跟我們在紐約 **in New York** 搭電車 **ride on the streetcars** 或走過一棟新建築 **walk past a new building** 的機會一樣大。」

GRAMMAR POINT

動名詞意思上的主詞 ⇨ 用所有格或受格來表示。

- What have old ivy leaves to do with **your/you** getting well?
  老常春藤的葉子跟妳的康復有什麼關係？
- -
- She was upset about **Johnsy's/Johnsy** giving up trying to live.
  她很擔心瓊西放棄努力活下去的念頭。

"Try to have some broth now, / and let Sudie go back to her drawing, / so she can sell it to the editor. Then, / I'll buy port wine for her sick child / and pork chops for her greedy self."

"You don't need to get / any more wine," said Johnsy, / keeping her eyes fixed out the window.

"There goes another. No, I don't want any broth. That leaves just four. I want to see the last one fall / before it gets dark. Then, I'll go, too."

"Johnsy, dear," said Sue, / bending over her, "will you promise / to keep your eyes closed / and not to look out the window / until I am done working? I must hand my drawings in / by tomorrow. I need the light, / or I would pull the shade down."

"Couldn't you draw / in the other room?" Johnsy asked coldly.

"I'd rather be here / beside you," said Sue. "Besides, / I don't want you / to keep looking at those silly ivy leaves."

"Tell me / as soon as you have finished," said Johnsy, / closing her eyes, / and lying white and still / as a fallen statue, "because I want to see the last one fall. I'm tired of waiting. I'm tired of thinking. I want to turn loose my hold on everything / and go sailing down, down, / just like one of those poor, tired leaves."

"Try to sleep," said Sue. "I must call Behrman up / to be my model for the old hermit-miner. I'll just be gone / for a minute. Don't try to move / until I come back."

Old Behrman was a painter / who lived on the ground floor / beneath them. He was past sixty / and had a long beard / like Michelangelo's Moses / curling down from his wide head. Behrman was a failure in art. He had been painting / for forty years, / but he had never produced anything noteworthy. He had always been about to paint a masterpiece, / but he had never yet begun it. For several years, / he had painted nothing / except for minor advertisements here and there.

- broth 湯　• port wine 紅葡萄酒　• fixed 不動的　• bend over 彎腰
- hand in 交出　• shade 窗簾　• I'd rather 我最好　• fallen 倒下的
- statue 雕像　• turn loose 鬆開　• call up 聯絡　• hermit-miner 隱居的礦工
- beard 大鬍子　• Moses 摩西　• failure 失敗　• noteworthy 值得注意的
- masterpiece 傑作　• minor 較小的；不重要的　• advertisement 廣告

CLOSE UP

1 **here beside you** 陪在妳身邊 / **Besides, I don't want you to . . .** 而且，我不希望妳
〈beside〉當介系詞，意「在……旁邊」。〈besides〉當副詞時，是「此外」的意思。

2 **I'm tired of waiting. I'm tired of thinking.** 我懶得等待。我懶得思考。
〈be tired of . . .〉是「厭倦／懶得……」的意思。

3 **except for minor advertisements** 除了小廣告
〈except for . . .〉和〈except . . .〉意思一樣，是「除了……之外」的意思。

「現在喝點湯吧 have some broth，讓小蘇回去畫畫 go back to her drawing，這樣才能賣給編輯 sell it to the editor，然後我會買一點紅葡萄酒 port wine 給她生病的孩子 her sick child（指瓊西），還會買一點豬排 pork chops 給貪吃的她自己（指蘇）her greedy self。」

「妳不用再買酒了。」瓊西眼睛繼續盯著 keeping her eyes fixed 窗外說。

「又掉了一片 another，不，我不想喝湯。只剩下四片葉子 just four 了，我想在天黑前看最後一葉掉落 see the last one fall，然後我也要走了 will go。」

「瓊西，親愛的，」蘇彎下腰 bend over her 對她說：「妳可以答應我在我完成工作前，閉上眼 keep your eyes closed，不要往窗外看嗎？我明天 by tomorrow 一定要交插畫 hand my drawings in，我需要光線 need the light，要不然我就把窗簾拉下來了 pull the shade down。」

「妳不能到另一間房間畫 draw in the other room 嗎？」瓊西冷冷地問道。

「我要在這 here 陪妳 beside you。」蘇說：「而且 besides，我不希望妳一直看著 keep looking at 那些蠢藤葉 those silly ivy leaves。」

「妳一畫完 finish，就告訴我 tell me。」瓊西閉著眼說 close her eyes，臉色蒼白、一動也不動地躺在床上 lie white and still，像一座倒下的雕像 as a fallen statue，「因為我想看最後一葉凋零，我不想等待 be tired of waiting，不想思考 be tired of thinking，我想要鬆開 turn loose 抓住每件事 my hold on everything 的手，飄下去，飄下去 go sailing down, down，像那些可憐、疲倦的葉子一樣。」

「試著睡覺 try to sleep，」蘇說：「我得和貝爾曼聯絡 call Behrman up，請他當隱居的老礦工模特兒 be my model。我只是離開 will be gone 一會兒 for a minute。我回來前 come back，妳別亂動。」

老貝爾曼 Old Behrman 是住在她們樓下 beneath them 一樓 on the ground floor 的畫家 a painter，年過 60 be past sixty，留著一把長鬍子 have a long beard，看起來像是米開朗基羅的摩西雕像，寬寬的頭 from his wide head 蓄著卷卷的 curl 鬍子。貝爾曼是個失敗的畫家 a failure in art，畫了 40 年 paint for forty years，卻沒有創作出 never produce 半點值得注意的作品 anything noteworthy。他一直想要畫一幅曠世傑作 paint a masterpiece，但他卻從未動過筆 never begin it。幾年下來 for several years，他除了到處 here and there 畫些小廣告 minor advertisements，什麼也沒畫過 paint nothing。

He earned a little / by serving as a model / for those young artists in the colony / who could not pay for a professional. He drank gin to excess / and still talked about his coming masterpiece. For the rest, / he was a fierce little old man, / who made fun of anyone who was soft / and who regarded himself as a bulldog / ready to protect the two young artists / living in the studio above him.

Sue found Behrman / smelling strongly of juniper berries / in his dimly lit den below. In one corner / was a blank canvas on an easel / that had been waiting there / for twenty-five years / to receive the first line of the masterpiece. She told him about Johnsy's fancy / and how she feared / she would, / indeed, light and fragile as a leaf herself, / float away / when her slight hold upon the world / grew weaker.

Old Behrman, / with his red eyes plainly streaming, / shouted about / how silly Johnsy's idea was.

"What!" he cried. "Are there people in this world / so foolish to believe / that they will die / when a leaf falls off a vine? I have never heard of such a thing. No, I will not pose as a model / for you. Why did you allow such a silly thought / to enter her head? Oh, that poor little Miss Johnsy."

"She is very ill and weak," said Sue, "and the fever has left her mind / filled with thoughts of death and other horrible things. Very well, Mr. Behrman, / if you do not care to pose for me, / you don't have to. But I think / you are a horrid old man."

"You are just like a woman!" yelled Behrman. "Who said / I will not pose? Go on. I will go with you. For half an hour, / I have been trying to say / that I am ready to pose. God, this is not a place / in which someone / as pretty as Miss Johnsy / should lie sick. Someday, / I will paint a masterpiece, / and we shall all go away. God, yes."

· **pay for** 付錢給　　· **professional** 專業的　　· **to excess** 太多　　· **for the rest** 此外
· **fierce** 火爆的　　· **make fun of** 嘲笑　　· **dimly lit** 昏暗的　　· **den** 小房間　　· **fancy** 胡思亂想
· **fear** 害怕　　· **fragile** 脆弱的　　· **float away** 飄走
· **slight hold upon the world** 對世界的留戀　　· **plainly** 顯然　　· **stream** 流淌
· **pose (as a model)** （身為模特兒）擺姿勢　　· **horrid** 糟的　　· **lie sick** 躺著生病

CLOSE UP

1　**regarded himself as a bulldog** 自認為是鬥牛犬
〈regard . . . as . . .〉是「認為……是……」、「把……看作是……」的意思。這裡的bulldog看作是「警衛」的意思也可以。

2　**with his red eyes plainly streaming** 紅紅的眼睛顯然在流淚
〈with＋受詞＋補語〉這片語，是表同時發生的狀況。受詞是his red eyes，補語是plainly streaming。

3　**allow such a silly thought to enter her head** 容許這麼蠢的念頭進入她的腦中
〈allow . . . to . . .〉是「允許……去做……」的意思。

4　**has left her mind filled with thoughts** 讓她心裡充滿念頭
〈leave＋受詞＋補語〉是「讓……成為／保持……狀況」的意思。

在藝術區 in the colony 那些年輕畫家負擔不起請專業模特兒的費用 cannot pay for a professional，於是他靠當模特兒 serve as a model 賺一點錢 earn a little。他毫無節制地喝酒 drink gin to excess，仍然一直提起他要畫的大作 his coming masterpiece。除此以外 for the rest，他是個火爆的小老頭 a fierce little old man，嘲笑 make fun of 那些軟弱的人 anyone who is soft，他卻認為自己 regard himself as 是保護 protect 樓上工作室兩位年輕畫家的鬥牛犬 a bulldog。

蘇在樓下他那間昏暗的小房間裡 in his dimly lit den 找到了渾身酒味的貝爾曼 smell strongly。在房間一個角落裡 in one corner 的畫架上 on an easel 一張空白的畫布 a blank canvas 在那裡等了 25 年 for twenty-five years，等待畫下傑作的第一條線 receive the first line。她告訴貝爾曼瓊西的胡思亂想 Johnsy's fancy，還說她怕瓊西真的像葉子一樣 as a leaf 又輕又脆弱 light and fragile。當她對世界的留戀 her slight hold upon the world 愈來愈少 grow weaker，她可能真的會飄走 float away。

老貝爾曼紅紅的眼睛 his red eyes 顯然在流淚 plainly stream，他大聲說道瓊西的胡思亂想 Johnsy's idea 有多愚蠢 how silly。

「什麼 what！」他大聲說道：「這世上有人笨到 so foolish 會相信一片葉子 a leaf 從藤上掉落 fall off a vine 時，人就會死去 will die 嗎？我從來沒聽說過這怪事，不，我不會為妳當模特兒擺姿勢 will not pose as a model。妳竟容許這麼蠢的念頭 such a silly thought 進入她的腦海裡 enter her head？喔，可憐的瓊西小姐。」

「她病得很重且很虛弱 be ill and weak。」蘇說：「發燒 the fever 讓她滿腦子都是死亡和其他恐怖的念頭 death and other horrible things。好吧 very well，貝爾曼先生，如果你不願意當我的模特兒 do not care to pose，那就算了 don't have to，但我覺得你真是一個糟老頭 a horrid old man。」

「女人就是女人 just like a woman！」貝爾曼大叫，「誰說我不擺姿勢了？走吧，我跟妳去 go with you，我不是已經說我準備好要給妳擺姿勢 be ready to pose 說了半小時了嗎？天啊 god，像瓊西小姐這麼漂亮的小姐 as pretty as Miss Johnsy 在這裡生病真是不應該，總有一天，我會畫出一幅曠世傑作，我們都可以離開 go away 這裡。老天啊，是的。」

GRAMMAR POINT

關係代名詞 ⇨ 一般來說，關係代名詞直接放在先行詞之後，不過有時候，在先行詞和關係代名詞之間會插入修飾片語等。

• ... for *those young artists* in the colony **who** could not pay for a professional
……那些藝術區的年輕畫家負擔不起請專業模特兒的錢

• ... *a blank canvas* on an easel **that** had been waiting there for twenty-five years ...
……畫架上空白的畫布擺在那裡等了 25 年

Johnsy was sleeping / when they went upstairs. Sue pulled the shade down to the windowsill / and **motioned Behrman to go into the other room.** In there, / they fearfully peered out the window / at the ivy vine. Then, / they looked at each other / for a moment / without speaking. **A persistent, cold rain / was falling / along with some snow.** Behrman, / in his old blue shirt, / took his seat / as the hermit-miner / on an upturned kettle for a rock.

When Sue awoke from an hour's sleep / the next morning, / she found Johnsy / with dull, wide-open eyes / staring at the drawn green shade.

"Pull it up. I want to see," she ordered in a whisper.

Wearily, Sue obeyed.

But, incredibly, / despite the beating rain and fierce gusts of wind / that had lasted throughout the entire night, / there still remained one ivy leaf / against the wall. It was the last one / on the vine. Still dark green near its stem, / but, **with its serrated edges tinted yellow** / as it was beginning to decay, / it hung bravely from a branch / some twenty feet above the ground.

"It is the last one," said Johnsy. "I thought / it would surely fall during the night. I heard the wind. It will fall today, / and I shall die / at the same time."

"Dear, dear!" said Sue, / leaning her worn face down to the pillow. "Think of me, / if you won't think of yourself. What would I do?"

- **windowsill** 窗臺　・**motion** 示意　・**fearfully** 恐懼地　・**peer out** 向外看
- **persistent** 不停的　・**take one's seat** 坐下　・**upturned** 翻過來　・**wearily** 無力疲倦地
- **incredibly** 不可思議地　・**despite** 儘管　・**gusts of wind** 一陣強風　・**remain** 留著
- **serrated** 鋸齒狀的　・**tinted** 染上顏色　・**decay** 枯萎　・**worn face** 倦容

CLOSE UP

1　**motioned Behrman to go into the other room** 示意貝爾曼到另一間房間
〈motion . . . to . . .〉是「示意……去做……」的意思。

2　**A persistent, cold rain was falling along with some snow.**
一陣寒冷的雨伴隨著雪花不停地下著。
〈along with . . .〉是「伴隨著……地」、「和……一起地」的意思。

3　**with its serrated edges tinted yellow** 鋸齒狀的邊緣染上了黃色
以〈with＋受詞＋補語〉組成的片語，表同時發生的狀況；受詞是 its serrated edges，補語是 tinted yellow。

他們上樓 go upstairs 以後，瓊西正在睡覺，蘇把窗簾拉至窗臺 pull the shade down to the windowsill，示意貝爾曼到另一間房間 go into the other room。在那裡 in there，他們膽顫心驚地凝視 fearfully peer 窗外那棵常春藤，後來他們一語不發地 without speaking 彼此對望了一會兒 for a moment。一陣寒冷的雨 a cold rain 伴隨著雪花 along with some snow 不停地下著 persistent。貝爾曼穿著他老舊的藍襯衫 in his old blue shirt 坐 take his seat 在充當岩石 for a rock 被翻過來的鐵壺上 on an upturned kettle，扮成隱居的礦工 as the hermit–miner。

第二天早晨 the next morning，蘇只睡了一小時 an hour's sleep 就醒來 awake。她看到瓊西無神的雙眼睜得大大的 with dull, wide–open eyes 盯著拉下來的綠窗簾 stare at the drawn green shade。

「把窗簾拉起來 pull it up，我想看。」她低聲命令。

蘇無力地 wearily 照做了 obey。

神奇地 incredibly，儘管整夜 throughout the entire night 不停地風吹 fierce gusts of wind 雨打 the beating rain，牆上 against the wall 還有一片常春藤的葉子 one ivy leaf。這是藤上最後一葉 the last one on the vine，靠近根部 near its stem 還是深綠色 dark green，但是鋸齒狀的邊緣 its serrated edges 已經枯萎 begin to decay 染上了黃色 tinted yellow。它勇敢地掛在 hang bravely 離地 20 呎高 some twenty feet above the ground 的枝條上 from a branch。

「這是最後一葉了，」瓊西說：「我聽到風聲 hear the wind，以為它昨晚 during the night 一定會掉 surely fall，它今天一定會掉 fall today，同時我也會死 die at the same time。」

「唉唷，唉唷 dear, dear！」蘇滿臉倦容地靠著枕頭，「如果妳不肯為自己想想，那為我想一想 think of me 吧！我該怎麼辦呢 what would I do？」

GRAMMAR POINT

despite : 不管……、不顧…… (= in spite of) ⇨ 注意不要錯誤地寫成了 despite of。

• **Despite** the beating rain and fierce gusts of wind, . . . there still remained one ivy leaf against the wall. 不管風吹雨打，……牆上還留著一片常春藤的葉子。

- -

• **Despite** my effort to keep her alive, she died. 不管我多努力讓她活下來，她還是死了。

But Johnsy did not answer. The most lonesome thing / in the entire world / is a soul / when it is making ready / to go on its mysterious, far journey. The fancy seemed to possess her / more strongly / as, / one by one, / **the ties that bound her to friendship and to Earth** / were loosed.

The day passed, / and even in the twilight, / they could see the lone ivy leaf / clinging to its stem against the wall. And then, / with the coming of the night, / the north wind again began to blow / while the rain still beat against the windows / and ran down the eaves.

When it was light enough, / Johnsy, the merciless, / commanded that the shade be raised.

The ivy leaf was still there.

Johnsy lay for a long time / looking at it. And then she called to Sue, / who was stirring her chicken broth / over the gas stove.

"I've been a bad girl, Sudie," said Johnsy. "Something has made / that last leaf stay there / to show me / how wicked I was. It is a sin / to want to die. You may bring me a little broth now / and some milk with a little port in it, / and . . . No, bring me a hand-mirror first, / and then pack some pillows about me, / and I will sit up / and watch you cook."

An hour later, / she said, "Sudie, / someday I hope to paint the Bay of Naples."

The doctor came in the afternoon, / and Sue had an excuse / to go into the hallway / as he left.

"**Even chances**," said the doctor, / taking Sue's thin, shaking hand / in his. "With good nursing, / you'll win. And now **I must see another case** / I have downstairs. Behrman, his name is / —some kind of an artist, / I believe. Pneumonia, too. He is an old, weak man, / and the attack is acute. There is no hope for him, / but he goes to the hospital today / to be made more comfortable."

· make ready to 準備好　· possess 佔據　· tie 連結　· be loosed 鬆脫　· twilight 星光
· beat 打　· eave 荷蘭式的屋簷　· merciless 無情地　· command 吩咐　· stir 攪拌
· wicked 壞的　· sin 罪　· pack 疊　· sit up 坐起來　· have an excuse to 有藉口去……
· even chances 五成機會　· acute（病情）嚴重的

CLOSE UP

1　**the ties that bound her to friendship and to Earth** 她與友誼和世上一切事物的連結
　〈bind . . . to . . .〉是「把……和……綁在一起」的意思。〈that . . . Earth〉這部分是修飾the ties的關係子句。

2　**Even chances** 五成機會
　even一般當副詞，是「甚至」或「連」的意思，也可以當形容詞，意「同一個的」、「平均的」、「對等的」、「偶數的」。
　形容詞：例 They are even in length.（他們一樣長。）/ an even number（偶數）

3　**I must see another case** 我得去看另一個病患
　case的基本意思是「（特殊的）情況、案例」的意思，它也有「患者」的意思，把它想成是「罹患疾病或受傷的案例」也可以。

可是瓊西沒回答，世上 in the entire world 最孤寂的人 the most lonesome thing 就是準備好 make ready 要赴上神秘、遙遠旅途 go on its mysterious, far journey 的靈魂 a soul 了，胡思亂想 the fancy 愈來愈強烈地 more strongly 佔據她全部的心思 possess her，且一個接一個 one by one，讓她與友誼及世上一切事物 bind her to friendship and to Earth 的連結 the ties 鬆脫 be loosed 了。

白天過去了，甚至到了黃昏 in the twilight，他們也能看見那孤單的常春藤葉 the lone ivy leaf 仍然緊抓著牆上的根 cling to its stem，然後，夜晚來臨 with the coming of the night，北風 the north wind 又開始呼嘯 blow，雨 the rain 不停拍打著窗戶上的玻璃 beat against the windows。雨水沿著荷蘭式的屋簷流下來 run down the eaves。

天色濛濛 be light enough 時，瓊西，毫不留情地 Johnsy, the merciless 吩咐 command 人拉起窗簾 the shade be raised。

那片常春藤葉依然在那裡 still there。

瓊西躺著看它 look at it 看了很久 for a long time，然後她叫了 call to 在瓦斯爐邊攪拌雞湯 stir her chicken broth 的蘇。

「我真是一個壞女孩 a bad girl，」瓊西說：「那最後一葉 that last leaf 留在那裡 stay there 是為了證明我 show me 之前多壞 how wicked。想死 want to die 是一種罪過 a sin，妳現在可以給我一點湯了 bring me a little broth，再給我一點加紅酒的牛奶 some milk，然後……不，先給我一面小鏡子 a hand-mirror first，幫我把枕頭墊高一點 pack some pillows about me，我就可以坐起來 sit up 看妳煮飯 watch you cook。」

過了一個鐘頭 an hour later，她說：「小蘇，我希望有一天 someday 能去畫那不勒斯的海灣 paint the Bay of Naples。」

下午 in the afternoon 醫生來了，他離開時，蘇找藉口 have an excuse 到走廊上 go into the hallway。

「有五成希望 even chances，」醫生握著蘇瘦弱、顫抖的手說：「好好地照料 with good nursing，妳會成功的 win，現在我得下樓去看另一個病患 see another case 了。他名字叫貝爾曼，好像也是畫家 some kind of an artist，應該也是肺炎 pneumonia, too。他又老又虛弱 an old, weak man，病情嚴重 the attack is acute。他沒有希望 no hope 了，但今天要把他送到醫院去 go to the hospital，讓他更舒服一點 be made more comfortable。」

GRAMMAR POINT

command that + 主詞 (+ should) + 原形動詞

⇨ 在和建議、請求、主張、命令等有關的一般動詞(suggest, demand, insist, command, etc.)後，在當作受詞的that子句中，動詞形態必須是〈should＋原形動詞〉或沒有should只留下〈原形動詞〉。

• Johnsy, the merciless, **commanded** that the shade **(should) be raised**.
瓊西，無情地吩咐人拉起窗簾。

• The doctor **insisted** that he **(should) go** to the hospital.　醫生堅持他應該要就醫。

The next day, / the doctor said to Sue, "She's out of danger. You've won. Nutrition and care now / —that's all she needs."

That afternoon, / Sue went to the bed / where Johnsy lay, / contentedly knitting / a very blue and very useless woolen shoulder scarf, / and she put one arm around her, pillows and all.

"I have something to tell you, / my dear," she said. "Mr. Behrman died of pneumonia / in the hospital today. He was ill / for only two days. The janitor found him / on the morning of the first day / in his room downstairs / helpless with pain. His shoes and clothing / were soaked and icy cold. They couldn't imagine / where he had been / on such a dreadful night. And then they found / a lantern, still lit, / a ladder that had been dragged from its place, / some scattered brushes, / and a palette with green and yellow colors mixed on it, / and—look out the window, dear, / at the last ivy leaf on the wall. Didn't you wonder / why it never fluttered or moved / when the wind blew? Ah, darling, / it's Behrman's masterpiece. He painted it there / the night that the last leaf fell."

・out of danger 脫離險境　・nutrition 營養　・contentedly 安心地　・die of 死於
・janitor 工友　・helpless 無助的　・be soaked 濕透　・dreadful 可怕的　・drag 拖
・scattered 散落的　・flutter 飄動

1　**on such a dreadful night** 在這麼可怕的夜晚
〈such a/an ＋形容詞＋名詞〉such 是強調程度的「如此……的」的意思。

2　**a palette with green and yellow colors mixed on it** 還有一塊混著綠色和黃色的調色盤
〈with ＋受詞＋補語〉的片語，是表同時發生的狀況，受詞是 green and yellow colors，補語是 mixed on it。

隔天 the next day，醫生跟蘇說：「她已脫離險境 be out of danger，妳成功了，現在她只需要 all she needs 營養和照料 nutrition and care 了。」

　　那天下午 that afternoon，蘇到瓊西躺著的床邊，瓊西愉快地在編織 knit 一條深藍色 very blue，且毫無用處的 very useless 羊毛披肩 a woolen shoulder scarf，蘇用一隻胳臂抱住瓊西和枕頭。

　　「我有件事要告訴妳 have something to tell you，親愛的，」她說：「貝爾曼先生 Mr. Behrman 今天在醫院 in the hospital 因肺炎過世了 die of pneumonia，他只病 be ill 了兩天 for only two days。頭一天早上 on the morning of the first day 工友 the janitor 發現他在他樓下的房間裡 in his room 痛苦又無助 helpless with pain。他的鞋子和衣物 his shoes and clothing 都濕透 be soaked 了，且覆蓋著冷冷的薄冰 and icy cold。他們無法想像 can't imagine 這麼淒風苦雨的夜晚 on such a dreadful night 他還能上哪兒去 where he has been。後來，他們找到一盞提燈 a lantern，燈還亮著 still lit，一把被拖來的 be dragged 梯子 a ladder，一些散落的畫筆 some scattered brushes，還有一塊混著綠色和黃色顏料 with green and yellow colors mixed on it 的調色盤 a palette。妳看看窗外 look out the window 牆上那最後一葉 the last ivy leaf。妳難道沒好奇過為什麼風吹的時候它從來不飄動 never flutter or move 嗎？啊，親愛的，那是貝爾曼的傑作 Behrman's masterpiece，他在最後一葉 the last leaf 落下的那一晚，畫上去的 paint it there。」

die of / die from：因……而死

⇨ 一般來說，因疾病而去世，用 of；因受傷或意外而死，用 from。

- Mr. Behrman **died of** pneumonia in the hospital today. 貝爾曼先生今天在醫院因肺炎過世了。
- She **died from** injuries after the car accident. 她因車禍重傷不治。

Super
Reading
Story
Training
Book

Answers
and
Translations

Step 4

What Men Live By

`pp. 2–3`

Stop & Think

- **Why couldn't Simon pay for the sheepskins?** 為什麼西門付不出買羊毛皮的錢？
  ⇨ His customers did not give him any money. 他的顧客沒還他半毛錢。

- **What did Simon see behind the church?** 西門在教堂後面看到什麼？
  ⇨ He saw a naked man. 他看到一個赤身露體的男人。

CHECK UP

1	Simon had five rubles.	F
2	Simon wanted to buy some sheepskins.	T
3	There was a robber next to the church.	F
4	Simon was afraid of the naked man.	T

1 西門有五個盧布。
2 西門想要買一些羊皮。
3 教堂旁邊有強盜。
4 西門很怕那個赤身露體的男人。

`pp. 4–5`

Stop & Think

- **What did Simon give the man?** 西門給那男人什麼？
  ⇨ He gave the man his coat, boots, and a stick. 他給那男人他的大衣、靴子和一根枴杖。

- **What did Simon's wife think about her husband?** 西門的妻子怎麼看她的丈夫？
  ⇨ She thought he had been out drinking. 她以為他出門喝酒了。

CHECK UP

1 The man said that — d. God had punished him.
2 Simon felt glad — b. to help another person.
3 Matryna was — a. very disappointed with Simon.
4 Matryna thought that Simon — c. was a drunkard.

1 那人說神懲罰他。
2 西門很高興能幫助別人。
3 瑪琪娜對西門很失望。
4 瑪琪娜以為西門喝醉了。

Stop & Think

• **What did Simon say to make Matryna calm down?** 西門說了什麼讓瑪琪娜冷靜下來？
⇨ He said that anger is a sin. 他說生氣是罪惡。

CHECK UP

1 What did Matryna feel for the stranger? (c)
   a. concern　　　　**b.** love　　　　**c.** pity

2 What happened after the man smiled? (a)
   a. A light came from his face.　**b.** Simon felt pity for him.　**c.** Matryna's heart softened.

1 瑪琪娜對陌生人的感覺是什麼？
   a. 關心　　　　　　**b.** 愛　　　　　　**c.** 憐憫
2 那人笑了以後發生了什麼事？
   a. 他的臉上發出光芒。　**b.** 西門憐憫他。　　**c.** 瑪琪娜的心軟了下來。

Stop & Think

• **What work did Michael know?** 麥可會做什麼工作？
⇨ He did not know anything. 他什麼也不會。

• **Who was in the carriage?** 誰在馬車上？
⇨ A gentleman in a fur coat was in the carriage. 穿著毛皮大衣的紳士在馬車上。

CHECK UP

1 Simon and Matryna had no more of <u>bread</u>.
2 The stranger's name was <u>Michael</u>.
3 Simon offered Michael food and <u>shelter</u> in return for work.
4 Michael became a very <u>skilled</u> bootmaker.

1 西門和瑪琪娜沒有麵包了。
2 陌生人的名字是麥可。
3 西門給麥可食物和住的地方，作為工作的報酬。
4 麥可變成了一個手藝很好的靴匠。

Stop & Think

• **What did Michael do when he looked behind the gentleman?** 麥可看到紳士後面的時候，他做了什麼？
⇨ He smiled. 他微笑了。

CHECK UP

1 The gentleman showed Simon some <u>expensive</u> leather.
2 The gentleman <u>terrified</u> Simon.
3 The gentleman wanted his boots in <u>two days</u>.
4 Michael made <u>slippers</u> for the gentleman.

1 紳士給西門看了一些昂貴的皮革。
2 紳士讓西門很害怕。

3 紳士希望在兩天內拿到他訂製的靴子。

4 麥可為紳士做了拖鞋。

pp. 12–13

Stop & Think

• **What happened to the gentleman?** 紳士怎麼了？

⇨ He died in the carriage. 他死在馬車上。

CHECK UP

1 Michael smiled two times in six years.   T

2 A woman with two girls came to Simon's hut.   T

3 The two girls were cousins.   F

4 The woman was the girls' mother.   F

1 麥可在六年之中笑了兩次。

2 有個帶著兩個女孩的婦人來到西門的木屋。

3 兩個女孩是表姊妹。

4 婦人是女孩的媽媽。

pp. 14–15

Stop & Think

• **How did the girl's leg get injured?** 女孩的腿是怎麼受傷的？

⇨ Her mother rolled on it and crushed it when she died.
她母親臨死前翻身壓到她身上，把她的腿壓壞了。

• **What happened as everyone was talking?** 大家說話的時候發生了什麼事？

⇨ A bright light filled the room. 強光充滿了房間。

CHECK UP

1 The woman said the girls   **a.** was not an ordinary man.

2 Michael asked Simon and Matryna   **b.** were precious to her.

3 Simon realized that Michael   **c.** to forgive him.

1 婦人說女孩對她而言很寶貴。

2 麥可求西門和瑪琪娜原諒他。

3 西門知道麥可不是凡人。

pp. 16–17

Stop & Think

• **Why did God punish Michael?** 神為何懲罰麥可？

⇨ He disobeyed God. 他違背神的旨意。

• **What did God order Michael to learn about?** 神命令麥可學習什麼？

⇨ To learn three truths: Learn what dwells in man. Learn what is not given to man.
And learn what men live by.
認識三項真理：認識什麼住在人裡面，認識神沒有賜給人什麼，認識人靠什麼活著。

1 Why did Michael smile three times? (a)
  a. He learned three truths.   **b.** He saw God.   **c.** He knew the little girls.

2 Whose soul was Michael supposed to take? (b)
  a. Simon's soul   **b.** the mother's soul   **c.** the girls' souls

1 為什麼麥可微笑了三次？
  a. 他學會了三項真理。   **b.** 他看見神。   **c.** 他認識小女孩。
2 麥可應該帶走誰的靈魂？
  a. 西門的靈魂   **b.** 母親的靈魂   **c.** 女孩的靈魂

pp. 18−19

Stop & Think

• **What did Michael *do* when he returned to Earth?** 麥可回到人間以後，做了什麼？
  ⇨ He took the mother's soul. 他把母親的靈魂帶走了。

• **What was *the second* truth?** 第二項真理是什麼？
  ⇨ Men are not given the knowledge to know what they need.
    人沒有知道自己需要什麼的能力。

CHECK UP

1 Michael could return to Heaven after he learned all three truths.
2 Michael learned the first truth from Matryna.
3 Michael learned another truth from the rich man.

1 麥可學會三項真理以後才能回到天堂。
2 麥可從瑪琪娜身上學會第一項真理。
3 麥可從富人身上學會第二項真理。

pp. 20−21

Stop & Think

• **What was *the third* truth?** 第三項真理是什麼？
  ⇨ All men live because love is in them. 人活著是因愛在他們裡面。
    All men live by love. 人靠愛而活。

CHECK UP

1 Michael learned the third truth from the woman.
2 A bright light surrounded Michael's body.
3 Did Michael fly away from Simon's house? (Yes)

1 麥可從婦人身上學會了第三項真理。
2 有道亮光包圍著麥可的身體。
3 麥可從西門家飛走嗎？（是）

How Much Land Does a Man Need?

pp. 22–23

Stop & Think

• **Why was the younger sister annoyed?** 為什麼妹妹覺得很煩？
  ⇨ The elder sister was boasting about the advantages of town life. 姊姊誇口鎮上的生活有多好。

• **How would Pahom feel if he had plenty of land?** 如果帕霍姆有很多土地，他會覺得怎麼樣？
  ⇨ He would not fear the Devil himself. 他就不怕撒旦。

CHECK UP

1 How did the younger sister feel about her way of life? (b)
  a. She felt anxious.　　**b.** She liked it.　　**c.** She wanted to change it.

2 Where was the Devil sitting? (b)
  a. on the stove　　**b.** behind the stove　　**c.** under the stove

1 妹妹覺得自己的生活方式怎麼樣？
  a. 她覺得很焦慮。　　**b.** 她很喜歡。　　**c.** 她想要改變。

2 撒旦坐在哪裡？
  a. 爐子上面　　**b.** 爐子後面　　**c.** 爐子下面

pp. 24–25

Stop & Think

• **Why did Pahom fine his neighbors?** 為什麼帕霍姆要罰鄰居錢？
  ⇨ They were trespassing on his land. 他們非法入侵他的土地。

CHECK UP

1 The Devil decided to　　　　　　　　　　**a.** and became a landowner.
2 Pahom bought a farm　　　　　　　　　　**b.** trespass on his land on purpose.
3 Pahom's neighbors began to　　　　　　　**c.** have a contest with Pahom.
4 Pahom took Simon　　　　　　　　　　　**d.** to court for trespassing.

1 撒旦決定要和帕霍姆比賽。
2 帕霍姆買下一塊地，成為地主。
3 帕霍姆的鄰居開始故意穿越他的地。
4 帕霍姆把西門帶到法庭，告西門非法入侵他的土地。

pp. 26–27

Stop & Think

• **What did the stranger tell Pahom about the village?** 關於村莊，陌生人跟帕霍說了什麼？
  ⇨ Anyone who moved there was given twenty-five acres of land for free.
  任何搬到那裡的人都可以免費得到25畝地。

• **Why was Pahom not happy in the village?** 為什麼帕霍姆在村裡不開心？
  ⇨ He had to rent other people's land every year. 他每年都要跟別人租地。

CHECK UP

1. The peasant came from a land beyond the Volga River.   <u>T</u>
2. The village beyond the Volga gave everyone 250 acres of land for free.   <u>F</u>
3. Pahom visited the village to find out about the land.   <u>T</u>
4. Pahom was ten times better off than before.   <u>T</u>

1. 農夫來自伏爾加河的另一邊。
2. 伏爾加另一邊的村莊免費送250畝地給每個人。
3. 為了解那塊地帕霍姆造訪了那座村莊。
4. 帕霍姆比以前富裕10倍。

---

pp. 28-29

Stop & Think

• **How much land did the peddler buy?** 小販買了多少地？
  ⇨ He bought thirteen thousand acres of land. 他買了13,000畝地。

CHECK UP

1. The <u>peddler</u> said that the Bashkirs sold their land for cheap prices.
2. Pahom decided to <u>visit</u> the land of the Bashkirs.
3. The Bashkirs pitched their <u>tents</u> beside a river.
4. Pahom told the <u>interpreter</u> that he had come about some land.

1. 小販說巴什基爾人用很低的價錢賣土地。
2. 帕霍姆決定要去參觀巴什基爾人的地。
3. 巴什基爾人在河邊紮營。
4. 帕霍姆跟通譯員說，他為了土地而來。

---

pp. 30-31

Stop & Think

• **What did Pahom say about the Bashkirs' land?** 帕霍姆覺得巴什基爾人的土地怎麼樣？
  ⇨ They had plenty of it, and it was good land. 他們有很多地，而且都很肥沃。

• **What did Pahom give to the chief?** 帕霍姆給首領什麼東西？
  ⇨ He gave the chief the best dressing gown and five pounds of tea.
    他給首領最好的袍子和五磅茶葉。

CHECK UP

1. The Bashkirs wanted to <u>repay</u> Pahom for his gifts.
2. The Bashkirs told Pahom to <u>point out</u> the land he wanted.
3. The <u>chief</u> arrived while the Bashkirs were arguing.
4. Did the chief speak to Pahom in Russian? (Yes)

1. 巴什基爾人想要答謝帕霍姆送的禮物。
2. 巴什基爾人叫帕霍姆指出他想要的地。
3. 巴什基爾人在吵架的時候，首領來了。
4. 首領跟帕霍姆用俄文交談嗎？（是）

Stop & Think

- **How much was the land Pahom wanted to buy?** 帕霍姆想買的地要多少錢？
  ⇨ It was one thousand rubles a day. 一天1,000盧布。

- **What was the condition the chief gave Pahom?** 首領給帕霍姆什麼條件？
  ⇨ He had to return to the spot where he started on the same day, or he would lose his money.
  他必須在一天內回到起點，不然他就會失去他的錢。

CHECK UP

1 What did Pahom want the chief to give him with the land? (a)
  a. a deed　　　　**b.** some money　　　　**c.** some servants

2 How far did Pahom think he could walk in one day? (b)
  a. 20 miles　　　**b.** 35 miles　　　　**c.** 50 miles

1 帕霍姆希望首領給他土地跟什麼？
  a. 一份契約　　**b.** 一些錢　　　**c.** 一些僕人

2 帕霍姆覺得自己一天可以走多遠？
  a. 20哩　　　**b.** 35哩　　　**c.** 50哩

Stop & Think

- **What happened to Pahom in his dream?** 在夢裡帕霍姆發生了什麼事？
  ⇨ He was lying dead in front of the Devil. 他橫屍在撒旦面前。

- **What did the chief put down to mark the starting spot?** 首領在起點放了什麼東西當作記號？
  ⇨ He put down his fox-fur cap on the ground. 他把狐皮帽放在地上。

CHECK UP

1 Pahom had a dream　　　　　　　**a.** on the fox-fur cap.
2 The Devil was　　　　　　　　　**b.** the night before the contest.
3 Pahom put his money　　　　　　**c.** laughing in Pahom's dream.

1 比賽前一夜帕霍姆做了一個夢。
2 在帕霍姆的夢裡撒旦在笑。
3 帕霍姆把他的錢放在狐皮帽上。

Stop & Think

- **Why did Pahom not lie down at lunch?** 為什麼帕霍姆午餐的時候不躺下來休息？
  ⇨ He did not want to fall asleep. 他不想睡著。

CHECK UP

1 Pahom walked for 100 yards on the first side of the square.　　　F

2 Pahom did not stop to have lunch.　　　F

3 Pahom made the first side and the second side of the square too long.　　T

1 帕霍姆走正方形的第一邊時走了100碼的距離。
2 帕霍姆沒有停下來吃午餐。
3 帕霍姆走正方形的第一邊和第二邊走得太長了。

pp. 38–39

Stop & Think

- What *did Pahom throw away while he was returning to the hill?* 回山丘的路上，帕霍姆把什麼丟掉？
  ⇨ He threw away his coat, boots, flask, and cap. 他把大衣、靴子、水壺、帽子都丟了。

- What *was Pahom afraid of as he returned to the hill?* 帕霍姆回山丘的時候害怕什麼？
  ⇨ He was afraid of death. 他怕死。

CHECK UP

1 Pahom thought he had tried for too much land.
2 Pahom kept his spade and used it as a support.
3 Pahom's heart was beating like a hammer.

1 帕霍姆認為他謀求太多土地了。
2 帕霍姆留下鏟子，用來當支撐的枴杖。
3 帕霍姆的心跳動得像鐵鎚在敲打一樣。

pp. 40–41

Stop & Think

- How much land *did Pahom need?* 帕霍姆需要多少土地？
  ⇨ He needed six feet from his head to his heels. 他從頭到腳只需要六呎地。

CHECK UP

1 The sun set at the bottom of the hill faster than at the top.
2 The chief said that Pahom had gained much land.
3 Pahom's servant saw that he was dead.
4 Did the Devil win his contest with Pahom? (Yes)

1 山丘下的日落比山丘上的還快。
2 首領說帕霍姆得到很多土地。
3 帕霍姆的僕人看到他死了。
4 撒旦贏了帕霍姆嗎？（是）

A Christmas Carol

pp. 44–45

Stop & Think

• **How did people feel about Scrooge?** 大家對施顧己有什麼看法？

⇨ They avoided him. 他們躲著他。 / They didn't like him. 他們不喜歡他。

CHECK UP

1　Scrooge was a greedy man.　　　　　　T
2　Scrooge and Marley still worked together.　F
3　Bob Cratchit was Scrooge's boss.　　　F

1　施顧己是一個貪心的人。
2　施顧己和馬里仍然一起工作。
3　鮑伯・克萊契是施顧己的老闆。

pp. 46–47

Stop & Think

• **What did Scrooge's nephew ask him to do?** 施顧己的外甥要他做什麼？

⇨ To go to Christmas dinner. 去吃聖誕晚餐。 /
To have dinner with his family. 跟他的家人一起吃晚餐。

• **What did Scrooge give Bob Cratchit for Christmas?** 聖誕節，施顧己給鮑伯・克萊契什麼東西？

⇨ He gave Bob Cratchit the day off. 他給鮑伯・克萊契一天的假。

CHECK UP

1　Scrooge said that Marley died seven years ago.
2　The men asked Scrooge to give them some money.
3　Scrooge paid Bob Cratchit his day's wages for Christmas.
4　Bob Cratchit promised to arrive early the day after Christmas.

1　施顧己說馬里七年前過世了。
2　那些男人要施顧己給他們一些錢。
3　施顧己付了一天薪水給鮑伯・克萊契過聖誕節。
4　鮑伯・克萊契答應聖誕節隔天早點上班。

pp. 48–49

Stop & Think

• **What went into Scrooge's room?** 什麼東西進到施顧己的房間？

⇨ Marley's ghost went into Scrooge's room. 馬里的鬼魂進到施顧己的房間。

CHECK UP

1　What kind of noise did Scrooge hear? (b)
　a. a screaming man　　**b.** a dragging chain　　**c.** a laughing woman

2 What could Marley not do? (a)

    a. rest   **b.** speak   **c.** move

1 施顧己聽到什麼聲響？
   a. 男人的尖叫聲   **b.** 鎖鍊拖行的聲音   **c.** 女人的笑聲

2 馬里不能做什麼？
   a. 休息   **b.** 說話   **c.** 移動

---

pp. 50-51

Stop & Think

- **How many ghosts will visit Scrooge?** 多少鬼魂會來拜訪施顧己。
  ⇨ Three ghosts will visit him. 三個鬼魂會來拜訪他。

- **What was the first ghost to visit Scrooge?** 第一個來拜訪施顧己的鬼魂是什麼？
  ⇨ The first ghost was the Ghost of Christmas Past. 第一個鬼魂是過去聖誕節的鬼魂。

CHECK UP

1 Marley said that Scrooge's chain was longer than his own.

2 The first ghost was going to come at one in the morning.

3 The first ghost looked like an old man.

1 馬里說施顧己的鎖鍊比自己的還長。

2 第一個鬼魂會在凌晨一點來。

3 第一個鬼魂看起來像一個老頭。

---

pp. 52-53

Stop & Think

- **What time of year did the ghost take Scrooge to?** 鬼魂帶施顧己到一年當中的什麼時候？
  ⇨ The ghost took Scrooge to Christmastime. 鬼魂帶施顧己到聖誕節期。

CHECK UP

1 Scrooge and the ghost   **a.** were not real.

2 The images Scrooge saw   **b.** in an office for Mr. Fezziwig.

3 Scrooge once worked   **c.** passed through the wall together.

1 施顧己和鬼魂一起穿牆。

2 施顧己看到的畫面不是真的。

3 施顧己曾經在費茲威先生的辦公室裡工作過。

---

pp. 54-55

Stop & Think

- **Who did Scrooge see with himself?** 施顧己看到誰跟他在一起？
  ⇨ He saw his old girlfriend. 他看到他以前的女朋友。

- **What did Scrooge tell the ghost?** 施顧己跟鬼魂說什麼？
  ⇨ Scrooge told the ghost to leave him. 施顧己請鬼魂放過他。

1 Scrooge never had a girlfriend in his entire life.   F
2 Scrooge loved money more than people.   T
3 The beautiful woman Scrooge saw was his mother.   F
4 Scrooge asked the ghost to show him some more scenes.   F

1 施顧己這輩子從來沒交過女朋友。
2 比起人，施顧己更愛錢。
3 施顧己看到的美麗女人是他媽媽。
4 施顧己請鬼魂讓他看更多場景。

pp. 56−57

Stop & Think

• **Who was the second ghost?** 第二個鬼魂是誰？
  ⇨ It was the Ghost of Christmas Present. 是現在聖誕節的鬼魂。

• **What did Bob Cratchit's family have to eat?** 鮑伯・克萊契家人有什麼可以吃？
  ⇨ They had a goose, some potatoes, and a small Christmas pudding.
  他們只有一隻鵝，一些馬鈴薯，和一個小小的聖誕布丁。

CHECK UP

1 There was a <u>giant</u> sitting in the middle of Scrooge's living room.
2 The ghost told Scrooge to <u>touch</u> his robe.
3 <u>Tiny Tim</u> needed to use a crutch to walk.
4 The Cratchits had a simple meal, but they <u>enjoyed</u> it.

1 有一個巨人坐在施顧己客廳的正中央。
2 鬼魂叫施顧己摸他的袍子。
3 小提姆需要用枴杖走路。
4 克萊契一家吃了一頓很簡單的晚餐，但他們得很高興。

pp. 58−59

Stop & Think

• **Who did Bob Cratchit propose a toast to?** 鮑伯・克萊契提議為誰乾杯？
  ⇨ He proposed a toast to Scrooge. 他提議為施顧己乾杯。

CHECK UP

1 How did Mrs. Cratchit feel about drinking to Scrooge? (c)
  a. pleased   **b.** nervous   **c.** unhappy

1 克萊契太太覺得為施顧己乾杯怎麼樣？
  a. 高興   **b.** 緊張   **c.** 不高興

pp. 60−61

Stop & Think

• **Who was the third ghost?** 第三個鬼魂是誰？
  ⇨ It was the Ghost of Christmas Yet to Come. 是未來聖誕節的鬼魂。

1 Fred wanted Scrooge to give Bob Cratchit more <u>money</u>.
2 The third ghost wore <u>black</u> clothes.
3 The third ghost said <u>nothing</u>.
4 Were the people the ghost showed Scrooge talking about a marriage? (No)

1 佛萊德希望施顧己給鮑伯・克萊契更多錢。
2 第三個鬼魂穿黑衣服。
3 第三個鬼魂一語不發。
4 鬼魂給施顧己看的人在談論一個婚禮？（不）

pp. 62–63

Stop & Think

• **Where did the three people get the items they were selling?** 這三個人是從哪裡拿到他們要賣的東西？
  ⇨ They got them from the dead man's house. 他們從死人的家裡拿的。

CHECK UP

1 The shopkeeper asked the women —————— a. what they had to sell.
2 One woman was selling —————— b. bed curtains and blankets.
3 The ghost pointed at —————— c. a dead body covered by a sheet.

1 店主問女人，她們有什麼要賣。
2 一個女人在賣床簾和毯子。
3 鬼魂指著一具蓋著床單的死屍。

pp. 64–65

Stop & Think

• **Why was the Cratchit family sad?** 為什麼克萊契一家人很傷心？
  ⇨ Tiny Tim died. 小提姆死了。

CHECK UP

1 The Ghost of Christmas Yet to Come took Scrooge to a churchyard. T
2 Scrooge wanted to know who the dead man was. T
3 The name on the grave was Scrooge's. T

1 未來聖誕節的鬼魂帶施顧己去教堂的墓地。
2 施顧己想知道那死人是誰。
3 墳墓刻了施顧己的名字。

pp. 66–67

Stop & Think

• **What did Scrooge tell the boy to do?** 施顧己叫男孩做什麼？
  ⇨ Go to the butcher's shop and bring the butcher back. 去肉販的店，把肉販帶來。

1 Scrooge realized that all three ghosts had visited him in <u>one night</u>.
2 Scrooge sent <u>the goose</u> to Bob Cratchit's house.
3 Scrooge went to his nephew's house to <u>have dinner</u>.

1 施顧己知道三個鬼魂的來訪只發生於一夜之內。
2 施顧己把鵝送到鮑伯・克萊契的家。
3 施顧己到外甥家吃晚餐。

pp. 68–69

Stop & Think

• **What did Scrooge tell Bob Cratchit he was going to do?**
施顧己跟鮑伯・克萊契說他要做什麼？

⇨ Scrooge said that he would raise his salary and assist his family.
施顧己說他要幫他加薪及幫助他的家庭。

• **How did Scrooge act toward Tiny Tim?** 施顧己怎麼對小提姆？

⇨ He became a second father to Tiny Tim. 他變成小提姆的第二個父親。

CHECK UP

1 What did Scrooge promise Bob Cratchit? (c)
a. a bigger house　　　**b.** a healthy family　　　**c.** a higher salary

2 What kind of man did Scrooge become? (b)
a. a greedy man　　　**b.** a good man　　　**c.** a silly man

1 施顧己答應鮑伯・克萊契什麼？
a. 一棟更大的房子　　**b.** 一個健康的家庭　　　**c.** 更高的薪水
2 施顧己變成什麼樣的人？
a. 貪心的人　　　**b.** 好人　　　　**c.** 傻瓜

The Last Leaf

pp. 72–73

Stop & Think

• **What kind of people went to old Greenwich Village?** 什麼樣的人會去老格林威治村？
⇨ Art people went there. 藝術家會到那邊去。

• **What happened in the colony in November?** 十一月的時候藝術區發生了什麼事？
⇨ Many people caught pneumonia. 很多人得了肺炎。

1 There were "places" in Washington Square.
2 People went to old Greenwich Village looking for low rents.
3 Sue and Johnsy lived together.
4 Did many people get pneumonia in May? (No)

1 在華盛頓廣場有「街道」。
2 人們到老格林威治村尋找低廉的房子。
3 蘇和瓊西住在一起。
4 很多人在五月得了肺炎嗎？（不）

pp. 74–75

Stop & Think

• **What *did the doctor say* Johnsy *needed to do?*** 醫生說瓊西該怎麼做？
⇨ She needed to want to live. 她需要求生意志。

• **What *did the doctor want* Sue *to do?*** 醫生要蘇做什麼？
⇨ Get Johnsy to think of something valuable to her. 讓瓊西去想對她有意義的事。

CHECK UP

1 The doctor said Johnsy had one chance in ten to live.
2 Medicine is less effective when patients think about death.
3 Sue cried very hard after the doctor left.

1 醫生說瓊西有一成機會可以存活。
2 病人不想活的時候，藥效會減弱。
3 醫生走了以後，蘇哭得很傷心。

pp. 76–77

Stop & Think

• **What was Johnsy *counting?*** 瓊西在數什麼？
⇨ She was counting the leaves on the ivy vine. 她在數常春藤上的葉子。

CHECK UP

1 Johnsy was counting backward.   T
2 Johnsy said she would die when the last leaf fell.   T
3 Sue said Johnsy's chances of living were ten to one.   T

1 瓊西在倒數。
2 瓊西說最後一葉掉的時候，她也會死。
3 蘇說瓊西存活的機會有九成。

pp. 78–79

Stop & Think

• **What *did* Sue ask Johnsy *to do?*** 蘇要瓊西做什麼？
⇨ Close her eyes and not look out the window. 閉上眼，不要看窗外。

• **Who was Behrman?** 貝爾曼是誰？
⇨ He was a painter who lived downstairs from Sue and Johnsy. 他是住在蘇和瓊西樓下的畫家。

1 What did Johnsy ask Sue to do? (a)
   a. draw in another room　　**b.** give her some broth　　**c.** pull the shade down

2 What kind of an artist was Behrman? (c)
   a. a successful one　　**b.** an average one　　**c.** a failed one

1 瓊西要蘇做什麼？
   a. 到別的房間畫畫　　**b.** 給她一點湯　　**c.** 把窗簾拉下來
2 貝爾曼是什麼樣的畫家？
   a. 很成功的　　**b.** 一般的　　**c.** 失敗的

---

pp. 80–81

Stop & Think

• **What did Behrman drink *too much of*?** 貝爾曼喝了太多什麼？
   ⇨ He drank too much gin. 他喝了太多酒。

CHECK UP

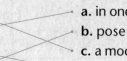

1 Behrman worked as　　　　　　　　　　　**a.** in one corner of Berhman's den.
2 There was a blank canvas　　　　　　　　**b.** pose as a model for Sue.
3 Behrman thought Johnsy's idea　　　　　**c.** a model for artists in the colony.
4 Behrman decided to　　　　　　　　　　　**d.** was silly.

1 貝爾曼在藝術區當畫家的模特兒。
2 在貝爾曼小房間的一個角落有一張空白的畫布。
3 貝爾曼認為瓊西的念頭很愚蠢。
4 貝爾曼決定為蘇當模特兒擺姿勢。

---

pp. 82–83

Stop & Think

• **What did Johnsy tell Sue to do *when she woke up*?** 瓊西醒了以後，要蘇做什麼？
   ⇨ She told Sue to pull up the shade. 她叫蘇把窗簾拉起來。

• **What did Johnsy and Sue *see outside*?** 瓊西和蘇看到外面有什麼？
   ⇨ They saw one ivy leaf against the wall. 他們看到牆上有一片常春藤葉。

CHECK UP

1 Sue and Behrman looked out the <u>window</u> at the ivy vine.
2 There was still <u>one leaf</u> left on the vine.
3 Johnsy thought the last leaf would fall during the <u>night</u>.
4 Was Johnsy ready to die? (Yes)

1 蘇和貝爾曼看著窗外的常春藤。
2 藤上還留著一片葉子。
3 瓊西認為最後一葉晚間就會掉落。
4 瓊西在等死嗎？（是）

Stop & Think

• **What did Sue and Johnsy see the next morning?** 隔天早上蘇和瓊西看到什麼？

⇨ The ivy leaf was still on the vine. 常春藤葉還在藤上。

CHECK UP

1 Johnsy looked at <u>the last leaf</u> for a long time.
2 Johnsy said it was <u>wicked</u> for her to want to die.
3 The doctor told Sue that Behrman had <u>pneumonia</u>.
4 The doctor said that Johnsy needed <u>nutrition</u> and care.

1 瓊西看著最後一葉看了很久。
2 瓊西說她一心求死很不應該。
3 醫生跟蘇說貝爾曼得了肺炎。
4 醫生說瓊西需要營養和照料。

Stop & Think

• **What happened to Behrman?** 貝爾曼怎麼了？

⇨ He died of pneumonia. 他死於肺炎。

CHECK UP

1 The janitor saw Behrman painting outside.　　　　F
2 Behrman was found with his shoes and clothes soaking wet.　　T
3 Behrman painted the last leaf.　　　　T
4 The last leaf was Behrman's masterpiece.　　　　T

1 工人看到貝爾曼在外面畫畫。
2 貝爾曼被發現的時候，他的鞋子、衣服全都濕透了。
3 貝爾曼畫了最後一葉。
4 最後一葉是貝爾曼的傑作。

Michael A. Putlack
專攻歷史與英文，擁有美國麻州 Tufts University 碩士學位

e-Creative Contents
專為非母語英語學習者研發教材的創意團隊

國家圖書館出版品預行編目 (CIP) 資料

FUN學英語故事閱讀訓練(合訂本) / Michael A. Putlack, e-Creative
Contents著 ; 陳怡靜、彭尊聖譯. -- 初版. -- [臺北市] : 寂天文化,
2020.03
　面； 公分
ISBN 978-986-318-902-2 (16K平裝附光碟片)

1.英語　2.讀本

805.18　　　　　　　　　　　　　　　　　　　109002273

作　　　者	Michael A. Putlack & e-Creative Contents
譯　　　者	陳怡靜／彭尊聖
校　　　對	黃詩韻
編　　　輯	陳怡靜
封 面 設 計	郭瀞暄
內 文 排 版	郭瀞暄／執筆者
製 程 管 理	洪巧玲
出　版　者	寂天文化事業股份有限公司
電　　　話	+886-(0)2-2365-9739
傳　　　真	+886-(0)2-2365-9835
網　　　址	www.icosmos.com.tw
讀 者 服 務	onlineservice@icosmos.com.tw
出 版 日 期	2020 年 03 月 初版一刷

劃 撥 帳 號	1998620-0 寂天文化事業股份有限公司
	訂購金額 600（含）元以上郵資免費
	訂購金額 600 元以下者，請外加郵資 65 元
	【若有破損，請寄回更換，謝謝】